W9-DAQ-990

DEATH AT GREENWAY

DEATH AT GREENWAY

A Novel

LORI RADER-DAY

THORNDIKE PRESS
A part of Gale, a Cengage Company

GALE
A Cengage Company

Copyright © 2021 by Lori Rader-Day.
P.S.™ is a trademark of HarperCollins Publishers.
Thorndike Press, a part of Gale, a Cengage Company.

ALL RIGHTS RESERVED
This is a work of fiction. Names, characters, places, and incidents are products of the author's imagination or are used fictitiously and are not to be construed as real. Any resemblance to actual events, locales, organizations, or persons, living or dead, is entirely coincidental.
Thorndike Press® Large Print Basic.
The text of this Large Print edition is unabridged.
Other aspects of the book may vary from the original edition.
Set in 16 pt. Plantin.

**LIBRARY OF CONGRESS CIP DATA ON FILE.
CATALOGUING IN PUBLICATION FOR THIS BOOK
IS AVAILABLE FROM THE LIBRARY OF CONGRESS.**

ISBN-13: 978-1-4328-9443-6 (hardcover alk. paper)

Published in 2022 by arrangement with William Morrow Paperbacks, an imprint of HarperCollins Publishers.

Printed in Mexico
Print Number: 01   Print Year: 2022

For the ten 'vacs of Greenway: Doreen, Maureen, Beryl, Pamela, Tina, Edward, and the others whose names we might yet learn, and to all those who have cared for and kept Greenway

With special thanks to the National Trust and the staff and volunteers of Greenway House

PROLOGUE:
AGATHA M. C. CHRISTIE MALLOWAN

*South Devon, England, 11:15 a.m.,
3 September 1939*

The mistress of the house was at work on the mayonnaise when the kitchen wireless began to speak of war.

"This morning the British Ambassador in Berlin handed the German Government a final note," the voice said, "stating that, unless we heard from them by eleven o'clock that they were prepared at once to withdraw their troops from Poland, a state of war would exist between us."

The others in the room had fallen silent. Agatha put down the bowl and whisk, the salad forgotten. She smoothed a strand of hair away from her face. Making mayonnaise was a physical task — it got the blood moving as well as calisthenics if done properly, though few put forth the proper effort. She insisted on doing it herself.

Down the hall, the infernal 'phone began to ring.

"I have to tell you now that no such undertaking has been received," Chamberlain was saying. *Is it Chamberlain?* Agatha thought his voice sounded quite reedy of late, an old man. "And that consequently," the voice continued, "this country is at war with Germany."

There were no gasps of surprise. At the table her husband and their friend Mrs. North sat listening, Max leaning forward with elbows on the kitchen table, his pipe jutting out of his mouth. Mrs. Bastin, in from the ferryman's cottage to help with the meal, curled her shoulders over the sink and cried into the vegetables.

"Oh, do be quiet," Max murmured, not as kindly as he might.

Later, Max would probably scoff at Mrs. Bastin's tears. Hadn't they watched the march of war arriving? It was nearly a relief to have the matter decided. What did Mrs. Bastin have to lose? But they all had so much to lose. How could it be war again, so soon?

The 'phone rang, rang. Agatha crossed to the wireless and nudged the dial in time to hear Chamberlain say, "You can imagine what a bitter blow it is to me that all my

8

long struggle to win peace has failed."

She stood back. It put one on notice to have the Prime Minister both hoarse and weary, defeated before they'd begun. She imagined Chamberlain sitting up all night committing these words to the page, to have them ready for the deadline, Parliament's ultimatum for Germany to release Poland from its grip. Would he have made another draft, too, in case the deadline had been met and all was well? They must have known no such plan would be necessary.

"Yet," Chamberlain continued, "I cannot believe that there is anything more or anything different that I could have done and that would have been more successful."

Strange to hear a man so publicly heartbroken. She listened as the PM mustered some vim for the pitch to the country to do their part. What could their part possibly be? She could wrap bandages, she supposed, but the brunt of it would hit the younger set. Rosalind and her friends.

But then even Max was all of thirty-five. Of all the reasons not to marry a younger man — she had gone through all the reasons — sending another husband off to war hadn't been one of them. When Agatha looked over, he plucked his pipe out of his mouth, his expression exultant. He would want to be a part of it — would be an absolute *nuisance* until he'd been given a job. And where did that leave her?

Agatha lost track of Chamberlain, thinking of distance, of separation. She tugged at her apron and hurried from the kitchen.

"Ange?" Max called after her.

The corridor, then through the house to the front hall, where the arch of light in the scallop window above the front door was bright. It was a fine day; all the worst days were.

She neglected the ringing telephone and opened the door, hesitating in the threshold. Outside, James, the latest of the Sealyham terriers, lay near a garden deckchair, white belly to the sun.

The first dog her father had brought home and placed at her feet, she'd gone nearly catatonic with happiness. She had never been able to take in news — not good news, certainly not bad — without seeking seclusion and letting the new information break upon the old, like the river's edge lapping at the shore.

Behind her, she could still hear Chamberlain. Never mind that now. She will hear his words repeated, reproduced, and read them in the evening edition.

Now she had time to wait out the cloud

that passed over the hill and darkened the magnolias. *Magnolia grandiflora.* She had time to let her thoughts catch up, her concerns be absorbed. When she felt she could take it all in, plans began to form. She could call on the dispensary, couldn't she? With a little brushing up, she could be useful, too. And of course there were always books to write. A Christie for Christmas, whether the Christie in question felt like writing or not.

When the cloud passed and the sun shone on the hill again, Agatha came out from under the portico, leaving the door wide, and crossed the gravel drive. She stood on the hill, chin pointed south toward the sea. She took it in: the river that led, so close, to the Channel; the fact of war; the eventualities. When she turned back, Greenway rose above her, the flat Georgian face catching the light like a temple of old. It seemed delicate to her just now. But hadn't it survived a century and a half? Hadn't it sent its sons to fight untold battles? The cannon mounted down the hill and pointed out toward the River Dart told the story. These grounds had already fended off wars long forgotten.

This time, however, they must expect bombs from the air, gas attacks. A modern

11

war with modern consequences, the likes of which no one had ever seen.

Agatha gazed over the warm white stone, stalwart on the high ledge of the river. An ideal house, a dream house. They'd barely had a chance to settle in, hadn't the chance to be happy here. Now she wondered if they would. A war was a rending, a death of how things had been. She had no concern for her life — but the life she had built? The people she had come to count on? Her marriage? This house.

She had traded her mother's house, the home of her idyllic childhood, to stand on this hill and call this house hers. Winterbrook, their residence in Oxfordshire, was Max's, but Greenway House was hers — hers in a way she knew might be seen as prideful, hers in her heart. Hers at last, since she'd come here as a child with her mother, visiting, walking the grounds that would someday be her own. Clever foreshadowing, *she* thought, credit to the author.

But that meant this was the *beginning* of the story, didn't it? If they were to have a proper story, Greenway stood, Max prevailed, Rosalind thrived, and she, Agatha, strung it all together, a book each year. If they were to have a proper story, then this simply couldn't be the end.

1
BRIDGET KELLY

St. Prisca's Hospital, near St. George's Gardens, London, early April 1941

Bridget sat on the bench in the corridor until the matron's door swung wide and the woman's stern face took in the sight of her, her apron marked with blood and bile. The auxiliary nurse who had been sent along as escort, as keeper, stood a good distance away and pretended not to watch for details she would deal out later to the others. Bridget walked alone behind Matron's swishing skirts as though to the gallows.

The matron's parlor was as sterile as any surgery. A chair for visitors stood in front of the desk, but Bridget wasn't invited to take it.

"You know of course you cannot be allowed to continue on," the matron said, settling behind the desk. "Hencewith, a decision must be made."

"Where," Bridget said. Her mouth was

dry. "Where shall I be sent, Matron?"

Matron Bailey studied her until Bridget could only imagine she would say the gaol.

"I can scarcely believe it of you," the matron said. "I've seen moments of great potential in you, and now — Do you have anything to say for yourself?"

Bridget nearly collapsed with relief for the opportunity to set it straight. "It must be an error, Matron —"

"Your error."

"No," Bridget said. "No, you see it's a mistake —"

"A mistake is the same as an error, Bridget."

"I mean it's a mistake to believe that I —" She sounded guilty, even to herself. "I administered as I was taught, gave the dose as written. If it was the wrong formulation, then —" She faltered, for she was not sure it would do any good to question the chemist's judgment. "I'm a good nurse."

"You are *not* a nurse," the matron said. "And you're a danger to say you are. A nurse. You're not through your probationary hours yet."

Bridget swallowed hard. "No, Matron."

"Therefore, it was not your job to administer treatment to that soldier."

"Sister Clare was run off her feet and my

only thought was to help —"

"You've got to the crux of the problem, well done. Your *only* thought." Matron Bailey's look was heavy. "You're single-minded on the ward, ticking the boxes. I've seen you. Arrogant with your peers, unfeeling with the patients."

Arrogant because she hadn't the time to chatter with the others? Because she didn't want to gossip or bring them back to hers for tea? On the ward . . . she'd only meant to be good at the work, hadn't she?

And unfeeling? Well, she wouldn't deny that. "Yes, Matron."

But even this answer came too quickly, she realized. Too quickly, without consideration. The matron shifted in her chair.

"And your striving with the sisters, reaching too far, going too fast, thinking too highly of one's own opinion . . ." The matron folded her hands together. "Have you considered, perhaps, that nursing may not be your calling? There are some fine positions opening for young women such as yourself in the factories —"

"I want to be a nurse, Matron! Truly I do," she said. "My mam . . ." She had a memory of her mam's hand, knuckles pink from the washing. A fluttering sensation started somewhere within her. "She wanted

15

it for me, Matron. She sacrificed a good deal to make it so. I . . . I want to save lives."

Matron Bailey sat quietly for a moment. "Only as a fully trained nurse would you perhaps have all the tools God has seen fit to give us," she said. "Fully trained and years of service. *Service,* Bridget. We are not the Redeemer, handing down decisions on life and death, playing God — even if . . . even if our mothers desperately wished it for us. What I see is a young woman trying to care for our patients with her fists clenched and her heart closed, and that is no nurse I've ever known. Nurses give care when there's nothing else, giving care, taking care. Care, Bridget, which, heretofore from you, I have seen precisely none."

They made jokes about the matron's pronouncements and timeworn words, calling her the Old Bailey behind her back. Judge of their crimes, warden of their time. But Bridget had only ever wanted to please her, to be useful, needed. Was that striving?

She lowered her head, showing her neck for the blade to drop. "What shall I do, Matron? I would do anything to make it right."

"Make it right?" the matron said. "Second chances are hard to come by in our line. A good man, and a good soldier from all reports."

"He's — dead?"

The matron was silent a moment but Bridget wouldn't look. Finally she said, "His family will arrive shortly, and I don't know what to tell them."

The flutter inside her began again, somewhere near her heart. She felt as though she were being shaken, gently.

Bridget clasped her hands together under her pinafore in case they trembled. A biological response, she knew from her training. She'd seen soldiers brought in, their hearts running on pure adrenaline when they should have given out. It turns out the same high anxiety that brought soldiers through catastrophe also rushed through the veins of the surgeons and sisters during a stitch-up. A shockingly bad time for one's hands to shake, with only a needle and boiled silk thread keeping a man's guts inside him.

"Are you all right, Bridget?"

"Yes, Matron."

"Have you been . . . run down?"

Bridget kept her face turned to the floor, the better to concentrate. "Matron?"

"Overwhelmed by the attacks each night, after your long shifts here."

"Yes, Matron, I suppose."

"Not sleeping well, headaches? Have you

17

experienced night terrors?"

Bridget finally looked up. She recognized symptoms, diagnosis. She was the best probationer they had, days put in or not. Great potential. "I don't suffer from battle fatigue, Matron. I'm weathering things, same as everyone." Same as everyone, which was badly. But she wasn't crawling the walls, was she? Hadn't resorted to the blue pills they gave to soldiers out of their minds. She had a thought. They'd never say she was, and send her as a lunatic to an asylum? "Missus?"

Matron Bailey, though, was somewhere else. "I just remembered that your mother . . ."

"Yes, Matron," Bridget said and was glad her hands were hidden.

"Yes, erm. You've got on with things, as well as can be expected but — you've encountered the symptoms of shell shock, surely?"

Bridget imagined herself made of stone. "In the patients, Matron."

The other woman seemed to be chewing on some thought. "It's a terrible quandary you've put me in."

"Yes, Matron."

"We can't have the scandal. No one wants to see our brave men survive a war zone

18

only to succumb to an overeager probationer acting on her own orders." The
matron's attentions had wandered to the
dirty window high in the room that showed
the cold white sky outside. "It may not be
right to send you," she murmured.

Bridget caught the scent of freedom, as
though the window had been cracked open.
"Send me?"

"The request is rather urgent . . . Have
you had experience with children, Bridget?"

"Matron?"

"Perhaps you helped around at home with
siblings?"

Bridget could track the tremor within as it
moved outward into her limbs, weakening
her knees, numbing her to her fingertips.
She concentrated harder. Every drop of
blood, every sinew under her skin vibrated,
ready to burst. The smallest movement
made, the slightest weakness shown.

"Yes, Matron. Five. There were five."

"I . . . I hadn't remembered it was five."

"Four girls and a boy, Matron."

The matron made a small noise in her
throat that Bridget had come to know quite
well as a condolence. Or something more
like an invocation against the same sort of
luck.

The matron smoothed a letter flat on her

desk. "And you *like* children, then? I mean to say, Bridget, that you could be trusted with children?"

"Whose children, exactly?"

The matron checked the note. "A Mrs. Arbuthnot is seeking my recommendation of someone to accompany some under-fives evacuated to the countryside. She wants a hospital nurse, but a trainee would be able to see to the care of *healthy* children, and I dare say the air will do you some good."

The matron opened her desk and pulled out a piece of paper and a pen.

Bridget didn't want to go to the countryside or take the air. Or spend time near children, in fact. But she had heard the word *recommendation* and felt herself stretch toward it, the barest hope blooming that she might yet get what she wanted.

"Do I have any choice in the matter? Matron?"

"You do, of course," the matron said easily. "You're under no obligation to accept any favor from me. You may seek your own fortune any time you wish."

Cut loose.

"*Or,*" the matron said, "you may have this — let's call it a *conditional* reference. Wheretofore you conclude this assignment to Mrs. Arbuthnot's full satisfaction, we shall see about reinstating you —"

Bridget opened her mouth to speak.

"— to begin again, that is." The matron looked back down at the note in progress before her and scrawled a few lines, murmuring to herself. Bridget had another fleeting memory, taking dictation from her mam for the letter sent to her da, telling him of the littlest's arrival and asking him to send his pay packet home for once. Learning too much, too soon, the complications of affection.

"Now." Matron Bailey folded the letter, crisp edges, put it in an envelope, and sealed it. "We are saving you from scandal, Bridget, and rescuing what I hope will be a fruitful career in the field."

Had she put that in the letter? "Yes, Matron. Thank you, Matron."

"On this assignment," the matron said, "you will need to be vigilant — absolutely vigilant, Bridget, for the children's safety, for the sake of your further improvement. Or you shall have to make your own way with no reference at all. Am I clear?"

The matron copied out a telephone exchange from the note on her desk and held out the letter and the number.

Herein lay her future.

Bridget reached for the offering, and the

matron looked her up and down. "Put that filthy apron in the rubbish before anyone else sees you," she said. "I shall trust you to see yourself out without delay. Without engaging in idle chatter, Bridget. This arrangement is between the two of us and that letter to Mrs. Arbuthnot."

Bridget pulled the stained garment over her head, rolled it into a ball as she moved across the room, and shoved it to the bottom of the bin at the door. She didn't partake in idle chatter, and none of the others would be looking out for her to do anything but stare and whisper.

Bridget looked down at the envelope in her hand. There was a dark smudge of blood across the flap. Did it matter that the arrangement was private? The scandal was beyond them already.

Dismissed. Disgraced. If she wasn't to be a nurse, she would very well like to know what she would turn out to be.

2
BRIDGET KELLY

A few minutes later

Bridget hurried past the looks and whispers
— she was a feast for them! — and went to
gather her things. Perhaps they would have
liked her cloak and kerchief for another girl,
but she needed the cloak, the only warm
thing she had to wear. She removed the pins
from her kerchief at the sink. She had
imagined the day she would graduate to the
cap, proper nurse, and now it would not
happen.

With her cloak buttoned to the neck, she
went to toss the kerchief for the laundry.
On top of the basket lay a white cap, still
crisp. She took it up. Couldn't she try it on?

But the door opened and in came some of
the other probationers, pretending they
hadn't come to idle and stare. Bridget hid
the cap in her pocket and hurried out and
toward home.

Home.

At the door to the courtyard, she stopped and held her brow until she got hold of herself again.

When the tear in Bridget's resolve was stitched up and she felt she might once again show her face, she stepped out into the chill and walked away from St. Prisca's, trying not to think it was for the last time.

At the street, Bridget chose to walk instead of waiting for the bus, where she might meet someone she knew or someone who knew her. She had walked the distance many times, early morning, late at night in the pitch dark of the blackout. Even with bombs making well-known landscape foreign overnight, when she ran out of pavement, out of familiar sights, she never made a wrong turn. Her London, remade each night by new destruction.

Her thoughts circled. What would she do?

As she approached the site of the old home place, her scraping footsteps in the rubble slowed, stopped.

Perhaps a change of air *would* do her some good.

She could still see the shape of their building, though it was gone, a thing that may never have existed. The rest of the row still stood and the lane had gone back to life as normal. In the next street, someone's sheets hung heavy and frozen on the line. Here, though, was a blackened crater, a pile of bricks that had once held everything she cared for in the world.

A breeze kicked up, blowing dust across the site. Down at the bottom, a scrap of fabric flapped. The landlady's tablecloth, perhaps. Mrs. Brown had been properly proud of her heirloom cloths.

Mrs. Brown had been out that day.

Someone had picked through the site since she'd last been to visit. There were shapes in the mud where boards and bricks had been wrenched up. Perhaps a few things had been saved, then. She had not been able to see to it herself, of course, thinking that if she'd crawled inside the scene, she might never climb back out. She'd left the lot to the swindlers and thieves, to the chancers. To the neighbors to take their share. She couldn't decide now if she minded a few of their knives were in service at someone else's table or gone to make aeroplanes.

So much was lost, it might as well be everything.

Bridget could feel the curtains twitching along the lane behind her, those deciding whether to invite her in, those who had already decided. She was freezing to her bones, anyway, and the sky threatened to drop another downpour. She couldn't risk sitting in a kitchen in this lane and having tea served to her, stirred by one of her mam's best spoons.

At her rooming house, Bridget let herself in and scurried up the back stairs before Mrs. Mitchell could hail her for the weather or the next week's rent. In her room, she hung the cloak as she always did, set aside the cap she'd taken.

What should she do? She might light the fire, warm up the room. Put on the kettle? She sat on the edge of her bed.

"You had a visitor," came a shaking voice through the wall. The man in the front room was frail, shuffling as far as the shared toilet down the hall and downstairs, only occasionally, for meals.

Not someone from the hospital. Not the police?

"Who was it?" she said.

"Your young man."

"He's not my young man." More gently, she said, "Thank you, Mr. Watson."

"I heard Herself getting the door," he said. "And I heard the visitor say 'Tom,' clear as a bell."

Bridget put her hands on the bed as though to stand.

She hadn't done what they said she had, surely. She had no way of making sense of it. And now her only hope was to care for children in the countryside? Scared children wrested from their parents while the Germans made craters of *their* homes? She was in no state. And anyway, why should she protect strangers' children?

"No one protected our houseful," she said.

"What's that?" Mr. Watson said.

"I said," she started loudly. But her voice faltered. "I said, Thank you, Mr. Watson."

She hadn't the Blitz spirit at all. People like this Mrs. Arbuthnot did their bit, taking on more than required. Collecting scrap and mending old clothes into new, firewatching at night. But instead of feeling expansive and generous as some seemed to, Bridget could only turn her back and curl over the softest parts of herself.

The matron had her dead to rights. *Closed fist.* Which is what worried her.

"All right, love?" Mr. Watson said.

If she stayed without her pay packet, she'd have to find a cheaper place to live while she looked for more work, and not the kind of work her mam had wanted for her. Not the kind she wanted for herself. If she stayed, she had no way to get back into the nursing scheme. No hospital in London would take her without some sort of acknowledgment of where she'd spent the war so far — and, beyond that, word would be out soon. Matron might keep the news out of the 'papers but not from the vine that twisted among nurses' dormitories. She would never be able to walk into another infirmary without wondering who knew, who had heard.

Not that she expected this Mrs. Arbuthnot to take her on — how could she? On the matron's reference, who thought her a killer? The envelope smudged with blood couldn't be an endorsement.

She needed a fresh start. In the country, if necessary, untethered. She gathered the letter and the telephone exchange. The number would reach Mrs. Arbuthnot, with or without the letter. How urgently did the woman need help?

Bridget turned her attention to the cold hearth. "Mr. Watson, shall I bring you a cup of tea?"

He didn't answer for a moment. He would die in that room someday. Is that what she waited for here in London? More death? Her own?

"Aye," Mr. Watson said. "Tea would be grand."

"With milk? I've got just enough, I think."

"You're too kind to me, Bridget."

While the fire under the kettle caught on the kindling of the matron's letter, Bridget went to the cupboard and brought down two cups. She had exactly two, mismatched from the charity shop, one chipped at the rim. She liked it even so. It was her own, something that had not come from the ashes of her old life.

When she served Mr. Watson in his room, and sat at his rickety little table for company, she thought about taking care of children again. She couldn't love them, obviously. It went without saying. But she saved Mr. Watson the last of the milk and took the chipped cup for herself.

3
BRIDGET KELLY

Mrs. Mitchell's rooming house, near Regent's Park, London

Bridget had been in bed an hour when thudding along the landing woke her. She sat up, confused, hearing shouts and voices, the sirens wailing. She threw on her cape, slid her feet into her shoes, and opened the door to find Mr. Patel, who lived in the back apartment and worked for Mrs. Mitchell — some said lived with Mrs. Mitchell — helping Mr. Watson gather himself. Bridget took the gentleman's other arm across her shoulder.

In chaos, she could be calm. Mrs. Mitchell thought it the result of her nurse's training, but Bridget knew the roiling sea was within. Nothing outside could hurt her, and if it tried, it hardly mattered.

The boarders hurried as best they could to the back garden where the corrugated arch of Mrs. Mitchell's Anderson shelter had been sunk into the ground. Under it, there was room enough for everyone, just, but they were forced into close quarters, shoulder to shoulder, knee to knee. Barely acquainted in proper fashion over Mrs. Mitchell's everyday china, they were strangers dressed in shadows and bedclothes, trying not to look one another in the eye.

They helped Mr. Watson to the bench and then Mr. Patel crouched at the door with the lantern. They had enough fuel for an hour or two. "It'll be another false alarm," he said. He glanced toward Mrs. Mitchell.

Bridget sat at the other side of Mr. Watson.

"Or it *won't* be a false alarm," said one of the widowed sisters who commanded the large double room at the front of the house, all the best views. They were Mrs. Henshaw and Mrs. Barden, but Bridget hadn't sorted them out in her mind. "Few of those to be had."

The groan of aeroplanes approached.

"And we'll be forced into another night in this trench," the other sister said.

"Better this trench than one in Belgium, Mrs. Henshaw," Mr. Watson said. "Or a grave."

Bridget couldn't look around to see which was Mrs. Henshaw. The Anderson was too tight quarters, not enough air. It was theater, tucking in like this. The Anderson in the garden of the old place was a twist of metal now, as much good as it had done. She closed her eyes and tried to keep still.

Mr. Watson said, "And for the unlucky, the trenches they dig will serve both purposes."

"Weren't you in the war, Mr. Watson?" Mrs. Mitchell said.

The sisters sighed and Bridget nearly gagged. To keep from turning herself inside out like the dead soldier at St. Prisca's took all her concentration. The effort she put in, she might as well be willing the 'planes above to stay in the sky.

"In the war to end all wars — quite wrong about that, we were — I was a young man and saw a bit of the continent," Mr. Watson said. There was a rustling as he sat up straighter. "They sent us in railway cars to France with some of their funny words on the side, so we started calling ourselves after them. Omms and Chevoos."

"Men and . . . horses?" said one of the sisters.

"Right you are," Mr. Watson said. "Forty men or eight horses, that's the top-off on one of those railcars. We didn't know the words, then, of course. Didn't know anything. Just went where they said and shot who they said to shoot." He stared into the dark corner of the shelter for a moment. "Bah," he said. "What are memories for? I have my souvenir. I earned my metal —"

"Oh?" Mrs. Mitchell sat forward. "A medal?"

"Metal, my dear lady. Iron rations in me leg."

"Oh," she said.

"It's no longer painful, I hope?" Mr. Patel said.

"Only when it rains, Mr. Patel," Mr. Watson said. It rained all the time.

One of the sisters jumped in, "If that was the worst you got —"

Antiaircraft guns thudded not far away. The 'planes raged overhead, the strikes banging like the world's largest tin drum, shaking the ground. Dust came down from the seams of the Anderson.

"No, indeed," Mr. Watson said after a few minutes. "No, not the worst by far."

Bridget cringed into the shadows. Must she brace herself even further to hear of fallen comrades? Every soldier in hospital had wanted to tell her their stories, but they never wondered about hers.

But Mr. Watson had said all he would tonight.

Mr. Patel held up the lantern. "We should

save the fuel. It might be a long night."

No one said anything. Mr. Patel snuffed the light and they sat in the dark, the permission to speak gone out, too. Waiting for the all-clear, Bridget could imagine she sat in another shelter, that the breathing in the dark belonged to those she longed for.

The signal finally came to return to their beds and Bridget and the others trudged in. The air tasted of dust, from the plasterboard of crushed homes. Dust and smoke.

Bridget spent the rest of the night turning from one side to the other, mashing her pillow into new shapes, thinking of the dead soldier from St. Prisca's.

He'd been a young one, probably ambitious and eager. He'd have signed on knowing the dangers, but never predicting the death that had come for him.

In all her plans for nursing, she had never considered she might harm someone.

Bridget spent the early hours as light crept in around the blackout shades going through her actions of the prior day, over and again until she thought she might go mad. Was already mad.

At barely a decent hour, the doorbell sounded. Mr. Watson's voice came through the wall.

"Our man Tom again," he said. He would be at the window, an early riser. "Very ardent."

Bridget dressed quickly and went to the parlor to receive him. When they met, he took her hand and kissed her temple. To avoid her lipstick, she had once thought. "Did you have some trouble last night?" he said. "Aunt says she was in the garden shelter again?"

Tom's aunt had been their landlady at the old home place down the street. She still lived near, a rented room. Acting the displaced royal with the owner, was Bridget's guess.

"Shall we go for a walk?"

"It's rather cold out, Bridget, and anyway, I'm in a dreadful rush," Tom said. He seemed to be performing for an audience, as though he knew the entire house listened in. Tom had a soft face, a soft middle, but a loud voice, like someone trained for the stage. An only child. "Just a few minutes to spare," he said. "Only I came to tell you I'm off this morning. I've new orders."

"So have I," she said.

He dropped her hand and recovered to a normal level of voice. "How do you mean?"

"Well, not this morning, but soon. Top secret."

"You're such a kid sometimes," he said. "Look, I'll write to you."

"I won't be here," she said. "I told you. I'm going on a mission of charity."

Tom stared dully at her. "What about nursing?"

"There are plenty of nurses," Bridget said, making it up as she went along and startled to hear the words coming out of her mouth. She had decided to go. "But I've a special assignment. Specially chosen." She did feel like a child and wished she'd never said anything of it. "Tommy," she said. "Do you plan to marry me?"

"I thought — well, that's rather —" He pulled at his neck, looking to the doorway in case Mrs. Mitchell stood by. "I didn't realize —"

"Several of the girls on the ward have been hitched up quickly before their men went to France." But she didn't want to talk about St. Prisca's. "Just something I thought of."

"I thought —"

"Wouldn't you rather I was taken care of? Just in case?"

Something passed over his face. "Wouldn't you rather be a wife than a widow?"

"Of course, but. At the moment I'm neither." That was the problem. She was nothing.

"It's only an office in Bedfordshire I'm off to," he said, his voice now quiet. "I'll be back in a week —"

"Never mind. I only thought I could be sure of something."

"None of us can be sure of anything anymore." He glanced at her from the corner of his eye. "Are you really on some sort of assignment?"

"You're doubting me. It's not enough to break my heart?"

"If I thought you were serious . . ."

He might do it, he might propose, and then where would she be? "I'm teasing," she said.

He looked relieved. "You shouldn't, not when I feel as I do, and when you — I shouldn't say."

"You can say what you like." If he said something that cut the binds and spilled her out, then perhaps it was for the best.

But he wouldn't. "I'd rather not. Let's part as friends, at least."

"Be safe, Tommy," she said. Bedfordshire.

"You'll write me? And send me a photo?"

He would do better to find a snap left behind in some bombed-out house. A photograph of her would impress no one.

"I'll send an address when I know it." Bridget turned her cheek for the kiss that would not touch her lips. She wished she loved him. It would have been far easier if only she could.

4
BRIDGET KELLY

Paddington Station, two days later

They were late leaving London.

Not on the day, of course. London still ran nearly on time, as well as it could. The Underground dislodged those sleeping on the Tube platforms every morning, switched on the electric, and started up again, no problem there. The trains into and out of the city still ran, a point of pride. That was the British way, everything suffered with a certain dignity — or a lie the papers would have them believe.

Bridget had decided on dignity for herself, as well. She was punctual, pressed, her best court shoes shined. The nurse's navy wool cape brushed and hair tightly pinned under a hat from two seasons ago couldn't be helped. The white cap she'd taken was tucked in with her things, something to wish on. She needed Mrs. Arbuthnot's good favor to return to London exultant, and she would have it.

In the crush of travelers, soldiers, and porters, she found the correct platform and set down the dressing case borrowed from Mr. Watson. It was nearly empty. Steam from the train had made the station hot, the air thick.

Nearby a woman crouched on her heels in front of a young boy, her face hidden by the wide curved brim of a red picture hat. Her Sunday best. Bridget turned away as the woman pressed the boy to her dark cloak like a lover, shoulders shaking.

No, it was a bright early morning, the train already waiting. But they were late in the *season* of escape, weren't they? The evacuations had begun the week war was declared, some children having to be sent out a second time once the bombing finally began. Thousands of children — hundreds of thousands, by now — had already been sent away from London for their safety.

Bridget looked for the time, tried not to make an accounting as she waited. If her biggest little sisters had gone with their school. If her mam had taken the babies to shelter somewhere else. If —

It never ended.

It *would* never end, if she let light in through the crack. She folded her arms around herself.

Along the platform marched a woman stuffed into a severe gray suit with gold buttons, trailed by two porters and a white-haired man wearing a beret, of all things. The woman's hat was small, pointed, and set too far forward, the sort of thing the probationers at St. Prisca's discussed as a character flaw. This woman hadn't the delicacy for fashion. She walked chest first, moving like the prow of a destroyer slicing through waves. The woman directed her hat toward Bridget and looked her over with less satisfaction than Bridget thought she deserved. "Which one are you?" she said. This was Mrs. Arbuthnot.

"Bridget Kelly, missus."

She was older than Bridget's mam would have been, but not a lady of leisure from the Woman's Voluntary, or if she was indeed, a different sort than Bridget had imagined. The woman's appraisal had moved on toward the mother and son on the platform. "Pleasantries later, if there's time after the other one arrives," she said. "Now I've raised five of my own, and when the time comes to part them, I'm afraid it will be difficult. Be gentle but firm. This is their child's last chance for safety, and they must understand the sacrifice, though difficult to bear, is necessary."

The man in the beret caught up. "They'll have the best of care, all the comforts. Far more satisfactory than they have at home, I wager."

"Malcolm, please," Mrs. Arbuthnot said. She turned back to Bridget. "My husband. You *will* be able to manage the mothers?"

The two porters arrived, weighed down. "I'll have that," Mr. Arbuthnot said, reaching to extract a small parcel from one of the helpers and nearly bungling the job for all. "What time do we arrive, darling? Joan? Where's the easel?"

"Sent ahead with the cots, Malcolm," Mrs. Arbuthnot said. "Don't fuss." She went to see to the mother and son.

He would, though, Bridget could see that. In no time he would gain permission to board early and have everything just as he liked.

Mr. Arbuthnot caught her staring. "Lucky getaway, eh?" he said. "Nearly criminal."

"Pardon me?" Had Matron Bailey had a change of heart? Had she telephoned Mrs. Arbuthnot herself?

"*Paid* to get out of the city as it falls down around your ears."

"Oh. Yes, sir." If the children would only arrive.

Mrs. Arbuthnot's voice rose over the noise of the station. "Mrs. Poole, I beg you!"

The mother in the red hat brushed past with the boy in tow and now Bridget caught a glimpse of her face, puffy and blotched from emotion.

"I'd rather he died alongside me," the woman cried over her shoulder, "than be left behind with no one." The linen identification tag on the child's coat fluttered behind.

"Mrs. Poole," Mrs. Arbuthnot called. "Please be sensible!"

The woman's hat disappeared quickly into the crowds.

"Silly woman," Mrs. Arbuthnot said under her breath. "Selfish woman. You see what we're up against, everyone losing their heads." She tugged the hem of her jacket. "Where *is* the other girl?"

"I don't know," Bridget whispered, the mother's words still clanging around in her head. *I'd rather he died alongside me.* How often she had wished —

"Oh, the children," Mrs. Arbuthnot exclaimed. "Here they are."

The children were tots, baby fat in their knees below shorts and skirts, socks pulled up or sliding, shoes scuffed or untied. They had tags affixed to their coats and child-sized gas masks in paper cases on straps around their necks. They wore caps and hats or bonnets and flung them to the ground in a tantrum. Those who were carried by their mums kicked to be let down. Two were *infants,* dear God.

Porters followed behind with pillowslips stuffed, picnic hampers, tiny cases ridiculous in large hands. Very few fathers were in evidence. Fathers were at the front, or already in hospital, or worse. It was best not to think of fathers.

Some carried bears or dolls or toy 'planes or tanks. Each child was allowed a favorite. As the platform filled, a young boy stopped running his pet locomotive along his mother's sleeve and looked on the soft toys the girls carried with hungry eyes. Comfort, too, would be rationed.

Mrs. Arbuthnot managed the group, her jacket riding up, her hat sliding further over her eye. The mothers had questions about visits, where they might send packages, telephone calls, visits again. Mrs. Arbuthnot reassured them and pulled Bridget aside as though for further instructions but actually to take a break from the mothers. "I can't imagine what's keeping the other nurse," she huffed.

"The other *nurse.*" Bridget glanced down

at herself, at the cloak she should have left behind. She hadn't meant to pass herself off as anything other than short-term help. Had the advertisement asked specifically for a nurse? Or was she to be rather a nanny? "Did the other — girl come recommended by Matron Bailey, as well?"

"Now don't be jealous. Your matron's good opinion of you is enough for me," Mrs. Arbuthnot said. "The other girl came through another source altogether."

Mr. Arbuthnot gestured to catch his wife's attention, his long coat flapping. "Yes, Malcolm, I see the time," she said.

"Mine is lost," Bridget said.

"What is?"

"My reference. My letter from Matron Bailey."

"Oh yes. I should have to request another one, I suppose."

Bridget tried to think of a way to discourage it. She had only wanted the new beginning, to leave all the blood of St. Prisca's behind her.

"It's too late now," Mrs. Arbuthnot said. "As you can see, we're under siege."

Bridget turned to find the platform rather crowded. "How many —"

"What I hoped for were extra hands at the oars, but I'm afraid we'll have to make do until new arrangements might be made," Mrs. Arbuthnot said. "It's time to board them, Nurse Kelly. Look sharp but be gentle — with the *mothers,* mind."

Nurse Kelly.

This development just as Bridget was meant to take control of the situation, to give the families confidence in her abilities to keep and care, to administer and tuck in, to guard, of course, to keep safe from the enemy, to serve tea and milk, to know proper temperatures and procedures. She should grab the porter who had taken her case and let the group go on without her. Could they? She imagined all the women yanking their children home, all those children *to die alongside* in London — and the matron hearing from Mrs. Arbuthnot, an earful.

"Nurse Kelly?" Mrs. Arbuthnot said.

She should be grasping hands and leading the 'vacs into the carriage, but Bridget had suddenly remembered doing much the same, one sister's hand on her left, another's on her right, off to church, off to market. *Home.*

Die alongside them.

She might never come back, that was it. She might never see the family grave again. That's what this woman was asking of her, to go without knowing what lay ahead, another item on the list to go without. Stockings, beef, her family, her livelihood, and now assurances.

The mothers said good-bye and then good-bye again, tousling curls and cradling until Mrs. Arbuthnot insinuated herself between a mum and child and motioned for Bridget to take the infant.

Bridget kept her face right and led the parade up the steps into the chocolate-and-cream-colored carriage. Inside, she sorted the children onto two benches, one on each side of the train, detaching mothers from children and sending them back out. All the while trying not to let her mind wander toward Regent's Square and everything familiar. Out of nowhere she thought briefly of Tom, of letters that may never reach her. Wherever she was going — the departure boards listed no town names, of course, the way of the world — there was no guarantee, not of His Majesty's postal service, nor of survival.

5
BRIDGET

A few minutes to departure

Bridget bounced an infant on her hip, wishing for a last gulp of London air — or an escape back to the city streets before the train lurched forward and made the decision for her. *You are not a nurse.*

Through the window, Bridget spotted the red, curved hat brim of the young mother who'd taken her son away. The woman had hooked a conductor and now gestured wildly at the train as he shook his head.

Madam changed her mind, did she?

But wouldn't Mrs. Arbuthnot be pleased to have the boy along?

Bridget hurried to the doorway and signaled until the harassed conductor looked up.

"There's still time, isn't there, sir?" Bridget said. "Madam, where is your son?"

The woman turned, the curve of her hat lifting to reveal a haughty face instead of a grieving one. "Pardon?" This woman was a few years older than Bridget, her red hat rather more posh than Mrs. Poole's had been. She had a cool manner, not the moist cheeks of a mother saying her good-byes, and cut a sleek figure with her dark cape thrown back over her shoulders, the bright red lining framing her slim skirt. Bridget felt dowdy, everything about her dull. Even in the same cape —

"Oh, you're the other *nurse.*" Bridget stepped off the train, and the mother of the infant she carried came near again to kiss and cry and pet. "We've only been waiting for you all this time."

The woman in the red hat looked at the baby, the mother. "I *am* sorry. I got caught up, as I was just explaining to this gentleman —"

"You can make your apologies to Mrs. Arbuthnot, but you should hurry."

"They say the train is full."

"It's been arranged. Mrs. Arbuthnot has it all sorted. Come now, I need your help straightaway." She couldn't very well see to two infants and a brood of under-fives all the way to the countryside. The Arbuthnots had first-class tickets, and she knew Mr. Arbuthnot would not be putting in a hand once they arrived.

The other nurse's bag was seen to and then she followed Bridget into the carriage. "And what's your name?" the other nurse said.

"I'm Bridget Kelly."

"That's me, as well," the other said delightedly, leaning down to look out the window as they went. "Isn't that something?"

"I had five Bridgets in my year at school," Bridget said. "And rather quite a lot of Kellys."

They dodged passengers and cases up the aisle to where Mrs. Arbuthnot tried to make herself heard to the ticket inspector over the shrieks of the other infant trying to launch himself from her arms.

"Here she is, missus," Bridget said. "You didn't mention we were both Bridget Kelly."

Mrs. Arbuthnot, frowning, handed the baby into Bridget's empty arm.

"Young lady —" When she looked upon the other Bridget, Mrs. Arbuthnot's words ran out. The other nurse was no girl, clearly, and, in addition to being the kind of glamorous that made the ticket inspector blush, she had the sharpish look of a woman who wouldn't be scolded.

"At sixes and sevens, Mrs. Arbuthnot,"

the other Bridget said. "My sincerest apologies."

"Ah, yes," Mrs. Arbuthnot said, finding herself again. "Did you say you were Bridget Kelly as well?"

"We can do a rota, which one of us gets to be Bridget Kelly." Bridget had a crying baby on each hip, and a stitch in her back. She glanced toward the rest of the children, who played with each other's toys, examined the next train over through the window, waved to mums on the platform. She counted heads, losing track as they moved about.

"Well, you both can't be Bridget," Mrs. Arbuthnot said. "It will be confusing for the children. And the staff."

"The staff?" The other Bridget's cool regard split open into a smile. She had a deep dimple in her cheek that drew the eye. It was a powerful force, armed to destroy like one of Hitler's secret weapons. She reached up and pulled off the red hat, revealing smooth, dark hair and high cheekbones. Bridget didn't need to be told how she would come out in the comparison of one Bridget Kelly to the other.

"I'm Bridey at home, missus." It was out before she could think.

"Then it shall be," Mrs. Arbuthnot said.

"Thank you, Bridey."

It stung a bit, the old baby name drawn out from the attics. The *children* would call her that name. She didn't feel herself, suddenly. Wasn't herself.

"Everyone calls me Gigi," said the other nurse. The dimple still sunk into her cheek.

Bridget stared. Another battlefront of the war had opened up before her very eyes. They hadn't even left the station and here this one had already given herself an adventuring name.

"Gigi, is it?" The slash of Mrs. Arbuthnot's lips pursed into something short of a smile. "Those names will do for the children, at least. Please go see to them, and I'll have further instructions when we get near our destination."

"Where is that final address again?" Gigi said. "Mrs. Arbuthnot? Ma'am?" Mrs. Arbuthnot would not be commanded back.

Bridget — now Bridey and a good deal sorry she had offered to be called it — pushed one of the infants at Gigi.

"I didn't —" The other woman took the child awkwardly and followed Bridey toward their benches.

"I didn't reckon for babies, either," Bridey said over her shoulder. The matron had said under-fives, and she had pictured them all four years old, like a set, standard and tidy. "And no one ever said *ten.*"

"Ten? *Ten* children?"

They arrived at their benches, the children clambering and inquisitive. When would the train leave, when would they have tea, when would they arrive, where were they going. Passengers along the carriage turned to look.

"Ten," Bridey said. Ten little lives in their hands, and herself a loaded weapon. The infant in her arms screeched. Bridget sat heavily as the train gasped into motion and raised the child over her shoulder.

"Good *night.*" Gigi sat on the bench opposite. "Did she tell *you* where we're headed?"

"The countryside, that's all I know."

"The West Country, isn't it? Cream and chocolate cars."

"Oh." She hadn't thought to ask and what did it say about her? That she trusted her betters, or that she had no option but to go along?

Outside the window, mothers lined the platform, the entire length. The children crushed into place at the glass to wave to their mums, who ran alongside, and then to other mums they didn't know.

Bridget held herself still. The children

would need her to be stoic.

When they were past the end of the platform, the children strained to see backward. At last they sat back on the benches, stunned as cows, questions at an end. They plucked at the violet fabric of the bench seat, some crying, some trying not to.

"Hush now, hush," Bridget whispered, jostling the one against her neck until it stopped caterwauling. She had helped with her brother and sisters, and she knew what she was about, nurse or no. If she needed to be skilled with children, then she would be. She could be anything she needed to be.

The train was picking up steam, and so were some of the children, in misery. "Let's be brave soldiers," she said. "For Mummy and Dad."

"And for King and country," Gigi said, not soothingly, more like she was raising a pint in a pub. She held the infant out from her as he began to pucker and scream, pink as a ham. "And in payment for all our sins thus far. Are you quite mad? You volunteered for this?"

"So did you," Bridey said. A warbling sort of laugh escaped her, and all the children looked her way, wiping noses on sleeves, smiling to themselves at the sound. They were innocents caught up with whatever she had agreed to, whomever she had decided to be. *Absolutely vigilant.* Yes, she would have to be.

6
BRIDEY

Somewhere southwest of London

The train passed out of London and its outskirts, laundry hung in back gardens, and then finally into fields with hedges, through smaller towns, each station with its name painted over. Then after an extended delay at a large town with church spires and hills, the train took a sharp turn, shadows dragging across the carriage to a new angle. The afternoon grew long, the view remote and empty.

Gigi begged off for the toilet and didn't come back. Meanwhile the children teased, kicked, cried, or turned inward. They had a messy tea right at their seats from the baskets. Bridey handed out biscuits for a makeshift pudding after, wiped dribbles from jackets, and dusted crumbs from the smocked fronts of dresses. When Mrs. Arbuthnot came by to check on them, they had turns at the toilet.

"Where's the other one?" Mrs. Arbuthnot said. "This Gigi."

"I'm sure she'll be back soon, missus." It was a train. Surely the nurse hadn't hopped off at the last stop, leaving them in the lurch. Bridey might better be able to pretend she was a real nurse if she weren't bothered by the constant companionship of the genuine article, but she hoped against it, anyway. She would need the help.

Mrs. Arbuthnot went back to her carriage, and Bridget changed nappies on the bench, ignoring glares from nearby passengers. It was a frantic business keeping all ten in order, and she was wilting, one infant wailing against her neck, the other propped against her on the bench, matching volume.

A man with striking blue eyes passed by, giving her a wink for her troubles. *The cheek.*

She got the babies settled and started a story for the older set, winding the tale out until all of them slept. The infants were tucked into a nest made of her cloak, and the rest of them draped across the bench or leaned against the window or cuddled together. It could be done, just, if this Gigi could be expected to take her allotment.

Now here was the Bridget Kelly the matron had spoken of. Keen-eyed and keeping score. She couldn't begin thinking of the children as bandages needing to be wrapped, dressings needing to be changed. Bridey looked down at the girl against her hip. The identification tag tied to the girl's coat button read *Doreen,* written in delicate, shaking script. She was a living doll, with a rosebud mouth and silken hair like something from a fairy tale.

Doreen should have reminded Bridget of her littlest sister, but that young one had been rather a skinny, sallow child, not unlike the foundlings at the hospital near their old flat. *These* children were loved and looked after, still fat at the thighs and wrists from mother's milk.

These children had loving parents. Among them, *Bridget* was the foundling.

She reached down and pulled Doreen into her lap as she would her sewing or embroidery. Something to keep herself weighted down, to keep the flutter beginning in her stomach from turning into tremors. Doreen's eyelids lifted, fought to stay open, and lost.

Gigi came along the aisle. She'd been gone an hour.

"Where have you been?" Bridget said, sounding more cross than she'd meant to.

"Chatting with some blokes I met in the

next carriage."

"I'll need your *help* —"

"Of course." She looked over the scene of sleeping children. "You seem to have it in hand. What do you need me to do?"

Bridey watched the countryside roll by, fuming. The girl Doreen was warm against her, and her eyes pricked with the effects of the last two days, readying for the journey and fighting off visions of the soldier from St. Prisca's each night. The lost sleep of several months of grief, more than a year of war. She closed her eyes.

Then Bridey jolted awake, finding the carriage dark. She sat up with a gasp.

"Tunnel," Gigi said.

They were out of it in two seconds, Bridey's eyes now dazzled by the light. She'd only dozed off. "I didn't mean to fall asleep."

"You didn't miss anything," Gigi said. "Except —" She lowered her voice and leaned across the aisle. "Some high drama two rows along."

Bridey looked among the benches until she spotted a couple sitting together but leaning apart, allowing more space between them than was proper, given how full the train was. They weren't much older than Bridey, perhaps still courting or —

59

"Do you think they've left that seat for the Holy Spirit?" Gigi said. "They disagree on nearly everything."

"Married, then," Bridey said. "How have you managed to learn what they agree or disagree about? Impressive range for eavesdropping, and their backs to you."

Gigi shrugged. "I chatted them up a bit earlier. But you picked them out, as well, and based on what?"

Bridey looked them over again. "Posture, I suppose. And —"

"Yes?"

"They're not reading anything or chatting or dozing or looking out the window. They're only *not* speaking to one another."

"That's rather good. You'd make a good one for — well, have you heard of Mass-Observation? I did some work for them."

Bridey hadn't. "Mass-*Observation?* It sounds rather . . ."

"Doesn't it?" Gigi whispered. "It's anthropology, only not in New Guinea or some other far-off place — here."

Now it did sound rather troublesome. "They're studying the culture of . . . us? In aid of what?"

"For the sake of — of the Register, for the record of what it is to be British. For instance, when Edward abdicated. We col-

lected then. The coronation, after? We collected."

"Collected?" Bridey said, her voice rather
high and too loud. "Collected what precisely?"

Gigi's eyes shifted up the carriage and
back. "Opinions. Attitudes. They had a lot
to say about the war posters, what people
will respond to, that sort of thing. If you
know what the nation's citizens think, you
can better talk with them."

"If you know what people think, you can
better change their minds to what you'd
have them think."

Gigi sat back. "Could do. And here I
thought all that work was used down the
line to, I don't know, sell soap flakes. Don't
concern yourself. I don't do such work anymore."

Except she clearly did, for her own amusement. Gigi's keen powers of observation
wouldn't work in Bridey's favor. How soon?
How soon before she revealed herself as a
fraud?

Mrs. Arbuthnot came along the aisle, tsk-
ing at the girl curled into Bridey's lap.
"Don't pet them, girls. It doesn't do for
them to get attached or to expect to be mol-
lycoddled."

Bridey smartened herself as best she

could, sliding Doreen off her skirt. "You said you have five children, missus?"

"Five," Gigi said, looking Mrs. Arbuthnot over as though she were a prize heifer.

The woman's face, already stone, had nowhere to go. "They weren't raised pampered little royals, I can tell you."

Bridey recognized it then. Under the airs and graces, Mrs. Arbuthnot had a hint of the wide accent of the working classes, same as Bridey's mam.

"All I'm saying is that you'll not have lap enough for them all," Mrs. Arbuthnot said, prim once more. "Better to teach them to . . ." She searched the fields rushing by for the right term.

"Buck up?" Gigi said.

"Something of that nature," Mrs. Arbuthnot said, turning to include her. Gigi was freshening the pins in her hair. She had lovely long fingernails. Bridey fixed upon them for a moment, wondering how she had managed to keep them. Matron Bailey had strict ideas about such things, and they broke often enough besides.

"It's our duty," Mrs. Arbuthnot was saying, "to make sure these children don't go back to their parents ruined by our influence."

Gigi's dimple threatened. "Which influence is that, ma'am?"

"They should be molded into proper British citizens," Mrs. Arbuthnot said. "It's a big job. We're doing nothing less than saving England, girls. Don't let anyone tell you otherwise."

Without Doreen on her lap, Bridey felt light and didn't recognize herself in Mrs. Arbuthnot's speech. Didn't recognize *children,* either. One would think, if she had raised *five . . .* Gigi, across the aisle, tried to hide the dimple that gave away she was smiling.

"Bridey, you look as though there's something you want to say," Mrs. Arbuthnot said.

"Well, missus, I — children pulled from the rubble of their own nurseries," Bridey said, swallowing hard to get through it. "They've been known to have the same shock as soldiers pulled from the battlefield. Don't you think small ones might . . . buck up a little more stoutly if they feel safe?"

Mrs. Arbuthnot swayed with the train for a moment. "Is that your training speaking, Bridget? Or life experience at age, what, twenty?"

So she would be Bridget, then, when she needed to be reminded of her place. She was nineteen. And to speak of her training — she should keep her mouth shut, good and proper, and let Mrs. Arbuthnot tell her how she wanted things done. "Four sisters and a brother, missus," she said. "I —"

"And do cuddles make your siblings safe when bombs scream overhead, Bridget?"

She couldn't think of it and deflected the woman's words by sinking deeply inside her own skin. "No, missus."

"Don't love them, girls," Mrs. Arbuthnot said, turning toward the first-class carriage. "A few less hearts broken, in the end."

Gigi leaned into the aisle to watch their employer march away, then turned back to Bridey. "In the *end*?" she said, stretching her mouth to mimic Mrs. Arbuthnot's revealed accent. "When the devil will that be, I wonder?"

The other nurse was sharp, much too sharp. Bridey turned to the window, wondering if her only allies would be the children, or if she should have any at all.

7
BRIDEY

On the train

After a long afternoon of hedges and stone
walls, of vast stretches of farmland dotted
by sheep, of pausing at stations to let more
important trains pass, trains full with soldiers or the wounded, of delays and more
tunnels, they ran alongside a vast stretch of
water. Gigi leaned over the aisle to study
the view on Bridey's side.

"That's the sea," she said. "Does it make
sense to take your charges to the *seaside*?"

Her charges, as though Gigi had never
signed on for the work.

The train turned inland along a river, the
tide out to reveal mudflats. Seabirds whirled
overhead.

The children played or fretted, asked
questions she tried to answer or questions
she didn't answer, fought over toys, shared
a snack, stared out the window in awe or
dismay. "What is that?" one of the little boys

asked of the landscape, once again dry. Flat, vast, and empty.

"Absolutely nothing at all," Gigi said.

"I wonder if it's the moors," Bridey said.

"How very Wuthering Heights."

"Eh?"

Gigi shook her head, her attention turned on two men and a woman coming down the aisle toward them.

"We thought you'd jumped the caboose," one of the men said, strolling with hands in his trouser pockets. Gigi, he meant. He was fresh-faced and jovial, while the other man was brooding and angled, the muscles in his jaw reminding Bridey of the skinless drawings in the *Gray's Anatomy* she'd seen at St. Prisca's. The woman had glossy red lips and a curvaceous figure. Something about her made Bridey think they'd met before. Was she from St. Prisca's? Or the old lane? Bridey turned her head to the window.

"I told you I'd have to get back to *work*," Gigi said. "I have responsibilities. With the children."

The group made themselves at home in between the sleeping children. The woman perched on the seat arm, her skirt riding up on shapely legs. She had a farmgirl's face, suntanned and freckled, but short black hair, modern and set into waves. She looked over the scene of their benches. "Quite a few responsibilities," she said. "*Too* many."

The jolly man wore a silver tie pin tipped with a sparkling bauble that might be worth something, but his shirt collar was too wide for his neck, his jacket too loose in the shoulders. One could tell a great deal about a man by his clothes. The ill-tempered one, for instance, dressed like a boy home from university, a bush jacket that did nothing to give him any shape.

The friendly one leaned across the aisle to include Bridey when he caught her looking. "How do you do?"

It was the blue-eyed man who'd stopped to have a wink at her expense. "Just fine, thank you." She turned her chin toward the window again, the only proper thing.

"Bridey, this chap reckons we're going to South Devon," Gigi said. "We've passed Newton Abbot already."

"My ticket's for Paignton," the jovial man said. "But the line goes as far as a place called Kingswear."

"As remote an outpost as you can imagine, then?" said the brooding one.

"You might continue to Dartmouth on a ferry from there. For a bit of *society,*" the first said. He stretched out his legs, taking up as much space as he could and kicking his dour friend in the knee with the toe of his battered brogue.

"Surely we'll alight before that," Gigi said. "What do you think, Bridey?"

They all took up too much space. Bridey looked up and down the aisle for a ticket inspector to move them along. "Surely we'll find out when we get there," she said. "If you could be careful of the children, please."

"Here now," another man's voice said.

Bridey thought he would be the inspector, but the voice belonged to another passenger, a man in a blue pinstripe suit who hurried along the aisle, not caring how the other passengers turned to stare. "Look out for the little ones, will you?" he said.

The winking man gave his apologies; the woman stood to go. The gloomy one grinned into his own chest.

"I hope they weren't bothering you," the new arrival said. He wasn't handsome but was well made. His suit was prewar, pre-restrictions, with cuffs on the trousers and a matching waistcoat — a smart look that signaled he cared more for the war effort than new fashion or money spent. He carried a walking stick that had the look of a simple branch stripped of its bark, and seemed to need it for a hitch in his left leg.

"They weren't," Gigi said.

"*Thank* you, sir," Bridey said. "It's already such a lot of work to keep ten children organized."

"You're doing a splendid job," he said, turning to gaze over the sleeping children. He had fresh shrapnel scarring on his neck, red and angry. A vet, home. "War nursery, is it?"

"Yes, sir."

"Thank heavens for women like you . . ." He leaned forward and reached out his hand.

"Bridget Kelly, sir," she said, standing to save him the stretch.

"Thank you, Miss Kelly. Nurse Kelly, I mean to say," he said, noticing her cloak. "Llewelyn Nevins."

There was the problem of rank. He'd be a lieutenant at least. "Thank *you,* sir."

"Ah, yes. Home a bit earlier than planned." He tapped his walking stick once on the floor. "Our boys will get the job done in the end and these children will be alive to see it. Thank you for seeing to these little angels while their mums and daddies see us all through it."

He couldn't know that what he said to her was both exactly what she would want and almost too much to bear. "Thank you," she

69

said. "Our employer says we're saving England."

The young woman rolled her red lips to keep from laughing. She turned toward the back of the train and the others followed, the ill-mannered one, the ill-humored one, all moving along the train sampling the headlines of strangers' newspapers, commenting on a book someone held, asking someone the time, drawing attention and reveling in it. The whole of the train for their amusement.

"We'll do it any way we can, won't we?" the man said. "Have a pleasant journey, Nurse Kelly, and good luck to you." He walked off toward the first-class car.

"What drivel," Gigi said as soon as he was gone. She stood.

"Where are you going now?" Bridey said.

"Powder my nose," Gigi said.

"Take one of the girls with —" But Gigi didn't wait to be told how she might take a shift.

Bridget was left to sputter and merely think the things she couldn't say.

8
BRIDEY

Somewhere southwest of Newton Abbot

Gigi didn't come back after a reasonable time or even an unreasonable time. The sun set, the carriage quickly turning gray and cold.

When would they arrive? Out the window, the sea had reappeared. *Does it make sense to go to the sea?*

Bridey consoled herself that, against Gigi's neglect of her duty, Mrs. Arbuthnot might see Bridey's quality more quickly.

She pulled one of the children's coats that had fallen to the floor over her for warmth and kept her complaints simmering, making room in her thoughts only for the blue-eyed wink, which she'd rather enjoyed now that she could look back on it. Tom Kent had never once winked at her. What difference would it make if he had? Tommy had a little extra around his middle, but he looked trim in his uniform, rather dashing. She imagined

Tommy winking with blue eyes, Tommy throwing caution and cheek kisses to the wind and taking her in his arms.

Then Tom swung open the door to a flat that was somehow theirs but not at all familiar, her mam crooning her happiness and the girls rushing in. Tommy Kent, handsome in victory, in battledress and bowler hat. His boots tracked large muddy prints into the bright kitchen but when Bridey knelt with a rag to clean the prints, they were not of mud. Tommy trailed blood, and the more she cleaned, the more it ran in red rivulets across the floor and down her arms. A bucket of sudsy water turned crimson, and then —

"Tom," she said. She sat up. The train was dark but this time they were not in a tunnel.

Gigi stood in the aisle, one of the older children, a boy, at her side. They rocked as the train slowed under them. "Who's Tom?"

"What's going on?"

"I found this one exploring the next carriage," Gigi said. She nudged the boy into an empty spot on the bench.

"I fell asleep for only a moment."

"No harm done," Gigi said.

The cool manner, no sign of vexation. This was what years of training looked like.

How could she hope to keep this woman from noticing that her nursing skills were not what they ought to be? She should have set Mrs. Arbuthnot straight back at the station, taken a chance she couldn't send her away on such short notice. All she needed was a chance to show them she could do the work. She could do the work well.

"Your stop, miss," said the inspector, coming in to reach for some of the bags. "Quickly."

So soon? It gave her nerves a jangle to imagine containing ten children outside the confinement of the train carriage. She shook the children awake, remembering to be gentle.

On the platform, the signs were blacked over. Bridey and Gigi, an infant each, gathered the rest of the children close to them. Bridey straightened caps and pulled up socks while their luggage accumulated at their feet. The Arbuthnots rejoined, other passengers disembarked, the all-aboard was called, and the train chugged away. Was that? It was. The man with the gaping collar had said he was ticketed for Paignton, and now he stood at the end of the platform. For a moment his gaze passed over their group, and Bridey thought Gigi might gesture or wish him well, but she didn't and the man moved on as though he hadn't seen them.

Soon their group stood alone on the platform with their bags and hampers around them, like a jumble sale of all their worldly goods. The night was dark and the world seemed to end at the edge of the platform.

"There's no war on here," said one of the little girls, looking out.

At last Mrs. Arbuthnot commanded the attention of someone helpful, and they were conveyed on foot, all of them too weary to complain.

Men smoking on the corner turned hard looks in their direction, glowering as a farm cart was procured, as a few discreet coins changed hands. "Did you pack the plague?" Gigi hissed at Bridey's back. "Why are they staring at us?"

"Some resent the evacuees," Mrs. Arbuthnot said. "And probably us for volunteering to bring them. It's nonsense."

One of the sisters at St. Prisca's had told of a cousin who'd taken in an evacuated mother and child in the first wave — lazy, dirty, complaining, expecting everything done for them, the cousin said. Surely not the norm, but then it might only be a clash between how one household was run against the customs of another. Bridey didn't want to think what a hostess would have made of her and her siblings —

Bridey put a hand to her mouth to keep her guts in place.

"Are you all right?" Gigi said.

She nodded.

As things went, the cart was pulled by a horse. Mr. Arbuthnot scoffed enough for all of them. "A *car* might have been sent —"

"Good heavens, Malcolm," Mrs. Arbuthnot said and reached for the baby sagging in Gigi's arms. "It'll have to do. Just this once."

They piled the luggage and the children into the cart and drove out of Paignton, along a dark road toward a village.

"The pub," said the cart driver.

Gigi paid particular attention. But then they passed by the village and Gigi turned her head to watch it disappear. "Do you mean to say —"

"Actual countryside?" Mr. Arbuthnot said.

"The village is better suited for children of school age," Mrs. Arbuthnot said. Explaining to Gigi but really, Bridey thought, her petulant husband. "We have comfortable lodging, don't worry. I have it all arranged."

"But *where* is it? Hiding from Jerry is one

thing," Gigi said. "But . . . surely we're not meant to be stored in a barn?"

"I think you'll be pleased," Mrs. Arbuthnot said, her tone ending the conversation.

The lanes grew narrow, the fields wide, the skies deep and spangled.

"Is that smoke?" one of the girls asked, voice rising up. In the sky was a sort of cloud, dense like white-blue vapor. "Is there a fire, miss?"

"I don't know," Bridey said.

"Those are stars," said Gigi.

Bridey looked again. "Are they really?"

They rattled along into the trees, which cast them into blackness. A way off, miles, something like lightning pulsed in the sky.

"They do have the war here," one of the children said. A girl whimpered into Bridey's skirt.

"They have war everywhere," Gigi muttered.

"Still, rather peaceful and all," Mr. Arbuthnot said to the cart driver. "Coming from London, a quiet night is an oddity." He sounded almost boastful.

"No need you wait for nightfall, sir," the driver said, his syllables soft and toothless over his shoulder. He had said his name was Albert. "Down'ere we've taken plenty of helpings at lunch. If you see my meaning."

76

"Direct?" Mr. Arbuthnot said.

"Oh, aye. Two children at the house was shot at, sir, like they was in the navvy."

"Sir. Please," Mrs. Arbuthnot said.

Was he joking? Children shot at? Bridey petted the back of the nearest child. Why had they come?

The cart horse made an easy turn past a little gatehouse, the children craning their necks to see, then at last came the crunch of gravel under the wheels. Bridey smelled water and listened closely for the sound of a stream. She heard only leaves rustling in unseen trees overhead.

The cart stopped and they all disembarked, the children clinging to Bridey's cloak. A little distance away, through a tunnel of dark hedges, a figure appeared with a covered lantern and beckoned.

"There you are," the man called. "Quickly now."

They moved through the imposing hedges, taller than any man. A corner of bone-white slab rose from the shadows and gave Bridey an ill feeling that she folded away. It was only a house, and an old one, a dwelling that had withstood much already.

They walked along a stone wall now and passed near a set of crumbling steps that curved up and into the dark. The children

77

edged closer to Bridey. She counted the children through the door as the man held it, hesitating, remembering suddenly her gran's old superstitions about entering and leaving by the same door, and wondering was this door, stepping down into the back of the house, the door she would use tomorrow? It was bad luck to move house overnight, too. The man made an impatient noise. "The luggage will be seen to, miss. If you please —" He gestured her inside.

In a dimly lit hallway with stone floors, their steps made scraping sounds. Overhead in the shadows, two sets of servants' bells hung silent.

"Is this a castle?" one of the girls whispered. Bridey would have to learn their names soon. The boy who had gone adventuring on the train inched up the hall toward a gong on a stand.

"Come away from that." The man from the door had put away his lantern. Stiff tweeds, white collar, he came to the front of their column and eased the Arbuthnots out of command. "Welcome to Greenway House," he said. "The rooms are ready upstairs, and I've laid out a bit of bread and cheese for the children. Perhaps some warmed milk? Better to get to sleep with something on the stomach. I caution you that we are under full blackout restrictions until dawn —"

"You'd think we'd be safe from attacks *this* far from civilization," Gigi said.

The man took her in, looked down at the crowd of faces. "The children should be in bed, miss."

"Agreed," Mrs. Arbuthnot said, adjusting the sleeping tot in her arms. "If you would, Scaldwell."

The bones of a large house surrounded them on the march up the tight, creaking staircase to the top floor. The stairwell was cold, as drafty as Mrs. Mitchell's rooming house the week the coal bill was due.

Upstairs, two rooms had been made into quarters for the children, with a sitting room between left open for their use. The rooms were all plainly decorated but well-suited. There was a separate room for the nurses to share, small with slim beds against the walls, and, the man called Scaldwell said, an apartment below for the Arbuthnots. Mr. Arbuthnot chewed on his unlit pipe, pleased.

The children clung to Bridey's cape. The infant in her arms woke, snuffled, and began to howl.

Mrs. Arbuthnot said to Mr. Scaldwell, "I hope we're not waking anyone. Is the mistress —"

"I hope you find it to your liking," Mr. Scaldwell said. "Your things will be brought up presently." He didn't offer to stay and assist.

At the door to the first room, Gigi counted off the three boys. "I've always liked the boys best," Gigi said. That dimple. "You like the babbies, anyway, right, Bridey?" Before Bridey could comprehend she was being left with all the girls and the two smallest as well, it was decided.

Mrs. Arbuthnot nodded Bridey impatiently into the second room. "You'll have to work it out between you," she said. "Just for tonight, let's get them to bed."

The room had high ceilings and tall, papered windows. Cots lined the room, a pillow and blanket each. A covered piano had been pushed into the corner.

They matched small luggage to owner, then coats off, hands washed, bread and milk consumed, crumbs dusted, faces and hands cleaned again. The snack revived the children, who had stored up a day's energy on the train and now wanted to explore the piano, the room, the hall, or wanted their mums. Bridey supervised tears and questions and pyjamas and more questions, folded each girl's dress away and stored cases under cots, children under blankets. Mrs. Arbuthnot went to check on the boys, a hand to her forehead.

"Are there ghosts living here?" one of the girls said.

"There's no such thing as ghosts," Bridey said. Not the kind the child meant. "Be still now."

At last Bridey turned the light low and sank into a nearby chair. She listened to sniffles turning to deep breaths and thought of the mums back in London, fretting the good-night rituals and the way the structure of their lives now lay wide open.

Her life, too, was riven. Bridey gripped the arms of the chair and held on. The soldier jerking in his cot. Her mam in her ear, her own opinion about ghosts. But if she cried now, Bridey knew, she would only be crying for herself, and she would never stop.

9
BRIDEY

Greenway House, near Galmpton, Devon
Mrs. Arbuthnot didn't come back from
checking on Gigi and the boys.

When Bridey's stomach growled, she realized she hadn't saved back any bread or
cheese for herself, hadn't had much of
anything all day. She crept out without the
girls or the infants stirring. Next door, the
boys snored in an otherwise empty room.

Bridey retraced their path down the stairs,
sampling the feel of the house around her.
She had a strange feeling, apprehension
perhaps, standing in an unknown house in
an unknown place. She paused on the dark
stairs, sensing the rooms of Greenway
House unfolding in all directions like a
puzzle to be solved.

Big houses had a sound to them, a taste
to the air. Not that she'd had much experience with big houses, except those cut up
into flats. She'd been to a stately home, one

turned to a Red Cross post, where she'd scanned the cots lined up in formerly elegant rooms for faces she knew —

At the memory, Bridey nearly missed the last stair. Her hand found and grasped at the newel post cap as she let a wave of nausea pass over her. In another life, she wouldn't have minded so much caring for *babbies.* What was gentling a crying girl or making a cup of milky baby tea to the smell of gangrene, to the sight of a man shredded by shrapnel? In her first week at St. Prisca's, she'd been assigned to clean the surgical theater, a test of her mettle. She'd carried an amputated leg to the furnace past the other gagging probationers and a few stunned sisters. The leg still wore its boot, tied into a rabbit's ears bow.

What good was such determination at Greenway House? What would they be doing but keeping the fine things in this house safe from grasping hands?

Bridey heard voices and reached into the darkness until she found the opening to the corridor. A strip of light showed under a door.

"Missus Arbuthnot?" she said into the hinges. The voices beyond stopped.

"Do come in, Bridey. There's tea."

The man called Scaldwell, the Arbuthnots,

and Gigi sat at a table with sturdy legs, tea things and empty cups in evidence. Mr. Arbuthnot still wore his ridiculous beret. Another woman stood at the sink with her back to them, busy at some task. Her arms below her turned-up sleeves were as roped and muscled as any man's, another page from *Gray's.* The woman turned at Bridey's entrance. "This is special circumstances, this is," the woman said.

"If this isn't special circumstance, what the devil would be?" Mr. Arbuthnot said. The cup too small in his hand.

"Yes, Mrs. Scaldwell, of course we understand," Mrs. Arbuthnot said. She looked small and weary next to the other woman, soft and directionless without her hat. "We'll observe household rituals tomorrow. It is special circumstances indeed, just this once."

"If you're a painter of views, Arbuthnot, we've a good one of Dartmouth," Mr. Scaldwell was saying. Another plate was found, a few bits of cheese and bread, no butter or marge offered. "Down the estuary on a clear day. If you don't mind swatting at German fighters."

"Not views, no," Mr. Arbuthnot said. "How many acres?"

"Thirty-six," Scaldwell said. "I walk them

twice a day, keeping lookout, especially with the master in London."

Mrs. Arbuthnot said, "Lookout for . . ."

"Invasion," he said. "But trespassers are sometimes a nuisance, even in peacetime. Folks coming through for the quay, bold as brass. You should watch for them as you go."

"We should guard the house and grounds, too?" Gigi lounged back in the chair, at her leisure. "Are the children in the Home Guard now? Shall we arm them?"

Gigi had a way of talking that confused Bridey. Was she teasing? Mrs. Arbuthnot hushed her and the Scaldwells stared.

"I only mean to say," Mr. Scaldwell said. "You should be careful of strangers about."

"That much call for caution?" Mr. Arbuthnot said.

"This close to the coast?" Mr. Scaldwell said. "There's a real concern the fifth columns might help the Germans stage a landing. Not on my watch, sir. Not at Greenway."

Bridey looked toward Mrs. Arbuthnot. *Spies* and strangers crossing the grounds and already bombs landing near? Children *shot* at. Why had they come to this place at all?

Mrs. Scaldwell poured some preserved apple slices on the plate in front of Bridey and watched as she reached with her hands.

"Apples from our own orchard trees," Mrs. Scaldwell said. "Mrs. M. likes her apples. Eats them in the bath."

"Thank you," Bridey said, mouth full. Shamed, her appetite revealed. But it was sweet and tart, crisp, the best thing she had tasted in an age.

Gigi leaned forward and nabbed a slice with her fingers, too. "Apples in the bath?"

"Had a ledge over the bath built, special." The woman went back to the sink.

Mr. Arbuthnot pulled a face.

"You'll find that this house is devised around the particular habits and tastes of our employers," Mr. Scaldwell said. He had a military bearing to him, proper —

The staff!

As far as Bridey was concerned, butlers were as likely as a fairie or a banshee, and here was one in the flesh.

"At least, it *was* arranged around them," Mr. Scaldwell said. "We've made adjustments around the needs of the nursery, but we ask that you and your charges respect the rules of the household while you stay here — as well as the privacy and property of the Mallowan family."

"Are we your first 'vacs?" Gigi said.

"We had two children here as a favor, just

after war was declared," Scaldwell said. "They moved on to their grandmother's after a few weeks." He and his wife exchanged a quick glance. "The mistress's goddaughter and her brother. Guests."

"Not vermin from London, then," Gigi said.

"Gigi!" Mrs. Arbuthnot said. "That will be quite enough."

But Gigi had the situation well in hand, didn't she? They were the dust of war, scrapings off city shoes into the home of a particular woman with funny ideas and probably a fussy parlor. *The mistress.* According to the *staff.* Bridey looked down at the thin edge of the bone china cup and saucer in front of her. Each piece on the table matched, petal for petal. What would happen if she dashed hers against the wall?

"We'll comport ourselves as guests, then," Mrs. Arbuthnot said. "Malcolm and I are grateful to have Mrs. Mallowan's patronage, to have some little part to play, and I know the children's parents are appreciative. The children are young and frightened, prone to tears, but we'll do our best to keep them tidy and contained to our assigned portions of the house."

Bridey stopped chewing, her cheek distended with apple. She looked across the

87

table to Gigi, whose cup rattled to its saucer. Prisoners, they were. The middle of nowhere, and nowhere to go.

10
BRIDEY

Greenway, late

In the night, a child woke and howled. Bridey stumbled out of bed, bleary, not sure where she was, thinking the cry was Evangeline —

Her arms and back were sore, and the bed across, empty. It all came back to her. She had agreed to a war nursery scheme, of all things, and they were highly outnumbered, even with the Arbuthnots' help. Down the corridor, two children cried. Perhaps Gigi had already gone to see.

But Gigi wasn't in with the children. After Bridey had changed and rocked both infants and then got one of the little girls to the lav and back in bed, she checked that all the children were in their beds and padded back to the room she shared with Gigi. No one was there.

Bridey crept down the stairs and along the dark corridor with no light under the door to guide her this time, the kitchen dark. She went as quietly as she could into the front of the house, feeling her way. Past the staircase that led to the family quarters and the forbidden sector of the house, a light burned through a wide, arched doorway. Within, a rustle of paper.

Inside, Gigi sat at a writing desk, pen in her fist.

"Can't you —"

"Bloody hell!" Gigi shouted.

"Sorry," Bridey said. "Sorry. My word. I didn't mean to frighten you."

"What did you *mean* to do?" Gigi said.

"Find where you'd gone." They were in a comfortable room, a library, perhaps. There were cases across the lower portion of the walls, all stuffed with books. Bridey felt like a child in her bare feet and nightgown when she realized Gigi was still fully dressed, blouse and skirt. She had let her hair down, though, long and black. "Are you going somewhere?"

"No."

"Only you're dressed for going out."

"I'm dressed for changing into my sleeping clothes. In a moment."

Bridey looked around. "I think this might be one of the rooms we're not allowed."

"Every room of this house is a room we're

not allowed. Didn't you hear?"

"It was never going to be a holiday, was it?" Bridey said. "Are you writing home already?"

Gigi set down the pen and folded the piece of paper in front of her. "Letting them know where I've turned up."

Bridey wished she had listened better to them talking of possible destinations. "Did Mrs. Arbuthnot ever say where precisely? Greenway. What *is* that? Where are we?"

"The front door of the Nazi invasion."

Bridey felt the rush of memory, dust from the site of their house in her throat. "They'd never take us somewhere truly unsafe."

"They have. They've brought us an arm's throw to the Channel."

"How do you know that?"

"Weren't you listening? 'This close to the coast,' he said. 'A view of Dartmouth.' "

"I don't know my geography," Bridey said. "I've never been far from . . . home."

Gigi watched her. "Who's keeping you so close to home, then? Tom, was it?"

"How do you — oh. No one."

"Not your fella?"

"No," Bridey said. "He comes around a bit."

"That sounds like he's your man."

"He's —"

"What?"

Bridey shrugged. "It's awful to say and he's handsome in his uniform but . . ."

"Doesn't set off the sirens? In your knickers?"

Gigi!"

"Is he at the front?"

"He's in an office somewhere — always stopped by and told the most tedious stories. His kind of war maneuvers. Nearly missed correspondence, lost files . . ."

"The misadventure of bad penmanship?" Gigi said.

"That's it," Bridey said, smiling. "All rather dire, in terms of romance."

"An office in London? He might be at the heart of it. Is he in Westminster?"

"Tom?" She stifled a wide yawn.

"Gad, does that clock say two in the morning?" Gigi stood, tucking the letter into her blouse sleeve. Bridey had never seen that before. What else could one secret away, literally up a sleeve? A handkerchief for little noses. "We should get to bed," Gigi said. "Do *you* not sleep well?"

"One of the children woke me. We'll have to take turns."

"I hadn't thought of that. They do require some attention, don't they?"

Bridey stared at her. "Have you never

been around children?"

"Not properly. Not . . . this young. Not at all, if I'm honest. What do we — well, what do we do with them, exactly?"

"Do?"

"I meant tomorrow's schedule. Have you given it a thought?"

"Well," Bridey said. "First we'll get them in and out of the lav, then dressed and brushed and fed." This part came easily, but she'd rather been hoping the other nurse would take on some of the management. What was expected? How quickly might they scrape the bottom of her training? "We should do a check for nits first thing or we might all suffer for it later. We might find a tape measure and do some measurements, if Mrs. Arbuthnot needs to report progress. We'll need to perform gas mask drills regularly —"

"Mercy," Gigi said. "I'm sorry I asked."

"— but then beyond that, I suppose we'll have to entertain them."

"Entertain them?" Gigi said. "We're expected to *amuse* them?"

"It's a job, isn't it? Away from red skies and nightly raids?" She hoped.

"Do you mean . . . teach them? Their letters and that?"

"They're too young. We'll only need to

keep them from trouble and harm. And then, if there's harm, that's where your nursing comes in. Our nursing, I mean."

"I see."

"Didn't Mrs. Arbuthnot tell you it was young children we were caring for?" Bridey said.

"She must have done. Perhaps I didn't listen well enough." Gigi smiled down at the desk.

"What's so funny?"

"I was rather a rotten child," she said. "I can't help thinking this is a joke played on me."

Bridey didn't see what was funny. "My feet are cold. I'm going back to bed, and so should you before one of the children starts calling for us again. Or the Scaldwells or this mistress we've heard so much about finds you where you don't belong."

Gigi snapped off the light at the desk. In the dark, she moved across the room. "*She's* interesting."

"She didn't see you?" Bridey said. The first night, and they'd broken the rules. She would never get Mrs. Arbuthnot's good favor.

"All this mistress this and that," Gigi said. She passed close by Bridey, stirring up a draft that gave Bridey a chill. Someone stepping on a grave, that's what her mam would have said. "Mrs. *M.* But it's the strangest thing . . ."

"What?"

Gigi stopped at the foot of the stairs reserved for the family. There was just enough light to see Gigi's head cocked back at the library. "Didn't you see all the books in that room?"

"What about them? Some like books."

"I like books, in fact. But every one of those books is about murder."

11
CECILIA POOLE

St. Pancras, London, April 1941

Cecilia Poole and her son had their tea late that day after the trip to Paddington Station and back. They sat at the kitchen table that wobbled, and every time Samuel moved, he kicked the table leg or knocked the edge with his elbow, and that was enough to set everything that should be still to moving. It righted soon enough, but if either of them put any weight on the table's edge, a wrist, or Samuel's little hand reaching for his cup, the table canted and corrected, and the tea in her cup sloshed. They were on a ship at sea, the two of them.

In the corner, the wireless played Vera Lynn's sweet voice. Cissy hummed along and used the towel tucked at her waist to wipe the dribble of tea from the tabletop.

"Mummy," Samuel said. "Whyn't I go on the train? You said I would go on the train with the nice lady."

"Not this time, love."

"When? I wanted to go on the train."

They'd said the countryside would be safe, and she'd believed them. The arrangements all made, all his things packed. She'd done all the mending and pressing to make sure he was turned out as well as he could be for the journey, and then folded everything into paper lantern shapes to tuck them into the nearest thing she had for a dressing case, a hat box with a handle from an old style she hadn't worn in years. She might have borrowed a dressing case but everyone she could ask had abandoned the building since the last raid. Gone to relatives, gone to America. Gone. Fine for them, having a place to go.

At the door, Sam's coat hung, the tag attached.

It had been all decided, all arranged. The volunteer couple, these Arbuthnots, had arranged a nice house in the south and hired the two nurses. She'd believed them when it was said she must send her boy, and then she had believed that woman when she'd promised she could take good care.

That morning, Cecilia dutifully dressed and fed Sam breakfast as though she meant to hand him over and went to the station with all good intentions to obey.

The station was teeming with children, and that's when she realized what was happening. This train was the *City of Benares,* a vessel sent into vast waters to save English children but with no guarantee — the ship under attack, the children drowned. She was meant to put him on it, was she? To send him away from her, with strangers, with no idea when or if she would have him back. She couldn't do it. She wouldn't.

"Sometime we'll both go on the train," she said. "We'll go visit your grandparents. Won't they be glad to see you?"

"Who?"

"Granddad and Nan. In Scotland."

He had no grandparents, or a father. Cissy had decided after Sam's birth on a cheap gold band and a story. A pair of doting grandparents in Scotland who sent occasional presents but never visited and a daddy with a grave in some far-off spot — that fit the pair of them down to the ground. They didn't need anyone else, not a father, not strangers offering a hand up into the door of a train going God knows where.

"Mummy, I don't like this song."

She blinked at him. Everyone liked Vera Lynn. That was the point of Vera Lynn. "Why ever not?"

"What are bluebirds?"

"Birds that are blue, I suppose?"

"I don't believe in birds that are blue," he said.

She'd never seen a blue bird, either, but then she'd never been to Dover. She'd never been anywhere. Maybe they should take a train trip, or a ship to Canada when the troubles were over. There was naught keeping them here. "I'd like to see a blue bird, wouldn't you?"

He pushed food around on his plate. "She sounds too sad."

"Well, that's all right because you know what? She's singing about how it's sad now, but won't we have good times soon?" She sang a few lines, got the lyrics twisted up. Her voice was thin and warbling.

"I don't like that."

He'd broken the song, cracking it open over the birds as he had. He was four years old, but he wielded such power over her. "I'm sorry you don't like it, but I do. Can't Mummy have one thing that she likes?"

Samuel looked up but said nothing.

They were on each other's nerves, that's all, together too much instead of separated by the evacuation. The children he knew downstairs had been sent to the country months ago, all the children from church and the lane gone and he wasn't allowed to go into the garden on his own. The war would steal his childhood from him. It would steal everything if they let it.

"Do you know?" she said, just as the air-raid siren struck up. Another night. They should go out to the shelter, but she could tell Sam hadn't the usual heart for it. It had been all adventure in the beginning, but now she had to fight him. She hadn't the heart for it, either. She'd promised him a train trip and new friends. How had she thought she could let him go? "Do you know what I like?" she said. "The one thing Mummy likes best is you."

He ducked his head to hide his smile, the darling, the table tilting as he moved and the tea splashing. But then his face was turned up to her, concerned and falling, and the table didn't correct itself but kept going, down, down, and they slid through the floor through the sky through the dark.

Cecilia had a headache as though she'd had a drink or two, like old days. Had she?

She had left the wireless playing, could hear the plaintive voice of Vera Lynn still singing her bluebirds.

Cissy hummed a note and slept.

Sometime later the lights came on and she blinked away from the glare. "Sam, get back in bed."

"Madam, stay where you are."

Someone was tugging at her. "Sam," she moaned, "what is it?"

"Who's Sam, love? Is Sam at home tonight?"

They were strangers' voices, and then she heard someone she knew, the woman across who swept her step every morning and always had a little treat for Sam. "That's Cissy Poole. Sam is her lad," the woman said. "He's evacuated this morning, thank God for it. They went to Paddington this morning."

Was the song still playing? But —

"No," Cissy said. She found her voice — she felt as though she had swallowed a spoonful of sawdust — and tried again. "No."

The light moved out of her eyes. She lay in her grave, all of them looking down. "No." They pulled her up and out of brick and wood, of stone and glass. She could still hear the song, that bloody song, singing about a boy and his little room, Vera Lynn singing and singing. "Where's Sam?" she cried into the light. "Where's Sam?"

Several hours passed. Or only minutes. The windows of the infirmary post were still dark but was it morning?

Cissy Poole sat on a cot with a cool cloth to her head. Someone behind her made a low noise that ended in a whimper. She hummed Vera Lynn and bluebirds, could hear the song even when she stopped, the high trilling notes coming as though from the back of her neck.

"Stop that noise," someone said.

She couldn't.

Where was Sam?

They went to Paddington, her neighbor had said. She remembered going to Paddington. She did, holding Sam's hand and the dressing case that was a hat box with a handle. Yes. She remembered the hat box with the handle. Ironing his clothes, placing them inside, the feel of the handle in her glove. Her fingers cold. And then —

She couldn't remember. Something had happened. "We went to the station," she said, in argument. Her fist pressed at her own leg.

Cissy was sure of nothing past that, certain only that they had gone to the station to send him away. She shouldn't have sent him away.

Nurses moved along the cots. When the ward sister's attention was turned to the far corner, Cissy stood and walked down the aisle of beds to the door and then out, hallway, door, dark night or morning, one could not tell. Outside, the air smelled of smoke. She lowered the cloth from her head, threw it away from her, but the people she passed blinked, stared, and asked questions after her that she ignored. She would be fine, thank you, if she could find Sam.

She walked until the streets started to come into focus, until she knew where she was and that was one more certainty. The sky brightened. Early morning, but she could still put Sam to bed properly. His own little room.

Someone was screaming.

No, it was a siren, and the people near her had started to hurry and push. She got caught up in them, no-madam and this-way-madam, until she found herself inside a Tube station, shoulder to shoulder when the lights went out. They all waited in silence for a long while, the smell of a stranger's breath stinking and hot on her shoulder.

Finally a string of bulbs came on, like Christmas in the shops. All around her, gray faces hovered in the gloom. Somewhere near her a little voice said, "Mummy."

"Sam?" Like the cry of a wild bird.

The man next to her edged away, eyes on

the floor.

"Sam?" When the lights came on, she would find him. She could hardly keep still for want of his hand in hers.

"False alarm," a voice grumbled.

The man next to her finally looked up. His eyes were black, shadowed. A haunt. His mouth opened, gaping at her for some reason. "Dear Lord in heaven," he said, his voice a rasp. "Madam, do you need help?"

"My boy."

The crowd was moving, then, toward the exit. Cissy shuffled along until she spotted him. There he was. Sam! Bless him, he'd been here the whole time. She would have to speak with him about slipping away like that. Didn't he know she suffered without him? That he was all she had?

Cissy pushed her way against the flow of people and down to the platform and onto the tracks, over feet and blankets of those still bedded down, taking no chances, down into the tunnel. They'd slept in the tunnel a few nights, hadn't they, she and her boy, when the shelter was full? "Sam!"

She caught up to him, grabbed at his coat.

It wasn't Sam at all.

"Why aren't you in the country?" She gripped the boy by the shoulders. The child fought her off and dashed for his mother.

"*My* boy had to go to the country."

She stumbled out of the tunnel. When? When would there be blue birds? That blasted song was still playing at the base of her skull, inside her bones. She could hear nothing but Vera Lynn. Vera Lynn and — crying. She could hear someone crying as though Sam would never come home.

12
MALCOLM ARBUTHNOT

The first day at Greenway House
Malcolm took the back stairs down but
didn't like to do it. The back stairs were
narrow and dim, and he and Joan weren't
the *servants*. They were guests in the house,
weren't they? Or if not guests, then the tenants, like a holiday let.

Never mind this do-gooding, this volunteering. They'd rented for the year in ad-
vance and the Mallowans should be happy
for the income in times like these. Might be
longer than a year if necessary, blasted war.
There was no telling, no telling at all, how
long they'd have to stay.

He should have the use of the proper stairs
if he wanted them.

Toward the front of the house, a little
daylight came in around a blackout shade
pulled up. Lovely light, that. The shade open
— did that mean the household was awake?
He had hoped to have a look around early,

before anyone could stop him, but the racket on the top floor had kept him from a good night's rest. Children wailing, footsteps all hours.

They couldn't stop him from looking around the place he lived now, could they?

He shuffled in his slippers toward forbidden fruit, past the gong and into the entrance hall.

He'd rather have stayed on at home, truth be told. They had a lovely house let on Jersey, but of course there was no denying it was a dangerous place, in German control now. This was technically their *second* evacuation, but he'd had no intention of becoming a prisoner of war, even in the comfort of his own drawing room. The other place, the chateau Joan's children preferred in the Antibes, was entirely out of reach now that France had fallen. Who knew what shape it might be in when they got into it again? The pile in Scotland would have been best, but it had gone to Joan's first husband's children with his first wife. Well, it was enough to keep a man up at night, thinking of all the landholdings just out of his reach.

Malcolm pulled back the shade. An open, rolling hill led down to the river, trees all around. A nice patch that Mallowan fellow had got for himself. Only six thousand pounds of his wife's money, he'd heard. One always had friends in common. If *he*'d had a chance at it for six thousand pounds, he'd have snatched it up, made a bloody palace of it. He looked around. He'd take down the dour-faced portraits, first thing.

He supposed he would never own a house like this. Or own one at all; he was at Joan's mercy. The money George left her was running out, she said. But Malcolm wondered what they were saving it for. Money wanted to be *spent.*

The first room near the door was a parlor of sorts, good simple bones, wainscot and built-in shelving, a nice fireplace mantel — but enough bits and bobs sitting all about to make a secondhand shop. Plates and saucers and little porcelain things people went in for, frowsy little tables everywhere he turned. He went in, picking up a piece and turning it over now and again, weighing things, pricing them. The children must be kept out of this area completely, and now he thought of it, they should put away anything the Mallowan chap had dug up in the desert straightaway. Malcolm wouldn't pay for any pagan idols these children broke, no.

He followed the carpets, a bit worn in

places, to the next room and found a drawing room, homely and well-used. Now *this* was a fireplace. It was cold, but Malcolm could imagine the evenings spent here. Would they, though? These Mallowans, so called — he knew who they were — had the gall to restrict them to certain parts of the house. If he'd known that to be the arrangement, he would have had Joan talk them down in price.

The restrictions were for the children, surely — their grubby, grabby hands. He had two grown children, aside from Joan's lot. He knew what children were about, and he didn't need this litter of brats from London to remind him he was glad those years were long past.

He and Joan might have spent the war years holed up in Coventry or Wales, some sleepy place away from London, but not so far as this. Painting, writing letters, reading, the two of them. If they desired proper society, they could have had it on their own terms. But Joan wanted her war nursery. They should volunteer, she said, get the rent paid for with war funds if they had to evacuate the Channel Islands. They should have a safe place to tuck away that her children might come to, she said. He wondered, though. Did she want to feel needed now hers were grown? Was it only a chance to cuddle and coo for want of a grandchild?

He opened one of the window shutters to have a better look around the room. Nice, this. Comfortable sort of place, room to put your feet up. If only he had a cup of tea and something sweet, this would suit him down to the ground.

A newspaper lay on the floor near the fireplace. "Ha," he said, pouncing. He could pay for a newspaper, of course, and no one had better suggest otherwise, but it was the luck of the thing, the happenstance. If he paid for a newspaper then of course he would have it, but if he *found* a newspaper, it was a matter of coincidence what all he might discover and know.

He chose a seat and gazed for a moment at the white light in the window. He should ask Joan where his easel had got to and take it out this afternoon, though he supposed the children might require some attention to get settled in. Those nurses should be the ones to see to the children's needs, or what were they hired for? Free room and board, too, and escape from living situations Malcolm could only imagine to be dire. His mind drifted, thinking of the dark-haired one. Flashing eyes. Something pagan there, as well.

His luck held out: the newspaper was from that week. The photograph reproductions were astonishingly poor, and many of the top headlines were the same as the paper he'd cadged on the train down the day before.

His attention drifted back to the window.

He woke to a clang. "What is it?" The paper lay on the carpets.

"Sorry, sir." A young woman with a humorless sort of face squatted in the hearth with a metal pail of ashes at her feet. "I was trying to be quiet."

"I don't see that you were successful, young lady. Who are you?"

"The daily, sir. Edith."

"Might you find a cup of tea for me, Edith?"

She looked at the pail miserably. "Yes, sir."

He needed the toilet but now that he had tea coming, he sat impatiently, making plans for the day. He should have asked what was warm in the kitchen.

When the tea arrived, the cup was on a proper tray, carried by the butler.

Malcolm coughed into his hand. "I didn't mean to bother you with it, Scarsdale."

"Scaldwell, sir. I'm sure the mistress won't mind you taking your refreshment here this morning, until you get your bearings. Sir."

Arbuthnot heard what was meant. "Very good, very good." They couldn't be kept to the service quarters entirely, could they? Around the clock? He would have a word to this Mrs. Mallowan, if he had to. He might make a little trouble. If he had to. "A good position for you here, is it?"

"I find it so. Milk and sugar?"

Malcolm noticed he'd dropped the sir. "Better than a stick in the eye. Yes, milk and sugar."

"Better indeed. One lump?"

"Two." He ignored Scaldwell's blinking face. He liked his pleasures, and he'd be damned if he gave them up. These Mallowans could afford a few fripperies from the looks of things. Yes, he knew what *she* was about. Fascinating the low sort of thing one might do for money, if one had to. "What time is *madam* awake in the morning?"

"She'll be awake now, working."

"Ah, she does that here, does she?" Tea was handed over. A shade dark to his liking. He could have poured his own milk, but the tray was out of reach now. On purpose.

"Her work? Sometimes. Her correspondence, of course. Contracts and proofs and such."

"Look, Scallwell, you're just the man I need to ask. It's good you came along. I'll need to set up somewhere in good light. I'm a painter, as I mentioned last night."

"You'll find exquisite light out on the hill over the river. Or if you like a hike —"

"I'm not one of those plain air types, chap."

"Is it some kind of studio you want? Perhaps the stables. Mrs. Arbuthnot can bring it up with the mistress when she meets with her."

"I could have a word myself," Malcolm said.

"She'll request you if she'd like to see you," the butler said. "She keeps her own schedule —"

"Now, see here —"

"— as these days her secretary works in a munitions plant." Scaldwell said this with a mix of wonder and distaste. "You'll find your breakfast served in your sitting room at the proper time. Perhaps you could take yourself upstairs? Before the ladies of the house come down? Sir?"

Malcolm's outrage dropped away. He was sitting in his dressing gown and slippers — like an old man, puttering about, senseless. Thank God the Mallowans hadn't wandered in yet, the daughter, if she was at home. A telephone started to ring somewhere in the house. He dug himself out of the low couch,

Scaldwell diving for the teacup as though he couldn't be trusted with it.

"I'm fine, I'm fine." He went quietly from there, passing only the daily maid, who waited outside the room for him to go.

He was nearly to the stairs — the service stairs, better not to run into anyone — when the butler caught up. "There's a call for Mrs. Arbuthnot."

"She's asleep," Malcolm grumbled. "Might you take a message? Here, I'll see to it."

The mouthpiece lay on a table in the entrance. It was a noisy connection. "Malcolm Arbuthnot here."

A tin voice, a woman's, came from far away. A trunk call, but then he wouldn't have expected to hear from anyone locally. "I'd rather talk with *Mrs.* Arbuthnot if I may. It's only that I owe her an apology —"

The connection was really rather bad, like the tide rushing up on the shore and some knocking as well.

"She's indisposed, I'm afraid," he said.

"Only I owe her an apology, you see," the young woman said. "And if she still wanted me, I could be on my way this morning."

"Wanted you for what?"

"I'm a nurse, sir."

How many nurses should they have to

114

feed and pay? "We've got a full docket of nurses at the moment, but I can have Mrs. Arbuthnot call around if we should need another."

Malcolm could feel the presence of Scaldwell, waiting behind him to be finished. It didn't cost anything to *accept* a long-distance call. Did it?

"Only I owe her —"

"An apology, yes, you said. I'll pass it along," Malcolm said. "Thank you for calling. I'll let her know."

After he hung up, he realized he had not taken the caller's name. Scaldwell gestured to draw him toward the back corridor and held out the teacup. It would be cold now, but he would protect it with his life to prove this fellow wrong.

And next time, he would get hold of the milk and pour it himself.

As he climbed the stairs, Malcolm selected a few sentiments to share with Joan about the so-called butler. He chose the words carefully and let everything else fall from his mind.

13
BRIDEY

The first day at Greenway

The first morning they had chaos.

The children under Bridey's care woke suddenly or groggily, and remembered to be sad or sullen, to be scared. The babies screeched and needed changing. One of the girls had an accident standing next to her cot in her pyjamas, and the others cried for their mums, for toys or dogs left at home, for the babies to stop wailing, for breakfast.

They had a lesson in *urgency,* a trip to the potties, a row of them set up, then another lesson on dressing, in storing their clothes in the cupboard. Each girl became the proud owner of a cubby Bridey marked with her name. The girls would need to learn their letters. They each had a one-piece siren suit to play in, the peak of each hood stitched twice in a bright color. The girls learned their colors: yellow, white, pink, blue.

"I have this color," said little angel-cheeked Doreen, plucking at the hood of her suit to show Bridey. It was lavender.

They had a lesson in how to say lavender, and what lavender was, then received breakfast with a good number of questions and ate in the room. Their table was a plank resting on a crate, covered with a third-best cloth. The meal was porridge, not at all hot, and milk. The children had plates, bowls, and cups, all tin, and bibs to tie around their necks. They were too old for bibs. Then Beryl's milk cup slipped from her hands and spilled, the first casualty of the children's war at Greenway.

They marched on the lav again, this time with toothbrushes. Sticky hands were washed and, back in the room, heads checked for lice and hair combed. Mrs. Arbuthnot came by to inspect. "Excellent work, Nurse Kelly," she said. "Er. Nurse Bridey, hadn't we better?"

"Yes, missus."

"You have it well in hand, well done."

Well in hand. Bridey calculated how quickly she might have Mrs. Arbuthnot's recommendation, how soon she might make her excuses. Summer?

Mrs. Arbuthnot remarked that the weather was fine. "Nurse Gigi has the boys out already," she said.

Ah. How many heads had she to comb? Three?

Bridey looked over the seven under her watch and despaired. It was almost too much. No, it was too much indeed. They needed another hand, at least —

"I'm rather fond of this age," Mrs. Arbuthnot said over the infants' cots. "Why don't I keep these two gentlemen today?"

Saved. On the older children, Bridey layered coats and mittens over the siren suits and formed a queue. She allowed the oldest girl to lead them through the corridor and down a set of stairs.

"Wait," she said, turned around. Again she had the odd unease of being released from the world as she'd known it. But they were only a *bit* lost. She hurried after the children. "Wait, please. Doreen? Maureen, Pamela?" But the girls had found another staircase and were down it, and sucked in their breath at a turn in the landing.

Bridey caught up and stared, too. The ceiling above was like something out of a country church, the blackout shades dimming the shapes of furniture below into hulking beasts and the doorways into caverns. On the walls were portraits of unknown faces, a petulant child, a grim old woman.

"Who *lives* here?" one of the girls whispered.

"You do," Bridey said. But she wondered the same thing, wondered who the stern pictures on the wall pleased, who had chosen the opulent chandelier, who used the walking sticks in the umbrella stand. Who had a library full of ghastly stories.

She led the girls around the corner and into familiar territory — past the gong and under the dual systems of bells and out the back door. Out the same door they'd come to keep their luck. There was an overhang that would prove useful, come rain, and a basin to rinse muddy Wellingtons.

Did the children even have galoshes? Or macs?

At this, her mam's voice was in her head. *A few raindrops. Will you melt away?* Her mam might be standing among the girls.

"Nurse?" one of them said.

Somewhere out of sight, the boys' voices rang out and a dog barked. The girls turned as one. Around the side of the house, here were the early risers. Bridey wondered how Gigi managed it, if she slept at all. But she looked as elegant as ever, hair pinned in place, her cloak draping far more dramatically than Bridey's did on her.

A white terrier ran around the outskirts of the crowd, yapping. Bridey glanced in its direction, wondering about bites and fleas, and when she looked back at the boys, she noticed shirts untucked, laces untied. There were not a few buttons missed that morning on their coats, and one of the boys wore short trousers, knees pink from the cold.

Was it some new school of thought, letting children run wild? "Good morning," Bridey said. "You're up rather early."

"I wanted a look around."

"And?"

"Well, it's a lovely prison, at least," Gigi said. "Come look."

She led them all around the corner to a steep, sloping garden. As they came around to the front of the house, a vista opened up, a long slide down to a green river, and trees on every side, bright spring leaves and early buds.

"Well?"

Bridey turned upon the house, expecting something monstrous. But Greenway was a wedding cake of a house, a flat traditional face in a confection color, clotted cream squared off into stone. Someone had trained vines up the front, with rather too much success.

The house was at once beautiful and innocent in its simplicity, untouched and unguarded. All hint of dread she'd had the night before was gone.

"Does it seem like a fortress to you?" Gigi said. "Without the bridge over the moat perhaps?"

"It seems like a fairie cake," Bridey said, blinking.

"With this view over the river," Gigi said. "And Dartmouth past that bend, I wouldn't have put babies here. I would have put sailors or antiaircraft guns."

A bright white target on a hill. They shouldn't be here. "Maybe it will be over soon," she said as brightly as she could. "And they won't have to put anyone here except the — what were the owners called?"

"That's the best part, Bridey," Gigi said. "You'll never guess."

The children were making their own games. Bridey counted them off, and noticed Gigi hadn't asked after the two left upstairs. *Her* charges certainly hadn't seen a comb yet this morning. The cutting of corners, while she minded twice as many and had been on her knees this morning cleaning first a pool of urine and then milk while the infants cried for their feeding bottles.

"Who, then?"

"Guess!" Gigi said.

"You said I would never. Minor royalty?"

"Not the kind you're thinking. Self-made."

"Do tell me, Gigi."

"A poisoner lives here."

"What?"

"Bridey, it's most ridiculous. Mrs. Mallowan, Mrs. M., the *mistress,* is Agatha Christie." Gigi was pleased with herself to be able to say it. "The queen of murder lives here."

"The authoress? The one who writes the — oh."

"Exactly the one. No wonder all the books were —"

"Gigi, the children."

The older girls had commandeered a yo-yo from the toddler boy. Doreen and the smaller girls were trying to coax the dog out from under a deckchair. One of the older boys toed the edge of garden where the hill rolled precariously. "You there, stop that," Bridey called. There were too many children, too many ways they might get into mischief in this new strange place. "Let's go for a walk, shall we?"

They took the nearest path, a slope that led away from the house toward the river.

"The house looks different once you

know, doesn't it?"

Bridey looked back. "It's smarter than I thought it was last night. Rather charming."

"Charmingly sweet on the outside but hiding sinister secrets, I'm sure. And don't you see? Ten children, Bridey. Ten little —"

"Gigi, really," Bridey said. They had entered the woods, and without the sun, she felt a chill in her bones.

"It's a story! Nothing will *actually* happen to them."

"Don't imagine the children dead, Gigi," Bridey whispered, sharp. The little ones were busy ahead, skipping, wielding sticks, chasing. Had Gigi no experience with children at all? How they listened, how they repeated your worst revelations back to you at the worst possible moment? "And best to remember there's a war on. That's —" She lowered her voice. "That's murder enough, without made-up stories."

Gigi pulled a face, disappointed perhaps. "Not a reader, then."

"Not specially." Who had the time to bother with make-believe? "Not with — everything going on just now."

The children had chosen a fork in the path, a steep plunge toward the shore.

"If the Nazis burn books," Gigi said, "it makes me think I should spend more time reading them. *Can* you read?"

"Of course I can read!" All the children's heads swiveled at her voice.

"Bridey, I didn't mean offense."

"I think you might have." Dull Bridget, dim Bridget. Was there no way to get through this without being compared to this other Bridget Kelly, now that they were thrown together? "We'll be redistributing the children before bedtime this evening," she said. Gigi had more training than she did, but she hadn't taken charge. "And we'll need a pram for the infants. Remind me to ask Mrs. Arbuthnot if she can manage one."

"I'm sorry," Gigi said. "I am, for being such a terrible snob. I've no right to be."

"Don't be daft, of course you do. In my experience, pretty girls get the privilege of being whatever they like to be."

"Except intelligent," Gigi said, raising her chin. "Or resourceful. Except anything *but* pretty."

Bridey looked toward the children. She'd already questioned the quality of Gigi's work, but it was only uncombed hair. What did it matter when Gigi was a proper nurse and she was a proper fraud? "Mrs. Scaldwell doesn't seem like she likes a chat. Who told you about Mrs. Christie?"

"A domestic named Edith," Gigi said. "I

124

found her polishing brasses in the dining room. *She* didn't mind a break."

"You went into the dining room? Gigi, you *know* we're to keep to our — Where were the boys while you were snooping?"

"Sleeping. It was only a quiet lark, no harm done."

Timid Bridget, craven Bridget. The path had grown rather steep, but the children only grew bolder. At the next branch in the path, they moved as one. "Well?"

"Lots of *things*. China and figures and silver. Rather more silver than any one family could use. Candlesticks and that. Souvenirs from all over, too."

"Must be a lot to keep clean," Bridey said.

"Do you honestly think only of the chores? Why not think of how they must collect it all, traveling the world? Imagine being rich enough so when war brats invade one of your homes, you simply move to another."

"Are they?"

"What the devil?" Gigi said. For all at once the path had opened up to reveal a view of the river, where the children had discovered a platform fixed with cannons pointed out at invaders.

"Dear God," Bridey said, and went to make sure they were antiques and harmless.

"Evacuate to a place built for war. What sense?"

The children clambered over the cannon, rode them like ponies, and cried out directions, pirate captains all. It wouldn't last. Let one of them think they'd not had a fair portion.

"Is she then?" Bridey said.

"What's that?"

"Is Mrs. Mallowan moving house?"

Almost at once a wail went up among the 'vacs, someone wanting a turn, not enough cannons for eight to divide among them. There was a push between the two older boys and a scuffle to the ground.

"Are you seeing to that?" Bridey said. There would be scraped knees and bloody lips, and on the first day. "You liked the boys better, didn't you say?"

"Oh," Gigi said, vaguely, watching the boys tussle but not moving to stop them. "I only meant that the boys usually like *me.*"

14
BRIDEY

Greenway House, later

They had an afternoon of air-raid trials, urging the older children and toting the small ones down from the nursery to the drawing room, far from the roof where an incendiary might start a fire. Timed and timed again, then gas mask training and play, then a messy meal and a fraught bedtime, one of the girls suddenly afraid of the dark. When Bridey finally had them all down, she only wished for her pillow. But Gigi goaded her downstairs, following the scent of baking bread, the promise of warmth. At the kitchen door, Bridey peered in cautiously. The mistress was the center around which the clock of Greenway turned, but she had no desire to meet her.

Mrs. Scaldwell looked up from the table. She had an empty cup in front of her and a shawl wrapped around. "Come in before the heat rushes out," she said. "Not a moment's peace."

Bridey sat down with her embroidery frame, a swatch of flowers half done. Busy work for fidgeting hands.

"Where's the mister Scaldwell?" Gigi said, warming herself at the oven. The Arbuthnots had presumably gone to bed but no one asked after them.

The housekeeper looked her over. "Home Guard. *I* wouldn't like to be out, day like this. The cold is in my bones tonight. Can you hear that wind?"

They listened to the howl and moan until it chilled Bridey more.

"Like the wisht hunt going by," Mrs. Scaldwell said.

"Which hunt?" Gigi said.

"The Devil's hunt, my lover," Mrs. Scaldwell said.

"Oh, is it a story?" Gigi said, settling in at the table. "Let's have it."

"Oh, no, Gigi," Bridey said. "It's too late and dreary for a story like that." She'd only been hoping to get warmed a bit, not be nattered at. Stories sometimes gave her a stomachache, anyway.

"It's no story." In the dim light, Mrs. Scaldwell seemed an old woman, her bagged eyes hidden in shadow. But they'd already heard about her nephew, a young fellow in the Royal Air Force lost in February. An aeroplane crash, four men. Another thing Gigi had from the daily girl Edith, who moved in and out of all divisions of the house in the performance of her chores. "The Wistman's Wood is fact enough," Mrs. Scaldwell said. "Not far of here, as it happens. There you'll find the stunted trees of the moors, bent into knots by a thousand years of wind like this. You'd be glad to avoid the old copse there any time of night or day, because the wisht man lives in that grove with his dandy dogs."

"His dogs?" Bridey said hopefully.

"Hellhounds, Bridey, do keep up," Gigi said.

"One night the Devil disguised himself as the huntsman Dewer and rode out his pack for the hunt. But he was not one for foxes, him. What *he* hunted was the souls of the unbaptized. Of the innocent child."

The sampler in Bridey's lap slid to the floor. She retrieved it, grasped it. "We shouldn't leave the children alone too long."

"Now it happens," said the cook, undeterred, "a man of the moors, a Mr. Todd, was stumbling back from the pub to his home, where he knows his missus will be sharp with him for the money he's drunk up. They've a wee one at home and nothing to eat for their supper. He's in trouble, this Mr. Todd. On his way home, Mr. Todd felt the wind blowing up around him and saw a pack of dogs stirring the air and howling. Why, it's his neighbor upon the moor, the huntsman Dewer, riding by in fine form! Todd called out to the master of the hunt in full voice, 'Have you had good sport?' "

Mrs. Scaldwell's performance of Todd's voice was the creak of an old nail coming out of a plank. It traveled Bridey's spine. This was why she hadn't wanted to hear about the hunt. She was done up, now. Stories strung one's nerves tight and plucked at them, tuning them for dread. Why should she be a plaything? But Mrs. Scaldwell's black eyes kept Bridey pinned in place —

" 'Why, yes!' answers Dewer," Mrs. Scaldwell said. "And he threw Mr. Todd a small bundle. 'Here, share our kill,' he cried and was away, the hooves of his ride and the paws of the dogs thundering off and shaking the ground."

There was a rumble of thunder, as though Mrs. Scaldwell controlled not just the room but the skies, too. She smiled. "Now Mr. Todd," she continued. "He believed this fresh joint of meat the huntsman has given him will keep his wife sweet when he returns, so he hurries home to present it to her. He'll be a fine provider then, won't he?"

Bridey had the thought that Mrs. Scaldwell was no longer the same woman inside her own flesh.

"Back home at last," Mrs. Scaldwell said, "the Todds unwrap the bloody bundle to begin their feast, and they find indeed fresh meat . . . the body of their own child!"

Bridey cried out, couldn't hold it in.

Gigi threw her head back and howled with laughter, and Mrs. Scaldwell nodded, pleased.

Bridey pulled herself in tightly, imagining the *Gray's Anatomy* chart of muscle groups, all flexed, taut. When she had herself stitched back together, when she could stop imagining a little child —

She turned to Gigi. "What was funny? It was horrid!"

"It's only a story," Gigi said.

"Everything is stories," Mrs. Scaldwell said. "But some are built on truth, or half-truth, at least."

"A half-truth is a lie," Bridey said, before she could think which side of that argument she might need to claim.

"Half-truths sometimes tell the truth better than anything else," Gigi said. "If you listen to a room of people boasting and telling stories, you'll find out what truly matters to them. What they're scared of. What they'll put up a fight about."

Bridey glanced her way. Listening to a room of people, a hobby now? "Well," Bridey said. "I've heard another tale near enough to it, but it happened around the corner from some other place."

"The Devil lives all places," Mrs. Scaldwell said.

"Well, that's the truth," Gigi said.

Bridey was surprised, as she hadn't got any sense that Gigi would believe in the Devil or hell, or even heaven, which some did, even as they ignored the rest.

"Never think the Devil can't be where you meet him," Mrs. Scaldwell said. "Whether he's called the wisht man or no."

Something scuffed outside in the corridor.

They all turned to the closed door, expecting Scaldwell to come through from his rounds of the estate. Or the mistress, perhaps. She liked a cup of cream as a treat, so said Edith.

When no one came through, Mrs. Scaldwell glanced between them and got up and Bridey imagined a dark figure behind the door, the wisht man, cloaked like Death and carrying a scythe, and then the figure was suddenly something worse, not a monster but the wounded, the destroyed, patched together and dragging —

Bridey stood, the sampler falling to her feet.

The door opened to little Doreen.

"What are you doing out of bed?" Mrs. Scaldwell said, but the little one had the bright eyes of fever. Strands of her hair stuck to her head and she had sick down the front of her nightdress.

"I've seen him," the little girl said. "I've seen the wish man."

"Good Lord," Gigi said.

This is what came of stories. Bridey was only happy to escape before Mrs. Scaldwell started another. "The poor dear," Bridey said. "Let's get you back upstairs."

"I'll send up some elderberry blossom tea," Mrs. Scaldwell said, going to light the hob. "That'll settle her stomach."

Send enough for two, Bridey wanted to say.

"He lives in the woods," Doreen said.

Mrs. Scaldwell stared. "And a cool cloth for that head."

Bridey scooped up Doreen and carried her upstairs, the girl's hot cheek against her own. A half-truth was a lie, she'd said so herself. But it might also be an opportunity. She would have to prove herself a nurse

133

now, ready or not.

At Doreen's bed, the blackout paper on the window was peeled back to reveal the dark trees of the wood that lay beyond the walled gardens. Bridey put the child in clean pyjamas borrowed from another's cubby and put her to bed, but for a moment, sitting on the edge of the cot, Bridey imagined Doreen had seen something, someone. She reached out to press the paper flat to the glass.

15
BRIDEY

---

11 April 1941 — a week at Greenway
She woke from deep sleep to Gigi shaking her.

"Stop," Bridey said. "Gigi, what is it?"

"You're shouting." Gigi retreated to her bed and perched on the edge. "About something on fire?"

The blackout coverings concealed the hour. It could be any time, any day of the week. "Sorry I woke you."

"You didn't." The grinding of aeroplane engines sounded in the distance. "The Germans did."

What had she been dreaming? "Should we gather the children?" But Doreen was sick and Bridey was exhausted after the week's exertions, air battles over the Channel a constant reminder of the state of things, then seeing to first one crying infant in the small hours, then the other, then the first again. The babies preferred Bridey

135

already and wouldn't be comforted by Gigi's sharp angles.

"*We* don't sound the alarm," Gigi said. "Do we?"

"I imagine Scaldwell is listening for them to get close," she said. "I thought evacuation would mean —"

"No raids. I don't think there's anywhere without raids at all," Gigi said. "I do wonder why the Arbuthnots chose this house for a group of 'vacs, don't you? A white house on a hill so near the hostilities?"

"They must have thought the same as me, that it was enough to be out of London," Bridey said. Was it disloyalty to her employer or to the house for already having come to the same conclusion? "It's a lovely spot."

"A single bomb would fix that up."

Bridey blinked into the darkness, listening to the 'planes. Were they closer? She got out of bed and went to the dresser to grab a pair of slippers. The drawer was empty, which made no sense until she realized it was Gigi's. But that also made no sense.

"Did you never unpack, Gigi?"

"Not much opportunity," she said.

Rather more chance than I've had. Bridey closed the drawer, opened the one she'd meant.

"Are you snooping?" Gigi said.

"I'm fetching socks. The cold's got in me. Do you not mean to stay at Greenway?"

"Haven't got 'round to it, that's all."

Would she? Already it was clear to Bridey that Gigi had no affinity with children, no interest.

They'd had gas mask training on the wide lush lawn of the walled south garden that day, all except Mr. Arbuthnot, who wouldn't be moved from his own plans. Mrs. Arbuthnot led the children on a march, making a game of it. She was quite good with the little ones, as it turned out, willing to romp with them. Mr. Scaldwell took it all seriously, maintenance of straps seen to, everyone fitted. Mrs. Scaldwell chanced a break and slipped away. The infants, who couldn't use masks, had bags with pumps that quickly exhausted the muscles in Bridey's arms.

"You and I have to keep them alive?" Gigi had said, alarmed behind her own mask. "Isn't there someone — I don't know — better suited?"

Afterward, the infants were returned to the house and Bridey and Gigi sat near the glass conservatory Scaldwell called the peach house while the older children played in their masks. "This is not for the weak," Gigi said, a cigarette lit, her hair mussed from the mask strap. "Is it?"

Bridey had suddenly wondered: Who could be better suited to keeping another person alive than a nurse?

So children were not Gigi's ideal. If she left Greenway, surely the Arbuthnots would send for a replacement. Wouldn't they? She might *encourage* Gigi to make herself more useful. It wasn't truly nursing, and someone with Gigi's training might naturally strain against the care of healthy children. But it was a job, and safe compared to —

In the dark of their room, the lamp rattled with the low thunder of another 'plane approaching. Bridey shut the drawer and slipped back into bed.

"Are you so cold?" Gigi said. "Your teeth are chattering."

It was possible to listen to one's death coming just like this. Bridey squeezed herself deeper inside her skin and tried not to imagine her mam pulling the children to her, how scared she must have been to see it coming.

She couldn't bear it.

If she'd been at home when the time came, she'd have died along with them. Sometimes she wished she had. That was a whole truth. How little it would have mattered to anyone left alive if she had.

And worse: now she thought of the soldier

under Sister Clare's care back at St. Prisca's. If Bridey had died along with her mam, he might still be alive, too, and all those he might have saved in his service. On and on, one person saved might mean another and another who lived. There was an invisible thread pulling through them, tying them together, wasn't there? She had snapped it.

Bridey threw back her covers.

"Where are you going?" Gigi said. "I thought you were cold."

"I think I hear one of the children. I'll check the boys, too."

In the corridor, Bridey leaned against the wall until she had control of herself, then peered into the girls' room. All was well, even Doreen was resting comfortably. She hadn't redistributed them as she'd threatened. The greater her sacrifice now, the sooner perhaps Mrs. Arbuthnot would notice her efforts.

In the boys' room, James lay facing the doorway, his eyes open. "Messerschmitts," he whispered.

"No, that's ours."

"It isn't."

The marvel of little boys and what they took in, collecting the sounds of 'planes overhead like marbles in their pockets.

"We're quite safe here," she said.

James closed his eyes, but, she thought, perhaps from disgust with her. She sat in the hard chair nearby waiting for his breath to go sweet, but the 'planes only seemed to drop lower. A clanging bell started up somewhere near the river, and then Mrs. Arbuthnot was in the door, saying, "It's time."

Bridey woke the next morning too early by far. She'd be like her mam soon, late to bed, up before the sun because it was the only hour she might have to herself.

The stab of memory caught Bridey sideways. She steeled herself against it, listening for what had woken her, then remembering the 'planes overhead in the night. They had come to Greenway to be far from such things, not to crouch in the drawing room in their bedclothes with crying children. Gigi still slept.

Bridey put on her dress and put her head out in the corridor. The children were quiet, for a moment. Had she heard someone downstairs? Edith, early to her duties? Mrs. Scaldwell, perhaps, an early riser to get the kitchen warm.

She crept down, but the cooker was still cold. One of the cabinet doors stood open, one of the drawers pulled out, rather surprising. She wouldn't have guessed it of Mrs. Scaldwell. She closed them. In the passage to the back door, she paused at the room Mrs. Scaldwell used as her office, but no light showed.

Outside the morning birds were cautious and the sky still smudged gray. Beyond the garden wall, the trees were colorless, wrapped in mist. How could the morning be so gentle after a night like they'd had? Greenway was still standing, at least.

She ought to be in bed, not wasting the last precious minutes before the children's incessant questions started up again. But the air was so clean, the world tranquil, like a gift only for her.

Something rustled far off in the woods, timid then thrashing, and the most awful noise ripped through the stillness, a high-pitched cry like a woman begging for her life. Bridey startled and stepped back, her hand stretching for the door.

On the flagstones at her feet was a man's muddy bootprint.

"It's only foxes," a man's voice said.

He crouched on the crumbling old stairs in the opening to the south garden, dapper in suit and tie.

"Rather late in the season for mating cries," he continued. "But not too late for hunting. Bad news, that. For the fox."

Foxes were mythical creatures, too, same as butlers. More stories Bridey gave no credence.

"Who are you?" she said. There were a number of people on the estate she hadn't had a good look at: the men who helped keep the grounds, the laborers at the farms. But the young ones had all gone off to the fight, or should have.

"No one to be frightened of." He took a handful of something from the pocket of his coat and tilted his head to drop them into his mouth.

She wasn't frightened. If she let herself be frightened, the seams would pull and she would be everything all at once. Some emotions were safe, but not the ones that reminded her —

She put her hand to her mouth.

"All right then?" he said.

When she had the bile down again, she glanced toward the woods. They were quiet now. Bad news for the fox indeed. "Are you helping yourself to the mistress's fruit? She won't look kindly on poachers. Or trespassers."

"I'm only having a look around." He talked around a mouthful. "How do you know I don't have business here?"

"At this time of morning? And I've never seen you before." He didn't need to know she hadn't been here long herself. But then suddenly she realized she knew him. He'd been on the train, grinning at her troubles as she cared for all ten children in Gigi's absence, and then theorizing with Gigi and the rest of his friends over the train schedule, feet up, all the time in the world. The neck of his shirt still gaped, and the shiny bauble on his tie pin looked quite out of place given the setting and hour. A rich man heading home after a late night? "You came down with us from London," she said.

"Did I?"

She couldn't say he'd *winked* at her. "We spoke to you about where we'd let off."

"We're old friends, then." He winked again. He remembered.

"We might be," she said. "Until the cook sees you stealing those berries from the garden or the butler catches you stomping through the grounds uninvited."

"The butler? Gracious, the *butler.*" He stood and cupped another mouthful of fruit into his cheek. "These are wild berries, I'll have you know. I wouldn't want to tangle with a butler."

The sky had lightened around them, and the fog in the trees had begun to burn off.

"You'd better go," Bridey said. "Take a friend's advice."

A branch snapped in the wood behind him, and they both looked.

"I'll just tiptoe through, shall I? Like a thief?" He shoved his hands into his pockets and started off, turning to keep talking as he went. "Only it's rather a good shortcut to the quay."

"Do be quick," she hissed, coming out to the path to see him away. "And don't try it at night."

"Why? Home Guard?"

"Watch dog." She thought of the small dog James and tried not to smile. "And a little terrier as well."

The man's blue eyes were bright, even at this distance. "If I come to the door next time, will the butler answer it?"

"The front door isn't for the likes of us."

He raised a hand and turned to continue toward the river quay. She watched him until he had gone from her sight, then remembered the muddy print at her feet. Like a thief, he'd said. She remembered the open drawers and cabinets and wondered, but the man from the train had not been wearing boots. His two-tone brogues had been battered, well-used, but clean.

The woods had been turned over to a

dawn chorus, birds for which Bridey hadn't the names. She should have gone back to bed, but instead she waited out the sunrise, listening for foxes and thinking, instead, of predators.

16
B<small>RIDEY</small>

Greenway, after breakfast
Bridey fetched the porridge and returned
with anxiety from below. "It's Kingswear,"
she said to Gigi. "They're all in the kitchen
thinking of who they know there." The
children were listening, she realized. "Everyone's safe, though. No one harmed."

They had moved their two makeshift
tables into the shared middle room so the
children could have breakfast together. Bibs,
milk. Gigi poked a feeding bottle at one of
the infants while the other wailed in a basket
at her feet. She nudged the basket with her
foot, trying for a rhythm. "Hmm," she said.

Gigi withdrawn made Bridey anxious to
make her jolly again. If Gigi left and Mrs.
Arbuthnot had to look for another nurse,
the matter of references might come up
again and Matron Bailey called upon for a
letter she'd already written. She needed this
job, this chance at redemption and a good

letter instead of a damning one. She needed Gigi, no matter how little help she was.

"There was a man," Bridey tried. "Trespassing on the grounds, bold as you please, as Scaldwell said. One of those blokes from the train."

Gigi looked up. "Too handsome for his own good or sour-pussed?"

"The handsome one." But she would have preferred the man who had come to her rescue, the one who'd sent Gigi's admirers scattering to their own seats. *He* had a healthy respect for what they were trying to accomplish.

Bridey worked her way around the table, serving out, then tidying, tucking, calling the boys back to the table when they wandered, putting spoons back in hands that forgot what they should be doing. "Do you know anything about foxes?"

"I had an aunt whose pride was a real fox stole," Gigi said. "Moth-eaten thing."

"I meant a real fox. A live one or — never mind."

Edith put her head around the door. "Have you heard about Kingswear?"

"Is there news?" Gigi said.

Edith came in, skinny arms and darting eyes. "I don't know any more than that. They're all in a state, rather close. You haven't been there but why it should be *bombed* — Mrs. Scaldwell's in a fit twice again because there's a jar of something missing from the cupboard."

The young man at the garden steps — was he perhaps a thief after all? "There was a bootprint at the back door this morning," Bridey said.

"Was there?" Edith's eyes grew large. "Mrs. Scaldwell will have his bones for broth. She thought you might have — Oh, never mind."

Gigi made room for Edith to perch with her near the babies. Edith loved the rolls of fat at the babies' thighs, their crossed eyes as they pulled her finger to their mouths. Gigi said, "The driver who brought us in from the train that first night said you'd had your fair share of bombs down here already."

Bridey sniffed. It wasn't proper talk in front of the children. And after a late night and early morning, she'd rather not have Edith prattling at them. But Gigi didn't mind. Her cool manner fell away, her droll jokes, and she reminded Bridey of some of the sillier ward girls at St. Prisca's, volunteers who wrote out letters for the soldiers and found too much time to flirt.

"Oh, we've had enough for two wars.

148

Dartmouth, Paignton, Brixham several times, Kingswear," Edith said, counting off her fingers. "Before Christmas, we had two hits not but up the hill. Two killed." She sounded thrilled, as though she'd met someone from the flicks on her own lane.

"Tsk," Bridey said.

"Poor lambs," Edith hurried to say.

"Still, it's safer than London," Bridey said, glancing over the children.

"I would rather be there anyway," Edith said. "If I ever got away from this place. Oh, Torquay! How could I forget *Torquay*?"

"What's there?" Gigi said. "A seaside resort, isn't it?"

"Mrs. M. was a child there," Edith said. "That's not the house she went missing from, though."

Gigi plucked at a thread from the baby's blanket across her lap. "I forgot about that."

"Missing? When was this?" Bridey said.

"I was just a girl," Edith said. "But when I started at Greenway, Mrs. Scaldwell made sure I knew all about it and then told me never to mention it."

"Never mention what to whom?" Gigi said, trying not to smile. "That was 'twenty-six or so," she said to Bridey. "I remember the newspapers went mad for finding her."

Bridey did the sums and realized Gigi

might be older than she'd supposed.

"Why did she go missing?" Bridey said.

"Her husband," Edith jumped in before Gigi could steal this hunk of meat from her mouth. "Her husband was having a love affair with another woman —"

"*Edith,*" Bridey said. "The children."

"— and asked her for a divorce. Can you imagine?"

"What happened?" Gigi said. "I can't remember."

"She lost her head and kidnapped herownself into Yorkshire, signed into a spa hotel under her husband's mistress's name, if you please. Mrs. Teresa Neale at the Hydro something. Mrs. Teresa Neal at the Harrogate Hydropathic, which is what — Oh."

"What?" Gigi said hungrily.

"I shouldn't say," Edith said, but one could see this was a story she wanted to tell.

Gigi leaned forward, rapt attention.

"Only that's what Mrs. Scaldwell calls the mistress's bath," Edith said. "With the shelf for apples? The Harrogate Hydropathic, right here at Greenway."

"That Mrs. Scaldwell does have potential," Gigi said.

"You can't kidnap yourself," Bridey said.

"You could arrange it," Gigi said.

"She ran away from home, then, if you like," Edith said. "Made like she'd been" — here she glanced at the children — "you *know,* like in one of her books, until someone told where she could be found for the reward. She pretended she couldn't remember a thing."

"One can't say she *pretended,*" Gigi said. "She might have got a knock in the head. There was a car accident, if I remember. Or maybe the troubles laid at her feet got to be too much and she — well, she wasn't the mistress you know today, you know, with a grand house and everything sorted just as she likes. She must have felt trapped in circumstances."

Edith's expression turned wary. "It's Mrs. Scaldwell that says she was only after a spa weekend."

"I'm not scolding you," Gigi said. "I simply don't like stories where the victim is painted with a brush that obscures the real villain." Gigi gave up on the feeding bottle with one babe and thrust it at the other. "I don't suppose you've ever asked Mrs. Mallowan about this adventure of hers?"

"Never! I'd be turned out."

"Then we only know she took flight and was found safe," Gigi said. "I hope I'm remembered for more than the worst moment in my life."

Scolded or not, Edith soon lost the taste for their company and trudged back to her duties. At the table, the children's feast had ended. Bridey gathered the dishes and cups and turned to hand Gigi her share but Gigi had gone. She was movement in the corridor, shadow on the stairs.

Villain.

Bridey didn't throw around such words. Back at St. Prisca's, they'd have said *she* was the villain. If she never got back there and proved them all wrong —

But now Bridey thought of the man on the grounds, cheerful but waiting where he shouldn't be. Yes, waiting, but for whom and for what purpose?

He couldn't be Doreen's wish man? Not a figment of imagination but real, a man sneaking among the trees. The matter of the bootprint had not been resolved. Someone crept into the house. *Someone* stole something from the larder. A chill lay itself across the back of Bridey's neck and wouldn't leave her.

17
SCALDWELL

Early May, nearly three weeks since the 'vacs arrived

Rather later than normal, Frank Scaldwell took to the top path on the lookout for Nazis.

He didn't expect to find any, but this was his duty. He had seen to the master until he left for London, to the mistress until she followed, as she might soon. If they'd gone to the house in Wallingford for the duration, Frank might have been expected to go and serve them there, but they had not gone to Wallingford. They had rented a *flat* — every time Frank thought of it, he felt himself wince — in *London,* at the heart of this trouble. As though there were no such thing as bullets or bombs.

He rubbed his hands together, cold. It had come to this. He relied on a woman and her typewriter to see him and Vera through the war.

He was no coward. He'd done his part the first go-round — Thirteenth Riflers — and he might still prove a crack shot, if the Brixham Home Guard ever laid in more than two old weapons. But this was a young man's war, not his.

Frank faltered, slowed on the path. A very young man's war.

Something moved above him in the woods, bringing him back. The sun had shifted, the temperature dropped a degree. "Who's there?" he called, standing straighter. The area was teeming with strangers of late. He'd chased off another trespasser using the estate as a shortcut to the quay not too weeks ago. Some had strange ideas about their rights on another man's private property. A woman's private property, in this case.

"Only me, Scarsdale." The voice came not from the trees but from down the path.

"Scaldwell. Sir." Arbuthnot, of course. He got the name wrong by design, to show he couldn't be bothered. "What are you prowling about for?" He glanced into the woods but saw nothing.

"Painting, of course. Give me a hand, would you?"

The man had his easel, a canvas, and a rather unwieldy case, but he would have carried them all out himself earlier in the day. Frank let the favor dangle. His duty was not to Arbuthnot, and they were certainly not friends. The night was darkening quickly, however. "You worked at the top of the hill today?"

"What of it?"

"Did you see any Nazis landing along the estuary?"

"What? No, of course not."

"Let's have it, then." Frank took the heaviest piece, the easel, rather than hear the old man's complaints. "You shouldn't stay out so late if you need help with your tackle."

"It sneaked up," Arbuthnot said, his voice thin with exertion as they climbed the gentle incline. "The light was magnificent, and then suddenly . . ."

Lost time. He thought Vera had suffered bouts of it since February, finding herself at the sink, hands in cold water. *He* had, peering through a shutter and the window gone dark, no idea how the last half hour had been spent. Ever since they'd had the news from Vera's brother about his son. Young Douglas, lost.

Nearly the same age as their Diana, who lived now as a series of letters, a telephone ring on the mistress's line of a Sunday. Incomprehensible that the next generation should be old enough to shoulder this, could be old enough to serve with the RAF to begin with. Douglas should be a boy skinning his knees at play, not a bloody air gunner smashed into high ground in Staffordshire. Diana should be here with them, still nine years old and plaits in her hair.

"I say, Scaldwell?"

Frank blinked into the dark, coming back. He'd done it again.

"I say, could you carry the case as well? It's just I'm rather . . . rather exhausted, if I'm honest. These children crying in the night, we're not accustomed."

He had not known the man to admit weakness. He was all bluster and pomp, turning every conversation to topics that suited him. In the three weeks they'd had the group in the house, they hadn't been able to escape the Arbuthnots. The man, in particular, seemed always underfoot and talking.

Frank had never listened closely to him until the day last week when Arbuthnot contradicted his own facts, trapping himself in a lie that turned in on itself like a snake twisting to swallow its own tail. Frank was listening to Arbuthnot these days, to be sure, on alert.

"Remind me again," Frank said, "*which* Arbuthnots are you from?"

The old man cleared his throat. "You're familiar with, er, peerage? The house of Arbuthnot?"

"Making conversation."

"Ah. My father is — was." He coughed, fingers at his mouth. "Percy Arbuthnot. Not the one in the papers, of course."

"Another Percy Arbuthnot. More than one." Unlikely, but there might be more than a few more Scaldwells unknown to him. Another Frank Scaldwell, another poor sod. "I thought you said your father was a *William* Arbuthnot."

"He was, ah," Arbuthnot said. "Sometimes called William. Yes, Percy William. Now that I think of it, he was much more widely known as William Arbuthnot. I would have called him neither, of course."

Coughing against the lie in his throat. What did it mean? He was no Arbuthnot at all? Times like this, things went slippery. A man might add a few years to his age on the Register and be saved the trouble of the war coming too near his patch. A man might enter the fray under a false name and turn up on the other side with a medal on his chest and the papers to establish a new life. How easy would it have happened in this fellow's time? Who was there to patrol it, to send you back to your old name? If you were God-fearing and law-abiding — or the new person you were trying to be was — you might live a quiet life.

This Arbuthnot, so called, an old man prone to bragging, grindingly boring — but what else might he be? A debtor, a confidence man? Something worse?

He realized he'd missed something Arbuthnot was saying. "What's that?"

"I said" — Arbuthnot took the opportunity to stop, catch his breath — "what do you think of these nurses?"

"I don't think of them," Frank said, not stopping. Vera didn't abide by the young women for some reason, but he had no feelings of his own. They were two more people crowding into the house, causing bother. He should be glad of the war nursery. If Arbuthnot's group hadn't come to Greenway, he and Vera might've been turned out.

For the children themselves, he had a secret fondness. He didn't mind them generally, and these were children with parents fighting on the front, working the factories, or dousing fires after air raids in London. His quibble with bringing them to Greenway was that the thin thread of the Channel, their last defense, nearly lapped at their shore. Oh yes, bring your children to safety, and Plymouth not as many as fifty miles away, pounded by German firepower nights on end. Hadn't they already had bombs dropped up the hill, hardly beyond the wall of the north garden? But by all means, bring all the innocent to Greenway, and a couple of old men left to defend them.

Frank glanced back at Arbuthnot.

Maybe he did have feelings — but about his own shortcomings, not those of the nurses. "What of them, then?"

"That one — she's sparky, isn't she? There's something about her."

How old was he? Good Lord, she was nearly as young as Diana.

But Frank knew which one he meant, and there was something about her, indeed. At the front in the last war, he'd seen little ones in the street with knowing eyes, and there was something inside Gigi Kelly of the beggar child, one that grew up dirty and too soon. He didn't trust her. He trusted none of the lot, but the other nurse, the plain one who had nothing bright to say and little to recommend her, was quiet. Almost absent. But she did her share and half again, and that was enough by him.

"Do you think she's trouble or what?"

"No trouble to you or I, happily married

men, of course, but she has a whiff of — of danger about her, if you know what I mean. Secrecy and dark looks, the stuff that tempts young men."

Was he aroused or afraid? A lady half his age and paying him no attention.

"She reminds me of the actresses I once photographed on Bond Street," Arbuthnot said.

Oh, yes, Bond Street. The celebrated photographer of bonny maids, society types, literary lions. He would soon mention Conrad.

"Have I ever told you I once photographed Joseph Conrad?" Arbuthnot said. "You know Conrad, of course."

"A pretty nurse reminds you of Conrad?" Conrad, author in repose, with his necktie four-in-hand and a monocle? Scaldwell turned his smile into the woods.

"No," Arbuthnot said. "Well, yes, in a way, she reminds me of *all* the subjects I ever sat. Lillah McCarthy, a great many actresses, George Bernard Shaw — great friend of mine, if I hadn't mentioned."

He had. "What do you mean, she reminds you of *all* of them?"

"Well, most people get twitchy in front of a camera, you see. Even those who are accustomed to being looked at on stage.

It's . . . intimate, having your likeness taken. You have to put them at ease, that's the trick."

"How do you manage it?"

"I talk with them, nothing to it," Arbuthnot said. "But that first moment when 1 moved behind the camera — the wall almost always went right up."

"The wall." Frank was interested, despite himself. He slowed so that Arbuthnot could better keep up. He could see the roofline of the house, the chimneys.

"The invisible barrier they put up to protect themselves, to keep me from seeing them for what they really were," Arbuthnot said. "I might be able to talk the wall down again, but it was almost always there at the beginning. Something false, you see — like a mask but — but of their own faces. Ah, I'm not saying it well. I deal in images, of course. If I dealt in words, I'd be a poet. A playwright —"

Like my friend Shaw.

"— like my friend Shaw."

They approached the house at Arbuthnot's shuffling pace. "Where did your wife find the nurses?" Scaldwell asked.

"The local hospitals, I believe. All their papers on the up and up, of course, nothing like that. Joan wouldn't have it."

161

At the house, the door stood open. He would have to talk to the household about lax practices.

Frank carried the easel and case through. He'd have to carry the lot upstairs, too, but he was tired now himself. They were not accustomed to babies in the house, either.

"What if we . . ." He found a spot in the larder for Arbuthnot to store his things, and the old man approved. Scaldwell reached for the canvas in Arbuthnot's hand only to have him hiss as though he'd been scratched.

"Careful now," Arbuthnot said. "The paint's wet."

Frank turned the canvas out and set it down. There was nothing at all in it he recognized, no landscape, no subject. For all the man's talk of light.

"How do you like it?" Arbuthnot said.

But Frank had nothing to say about art. He dealt not in pictures, nor in words. Just now he was not at all sure what he did deal in. What would be said of this Frank Scaldwell, among so many? He was singular in almost no way, except that he had stumbled into a life that granted him access to this grand home, not his own.

Later, it troubled him. As he walked the ground floor, making fast doors and shutters, tucking in blackout coverings, as he headed to the kitchen afterward for a bun and some milk, like a child, it worried at him. Not knowing, not having a single idea who he might be, if not for this house.

18
BRIDEY

A month at Greenway House, May 1941
The telephone began to ring day and night
with inquiries and arrangements for Mrs.
Mallowan to join her husband in London.
He might get a post with the Air Force, all
hush hush, but not hush enough to Mrs.
Scaldwell. And now the mistress was going
to be of help as a chemist, of all things.

"Poison," Gigi said. "Remember that she's
an expert."

Bridey hadn't forgotten, not for a minute.
"She's an apothecary's assistant in a hospital
dispensary," she said. "She's an expert in
medicine."

"Any pill's a poison if you take too much
of it," Gigi said.

They had barely seen Mrs. Mallowan in
the house, keeping to their portion as they
had. But now Bridey watched through the
rainy nursery window as Hannaford the
gardener tucked the silver-haired woman

into the backseat of her black estate car. A heavy sky had settled in simultaneous to Doreen's fever, which had made a quick run of them all, children and adults. They'd all been sticky, cross. Sleepless. The milk spilled. Toes stubbed and fingers splintered. Toys broke. Nothing was safe.

Gigi sat with feet tucked up, a book in her hands. She always had one of Mrs. M.'s books open these days, reading into the hours of blackout with a candle, if she could get one. The candles were hard to come by, but Edith had nicked a few stubs from other parts of the house.

The children fought over jacks, over the boys running their toy tanks through the girls' imaginary tea party.

"One of Hannaford's men has his cart out in the rain," Bridey said.

"Hmm," Gigi said.

"The work has to get done somehow," she said. Or did it? If Greenway's paths grew over with tendrils, and the trees hung heavy with fruit until it dropped and wildlife fell upon it, what harm? At the top of the house on the hill, Bridey imagined herself a phantom in a house already reclaimed by the land.

"Maybe one of Hannaford's men is Doreen's wish man," Bridey said.

Gigi read on.

"I didn't know you liked to read so much."

"That was you, I think," Gigi murmured. "I love a distraction."

A distraction from the children, from her work. Gigi never turned down an amusement. "You'd be better off reading history or — the classics. I don't see the point of this silly nonsense."

"You don't like a story?" The children perked up. "I thought I saw you with one of Aggie's books, too."

Scaldwell wouldn't like that, not one bit. "Should I spend every evening darning socks for the entire household?"

"You offered to do that. You could have kept up with your embroidery, done something *you* wanted to do."

Bridey didn't know what she wanted to do. She had carried that unfinished sampler in its frame all over the house, but her needlework seemed a precious old-maid sort of pastime in the days of make-do and mend, slim skirts and no fuss. She felt as cooped up as a hen, scratching for a fight.

She wouldn't admit reading was hard going for her, that she couldn't let herself fall into the story for fear of where her mind might go. Abandon was a luxury for *some.* Gigi could spend hours, barely moving, her breath shallow. When Gigi read a book, she wasn't there in the room any longer, and Bridey knew she'd been left behind.

"A month in this house and you're ruined already, plump and spoiled for the books," Bridey said. "I'm worried for the —" She gestured toward the children.

Gigi set the book aside, and Bridey tried not to be pleased. "Worried because of the —" Gigi nodded her head toward the window, toward Dartmouth, the open sea, France. They had a practiced panto at this point, trying to avoid using certain words to speak of the war in front of the children.

"*That,* yes, but also *this.*" Bridey swung an arm outward, encompassing the house, the elegant things of the Mallowans. "They've come from another life altogether, and they'll have to go back. We'll all have to go back."

Gigi's eyelids fluttered. "Did you call me *plump,* darling?"

"I only meant," Bridey said, "satisfied, like a cat in a sunbeam. But it can't last. We'll have to get back to real life."

Gigi's look was inscrutable. "Can you imagine?" she said. "Going back home now, listening to your mam?"

Bridey turned back to the window and caught her own reflection, mouth turned down at the corners.

"Scrubbing the floors," Gigi said, "and hoping some dull, ruddy-cheeked lad will take you to the church?"

"Stop," Bridey said.

"*Tom,* is it?"

"No." She had wanted Gigi's attention, but now it was too much.

"That's not all you dream of? After you've seen what it's like to live in a grand house? To have as many books as you want and an hour in the bath with apples to eat?"

"Wasteful."

"It's not *lavish,*" Gigi said. "Apples literally grow on trees. And to read all the books you want in the bath until the water's cold and your fingers wrinkle? Bridey, it's a dream."

"All the books I want is not many books."

"Or your needlework. I only speak of the *time,*" Gigi said. "The time to do as the great woman herself does. A life you built yourself with your own wiles and talents, in a house you bought with your own money. And with no one at all to bother you."

Bridey went to the table and thumbed at the thin ribbon marking Gigi's spot in her book. "No one at all? Don't you want a husband?"

"I haven't met the man yet," Gigi said.

"Mrs. Mallowan is a married woman."

"She is," Gigi said. "And she's still a writer, that's what I'm getting at. Tell me you're not one of those women who wants to be a nurse only until she meets the right man, and then all the hours of her days are given over to the kitchen and clothesline?"

"No." It was her mam Gigi meant, her mam and all the women like her. It couldn't be a bad life. It hadn't been. She couldn't bear to think her mam had other plans. "I want to be a nurse, and I will be, soon enough."

"Well, you *are*," Gigi said.

"Yes, of course." She kept losing track. "I only meant — *after* the war, you know. Set up proper."

"Though right now you could probably be put to better use somewhere nearer the boys coming home injured." Gigi stood and drew Bridey back toward the window, where they might talk more freely. "I'm sure you didn't expect to spend the pivotal moments of the" — she nodded her head out the window — "minding *children,* and healthy ones at that. If I could be, I'd be back in London near the center of things."

Bridey had thought as much, so what was stopping her? She yearned to be back, too, but on her own terms. She couldn't seem too eager, not without Mrs. Arbuthnot's good word. "The center of things," Bridey said. "Like a bull's-eye."

"Do you know . . . ? It's in the center of things that I always feel most sure," Gigi said. "Have you heard that sailors in the center of a cyclone can look up and see the stars? It blows all around, but they know who they are, where they are, because the tools that guide them are larger and outside the wind. The war can rage on around me, but if I'm at the center —"

"The center," Bridey hissed, glancing to make sure the small ones were out of range. "The center is next to Hitler."

"Fine," Gigi said. "Send me to Mr. Hitler's side. I like his funny little mustache, don't you?"

"Gigi! You can't — he's — That's *treason.*"

"I don't think they'll hang me for imagining a mustache tickling the inside of my knee."

Bridey stared. "How would a mustache tickle your *knee?*"

"Oh, *darling,*" Gigi said. "You and your Tommy might excite each other more if you tasted the pleasures."

"You can't talk about Hitler like — *that.*"

"Why not?" Gigi said, dimple making an

appearance. "I talk about everyone like that."

"Everyone?"

"Well, the retired gardener at the ferryman's cottage is eighty soon, so *he's* probably safe."

"Gigi!"

"Probably," Gigi said. "It has been a *while*. The Mallowans weren't my type, though I do appreciate a woman in pearls and furs."

"Are you a —"

Gigi leaned closer. "Am I a *what*?"

"One of those women." Her voice, weak.

"I've been called worse. You didn't let me finish my plan. Hitler, mustache, knee —" She swiped the inside of her knee through her skirt. "Gun."

"You would kill someone?"

"We *are* speaking of Hitler, still?"

"But . . . you think you could?"

Gigi looked toward the window, the square of light that had come to represent the war raging on. "If I had to, I could. If I had the chance to end suffering, I would have to try."

Bridey thought of the soldier at St. Prisca's, convulsing in his bed. "I don't think I could."

"It's a good thing you've chosen nursing as your calling, then," Gigi said. "You'll have the opposite. You may have to save someone who turns your stomach." Gigi was thoughtful. "I would do it, I think. Even if it meant my own death. If I could end this slaughter and bring the men home? Your Tommy home, so that he might . . . start to grow a *magnificent* mustache?"

Bridey slapped a hand to her mouth but too late — a trumpet of laughter escaped. The children came running to see, smiling as though they might be included.

Bridey doubled over snorting, laughing with her full body, something she hadn't done in so long. She couldn't stop, couldn't remember the last time she'd laughed with a friend, and had begun to remember she had no right to joy when Gigi put a hand out. "What's that? Do you hear it?"

Bridey sobered, straightened. It was a bell clanging. "Not a church bell?" In London it would mean Armistice. Here, a raid.

"I don't think so," Gigi said. "It's more like —" There were footsteps on the stairs and then Edith, breathless, in the door.

"Come quickly," she panted. "There's a dead man in the river."

172

19
BRIDEY

They hushed Edith and drew her into the corridor, further away from little listeners.

"Why should we go and see a dead man?" Bridey said.

Edith looked at her oddly. "But you're a nurse!"

"I meant — you'll want the undertaker," Bridey said. "If he's indeed dead."

"They're sending for the doctor, but you're already here."

Bridey was not afraid of death but of the spectacle, of acting the role in front of the others, in front of Gigi and a doctor. She'd be found out. "I'll wait with the children, Gigi," she said. "You go."

"We should both go," Gigi said. "Edith can watch the nursery."

"But I can't see to them all," Edith said. "Not all ten."

"I've had to," Bridey said. But she didn't want to encourage Edith to stay, did she?

"You two go, and I'll stay."

"They're having naps soon," Gigi said. "We're better as a pair, aren't we?" It was decided.

On the walk down to the quay, the clanging bell died down. Gigi said, "You've *had* to? You've had to watch all ten, you say? Have I let you down so thoroughly?"

"You have been known to lark off."

"On the train, when they couldn't get away from you?" Gigi said.

"You took an hour the other day, and *three* hours later —"

"Yes, all right."

They overtook Mrs. Arbuthnot on the way down the hill through the woods and learned how Mr. Bastin from the ferryman's cottage had come for Hannaford, who had gone for Scaldwell, who had called on Mrs. Arbuthnot for the nurses and Edith to fetch them. Now as they came out upon the road from the trees, they came upon the whole of Greenway Road — the tenants and horsemen from the upper and lower farms, their wives hanging back out of decorum, and even a few cars from the village — all coming to have a look.

"The nurses are here," Mrs. Arbuthnot called out. Shoulders parted and they were nudged forward through the crowd, all eyes

174

upon them. They made their way past the bell stand to the packed earth of the quay, Gigi dragging behind.

A small party of men stood over an uneven shape draped in white.

"No nursing to be done here," one of the men said. Boats tied up at water's edge scraped against the pilings. A few small craft bobbed out in the river, the men at the oars watching.

"He's — dead then," Gigi said.

A few of the men turned to answer, and the effect of Gigi rippled through them. They'd perhaps imagined the rumored nurses from London to be something different, Bridey thought. A motherly bust and comforting ballast, like Mrs. Arbuthnot.

One managed to speak. "Yes, miss. He's dead." He took off his hat, and the others followed.

"Is it someone from Greenway?" Mrs. Arbuthnot said. "Or the village? Do any of you gentlemen know him?"

"If you'll beg pardon, missus," one of the men said. "We can't tell if we do."

"*Can't* tell?"

"Bloating," Bridey said. "The body will take on water and the face will lose distinct characteristics as decay sets in."

Mrs. Arbuthnot took a startled step back,

and hands reached out from all directions. "Oh," she said.

Some at the edge of the crowd glanced between themselves. The problem, Bridey knew, was that a man was something solid, with edges, something definitive like a number on a ledger. He could not be something porous, even dead, not a water-logged loaf of flesh washed up on the shores of their safe haven.

"How long in the water?" she said.

"Waiting for the doctor. He'll know."

"May I?"

The crowd shifted uneasily. They were not ladylike to arrive at the dock, to speak of decay, to offer professional assistance. As many ways as there were to be a woman now, there was still only one correct way.

Gigi said, "Let her give her assessment."

Bridey hesitated, wishing she had let Gigi take charge. But it was not the same as identifying someone you knew and loved. She was a good nurse — she might be. She stepped forward, crouched, and lifted the sheet at its edge, working to keep her face blank. Her hand shook a bit from having an audience.

"He warned you right enough," one of the men said, and the others laughed.

Bridey cataloged the details. His features

weren't as much waterlogged as walloped. He had an ugly pallor to his skin and one eye swollen shut, but the other, open and staring, was a stunning, winking blue.

"Nurse," Bridey said. "Could you come assist me, please?"

Gigi hesitated, as though she weren't sure Bridey could mean her. Bridey looked up to find the Scaldwells, Mrs. Arbuthnot, the Bastins, of course, with the ferryman's cottage behind. Mrs. Bastin wept, pulling the edge of her pinny to wipe her face. It didn't matter to her who the unfortunate would turn out to be.

More strangers had gathered on the road, too. The whole of South Devon should turn out for a single dead man. Were there not yet telegrams arriving at Galmpton and Churston homes? No sons lost?

Her eyes landed on Mrs. Scaldwell, stoic though her loss was recent. Those with telegrams could weather a body in the river, while Gigi still hovered among the folks from the estate, her face pale.

"Nurse Kelly? Please?" Her voice seemed not her own. What could she say to these people? The matron was right: she put herself forward too quickly, and now she had the attention of the entire county.

Gigi moved forward uncertainly, coming

to stand behind Bridey. At the sight of the man on the ground, her breath caught. She fell to her knees, closely so that her leg knocked against Bridey's, and pressed her hand to her lips.

The man looked much as he had the day they'd met him on the train, as he had the morning he had crossed the estate to the quay and spoken of foxes — except that his handsome face was pummeled and stark. His shirt collar still gaped.

Bridey flipped his tie around. The clear stone on his silver tie pin sparkled in the sun.

Near his throat, there was a bruise. Bridey reached in and pulled back the man's collar. It was a rounded bruise, a crescent moon of color, and a match to the one on the other side.

A low murmur in the crowd signaled impatience or disgust.

Gigi had said nothing, but surely —

Bridey lowered the draping. It was a bedsheet, with small hand-worked flowers on its edge, delicate stitching. Bridey imagined the sheet taken down from a cupboard in the ferryman's cottage. Dear Mrs. Bastin, using her best sheets for a river-soaked corpse.

Bridey stood and dusted herself. Out in

the river, one of the pleasure steamers churned upstream, the people crowded to starboard to see what happened on the quay.

"Not long in the water," she said at last. "None of you recognize him?"

The crowd murmured, conferred. Gigi stayed on her knees, offered nothing.

"Probably a seaman from the turned over boat they had downriver," said one of the men. He put his hat back in place. "Di'n't recover them all. Norwegian men."

"That was two months past," Mr. Scaldwell said.

"One of 'em turned up weeks later near Old Mill Creek," the first man said, defending himself.

"Poor lamb must have got beat up on the anchor stone," Mrs. Bastin said. "And caught up under a dock or summat."

"But *she* said not long in the water," someone in the crowd said.

"And you said *down*river," said another. "Where's the sense in the body washing upriver?"

"Best wait for the doctor's opinion after all," Bridey said.

"His expertise does seem to be dead men," someone in the crowd said, and those around him laughed.

Bridey tugged Gigi to her feet, searching

among them for what was funny. One man had a dark look to him, familiar. A glum face, one that should not have been there.

She ducked her head and conveyed Gigi through the onlookers, who stepped aside but reluctantly now. Bridey had the feeling of escape, of stealing between stones in a graveyard hoping nothing tugged at her skirt. This was nothing to do with Greenway, nothing to do with them. She had already inserted herself too much when she should keep her head down.

She cut through the crowd and made toward the path that led back up to the house. Why had they said nothing? Gigi she could nearly excuse for not speaking out for a stranger, but the other one, his friend from the train —

"Girls," Mrs. Arbuthnot said.

"We should get back to the nursery," Bridey called over her shoulder, hooking her arm through Gigi's. "We're no help here."

They turned into the path as a rather posh motorcar appeared along the road. The doctor. Behind them, the Norwegian sailor's story gathered steam. By the time the medical man arrived at quayside, the dead man would be a war hero and a credit to his nation and theirs.

She dragged Gigi up the hill and through a switchback, the grade punishing.

Gigi pulled loose. "You're hurting me."

"You recognized him, surely?"

"Why should I?" Without conviction.

There was a snap of a branch somewhere below. Bridey grabbed Gigi's hand and towed her up the incline. The trees around them seemed close and behind every one a figure until proven a shoot or vine. Was it not safe here at Greenway? The whole point of bringing the children here was to keep them from harm. Bridey felt the stitches keeping her panic tied down start to tug, her mind leaping toward memories she couldn't spend a moment on just now. She regained herself. "You know very well who that was."

Gigi yanked back her hand. "Do I? My, you like the drama of it, don't you? All that life and death, you're pink-cheeked and quivering for it. I've never seen you so animated. No wonder you'd rather be a nurse than a wife. Tommy surely can't compare to dashing death and carnage."

Bridey spun to face her. Gigi might have been stone — a chiseled maiden there among the trees and ferns, pale, lovely, empty.

She didn't know Gigi at all. They had

become friends, but what was that worth in wartime?

What would happen now? The police would be called, questions asked, identities scrutinized. Perhaps a telephone call to Matron Bailey, just to square the corners on things — and the truth spilled out. The end of her time at Greenway. The end of her options.

"You and I both know for certain," Bridey said. "That boy is no Norwegian sailor. Should he be buried so far from kin? A nameless grave?"

For a moment, Bridey thought Gigi might dig in. Then the façade of her countenance split, her color rising as she seemed to return to her body. "No."

"All right then." Bridey's thoughts whirled. Gigi had protected herself, kept quiet when she might have helped. Matron Bailey's words returned to her: it was no nurse she had ever known.

But the dead man's friend, the ill-humored one, had stood there on the quay and said nothing as well.

"How do you think he died?" Gigi said.

"Well, those bruises on his neck —"

Gigi stood back, her eyes sliding across Bridey but not alighting. "Bruises."

"Just the shape of a thumb along his

windpipe —"

"No!" Gigi's hands flew to her mouth.

Bridey stared at Gigi's hands, some little thought tugging at her attention but darting away when she tried to snap it out of the air. "You didn't see the bruises?" She had done everything but point them out. "Your small hands should rule you out," Bridey said. "And your sex. It will be a man able to strangle another man. You didn't invite him to Greenway?"

"Never! I — only saw him on the train."

"But he was here that morning, waiting. Did you tell him you'd be at Greenway?"

"How could I?" Gigi said. "I never heard of the place until we arrived."

She remembered Gigi's dismay as the pony cart took them away from the village. "What's his name?"

"I-I don't know it."

"Why did his companion, the sullen one, say nothing?"

"I wouldn't know."

"I don't understand," Bridey said. "Why not tell them you've seen the man before? They'd at least know he was from London and have a better search for who he is."

"I don't know he's from London," she said. "He might have been only passing through Paddington."

"But —"

Bridey caught a flash of movement and color below them on the path. Mrs. Arbuthnot, struggling up the steep path, or some chancer from the village taking advantage of distraction to walk over the estate. "Come on, let's go and relieve Edith of the children."

"I shouldn't be anywhere near the children."

That made two of them, then. "Shirking again. It won't work. Come on."

20
JOAN ARBUTHNOT

At Greenway Quay

Joan decided to stay on until the young man had been seen to. Only right. She'd been embarrassed by the nurses' quick exit, as a matter of fact. She'd asked for *quality* when seeking the right applicants, hadn't she?

The doctor came. Too young a man for her taste. She liked an old doctor, a man who advertised his services with his own longevity.

The constabulary arrived soon after and shuffled all the witnesses away from the quay. The crowd broke apart, but Joan hesitated. The same impulse that had brought about the Greenway war nursery wouldn't let her abandon the boy.

Mrs. Bastin stood near the gate to her cottage talking with Mrs. Scaldwell. How terrible to have a dead man on one's doorstep — but the chat was giving Mrs. Bastin her color back. Joan tried not to look as though she were hanging about hoping to be pulled in.

The society at Greenway was rather slim since Mrs. Christie had gone off to London. Malcolm couldn't be counted on; he was always off painting, was off painting now in fact. The Scaldwells acted as though they were the landowners and were not simply implements to keep the estate tidy and hospitable, and the woman had all but accused Joan's evacuees of snatching a misplaced pot of jam, when Mrs. Bastin herself was in and out of the service corridor all day.

The young nurses' company she didn't care for, one too eager to please and one — well, she hadn't had the measure of Gigi yet. Something in Gigi's stunning cheekbones made Joan wonder if she might not have a bit of traveler ancestry. Not that it mattered, of course — only she was quicksilver, one minute something Joan recognized and the next, something else.

For companionship, that left Joan with the children. She rather enjoyed the children, as she had known she would. Of all the ways she and Malcolm might have spent the war years, she knew getting up a war nursery would be the most natural way to do their part. A private arrangement, not that Women's Voluntary Services scheme, where they placed one *heaven* knew where. She'd brokered the house herself and now they had the comforts of a fine home while they couldn't be in their own on Jersey. A place her children might come to if their own wartime plans fell through. She tried not to hope for it.

But oh! She so wished Mrs. Christie had stayed on. They might have been great friends.

In not a few letters to the relatives, Mrs. Christie's name *had* come up.

"Mrs. Arbuthnot," Mrs. Bastin called out from the cottage gate. Mrs. Scaldwell turned a cheek as though she didn't care one way or another if Joan joined them. "Is it not horrid?"

"Unconscionable," Joan said, walking over. "A young man with his life ahead of him. What more trouble can youth bring upon themselves?" She remembered Mrs. Scaldwell's nephew too late. "Er. When one thinks of the loss we already suffer weekly among our men in uniform . . . as with your family's great loss, Mrs. Scaldwell."

"Thank you."

"I suppose I'm grateful it's an incomer and not one of our bueys," Mrs. Bastin said, her Devonshire accent thick with feeling.

187

"But I can't help feeling sorry for his mum."

The woman had wide-set eyes like a sheep. Did she realize what she had said? An outsider's life was less valuable, less cause for concern? Was the boy any less dead?

How could these people feel such a way, when they were fighting together with the Poles and French, when it was rather the entire point that they all stood as one against common enemies? But here in Mrs. Christie's patch, they'd their gazes canted at any stranger. Probably their neighbors as well, come to it.

"I don't know why he wasn't at the front to begin with," Mrs. Bastin said.

"Not all young men go to the front, Elsie," Mrs. Scaldwell said.

Joan thought Mrs. Scaldwell stared daggers at her. How would she have heard? She couldn't have.

"Some have other roles to play, that's true," Joan said, carefully. "But this. This seems naught but senseless death." Mrs. Scaldwell's nephew again. "As with —"

"Douglas," Mrs. Scaldwell said.

"May he rest in peace," Joan said. "This war will have taken its toll on an entire generation when it's done."

"On every generation," Mrs. Bastin said.

"Have you heard about Old Brian down Stokes Gabriel?" she said to Mrs. Scaldwell. "Died in his own bed during that last tip and run raid."

"Bill Brian, too?" Mrs. Scaldwell said. "There won't be a man over fifty left in the village. One does wonder —"

"His house was bombed?" Joan asked.

"Heart trouble, they say," Mrs. Bastin said. She glanced toward the high window of her cottage. "But what should happen, if you drop bombs near the houses of aged folk?"

"What good is it having a doctor with his newfangled ideas —" Mrs. Scaldwell started.

"He still does house calls," Mrs. Bastin said.

"When was the last time your father received one? House visits are reserved for those who can pay him what he thinks he's owed." Mrs. Scaldwell noticed Mrs. Bastin's fluttering eyelids. "Elsie, John Hannaford is fit as a fiddle. Your father will live to be a hundred."

"Old Brian and Mr. Prescott in Churston last month, they weren't sixty," Mrs. Bastin said. "The doctor said the stress of the attacks . . . it's a silent killer, the doctor said." She paused over the words, perhaps pleased with them. "Silent killer, like one of madam's books."

"Not at all like," Mrs. Scaldwell said. "Ill health makes for a rather less mysterious story."

Mrs. Bastin said, "I don't suppose it could be the same thing with that young man . . ."

The stress of the water, perhaps. "Perhaps it's not ill health stalking the county," Joan said.

"What are you saying?" Mrs. Scaldwell said.

"A great number of your friends have died? Cause for alarm, is it not?"

"The doctor does know what he's about," Mrs. Bastin said. She looked hopefully to Mrs. Scaldwell. "Vera, don't you think so? University trained and all."

"What good it does. He's an upstart," Mrs. Scaldwell said. "But he probably knows heart trouble when he sees it."

"Well, I'm sure. I didn't *speak* with him," Joan said. "Maybe I should have done."

"What need?" Mrs. Scaldwell said. "*Frank* spoke with the doctor and will notify the mistress."

The mistress, if you please. Even when she was off in London, they bowed and scraped. Joan surely had more in common with a doctor than a butler. Her first husband had made a comfortable life for her, then and now, and she was a woman of property, even if she couldn't access much of it at the moment. Not that these women knew anything about such things. They made her think of her own low beginnings, all the pieces of herself she had tried to leave behind.

She made apologies — the children, always the children — and bid the women good afternoon, sensing the circle of their confidences close off at her back.

Joan took the same path as the nurses had, the shortcut through the woods, but slowly, her feet going out from under her a bit. A Norwegian sailor, three weeks in the River Dart? But at least then he would have gone in somewhere downriver. Not a matter of having been killed *here*.

Joan felt the shadows of the trees upon her neck. She knew the way, and yet Greenway's flat white face loomed far above her, out of reach. Mrs. Christie couldn't enjoy heaving herself up such a hill as this. But no, Joan supposed Mrs. Christie and her husband did enjoy the grounds; there was the tennis court, and Mrs. Christie was hardy enough for expeditions to Iraq, heaven's sake. The things Joan disliked about Greenway were the precise reasons the Mallowans preferred it. One chose Greenway to stalk hill and dale for sport, to be free of the society of other people and their noise. And when the people and their noise came to Greenway, the owners packed their belongings and made for London. Chose London, even as the Germans turned it to rubble.

In every way, spending the war at Greenway had seemed a cheat — safety for them, the satisfaction of doing some small duty, comfortable surroundings. It was almost as though they were guests of Mrs. Christie. Invited. She might have suggested as much in a *few* of the letters.

And yet — bombs in Plymouth almost every night, and the young women she'd hired to protect the children administering to *corpses*.

Joan stopped.

Why had Bridey forced Gigi to examine the man? He was dead enough that one nurse could not save him, so what purpose was a second opinion? And Gigi pale and shaking. Had she never encountered death? What lucky training she must have had.

Ahead Joan saw a stone wall with an arch and moved toward it, through it. Here were the ruins Mrs. Bastin had once mentioned to Malcolm, for painting. But Malcolm wasn't interested in painting likeness. It was all shape and abstraction he favored now. Joan walked along, thankful for the even ground, a chance to catch her breath from the climb. The level ground and the wall the work of captives of Sir Francis Drake's, enslaved Spanish labor from the Armada, so said Mrs. Bastin.

"Just a story, surely," Joan said.

But there was something in the myth of the place that made her uncomfortable. Was every place a site tainted by past cruelty?

The wall had an arched niche and a bench and, further, an open doorway, partly covered with overgrowth. Inside was a small stone room, open to the sky. There were notches where beams might have held a roof of some kind, perhaps wood that had rotted, or tin sent to be made into Spitfires.

All resources, everything they had and were, fed to the flames of war.

As soon as she thought it, the walls closed in, the trees overhead pressed down. Joan felt her way back to the niche and slumped onto its bench.

She was fine. All would be well. Although sometimes she remembered that her children were all at an age to be destroyed by it all: to be put on the front line, to have their sweethearts not come back from the RAF.

Her sons, adopted with George, were objectors — leanings quite like his, though she would never say *socialist* aloud. They were kept from the fighting but not from — well, she didn't want to say shame. Not from fear of reprisal, from looks like Mrs. Scaldwell's: knowing, judging.

It was not *shame.*

When she was quiet again, she heard birdsong, and leaves shivering in the trees above. She caught a voice down on the river, someone going by in a boat, fishing for the evening's supper or, more likely, coming by for a look at the quay and the rumored body. A South Devon chap who existed outside the periphery of her attention and knowledge, going about his day. Wasn't it remarkable that one might go about one's life, thinking oneself at the center, barely looking right or left, only to discover that everyone else was exactly the same?

The curved bowl of the niche in the wall above her head made her think of some Italian Madonna, posed in a grotto, like something Malcolm might have arranged back in his photo studio days —

Someone was scuffing along the path toward her.

It would be Mrs. Scaldwell, wondering why she'd hurried away from their conversation, only to break here in the ruins. But the footsteps were rather heavier than a woman's, and the breathing far more labored than Mrs. Scaldwell's was likely to be.

Some bystander at the quay using the disturbance to traipse through Greenway's lush woodlands? Someone with an interest in the dead man? Prurient interest?

Malicious?

Joan pulled herself deep into the niche.

Or might it be the constables, stalking the grounds for clues. Rather like one of Mrs. Christie's books. Why, Mrs. Bastin had been rather on the nose there, hadn't she?

It *should* be the constables. And while Scaldwell might have talked with the doctor, she as the tenant was the proper surrogate for Mrs. Christie, not some hired man. Anyway, she should be kept informed. She protected a brood of innocents and answered to their parents. And Parliament, really. Churchill. The King, if one truly considered the matter. As she liked to remind the nurses, they were doing no small job here at Greenway. The future of England depended on women like them.

Joan stood and emerged from the niche, on behalf of Mrs. Christie, a deputy as it were, ready to be helpful.

The path was clear, dappled sunlight waving with the tree branches above.

A twig snapped higher on the path, and Joan lifted her chin. Whomever it was had bypassed the ruins for the house. She was alone.

21
VERA SCALDWELL

Greenway Road

Vera took the long way back to the house, up the hill past the doctor's motorcar — a bit grand for the country, she'd thought, and how did one come by a new model these days? Frank would like nothing better than to report the fellow for not installing headlamp covers.

The last of those come to see what had happened at the quay had their heads together now, farmers' wives who all but fled back to their chores at the sight of her. Perhaps because she lived at the great house and had the mistress's ear, she couldn't be trusted? Vera thought herself pleasant enough company, when she had the time. She never had the time.

More to the point, she hadn't been born across the river, raised to live no more than a stone's throw from Mother and Dad. She had no patience with those that thought their history in a place made them the owners of the land they still farmed for someone else. They were tenants. Squatters, rather, and couldn't admit it.

She turned the hook of the drive through the gate and around the pretty little gatehouse.

For instance.

"All of it settled, then?" Alice Hannaford called from the garden, as though she hadn't been down at the quay an hour herself. The gardener's wife. The gardener, George, was the son of the former gardener, John, who now lived in the ferry cottage with his daughter, Mrs. Bastin, whose husband was a laborer at one of the estate farms. Hannafords stuffed into every corner of the place as far as the eye could see but, still, they were in service, same as her.

"As well as it can be," Vera said, gazing over the gate lodge. She had plans for that pretty little stone chalet with its lacy pediment in the gable over the door. The kitchen was small but what she wouldn't give to have her own again. The gate lodge should be theirs by rights and when the old gardener died, she would send Frank to put a flea in the mistress's ear.

The gates to the great house stood open. Rather sloppy. The mistress didn't like the gates left open. "Is someone in, Mrs. Hannaford?" Vera said. "The fishmongers? Only they've left the gate hanging."

"So they did. It was *constables*," Alice Hannaford said. A little too pleased, it seemed to Vera.

"Ah yes, I suppose they would stop in," she said.

"Enough trouble on, without constables at Greenway," Mrs. Hannaford said.

"I agree with you." Vera gritted her teeth wishing Mrs. Hannaford a good day and tried not to hurry up the drive too quickly.

They were meant to keep order, she and Frank. Order of the sort the mistress needed when she was in, order that kept everyone else at bay when she was out. But already there were too many feet heavy on the floorboards.

And grimy hands in the larder.

She knew the Arbuthnot woman thought her daft for caring so much about a jar of plum preserves, but it was the principle of the thing. They were all making accommodations and sacrifices, but the scoundrel who'd taken the preserves wasn't making any consolations to anyone else. You put up jam for the future, didn't you? Captured the moment, conserved it as berry purple-red, and saved it for a long-off day. It was a promise, was preserves.

With a pang of grief, she recalled a time Douglas had got into his mum's pantry, just a little mite, and had a feast. They'd found him asleep under the stairs with jam still packed in his cheeks, sticky from head to toe.

Children were a promise, too. Or she had thought. Her steps slowed on the cobble.

If you raised a child, you were plunking down a wager in favor of the future, choosing your horse. But he would always be dead now, was that it? Always twenty, no matter how often her thoughts turned to him? She'd gone to help Katie in her confinement with Douglas, had nestled the boy in the crook of her arm when he was minutes old, ahead of the child's own father, Vera's dear brother. She and Frank had their Diana not a year later.

Her brother Leslie worked at the undertaker's. He might have laid out his own son for burial but certainly someone else —

She couldn't bear it. Douglas's death had no message to send, no lesson to teach. It only meant the gambles they made might be risky. The choices, bad.

She looked up. And now the police, as well.

Vera entered the back of the house and

trailed along the service corridor, following the sound of voices to the kitchen. Cups of tea all around and at the table, two policemen with caps sitting on the table linen, the two nurses, and her husband with sleeves rolled up. Frank's eyes flicked to her as she came in. "My wife," he said to one of the men, who wrote a few words in a small pad.

"Gentlemen," she said. These were young ones, fish-belly pale from sitting in some pub and calling it policing.

"Now where were we?" the one with the pad said. His hair was a copper shade, comb tracks still neat. "You're certain you're not familiar with the bloke?"

"Familiar?" This was Gigi. "What are you insinuating?"

"Nothing," the chap said, startled enough. "Nothing at all. I only meant —"

"We said we didn't know him," Gigi said. "Is the Greenway Quay not a public port of call?"

The dark-haired nurse didn't fool Vera. She had a fox face, made Vera think of tales of beguiled men choosing their own deaths, bashing their ships into sea cliffs. What did they know of these women? This one had no shortage of smart things to say, all jokes and flirtations, but Vera hadn't been taken in. Gigi, ridiculous name. It all had a whiff

201

of the alley-way confidence man.

"I only meant," the policeman stammered, "I only meant was there anything you wanted to let us know, like."

Vera looked to the other nurse. Different sort here. This girl had a way of disappearing before you, the life in her eyes falling away until you weren't at all sure she was inside there somewhere. She might as well not be there, letting Gigi take the brunt of the questions, except — as Vera watched, something rose to the surface of Bridey's expression, some animation to her not always there, and then fell away again. Like a single ripple in a still pond.

"I'm sure these girls would let you know if they had anything worth sharing," Frank said. "We only wish we could be of any help but we don't know the boy. We've never seen him before."

But hadn't he said —

One look from Frank kept her still.

"Well, I suppose if you think of anything." The other policeman was thick-lipped and soft-shouldered compared to his partner, as malleable as raw dough.

"Is there a good deal of crime down in this area?" Gigi said.

The other nurse looked at her sharply.

"No more than there ought to be," said

the ginger one but the thick one was already listing the recent occurrences.

"Spot of robberies, a few wild theories to explain away a valuable missing after family's in for a funeral . . ." He realized he'd spoken out of turn, coughed, and sat up straight, all courtesy and business. "Nothing we can't handle."

"Do you mean break-ins?" Bridey said.

The policemen startled at her voice. "Miss?" the ginger one said.

"Has there been someone skulking about?" she said. "Someone . . . troublesome?"

"You mean fifth column, like? Or Germans?"

Frank spoke up. "The Home Guard hasn't seen any sign —"

"One of the children said she saw someone is all," Bridey said. "We've had a theft, as well."

"It's only a jar of jam," Gigi said.

The thick officer leaned forward. "Might your girl describe the bloke to us? As if these folks haven't lost enough, they're to do without the hair-looms, too?"

"Evans," barked the other copper.

"She's barely four years old," Gigi said. "She said she saw the *wisht* man."

Evans sat back, his mouth open until he

could find the words. "No, I wouldn't have her saying that. That's not faerie stuff. That'll call the devil to you, right enough."

"Evans."

Frank soon saw them out and the nurses fled the kitchen while Vera stoked the fire for the oven and cleared the cups from the table. The one called Evans had barely touched his tea.

Frank returned with a bottle of whiskey he had squirreled away in his office.

"Didn't you say you saw someone on the grounds?" Vera said.

"I said —" He was about to lie, she could always tell, then changed his mind. "Yes. I saw a man on the grounds, but it's nothing to do with this."

"Nothing? Couldn't it be the same man?"

"Nothing to do with us, and it was not the same man. I saw the body, remember? The village is on fire with suspicion, every stranger a threat. Someone fancied that gentleman a German operative and pounced, you mark my words. Let's not get mixed in."

"You think he was a —"

"I think someone out there thought he was. Things move quickly when some fool's jumping at shadows."

She tipped the full cup of tea left behind

and clucked. "Waste."

"I think that copper didn't want to risk it." Frank took the cup, dumped it into the sink, and filled it again with whiskey.

"Eh?"

"Risk drinking anything from the poisoner's kitchen," he said, raising the cup. "Cheers."

The bell rang. What now? Vera went for the door and heard someone coming along behind her. Mrs. Arbuthnot, thinking herself the hostess.

"If you'd like to open the doors for visitors," Vera said, "you'd save me the bother."

"You may open," Mrs. Arbuthnot said.

Granting her the favor of doing her own job!

Oliver Hart stood on the step, country tweeds and hat in hand. Should have known he'd take the occasion to come up to the house.

"Why, you're the doctor," Mrs. Arbuthnot said. "Do come in. Mrs. Scaldwell, please fetch Bridget?"

"That's right." The doctor leaned over Mrs. Arbuthnot's hand. "Dr. Oliver Hart."

"Mrs. Malcolm Arbuthnot."

"Not the photographer Malcolm Arbuthnot?"

Vera wouldn't miss this for the world. It was a test of Mrs. Arbuthnot, who was still a puzzle.

"Indeed." Mrs. Arbuthnot was blushing. "He's painting these days. Right now, in fact, or I should have him down to say hello. Another time, perhaps."

"I welcome the opportunity." Hart glanced her way. "Mrs. Scaldwell. I trust you are well?"

"Rather busy," Vera said. She walked to the corridor and called for Elsie to send the nurse down.

Behind her, Mrs. Arbuthnot tried to laugh off the exchange. "Can we help you with anything, Doctor, or were you only looking in on the Mallowans? They're away, I'm afraid. Perhaps you hadn't heard."

"Looking in on you, actually. Giving my professional regard for the nurses, as I heard they were helpful at the quay."

Vera arrived back in time to see Mrs. Arbuthnot's simper in the presence of the doctor's good looks. She was failing the test. Was she a society woman with a husband who trailed along after her whims? Or someone more interesting, who could be expected to be circumspect of the doctor's flattery. "Oh, I *am* glad," Mrs. Arbuthnot said.

"I'm only sorry to have made your acquaintance in such tragic circumstances," Hart said. "And so soon after your arrival."

"And to have happened to someone so young," Mrs. Arbuthnot said.

"We've had a few losses locally these last months, all of them tragic. The war, some natural disorders of the heart, lungs." He shook his head. "We'll never know precisely."

"Tragic indeed," Mrs. Arbuthnot said.

"I suppose I'm also here to put in an early bid," he said.

Ah, here it was. He was a *salesman,* as though they had any sort of choice in the matter. The nearest doctor otherwise was in Dartmouth or Brixham.

Bridey was coming down the corridor, and Vera stepped out of the way, hoping to be forgotten.

"Even with exceptional nursing," Hart said, "you may find need for my services. Any troubles at all, man, woman, or child." He looked around the room. "I've been known to perform house calls, too, for particular friends."

"Why, you're too kind," Mrs. Arbuthnot cooed. "And here's our Nurse Kelly."

"Nurse Kelly, Dr. Oliver Hart. Pleased to make your acquaintance," he said. "Why you're quite young! You're nearly the same age as the man on the quay. You'd not encountered him in your stay here?"

"No, sir," Bridey said. "We're rather — outside of town. But I thought someone said he might have been down from London."

"Indeed?"

"I hadn't heard that," Mrs. Arbuthnot said. "A long way to come, only to drown."

The doctor's eyebrow twitched. "What was your assessment of the situation at the quay, Nurse Kelly?"

Bridey spoke to the window over his shoulder. "I wouldn't like to say, sir."

"Go on, Bridget," Mrs. Arbuthnot said. A stage mother pressing her star into the center.

"Was he drowned, Sister?"

"No, Doctor. I don't think he was drowned at all."

Mrs. Arbuthnot turned. "But —"

"He was killed before he went in," Hart said. "The lungs will be absolutely empty, mark my words. And now — London. I wish he hadn't brought his troubles here."

"The troubles may have awaited him here," Bridey said. "Sir."

"Astute," Hart said.

Mrs. Arbuthnot fanned herself. She'd be thinking of all the other places her war nursery might have been received, wouldn't she? Just as Vera had been doing all along.

She went to get the kettle. The sooner he was served a cup in the drawing room, the sooner they'd see the back of him.

22
Bridey

Gigi stood at the top landing when Bridey came up the stairs from meeting the doctor. "I need to get to that pub," Gigi said. "Tonight."

"Which pub?" Bridey said. The cart driver had mentioned a pub as they drove into Greenway the first night — Gigi had had it stored away all this time? "You mean to leave me alone with them all again?"

"No, I mean for you to go with me," Gigi said.

"I don't see how that's possible."

"I do," she said as they entered the nursery playroom to find Edith happily dandling the youngest baby and the Jackson girls entertaining the rest of the children.

"*Galmpton?*" Edith said. *Gam'ton.* "You know there's naught to do there?" Gigi offered a pair of new shop-bought stockings, perfectly smooth, under which Edith's campaign of discouragement never gained steam.

"What if I don't want to go?" Bridey said, pulling Gigi out of the doorway. "What if I'm happy here?"

"Aren't you even the slightest tired of these four walls?"

"But there's a — a killer on the loose."

"Fair point," Gigi said. "What did Mrs. Arbuthnot want?"

"To have me tell the doctor —"

"The *doctor*? And what's he like?"

Bridey didn't want to say and tried not to blush. "What you might expect. I did manage — don't be angry with me — to hint the dead man might have been from London."

"Did you? Well, it's only gossip, I suppose. No harm, especially if it helps them find out his name. Let's go see who's in the kitchen," Gigi said.

They'd just been in the kitchen, hadn't they? If they had an hour, Bridey had been hoping to get some of her personal chores seen to, a bit of washing perhaps. But they'd be talking about the dead man, wouldn't they?

In the kitchen Mrs. Bastin sat shucking early spring peas from the garden, and the man in the river was precisely what *she* wanted to discuss.

"It's like one of Mrs. Mallowan's stories," she said when Gigi sat herself across at the table and reached into the pail to help. "I was telling Mrs. Scaldwell. 'Death at the Quay' or summat like that. That's her all over. Though of course he wasn't murdered."

Bridey looked at Gigi.

"*Was* he?" Mrs. Bastin said.

"He might have been," Gigi said.

"Well I do wonder," Mrs. Bastin said, her hand drifting dreamily to the pail. "And Mrs. M. missing her chance to sniff it out."

"Is the mistress a detective?" Gigi said.

"She has the mind for it," Mrs. Bastin said. "The twisting mind. One wonders where that came from."

"What would a twisting mind make of all this, d'you think?" Gigi said.

Bridey stared. Gigi's accent had slipped south or — no, she was only mimicking as she often did. But to the woman's face!

"Oh, I don't know," Mrs. Bastin said, not seeming to notice. "I never thought a second on intrigue and murder until Mrs. M. came to live. This house stood a hundred years, but now there's murder in the curtains and carpets, stitched into every sampler and tea towel, baked into every crumb. It's the home that murder made now, right enough."

"You've never read one of her books?"

"You've caught me. I've lived here the whole of m' life, but the Mallowans, they've only had the house these three years. I should do, I suppose. I'd only fall asleep, to try and read a book."

"I do, too," Bridey said, and was rewarded with a smile from Mrs. Bastin, genuine and sweet, a tooth missing.

"They're just stories, you know," Gigi said. "You *tell* stories, I wager. Like Mrs. Scaldwell and her wisht man —"

"That's not stories," Mrs. Bastin said. "That's truth."

"There's truth in stories, and stories in truth," Gigi said. "You must tell stories all the time, true ones. When you say to Mrs. Scaldwell what people you've met at market or what someone was wearing at church, or tell your husband what's happening in the big house."

Mrs. Bastin snapped alert. "I don't gossip about what's happening here."

"Oh? I would. I would gossip all the livelong day," Gigi said, sitting back. "What else is there to speak of?"

"Well," Mrs. Bastin said, relenting. "I don't mean to."

"Not maliciously, of course," Gigi said. "Only to make conversation, like we're doing now."

"Never — no, not unkind. Not maliciously." In Mrs. Bastin's mouth, the word was softened until it tangled.

"You're a bright one, I think," Gigi said. "And having lived here so long, you're like to notice things no one else does."

Mrs. Bastin plucked a handful of peapods. "That's what he said, too. He said, 'You've lived here longer than anyone in the house,' he said. And he was right. My da, my brother, me, we're here longer than anyone." She sniffed. "Some don't think it matters."

"Who's this asking?" Gigi said.

"That buey."

"The boy? From the river? You know him?" Bridey said. "Did he tell you his name?"

Gigi cut her a look that made her quiet.

"I met him once," Mrs. Bastin said. "Told the constable, too. If he gave his name, I don't remember it. And —" She stopped.

Gigi allowed the silence in the kitchen to swell. Bridey began to ask, but under the table, Gigi reached over and put a hand on Bridey's arm.

"Well, I don't like to speak ill of the dead," Mrs. Bastin said at last.

"He's no friend of mine," Gigi said.

Bridey wasn't so certain about that. *Stories in truth.* She shook off Gigi's grip.

"Well," Mrs. Bastin said, glancing toward the door. "He had a lot of questions, and folk down this way don't abide it. They keep theirselves to theirselves."

"What kind of questions?"

"About the men away at the front, and no one minds if you're asking after one of our own bueys," she said. "But he wanted to hear about — well, anything anyone might normally say behind their hands, do you know what I mean?"

"I do," Gigi said. "This is down at the quay?"

"Rumors and scandals," Mrs. Bastin said. "Yes, the quay. Any wary word at all, he wanted to hear it. What did we think about this and that. As though the Register was being taken again, all the questions he had."

"Were there any rumors or scandals he was particularly interested in?"

"Well, it's like I said. I don't gossip."

But wasn't she —

Bridey held her tongue, recognizing Gigi's game. She was giving the exchange air, letting out the line so that her catch would bite.

"But I did mention a few things to him,"

215

Mrs. Bastin said. "Common knowledge and all that. Anyone might have told him, so I told him d'rectly."

"Only right."

With a little more silence, Mrs. Bastin reeled out her facts. The Freebys at the higher farm had three sons the right age for war but the widow Mrs. Jackson at the lower farm only the one son, and the whispers held that the scales of justice were sometimes heavier for some. There were the usual things: the wives left behind, what they got up to, and what they might be like to live with when husbands returned. Illnesses long and short, funerals well attended and not. The slights of small places, waged for generations. Mrs. Bastin wouldn't be stopped, and Gigi didn't try.

When the woman finally wound down, Gigi thanked her. "Talking with you has been so rewarding. You make us feel at home here."

Mrs. Bastin looked up from her peas and gave Gigi a sly version of her gapped smile. "Not like some, you mean."

In the corridor, Bridey whispered, "Not like some?"

"Those who don't want us to settle in," Gigi said.

"The Scaldwells," Bridey said.

"Where is Mrs. Scaldwell now?"

"Gigi, you'd *never.*"

"Chat up Mrs. Scaldwell? Why not?"

They couldn't find her. They checked her office first, then poked their heads in the larder and knocked at the door of the pantry, with the butler's office beyond, the little cupboards under the stairs that were the Scaldwells' domain. Outside on the hill, Edith and the Jackson daughters had the children turning somersaults, the babies on a blanket.

"We could try their apartment," Gigi said. "I've always wanted to have a look in there."

On the next floor outside the Scaldwells' living quarters, they heard footsteps overhead on the children's floor.

"Well, I doubt it's the wisht man," Gigi said.

Mrs. Scaldwell was in the girls' room, going through a dressing case pulled out from under one of the beds.

"Good afternoon, Mrs. Scaldwell," Gigi said.

She hadn't been expecting them. "I thought you went out. I'm tidying."

Snooping. Bridey saw Gigi hesitate.

"You said you were missing a few jars of jams," Bridey said. "I dare say it's not the children doing it, but why don't we help you look?"

Mrs. Scaldwell took this as permission to keep searching. "Damson *preserves,* grown right over on the hill in Dits'm. We didn't have to guard the plums before your lot showed up."

"Their hands are so small," Bridey said, cheerfully going through the cubbies. They could use neatening anyway. "They're more like to smash a jar of preserves than get away clean."

Mrs. Scaldwell sighed. "It's not even about the preserves."

"Meanness," Bridey agreed.

"No, I — I'm not sure what I mean."

"When did you put up these preserves?" Gigi said. She had gone over to the piano, but there weren't any hiding places there.

"We put up berries most years," Mrs. Scaldwell said. "Not *this* year, of course, with all the mouths we'll need to feed. Vegetables at the end of summer. Courgettes into pickles, marrows. Leeks and onions and swede. Plums and peaches, late. Apples in the autumn."

Bridey's mouth watered.

"I understand why it upsets you," Gigi said. "Laying by, pickling and bottling — that signifies there's a day of feasting out in the future. That the future will come." Gigi went to Doreen's cot, sat on the edge, and gazed at the papered window, at the tear Bridey had fastened with cellophane tape. "It's an act of hope, isn't it, to imagine a crowded table devouring last summer's harvest?"

Bridey had never considered onions nor apples in such a way. "Then stealing them . . ." Bridey said.

"Yes?" Gigi said. Not stopping her this time, but encouraging her.

"Then stealing from the larder," Bridey said, "is the same as saying my today is more important than your tomorrow."

The dimple popped, like a wink. "It's war profiteering, is what it is."

Mrs. Scaldwell's cool demeanor had dropped several degrees. "I expect you're right about the children having naught to do with it. I had to be sure. There's so little to be sure of now."

"We were just talking with Mrs. Bastin in the kitchen about this very thing," Gigi said. "So much happening, strangers about, bad news from all corners." She paused so that Mrs. Scaldwell knew they included the nephew. She nodded, once. "The man in the river. Mrs. Bastin even said he'd been nosing about the village before he died."

"Was he? For what?"

"She didn't know," Gigi said. "Gossip, at best. Leverage, at worst."

"Leverage?" Mrs. Scaldwell dragged herself up from her knees to the nearest cot. "What in the wide world does that mean?"

"Digging for dirt, sniffing around for tales to tell or not tell. For a price."

"*Here?* I never. Galmpton's hardly a spot for crimes worse than hurt feelings." She thought. "But then again, times is different . . . recently."

Bridey thought she meant to blame them for the dead man now. How did they have the time to steal jam, too?

"Any place with people has secrets kept," Gigi said.

"I suppose," Mrs. Scaldwell said. "But I can't think of any secrets here some fellow from London would be interested in. They're always scraping at that old story about the mistress, but it comes to nothing but embarrassment for a good lady. You know that story of course."

"Of course."

She seemed disappointed they already did and she couldn't tell it.

"Did you ever meet him?" Gigi said.

"Who? Her first husband?"

"The man pulled from the river."

"Can't say I did."

The blanket from Doreen's bed dragged the floor, even if Gigi hadn't noticed. Bridey crawled over and lifted its edge. There was a pile of dust, fallen from a rough spot on the wall.

"I met him," Bridey said. She ignored the look Gigi gave her. "He passed through the property one morning."

"Did he?" Mrs. Scaldwell said.

"Early, before anyone was about."

"Frank runs off blokes all the time." Mrs. Scaldwell looked troubled. "But he would have seen the back of him to the road. Safely. If Frank had met him."

"Of course," Bridey said.

Gigi said, "Has Frank — Mr. Scaldwell, I mean —" Mrs. Scaldwell looked at her sharply. "Has he escorted anyone off the grounds lately?"

"None I know of."

The conversation, which had seemed like a game at first, now seemed as though a door had slammed. Mrs. Scaldwell stood. "I'd better get back to work. Cooking for ten children is a toil."

"Caring for them, too," Bridey said.

Mrs. Scaldwell looked between them, Gigi lounging on the cot and Bridey sitting on the floor. "Well, you both make it look so easy."

Gigi held her laughter in until the woman was down the stairs. "She's my favorite, I think. Not a bit of subtlety to her." She sat up on the cot and looked toward Doreen's window again. "Shouldn't we go to Galmpton?"

If this was collecting, it *was* rather diverting, Bridey thought. She had arrived at Greenway wanting Mrs. Arbuthnot's approval but now she also wanted Gigi's.

"Mrs. Arbuthnot can't find out," she said.

Gigi's dimple popped. "*I* won't tell her."

23
BRIDEY

Toward Galmpton

"How you convinced me of this," Bridey gasped, trying to keep up with Gigi through the shadowy woods that night. They were taking a shortcut, more of a rumor than a path, and the way was rugged. Back at the house, the children were in bed, Edith on duty, the Arbuthnots retired upstairs, and the Scaldwells none the wiser. "I should have realized it would be entirely uphill. We'll arrive smelling high. Like farmhands."

"We'll be blushing pink, like brides," Gigi said. "We should have worn white."

Bridey tramped behind, keeping a keen eye on Gigi's back so as not to lose her in the dark. There was a snap of a twig in the woods, but when Bridey turned, there was nothing to be seen but the deep silhouettes of the trees, more blackness. She remembered the screams of foxes, then the young man's wink, and shivered.

"In white, we'd have been able to see one another on the dark walk home," she said.

Gigi said, "Maybe we'll ride some sailors home."

She was supposed to be shocked. Decent Bridget, ladylike Bridget. She could be, but most of all she enjoyed that Gigi teased her as though she was just another girl, a regular sort of girl and not one whose life had slid off the road into tragedy. In such a life, she would already know all the secret things Gigi seemed to. She'd already be a bride, perhaps, and why not? Tom had put in his time, ticked the boxes. Asked little of her. She could wear a smart suit and a hat with a veil, something suitable for the registry office. That was the tidy thing to do. A witness snagged last minute, no fanfare. No well-wishers. No crying mams, no little sisters all vying to carry the flowers —

Bridget nearly gagged on the grief that rose up in her throat.

"Did you say something?" Gigi said.

"No."

Gigi stopped to take a look at her. "If you're that miserable, you can turn and go back."

She was not miserable. If she kept her wits about her, she was neither this nor that.

"You could tell me, if you had something

on your mind," Gigi said. "I'm a good listener."

"I won't sit for examination like Mrs. Bastin and Mrs. Scaldwell," Bridey said. "You spent all afternoon wringing information out of them. Are you playing at detectives like one of the mistress's books? Is this all for your amusement?"

"I was only having conversation."

"You weren't. I was there. I saw what you were doing."

"I *like* talking. I've always had a knack for getting someone to chat," Gigi said. "I used to use it in school, to get the teacher reminiscing until we'd run out of time for lessons and the school bell rang."

"What do you use it for now?"

Gigi stopped. "Aren't you a bright one?"

"You said the same to Mrs. Bastin," Bridey said. "And you didn't mean it. Is it more of your *observing*? Why are you still doing it?"

"Asking questions is a difficult habit to break," Gigi said. "And I'm interested in other people, aren't you? Their oddness, the things they think bog standard that no one else would recognize. It's thrilling to know what people feel, to know who they really are. It's rather an addiction. Once you start collecting, it's difficult to stop. It's difficult,"

Gigi said, "not to take in what people don't want you to know."

Bridey couldn't tell anymore if Gigi confessed her own sins, or if she laid a trap for Bridey to declare hers. She was glad of the dark.

"The danger is accidentally taking in something you shouldn't," Gigi said.

She'd been found out. It was slipping away from her: her position, her reputation, her hopes. All. Her tongue felt thick in her mouth. "Did you?" She would be consumed whole by Gigi's silence. She could barely choke out the words. "Did you take in something? Tell me."

"I shouldn't. It doesn't make you any safer."

"How do you mean?"

"What trouble I got up to in London shouldn't be left at *your* feet."

The tightness in Bridey's ribs loosened. Gigi hadn't been speaking of her at all.

"What kind of trouble?" she said as they carried on toward the village.

"Spot of bother, that's all," Gigi said at last. "With a man."

How tiring it must be to be an interesting person.

"A German?"

"He wouldn't have to be a Nazi to be

trouble. Think of her books, Bridey."

"The *mistress's* books?"

"There's evil everywhere, on a boat, on a train, at home. They were all regular people doing vile things when they might get away with it."

"They're *stories,* Gigi." She couldn't keep from laughing. "You're not reading them as fact, are you? Her stories aren't *real.* None are."

"Stories teach you what life is, so that you can survive the world. In her books, one person seeks the truth and serves justice. Inspiring, really."

"So you're . . . dressing down all the cooks, cleaners, and housewives of Greenway for stories?" Bridey said. "For justice?"

"And butlers and gardeners and whatever Mr. Arbuthnot is," Gigi said. "That's who I can reach from this gilded cage. The women always have more to tell, though."

"More they will tell, more like."

"Women pay more attention, and they're never asked what they think — and when they do share an opinion, they're told in a hundred ways their thoughts don't matter. Women always know more than they let on, and the smarter they are, the less they'll say."

"That doesn't seem right."

"The smarter they are, the more they know their intellect will never reward them."

Through the woods, they bypassed the farms and any barking dogs the families might keep, but it was slow going. Back on the road at last, Bridey started to recognize the village building up, the hulking shapes of houses in blackout, the curve of the deserted road, looming branches of black trees. And then the inn. With shades pulled, it was a squat box on the dark road. A door opened in the face of the building and they saw the door pulled and the figure of a man parting the blackout drape that kept light from spilling into the road. Beyond him, the low-ceilinged pub.

Gigi pulled up, and Bridey nearly ran up her back.

"What —"

"Nothing," Gigi said.

"Someone we know?"

"The only person we know here is the cart driver," Gigi said.

Bridey thought she might like to know a cart driver, for the road back.

A car slid by, headlamps capped, like a snake slithering along the road. Gigi linked her arm through Bridey's and started them toward the inn. "Let's just have a laugh tonight."

"A laugh how?"

"Let's say we're someone else tonight. Not nurses."

This came dangerously close to the truth of the matter. "Some of them will have been at the quay," Bridey said.

"Pretend."

"Who should I be, then?"

"Anyone you want," Gigi said.

24
BRIDEY

At the Manor Inn

Bridey reached for the door and slipped through the drape. The pub was crowded and loud, the air dim and yellow from oil smoke.

"There's nowhere to sit," Bridey said.

"Get to the bar and I'll do the rest." But the dimple didn't pop in her cheek. She lifted her chin to scan the room.

Bridey aimed herself into the crowd and broke through wherever weakness might be found, reaching back for Gigi's hand and pulling her along through the attention she drew. A sliver of space at the bar opened up, a miracle, and Gigi rewarded the man who'd created it with a smile.

"I'm Lorraine," she said.

He couldn't believe his luck. Nothing to look at, sunburned and stout. Rather like Tommy, in fact. Uniform or not, he had that military bearing to him that so many boys had now, his hair cut too short, showing ears that should be under the brim of a hat in the fields.

"Fiona," Bridey said. The lie came easily.

"Charlie," he said. "This good lad is Arthur."

He was the reedy kind, half his body weight in the Adam's apple. "How do you do?" he said with a hand out. The other half in manners.

A girl on the other side of this fellow peeked around. "*Lorraine,* was it?"

Bridey recognized her at once — the woman from the train.

"Why *hello,*" Gigi said. "Nice to run into you here —"

Gigi stood back to take in the woman's dowdy skirt and a double-breasted jacket, like a man's. "Darling," Gigi said, "are you a *bird*?"

The woman laughed and said yes, she was. "They've made me a messenger in the signals office. Look at these pegs, I ask you. Running up and down that hill, I'll be muscled as a shoreman. And when they get around to teaching me semaphore, I'll be able to fly on the strength of these wings."

The woman waved her arms this direction and that, the arms of a clock. Gigi found this terribly funny and Bridey tried to ignore a slim dagger of jealousy poking at her. She had never had such friends, not her own age. Only Margaret, her oldest little sister —

Charlie leaned close to her ear. "A Wren," he said. "Royal Navy."

"I *know,*" Bridey said. She hadn't but now she might feel annoyance at him and not grief.

"Willa," the woman from the train said, putting her hand out to Bridey.

"Uh, Fiona."

"What's brought you to this distant outpost, Fiona?"

Bridey didn't know how to answer. Was she not the woman from the train? Gigi jumped in. "*Fi* is *also* a hospital nurse sent down with 'vacs from London. You met on the train, remember? With all the children we're caring for . . ."

Something passed between the women, then. "Oh, right. I remember you now," Willa said, squinting at her. " 'Vacs from London, what fun."

"I'm sorry about your friend," Bridey said.

Willa and Gigi turned in opposite directions. Willa considered the room. "We'd only just met, but thank you."

"Did you catch his name?"

"I think someone said his name was Thorne," Willa said. "Something like it."

"Did they? What about the other one?"

"Which other one?"

"The other young man from the train."

Willa cut her eyes at Gigi.

"He went on to Dartmouth," Gigi said. "Didn't he say? The Naval Academy, I believe it was."

She'd seen him at the quay, though, a witness at the scene who had refused to give any bit of information. But then, so had Gigi. "But —"

Charlie handed the women half-pints of lager. "That's where Artie and me are off to tomorrow."

Artie's Adam's apple bobbed.

"What is? Oh, the academy," Bridey said. When no one else offered a word, she added, "It's a brave thing you're doing."

"Or blindly stupid," Charlie said, raising his glass. "Lead the toast, Artie, you're youngest."

"To our wives and sweethearts," Artie said. He held his glass high.

"May they never meet," Charlie said.

Artie took a drink and said, "We don't have either one, truly. It's only tradition."

Charlie took a long drink, watching Bridey over the rim, and when finished wiped foam from his lip. "You're up at Mrs. Christie's house."

She wasn't supposed to be precisely who she was. "How do you know that?"

"Everyone knows everything that happens around here."

"We'll have new accommodations soon, anyway, I imagine," Gigi said. "Better ones, right, Fi?"

Was *this* part of the story? She had to pay attention to the lies so she wouldn't lose track of them. *Fiona and Lorraine. Fiona and Lorraine.* And Willa. But was that her name, or was she pretending to be someone else, as well? And why should they be looking for a different place to stay? It was games for the sake of games, without scores kept.

"Shall we find a place to sit?" Artie said.

"We don't mind standing," Gigi said.

Bridey would have liked a seat. The other women were keeping their options open, drifting away from the baby-faced sailors now that they had a drink bought for them. Or they were hoping the table at their backs would come available. The men there leaned over their beers in earnest conversation, no sign of going.

"Better accommodations than Greenway House?" Charlie said. The way he said it, Bridey could tell he was local, had grown up thinking of the house as the center of the county, the manor and seat of power.

Had taken the ferry to Dartmouth all his life, craning his neck to see the great house through the trees.

Gigi and Willa had gone back to quiet conversation. So quiet, Bridey could better hear the men at the table behind them. Were Gigi and Willa saying anything at all, or only pretending so they didn't have to talk with Charlie and the other one?

And then she knew. Gigi was *eavesdropping.* Tuning into the local men's conversation like it was time for the King's speech on the wireless. Willa, a prop, didn't seem to notice.

"I can't think of a better house around than Greenway," Charlie said. "Not one you could have for a war nursery in any case."

"I think she's joking about better accommodations," Bridey said. She would have rather heard what the table of men had to say. They would be talking of the dead man. The entire pub might be. A Saturday night and a scandal, too. "It's a lovely house."

Charlie was appeased, but had a lot of questions about the interior of Greenway, as not many in the area had seen the house since the Mallowans had moved in.

"Was it the billiards room she took down?" Charlie said.

Bridey didn't know they had taken down

any rooms and found herself impatient to be saddled with the sailors on her own. "There's no billiards room I've seen."

Gigi reached in and claimed Charlie's arm. "Darling, where might a girl go to spend a penny?" Her words landed on him like a weight. He nodded her toward the back corridor. "And why don't you get us something else to drink?"

Suddenly they all wheeled away, Gigi pulling Willa toward the ladies' and Charlie and Artie, to see about a bottle. Bridey stood alone in a room of strangers and wondered why she had come at all.

25
BRIDEY

Suddenly a man stood at her elbow. "Thought that was you."

"Oliver Hart. We met this afternoon."

Her head buzzed. She was not a drinker and had finished her drink too quickly.

"*Doctor* Oliver Hart?" he said, his face falling a bit.

"I remember." The only person in the county other than Gigi who might be able to see through her lies, the real ones, the lies that mattered. He was also rather dashing, tall with good jaw and hair. Did she imagine that the room seemed to tilt in his direction, everyone admiring? He expected to be remembered.

"You don't seem to be enjoying the *manner* of the Manor Inn." His smile was renewed now, with a coy twist to one side of his mustache.

I like his funny little mustache, don't you?

"Have you —" The image in her mind sent

words scattering.

"Have I?" he said.

"Have you learned the name of the man pulled from the river?" The doctor frowned. Could she not manage social banter? Was she a lost cause? She thought quickly. "Only I did hope he'll be buried among family. It's the only thing, really, the only thing one can be certain —"

Tears were in her eyes before she knew what was happening. Without a word, the doctor produced a crisp white handkerchief, a monogram and fine stitching in ivory at the edge. He took her empty glass, set it on the bar, and led her by the elbow, gently, to the next room, which was quieter and far less crowded. A cold, blackened fireplace took up the wall, and near it, a table was empty. Hart directed her to the nearest chair and sat across.

"I'm so sorry," she said. "We're all of us in the house not sleeping well with the children and the raids —" But she had already tucked it all away, eyes dry, by the time the handkerchief reached her face. When she offered it back to him, he gestured she keep it. "Thank you."

"A big assignment you've taken on," he said. "With the shortage of nurses, you'd think you'd have your choice — well, it's none of my business."

"A favor," Bridey said. "For my matron. Mrs. Arbuthnot was in rather dire straits." She gritted her teeth and plowed ahead. "And I do so love caring for children."

"I knew it must be something like that." He glanced around and leaned lower over the table. "He's a young man from London, as you suggested," he said. "The authorities there have taken matters into their own counsel."

"But surely they'll be down soon? To investigate?" Whenever she thought of the police coming, she suffered a wave of nausea. Constables asking questions could strike up against the dead soldier back in London.

"I shouldn't think so," Hart said. "One young man's death is rather difficult to prioritize now."

Like the robberies the policemen had mentioned. Everyone on high alert to make it through the air raids, to sandbag municipal buildings and hospitals, to beat out the rooftop fires. No one had time to search for missing silver or to attend to one dead man when there were so many.

"Why should a man from London come all this way to be killed?" Bridey said. "Are there no clues at all to his death?"

"Clues? Strains of Mrs. Mallowan's favorite tune."

Bridey rubbed her thumb across the monogram. It was lovely work. A wife, perhaps. "I suppose I'm . . . looking for some sense in it all."

"Often there is no logic to be found," Hart said. "You must know that, coming from London and what's happening there. Very little point to death at all. Your entire generation of men will be devastated by it, and the repercussions will last decades. Perhaps longer."

Your generation. As though she were a child. "I don't disagree," Bridey said. "Only if we think there was no purpose in any of it, well that's —"

"Yes?"

"Miserable."

"Ah, yes."

"There would be nothing left to cling to . . ." If there were no sense to it, what was she doing? If she was not saving England, what was the point of being far from home, what was left of it? Far from the grave in need of decorating. The pub at her back roared with drunk voices, bursting laughter turning to ragged coughs, chairs dragging. Their table was an oasis.

"Are you all right?" he said.

"A bit light-headed. The air will be good for me, I think."

"You're not walking home?"

"I meant to," she said.

"Let me take you. No, it's no bother."

"Thank you but I'd like to wait for my friend."

He looked surprised. Not used to being turned down, she thought. "Another time, then."

"Dr. Hart," she said.

He turned as though he had expected her to call him back.

"I heard someone say they thought the man's name was Thorne. If it helps."

"I — Yes, I think it will. My, you *are* drawing from Mrs. Mallowan's bag of tricks. I'll pass it along."

In his absence, the room around her shook with company she no longer wanted. Another time? He might find it difficult to catch her here or in any corner of the village again. She would go back to Greenway and be glad of her duty. She knew no other escape. She had no other plan.

Charlie and Artie arrived back, the requested bottle tucked in a pocket after both men had a swig. There was a second drink for her that she'd not asked for.

"Only the best of company for you," Charlie said. "Are you friends with the village doctor?"

"Professional courtesy," Bridey said.

Artie looked stumped.

"Doctor," she said. "Nurse."

"You're a real nurse, then," Charlie said.

What had Gigi said? "We both are," she said cautiously.

"Only meant — not a nursery nurse. You know." He looked uncomfortable. "How did you meet the local sawbones?"

"The doctor was consulting at Greenway this morning."

"To see to the drowned bloke." Charlie's breath pickled the air between them. "That were awful."

"The dead man was from London," Bridey said. "If you worried you should know him."

"A good number down from London now," Artie mused.

"Too many at that," said a voice from a nearby table. They looked over to find three men sitting in front of empty pints. More attitudes against evacuation? Against evacuation meant for arrival in their town. What old men had against little children being rescued, she would like to know. "Too many by a far sight," the man said.

"Shouldn't like to start rumors, *Artie,*" Charlie said pointedly.

"Do they think it's to go unnoticed?" Artie said under his breath. "When the ground-work starts —"

"Not for you or me to decide."

Bridey tried to catch their meaning as it passed between them. They were not speaking of the war nursery, the evacuees, at all, so who did they mean? She and Gigi? Willa and those ones. "Which folks down from London?" she said.

There was a commotion somewhere in the next room, a dropped pint or a hurt feeling. Artie looked around. "I rather think it's time to go somewhere else," he said.

"There isn't anywhere else," Charlie said.

"And those girls not back yet."

Bridey knew then that all their attention had been pitched to the missing women the entire time. She was the half crown on the barrel so the other two were guaranteed to return.

"I'll check on them." She needed the lav before the walk home anyway.

When she stood, the whole of the room tilted toward *her.* Maybe that was the second drink. She'd had it anyway.

The ladies' toilet door stuck, wouldn't budge at all. She looked around helplessly, then threw her shoulder into it and tumbled in.

For the blink of an eye, Bridey didn't know what she was seeing. Against the wall, a dark shadow split into two. Willa straightened her skirt hem.

Gigi went to the sink and washed her hands and face, drew out her lipstick. "Don't stand there staring, Bridey, if you need the throne."

Bridey still had her hand on the door. "I'll wait." Her voice sounded small and stiff. She thought about the long walk home, squatting at the side of the road. Wait for what? Who knew what would happen next?

She went to the toilet and hitched up her skirt. She'd had four sisters, for one thing. She kept her head down. "So not strangers at all, then."

"You don't seem bothered," Willa said.

"She's not bothered by anything," Gigi said. "You should see her when the Germans fly over. Ten children marched to safety in two seconds flat. Not a ripple of concern." Bridey thought she heard not pride, not envy, but accusation. Or nerves, that she might create a scene or find disgust or alarm.

"Five under each arm, I suppose," Willa said. "With nerves of ice, she shouldn't be a nanny. She should be a —"

"I'm not a nanny," Bridey said. "We're nurses. Proper nurses."

"Right, of course," Willa said.

Was she bothered? Surprised, maybe, but surprise was something she was allowed. Of all the things she'd had to fold in and absorb, this was only another. At the hospital, they said it was a mental defect, with treatments, and there were laws. But Parliament, as far she knew, had never enacted a law against — whatever two women got up to.

When she got near imagining it, she only wondered how much about the world she hadn't encountered, what she missed by being exactly who she was, not a laugh at all. She pictured the dark of the doctor's car, her hand reaching for the waves of his hair. He could ruin her, if he wanted to. Twice over and completely, but even this small rush of desire threatened to break open everything else she kept at bay.

"You won't say anything?" Willa said.

She should be more bothered by why they had pretended not to know one another on the train. Had they all known one another? Was Thorne a stranger, or had they all stood by as a friend lay dead on the quay?

At the sink, Bridey nudged Gigi aside. In

the clouded mirror above, she caught Willa's profile. On the train, Willa had looked familiar to Bridey, someone she had met, but now she saw the likeness for what it was. Something else to take in, there, but it mattered not a whit to her. The war made things possible that hadn't been before, didn't they? She would be a nurse, trained or not, and Willa would be a Wren, maybe the first, integrated without fanfare. She would say nothing. They were all just chancers, weren't they, taking advantage of the situation? If they were saving England, couldn't they have a little something for themselves, too? "Say anything to whom?"

The divot of worry between Gigi's eyes disappeared.

"Hadn't we better get back, though?" Bridey said.

"Come, Bridey. You're having fun in there somewhere, aren't you?"

"I thought her name was Fiona," Willa said, lighting a cigarette. "I like you better as Fiona."

"I don't feel at all like staying out —"

The door opened and a woman, haggard face and ugly dress, a pitcher in her hands, tried to come in. She reared back at the sight of them and stood blinking.

"What is it, flower?" Willa said.

"They need water," the woman said.

"Who does?"

"The doctor, and hurry. He's having a surgery in the lounge."

26
BRIDEY

The front room

In the front room of the pub, Dr. Hart sat at a table, flickering oil lamp brought close, arm wrestling with a burly, greasy man, legless from drink and outraged at the attention. The man had a friend on either side to hold him still. They had an audience as well, men pulling up chairs and coming in from the other room. She thought she recognized a few faces from the quay.

Hart looked up. "Nurse Kelly, could you assist? We're the enemy of a broken pint glass."

"Of course, Doctor." The words to her were music, a song she knew so well she'd had no conscious decision to make. That was retention — her body and mind responding to the call they remembered. She rushed to Hart's side, where he held the thick wrist of a hand covered in blood.

There was an odd noise, a shout. Bridey

looked over to find Gigi in the doorway, her knees buckling. The sailors caught her, one each arm, and with Willa, they hurried through and outside.

Hart hardly glanced in their direction. He had his kit, needle, and thread and a boiled kettle quickly delivered from the kitchen to soak the lot. He nodded into the depths of his valise. "Something in there for the gentleman's general demeanor."

She found forceps, curettes, scapula, scissors, and sutures; a leather wallet of syringes; sewing needles; and clamps lined up, one with a spangle at its end, rather flash. Finally the tin with ampoules of morphine. She paused to read the labels. Wouldn't make that mistake again, would she? She broke the neck of the selected ampoule, inserted the syringe, drew out the liquid, considered the man's bulk. Hart nodded her onward.

"Here now," the man was able to say before the syringe plunged in his arm. He had a few words for her then and, for his two keepers, a more difficult job.

But soon the man was slumping where he sat, quite genial, and his hand could be seen to. Bridey held his wrist and stretched back the last finger, thick as a sausage, to give Hart the best angle. She watched as the stitches went in, two, three. Hands were tricky.

"It's certainly bleeding enough, Lydell," Hart said.

"I've always been a good bleeder," the man said, his syllables soft.

"Nicked an artery?" Bridey said.

"Possibly. We'll pull it tight to stop it gushing."

Bridey leaned in for a closer look.

"You've the stomach for it," Hart said.

Should she feign a demure posture, collapse to see how many reached to steady her? What *good* was being a woman?

"It was a compliment. Was that the other nurse at Greenway?" Hart said. "Looked a little green. You've not had any illness up at the house?"

"Too much drink," Bridey said.

"I believe I have this under control, if you'd like to see to her."

"She has as much attention as she needs," Bridey said. She saw Hart's smile through his patient's splayed fingers. "But if you're sure . . ."

"Do let me know if I can be of help with the children's good health. Or yours."

Was he flirting? He reminded her of one of the doctors at St. Prisca's, a cad who courted his way through the nurses, down

250

to the probationers.

In the ladies' lav again, Bridey scrubbed blood from under her fingernails and looked at herself in the old mirror. Her hair had fallen out, and she had a smear of blood on her chin. She looked rather daring.

She's not bothered by anything.

Her composure should make her a better nurse, shouldn't it? When even the self-possessed Gigi, for all her training, wobbled? Bridey wiped the blood away, saw to her hair.

The doctor had things nearly resolved by the time she made her way through again. He lifted his head briefly as she went by, and she allowed herself the sense of satisfaction. She had done the job well. Perhaps Dr. Hart could recommend her —

But it couldn't be. To plead her case to Dr. Hart, she would have to admit who she was, what she was.

Outside the pub, the air was clean. She filled her lungs, basking a bit. Was it striving, what she had done? To have helped someone? Call her the names, then.

Down the lane a match flared and illuminated only briefly a man's profile, a jacket shoulder. She knew him, didn't she? Not from the quay . . .

By the time she realized the man was her

251

rescuer from the train, shooing the merrymakers away from the children, he had edged around the corner on his walking stick.

They had all ended up in Galmpton, had they? Willa. The handsome man who'd ended up dead. The sullen, watchful one standing aside on the quay while his friend lay nameless. And now her rescuer as well. Had everyone from that train come to this small village? Artie was right. A great number of Londoners converged in the area and not only 'vacs and those who kept them, not only naval recruits.

"Fiona!" Charlie called. "Lorraine figures she'll have another drink."

The poor hopeful lad. Gigi sat on the edge of the open bed of Charlie's lorry as though she'd been tossed there, limbs loose.

"Isn't she already tight?" Bridey said. "She was swooning."

"That was only the blood," Willa said.

"The pub air was close," Gigi said. "Let's go."

Charlie took charge. The five of them squeezed in with Willa on Gigi's lap and Charlie throwing his arm around Bridey. She pulled herself in, narrow as she could.

The headlamps on the lorry were fitted with slotted shields, barely enough illumination to keep on the road. The bottle went from hand to hand, Bridey passing it along without temptation.

"Charlie," Gigi said, "find us a nice spot to pull over. We needn't race the bottle to the last drop. Let's have a chat."

"They aren't chatty in these parts," Willa said. "I noticed."

"I thought they'd all be talking about the week's big catch down at the quay," Artie said.

Willa tried to laugh and caught Bridey watching her.

Charlie leaned into Bridey. "The man in the river."

"I *know.*"

"Were they, Artie?" Gigi said. "Did you hear anyone discussing it?"

"Dr. Hart said London had charge of the investigation," Bridey said.

"Dr. Hart!" Willa said. "I wonder if it's his real name. He might as well be Dr. Bladder, hadn't he?"

"He's the new one," Artie said. "My mum won't see him."

"She doesn't want to strip to her knickers for such a handsome fella?" Willa said.

"Lord," Artie said. "I didn't need that in m' head, thanks."

"Here we are," Charlie said and pulled

the lorry to the side of the road.

Bridey crawled out after him. "Where are we?

"We're over the train tunnel," Charlie said. "Goes to Kingswear under Greenway land here. If the owners had allowed it through regular . . . The old owners, I mean, not the new ones. If the train had gone through to Dartmouth, this area might be a different place altogether."

"Better? Or worse?" she said.

Charlie blocked her into the lorry's door. The others were getting out on the other side. "Is your name really Fiona?"

"No."

"I didn't think so," he said.

"I don't seem like a Fiona?" Bridey said.

"You don't seem any certain way to me."

"I'm — I have a sweetheart already, that's all."

"Thought maybe you had," he said.

"But even if I hadn't —"

"You don't like the looks of me."

"No," Bridey said. "I mean, that's not it. I . . . I'm not —"

"You don't have to explain. Is your man at the front?"

"I don't know where he is," she said and felt the truth of it in her stomach. Tom had been sending letters as soon as she sent the forwarding address to Mrs. Mitchell, but he might be anywhere. She was living her life out of reach of everything and everyone she had known, untethered from this world like a ghost. Were they all? Tom off somewhere; she didn't know where her da had ended up, dead or alive. And she had no idea where the beautiful parts of so many lives that were precious to her had disappeared to. The boneyard, of course, with one stone and not enough money for anything but the family name. That was where their bodies had gone, but what had become of the rest?

She'd been living under so many lies, all evening and since they'd left London, she'd forgotten the single truest thing about herself.

Bridey reached for the bottle.

"All right, my lover, easy," Charlie said when she had her second pull.

She should be feeling their loss every moment of every day, the loss of their voices, their laughs, their shining eyes, but there were some days she forgot, and when she recalled like now, sometimes in the middle of enjoying herself, of being alive, she wondered how she could have dared keep going. "I haven't any idea where he is," she said, to explain away her wet eyes. "He might be dead."

"But he might be fine."

She'd forgotten the sailor's fresh haircut and exposed ears. "Yes, of course. He probably will be."

They converged with the others at the front of the lorry, shared the bottle around in the dim light of the headlamps.

"Do you ever think," Artie was saying, "right now, out there somewhere, Adolf Hitler is shaving? Having a slash? What do you think he's doing?"

"Not bombing South Hams, for a change," Charlie said.

"Sitting at home, glass of wine, burning a nice book in the fireplace," Gigi said.

The bottle was passed to Bridey. She handed it off to Gigi.

"That bloke in the river," Gigi said. "That must happen all the time so near the sea."

"Occasionally you get a bit of misadventure or a visitor falls off a steamer," Charlie said. "The locals know what they're about."

"No other drownings recently?"

Bridey started to say Thorne hadn't drowned — but someone grasped her arm in the dark. Gigi, steadying her as though she were a child. She shook off Gigi's hand.

"None I know of," Charlie said. "Artie?"

"My uncle died a few months back, but not in the water. Something wrong inside, you know. One more reason my mum won't see the doctor, I s'pose."

"More expected then," Gigi said, so gently it was almost sound instead of words.

"He was plowing his back field the day before! My da's side lives a long life normally. My da blames the war."

"Was the uncle in the war?" Willa said. "Not this one —"

"Nah, he's younger than my da by years and missed out," Artie said. "Some say he should be in this one, that's how fit he is. Was."

With this, the silence opened up and consumed them all. Above, a clear sky, quiet for once, and a cloud that was somehow stars.

Was that what she was doing? Missing out? Sitting out the war at Greenway when she might have been more helpful, save one deadly mistake? Sitting out her life.

"It's all so short," Willa said, head turned to the sky.

"What is?" Bridey said. She was fuzzy-headed, tired, and impatient for her bed. Petulant at being scolded again.

"The time we have. Short and bright like one of those, what do you call it, on Bonfire Night?"

"Penny banger," Artie said.

"Sparklers," Bridey said at the same time and saw her sisters' faces lit by the sizzle and flash —

One second she was not bothered and the next she was a split sack and spilling herself, hands and knees on the road. The sound out of her was barnyard, then siren.

"Is she having a fit or summat?" Artie said.

"Boys," Gigi said. "Party's over. We'll walk from here."

27
BRIDEY

Greenway Road

"Walk?" Willa moaned.

The sailors put up a weak fight to take them on to Greenway. Bridey listened, sniffling, sitting on her heels.

"We can't have you drive up to the door," Gigi said. "No, I think Fiona would like a chance to compose herself."

With a few best wishes to the men, they parted ways. Bridey, pulled to her feet, had the doctor's handkerchief and was glad. They were twenty minutes away from her bed. Some sleep would put her right again.

But then the memory of her own grief there on the road nearly started the process all over again. Who did she cry for, then? The innocents lost to the world or herself?

Grief was a game played so that one might only lose. Bridey gathered the last of her resources and tucked the handkerchief into the sleeve of her dress.

"Well, Fiona, *something* finally bothered you," Willa said.

She couldn't use Tom as an excuse or the yellow pub air. "I've only had — a lot to do. A lot to take in. And those boys, off to serve. They break my heart."

"I think that Charlie might have found a better send-off for him, if you hadn't soaked the road," Willa said.

"Well, he did try," Bridey said. "But he's not for me."

"Ah, now, that sounds like a lady who's got her eye on someone," Willa said. "Handsome sawbones for the nurse, is it?"

"I have an interest in Dr. Hart's work," Bridey said. Willa's silence was doubt. It wouldn't do. "At St. Prisca's I assisted in all manner of surgery —"

"Were you *bombed* in the war, Bridey?" Gigi said.

The question was so abrupt, so head on, Bridey couldn't find an answer. She couldn't speak of it, certainly not in front of a stranger.

Without a word exchanged, the third woman was lagging behind.

"What, because I had a little cry?" Bridey said.

"*Were* you?" Gigi linked arms with Bridey and spoke in a low voice. "You seem anxious to be in the fray instead of wiping noses, but here you are. When I said you could be put to better use somewhere nearer the action — was that a terrible thing to say?"

"No, I do want to be helpful." Once she had secured a way to be there, once she had what she needed. "Wherever I'm necessary. Just now, it's here."

"So you weren't bombed?"

"Of course I was bombed," Bridey spat. "The whole *city* is pockmarked with his bombs."

"I mean —"

"I wasn't," Bridey said. This was the truth, but a narrow thing. "Not me."

Their shoes scuffed along on the road. Bridey couldn't quite fill her lungs. Her rib cage still ached from the torrent in front of the sailors.

"In your nightmares, Bridey, when you wake shouting?" Gigi said, as though she asked the weather. "Whose house burns?"

Willa was twenty paces back.

"My mam's flat," Bridey whispered.

"*Your* flat," Gigi said. "Ah. Who was . . . home? Your mam? What did your mam do for work?"

"Took in laundry," Bridey said.

"And your father —"

"He came and went as he pleased, didn't he?"

"Right then," Gigi said. "So. Your mam was at home?"

Bridey was so tired. The night had grown long and the morning would still be as bright. She couldn't face another question. "Yes," she said.

Bridey could nearly hear the calculations in Gigi's head.

"On the train," Gigi said. "The little brothers and sisters you said you helped raise . . ."

Bridey, outside of her own body suddenly, the only way to take the direct hit, recognized that Gigi remembered everything she had ever said. She could not be flattered by it. The other Bridget was only observing. She had been warned.

"All?" Gigi said.

All. She hardly thought of them as individuals anymore, not of Margaret's dancing from place to place, of Helen's love of reading, of Simone's lisp, or Evangeline's tiny little hands, or Michael trying to be stout, trying to shoulder being man of the house. He wasn't yet eight. Would never be eight. The same auburn hair as their mam, all.

They were a collection, like Mrs. Mallowan's silver, something she had put on a shelf.

Bridey kept the silence long enough that she wondered if Gigi might have given up needling her for details. She wished for it. Gigi's voice, when it came, was as small and surgical as a needle jab. "Bloody hell," she said.

If Bridey had not already emptied her heart on the road, she would have then. Would Gigi treat her with white gloves now? She was back inside herself, then, full inside her skin, if tender. She couldn't bring herself to dump the dead soldier on the scales, too, to be ruined for a fraud and worse. To lose Gigi's good opinion of her, to have all of Greenway know, all of Galmpton. Bridey felt for the handkerchief in her sleeve.

"My family is lost for me as well. Not in the same way." Gigi glanced back at Willa. "They're alive but — I have nowhere to return to."

Bridey didn't know what to say. "If they live, why wouldn't you have a place with them? Gigi, I would give anything."

"Yes, well," Gigi said. "While we're trading confidences, I should tell you something else."

"Lorraine," Willa said.

"This isn't who I am," Gigi said.

263

Did she mean the drinking, the carrying on in the ladies' toilet?

"Of course not," Bridey said. But she didn't want affection and truth-telling. It all had to be packed away. She couldn't live like this, an open wound. She heard a motor far up the road.

"Not that," Gigi said. "That's me, right enough. But you should know the truth."

Headlamps, high on the hill.

"Bridget," Willa said.

Bridey looked over. "There's someone coming."

"We told them we didn't need a ride," Gigi said.

These headlamps were full and rounded, not slits. "That's not Charlie," Bridey said. "Who doesn't have their lamps capped? The wardens will —"

"Let's go," Gigi said. She grabbed at Bridey's hand and dragged her out of the road and over a stile. Willa scrambled after them.

There was nothing to hide behind in the field. The beams of light sliced at the road above them. Gigi pulled Bridey low to the ground, flat against the hill. Willa lay on her back on the other side.

The motorcar slowed to a crawl and stopped above them. Gigi's hot, whiskey breath blew into Bridey's face.

"What?" Bridey whispered.

"I'm sorry."

Bridey listened to the car on the road above — a soft hum, a tick as the engine cooled — to keep from thinking of anything else.

At last the motorcar eased away. When Bridey was sure they were alone again, she said, "What was that about?"

"Stay down," Gigi hissed. "They'll have nothing to do but come back through, won't they?"

"Who is it, Gigi?"

"Not yet."

Bridey waited, the front of her dress pressed into the ground. Her patience wore to a sharp edge until she thought they might have to stay the night on their stomachs in the meadow and wake with the sheep.

Then the motorcar could be heard from far off and then overhead again, quickly now, taking the narrow turns of the road too fast.

When all was silent again, they waited some more.

They sat up slowly and crept toward the road. At the stile, they paused to be sure, then helped each other over, all of them silent as they walked toward the house, stretching their senses out and across the hills.

The gates were closed. Rather than open them and wake the Hannafords, they tiptoed past the gatehouse toward the quay and then up the hill, switchbacks taking on new danger in the dark. They reached the top of the path, and stole around the side of the house, three instead of two.

Bridey stopped. "What are you sorry for?"

Gigi hushed her.

They were nearer the gardener's bothy than the house, but the lean-to would be empty. Bridey checked the windows, the one through which Doreen watched her wish man. All were dark. Too late for Scaldwell's rounds, too early for anyone but the sleepless.

"You said you were sorry," Bridey whispered. "You said I should know the truth and that you were sorry. What are you sorry for?"

"For dragging you into the mud."

"I don't think that's it." Bridey's chest hurt again, as though her ribs curled inward and poked at her lungs. She was not a child, and she was being lied to.

No one said anything. She couldn't see their expressions.

"When you have nightmares, Gigi, whose

house is on fire? Is it this one? Do you hold the match in your own hand?"

Bridey turned and made her way alone to the back of the house, the door, into the service corridor. Someone had left the door to the stairwell cracked and a light on, and she sailed toward it, safe harbor.

28
DOREEN

Greenway House, long past bedtime
I am supposed to be sleeping but I can't sleep.

Dor-may-voo. That's a thing I learned, a song about a brother named Jack. Are you sleeping are you sleeping dor-may-voo. I remember it because Dor is like my name. I hum the words because I can't remember them all and one of the other girls makes a hissing noise for me to stop. Probably Pamela.

There are bells in the song and our voices are the bells ding dong ding and it's lovely.

We had bells in London but here the bells might mean aeroplanes.

I want a drink of water.

Nurse Bridey is not in her chair. Miss Edith sent us to bed tonight but she is not in the chair, either. It's late and I'm not sleeping ding dong ding.

My cot is in the corner of the girls' room

and so is a piano! We're not allowed to leave our cots. We're not allowed to touch the piano, but we do. I have a window next to my cot, and no one else does. There's a rip in the paper over the window and sometimes I pull at it so I can look out at the forest and watch for the wish man.

I have a wall next to my bed, too. There's a little hole in the plaster and sometimes in the night when I can't sleep, I pick at the hole and make it a bit bigger.

The hole gets bigger and there's dust on my finger. I still want a drink of water and now also one of the little potties.

I walk back and forth on top of my blankets on the cot, seeing what there is to see, which is nothing since it is dark and my window is covered for the Black Out. And then I'm cold and I get back under the covers and it feels soft and warm.

If Nurse Bridey was in her chair, I could ask politely please. Nurse Gigi does not like us to ask questions. She has lovely long fingernails and when water drips off them, they are even longer. I will have long fingernails when I'm big. Nurse Gigi never sits in the chair in our room.

Miss Edith was in the chair when we went to bed. She said another jam is gone.

The jams gone is what is called a mystery,

Nurse Bridey says. The jams go and no one knows who has them but it's not me and not Maureen and not any of the girls. Maybe the boys.

Maybe the wish man!

I need a drink of water.

I get out of the blankets and walk up and down my cot and then jump down and go to the door. It's dark. I don't like the dark. Nurse Bridey would turn on the light for me.

But the stairs aren't dark, so I go to the stairs and down and then to the other stairs and down, down, but not all the way down. I stand on a step and look at the door and wish for Nurse Bridey or Nurse Gigi or even Mrs. Ar-buth-not but mostly a glass of water and then the door opens and the man, Mr. Scaldwell, is there looking up at me.

"You shouldn't be out of bed."

"I wanted a drink. Of water." In the empty stairs that go up and up, my voice sounds like it did on the stairs at home and I miss Mum and Daddy now, Granny and Grand-dad, Aunt Cis, who works in a factory. They would all of them get me a drink of water and turn on the light for the toilet. "Please."

"Where is your nurse?"

"I don't know, Mr. Scaldwell." He is a *butler* and I never met one of those before.

270

What a *butler* is, that's also a sort of mystery, I think. "Sir."

"Stay there for a moment," he says and disappears.

I walk on the step, back and forth, but I stay there. I am ready for my covers now. But then I wonder if Mr. Scaldwell is getting Mrs. Ar-buth-not or Nurse Bridey or Nurse Gigi and I'm in trouble. If I got into trouble, would they send me home? Sometimes I want to be home and sometimes I forget Greenway is not my home.

The door opens a bit more and Mr. Scaldwell is back with a cup. It's a nice cup, not one of the tin ones we have for our milk.

"Hold out both hands," he says. "Drink it where you are — stand still, please, be careful — and then you'll visit the water closet on the way back to bed. Do you understand?"

I am drinking the water so I don't stop to answer. I am holding the cup with both hands, a cup fit for a princess. On the cup is a flower and vines in purple, in lavender —

"Are you finished?"

I gulp the last little bit and use both hands to give the cup back to him. "Thank you, Mr. Scaldwell, sir."

And then Nurse Bridey is standing in the

doorway behind Mr. Scaldwell. She's got a smear of red on her neck and dirt all down her front, on her nice dress. She might not like to talk to Mr. Scaldwell but it's too late. He's talking to her.

No, he's talking to me. "Go to bed," he says. I am in trouble. Will they send me home? Is it awful that I don't want to go? "Now," he says, but when I climb the stairs, Nurse Bridey watches me go and doesn't come, too, and I think it's not me who is in trouble.

29
BRIDEY

Greenway, the next morning

Bridey woke early the morning after their trip into the village, angry and uncomfortable in the chair in the playroom, where she'd bedded down after a good scolding from the butler. She'd chosen the chair for spite, some misguided effort at being noticed missing, but who was the victor? She had a thick head and tongue, a crick in her neck.

In their bedroom, Gigi and Willa lay entwined in Gigi's bed, faces of angels.

She didn't tiptoe. Bridey opened the shutters and let the hot sun glare in, allowed her feet to fall heavily.

Gigi shifted in her sleep. "Bridey, my God," she groaned. "What are you *about*?"

"Get dressed. I'm not watching all the children by myself so that you can have a lie-in."

"Bridey, of all mornings. Think of my head."

"You might have thought of your own head last night. Do you think I don't have a headache? It's *Sunday.*"

"Is that your judgment?"

"We're taking the children to church."

"You must be joking."

"It can't be morning already," Willa said, burrowing in.

"And you'll want to see your friend out before Mrs. Arbuthnot wants an explanation," Bridey said.

Gigi sat up, her eyes slits. The sheet barely covered her, and Bridey looked away. "Wills," Gigi said, her voice hoarse. "Wills, wake up."

"The children should be your priority. Not visiting pubs, not listening for hints and codes in parish gossip. Not sneaking . . . *strangers* into the very house you're to keep safe."

"I don't keep the *house* safe," Gigi said. "You make me sound rather cloak and dagger, someone Aggie conjured with her stories."

"It isn't amusing," Bridey said. "Intrigues and ruined dresses and —"

"Say what you mean to."

"Vulgar acts in a public toilet. It's not a

regular way of life."

"I don't think you would know a regular way of life," Gigi said, "if it wrote you a letter every Tuesday whether you answered it or not. Are you jealous?"

"Jealous of who, then?"

"All right, if not of *my* attention — of feelings, of desire. Of being alive and young and hungry and having someone take you in their arms and feed you precisely what you need." Gigi gazed down at Willa, a look of such tenderness that Bridey had to look out the window. "Of having a moment of calm and relief in which you can believe all will be well."

Is that what romantic love was? Freefall, hoping one would be saved by another? It sounded rather childish.

"I'm glad you had such a good night," Bridey said. "I took last night's expedition on the chin with Scaldwell, slept in a *chair* in the girls' room so I wouldn't have to listen to —"

Gigi laughed. "You heard a bit of that."

"You're a fool if you think I'll take the full serving for you today."

"All *right,* Bridey. Will you please be still? *Wills.*"

There was a sharp rap at the door.

Bridey went to answer, heard exclaim and

scrambling behind her. The doorknob turned as Bridey reached it. She stepped into the door's path to keep Mrs. Arbuthnot from putting her head in.

"Girls, please," Mrs. Arbuthnot hissed through the opening. She had her hair set in rollers, night cream across her nose. "You've woken the entire household. Will you not let me in?"

"Gigi's not decent," Bridey said, enjoying it.

"One of the children is crying, Bridey."

"Is Gigi not *also* employed to take care of crying children?"

Mrs. Arbuthnot stared at her. "Just this once —"

"Just this once, just this once. It's been nothing but just this once since we arrived. I would like to request that *Gigi* do her share of the work or — or I'll have to find another position."

Mrs. Arbuthnot pressed at the door, and Bridey let her in. Gigi sat in bed, blankets pulled up to her chin, alone.

"Bridget," Mrs. Arbuthnot said, rigid in posture, "I would appreciate if you would go see to the child who is suffering, alone, without his mother to comfort him. Or you *will* have to find another assignment and without my reference. Do I make myself clear?"

Bridey swallowed around all the things she wanted to say. "Yes, missus."

She turned and fled. Behind her, Gigi was receiving a few words from Mrs. Arbuthnot as well. Where had Willa been stowed? In the cupboard? Under the bed?

She didn't care.

Who was she? She'd arrived a month ago knowing what she wanted, who she wanted to be, knowing what she had to do to get there. Thinking the matron was wrong about her, thinking she had been nothing but maligned and unfairly treated. And now she didn't mind if she lasted the day, if she was put back on a train for London, if —

She *did* mind. Despite all her defenses, the children had sneaked under her skin. She didn't love them, of course — she couldn't. But they were innocents in all of this — all of it. She couldn't leave them to fend for themselves with only Gigi and her intrigues.

And there was her own reputation. Her future.

Bridey thought of working alongside Dr. Hart in the pub, of feeling capable and in partnership — of his surgery in Galmpton. Her future was so close and so far away at the same time. *Was* there a wife? Why couldn't she still become who she was meant to be? She was not the one who had cracked the smooth surface of this arrangement. *She* was not messing about in conspiracies and secrets.

With a black cloud over her head, she went through her duties, the babies changed, girls dressed and brushed, all of them fed. She wouldn't punish the boys for Gigi's sloth. She wouldn't punish herself, either.

"Let's have an outing," she said, and then the questions began. "Edward, please sit down." Bridey went to seat the boy back in his place, then someone's milk was spilled. The rest of the meal was a tumble downhill.

They went out to the ruins on the hill and Bridey let them gather as many violets as they wanted, to play war games in the roofless stone room. Through lunch, she still hadn't seen Gigi. Perhaps Willa had been discovered and Gigi sacked?

When Bridey had the children, all of them, down for an afternoon nap and order nearly restored to the playroom, Edith appeared at the door.

"There's someone downstairs for you."

"For me?" Bridey said.

Gigi appeared over Edith's shoulder.

"Who is it?" she said.

"Where have you been?" Bridey said.

"I didn't see who it was," Edith said, looking between them. She had bags under her eyes and a foul expression. "Only Mrs. Scaldwell fetched me upstairs to tell you and now I'll get back to the dusting."

"Perhaps *your* guest has returned, Gigi," Bridey said.

"Is it a man or a woman?" Gigi said.

"I'm sure I don't know," Edith said from the landing, not stopping. "I know how you might find out for yourself."

"The cheek," Gigi said. "That was a good pair of stockings I gave up for a few hours out."

"She hasn't forgiven you for scolding her for gossiping about Mrs. M."

"Maybe it's Tom," Gigi said. "You go."

"It won't be *Tom.*"

Gigi crouched on the rocking chair, curled in on herself. "Well, you'll have to go."

"Another chore you can't do? I have to receive visitors for the both of us now?"

"I'll watch the children while you see who it is," Gigi said.

"Now I got them asleep? How generous."

"Maybe it's someone for Mrs. Arbuthnot." Gigi stood and brushed past Bridey to the window.

No one would come to Greenway House to see *her,* in other words.

"Don't mention my name," Gigi said.

"Our name, you mean. Shouldn't be difficult at *all.*"

"Right. I'm not here, just in case."

"In case of what?" Who would come looking? She felt the tremor start up, deep in her guts. "In case the police are back and want to speak to us, you'd have me see them alone."

"You're much more stoic than I am. You're a sphinx," Gigi said. "And you're such a good girl. You'll be much better with them than I was. If it's them. It might not be."

Bridey went down slowly, fighting a rising panic. What if it *was* the police? What if it was —

The image of Matron Bailey came to her, traveling cloak billowing vengeance as she stood at Greenway's front door.

Edith and Mrs. Scaldwell stood in the entrance hall peering around the doorway into the morning room.

"What's happening?" Bridey said.

Mrs. Scaldwell raised her chin as she turned toward the kitchen. "Do tell me if this . . . *guest* will be staying for tea. We barely have the rations for ourselves, what with the thief taking an extra share."

"Mr. Scaldwell's up to the higher farm," Edith whispered. "Should Mrs. Arbuthnot be called for?"

Now she was curious. "She's gone for a walk," Bridey said. "And Mr. Arbuthnot's off painting, of course."

"We could get Hannaford or one of his men to go fetch her."

Bridey looked in. A hatless woman sat in one of the parlor chairs, leaning forward over her knees. Her ankle showed a scuff where she might have taken a tumble on the road and her long dark hair had started to fall out of its arrangement. She wasn't quite ready for visiting, but otherwise Bridey could see no reason to panic. She was lost or had motor trouble.

"I'll see to her." She pulled off her apron and handed it over.

"But — miss, wait —"

Bridey entered the room with authority. She might be the mistress of the house as far as this woman knew. "Madam," she said, attempting Mrs. Arbuthnot's abrupt way of speaking. "Welcome to Greenway."

The woman looked up, as startled as a deer on the road. Her eyes were bright, and she had a bloody gash at her temple.

"Oh," Bridey said. "What's happened,

missus?"

"Do you have the children from London?" the woman said.

"That must sting," Bridey said. "Let me take a look. Edith, will you fetch some bandages from — from upstairs?" She'd almost said Gigi's name, but Gigi was not here. "What's your name, madam?"

"You're not the woman from the station. Where is she?"

"No, I'm not from — I'm Bridget. I'm the nurse."

"Nurse!" The woman bolted up and put the chair between them. "I won't go back without him. They said they would help but they didn't help."

"Madam, please. Your name?"

"Cecilia Poole," the woman said, like a child called upon in school.

"And what happened to your head, Mrs. Poole? Did you have a fall?"

Mrs. Poole closed her eyes. "The floor went out."

Bridey thought she finally understood why they'd wanted to call for Mrs. Arbuthnot, or anyone else.

She'd seen worse at the hospital, of course. Grown men who'd lost their minds, who called for their mams as though they were little children. Men who thought they were still on the battlefield and raged against any efforts to patch them up. Women with blood dripping from the ears, carrying their dead children into the ward.

Bridey swallowed down her own memories as they rose, bile in her throat. "That's too bad about the floor. Generally speaking, one does expect the floor to stay put."

"It always had before."

"What brings you to Greenway, Mrs. Poole?"

"I've come for Sam," the woman said.

"Sam. I'm afraid I don't know who Sam is."

"My little boy," the woman said. She stood and walked toward Bridey, her wild eyes barely contained in her skull. "You took him," she said. "You took my little boy."

Mrs. Poole was so convinced, Bridey wondered — *my God, have we been calling one of the boys by the wrong name?* Her eyes were so hot with fervor, Bridey was inclined to believe she was right and backed away as the woman reached for her.

30
BRIDEY

The morning room

Bridey stepped backward from their desperate visitor until she struck the couch and could go no further.

But no, on second thought . . .

"Oh, *Sam,*" Bridey said for time. "Of course."

Mrs. Poole stopped, slumping with relief. "Sam, yes."

"How, uh, how old is Sam these days?"

"Almost five. Almost ready for school. So I . . ." Mrs. Poole drifted away and then snapped back. "I need him home. I need him safe."

"That's paramount, that is, keeping them safe."

Someone stepped into the room behind Bridey and Mrs. Poole reared back.

"Mrs. Poole?" Mrs. Arbuthnot said. "Is that you?"

Bridey, shaking, sank against the couch.

Mrs. Arbuthnot took in the scene. "My goodness, what — what are you doing here?"

Now Bridey recognized the woman from Paddington. But this was more troubling, not less. Hadn't the woman taken the boy back with her? Edith came in with the wrappings. Bridey sent her back out for towels and water from the kettle.

"I've come for Sam," the woman said again, dodging forward and clutching at Mrs. Arbuthnot's arm. "You remember? My little son."

"Of course I remember Sam," Mrs. Arbuthnot said. "You've come for him? Here? What a long journey."

"The train," Mrs. Poole said vaguely. "I had to come. The floor. The floor went out."

"Maybe you'd like to sit down and rest a bit," Bridey said.

Mrs. Arbuthnot gentled the woman into the chair and pulled up a footstool to sit at her side. She transferred the woman's grip on her arm to her hand, squeezed it. "The floor, you said, Mrs. Poole?" They might be talking of the latest fashions.

"It went out from under our feet."

Bridey and Mrs. Arbuthnot exchanged a glance. Edith returned with the supplies and held the water as Bridey dipped the edge of a towel into the basin and eased Mrs. Poole's head back. The woman closed her eyes.

"The floor went out from under whose feet?" Bridey said.

"Ours."

They waited. Mrs. Poole's eyes fluttered open. "Mine."

"Is there anyone back home we should call? To let them know you've arrived?"

"No one. I — I only want Sam. I only have Sam."

Mrs. Scaldwell brought in a tea tray, rattling cups and saucers, taking her time. "Thank you, Mrs. Scaldwell," Mrs. Arbuthnot said. "That *will* be all."

Bridey cleaned the dried blood away from the woman's hairline and administered to the wound. She might do without stitches. Edith had brought in a packet of aspirin. Bridey fed the pill to Mrs. Poole along with a cup of hot, milky tea that Edith made from Mrs. Scaldwell's tray.

Mrs. Poole took the cup in both hands.

Released from the woman's grip, Mrs. Arbuthnot slid off the stool and out of the room. They were soon listening to a demand into the telephone for a London exchange.

Mrs. Poole sat with her eyes focused somewhere low on the wall. The teacup moved to her knee, steady enough.

"Tell me about Sam," Bridey said, to cover Mrs. Arbuthnot's conversation in the hall. "Is his daddy in the war?"

"Yes," Mrs. Poole said. Then, "No." She sighed. "He might be. I don't know."

To Bridey this seemed like a good start, the window of truth widening by a degree or two. "Do you have any family? Any particular friends you'll be glad to see when you get back?"

"No. No family. The neighbors . . ."

"Does Sam have any brothers or sisters?"

"It's just the two of us," Mrs. Pool said, impatient. "And now . . ." She thought a moment, seemed on the verge of remembering something. "I do need to get back."

"Do you have work in London?"

"I — yes, of course. I can't remember — What's the time?"

"The time? It's tea soon. We'd be pleased to have you join us, no need to rush off. Plenty of room at the table."

"Table," Mrs. Poole whispered, and then she was on her feet, her cup hurled away. She stood, dripping tea, and howled into her hands.

"Mrs. Poole, please!" Bridey reached in, took a fist to the cheek, and fell to the carpets.

When the stars cleared from her eyes, the door stood open, and a figure stood there. The wisht man, Bridey thought.

It was a man with wide shoulders in tweeds, backlit in the doorway. "Are you all right?"

"Did you not stop her?" Bridey said and swooned.

"Here now, Sister." The doctor rushed to help her up and guide her to the chair, a hand at her waist.

"Thank you," she said meekly. "Sir."

"She surprised me. Bashed into me. Did she strike you?"

"She didn't mean to." Her head spun. She blinked away from his mustache.

"You'll have had some experience being knocked about by patients, I suspect," Dr. Hart said, touching gently at her face.

Mrs. Arbuthnot burst into the room, sharp-eyed. "What's this all about? Where is Mrs. Poole?" Hart stood back from Bridey and Mrs. Arbuthnot's eyes boggled. "Dr. Hart, whatever is going on?"

"Mrs. Poole is heading toward the road," Bridey said.

"Bother," Mrs. Arbuthnot said. "Doctor, was there something you needed or could I beg your forgiveness? We'll need to see about our visitor."

"No forgiveness necessary. How may I help?"

"Did you drive here?" Bridey said. "Could you drive us toward the village to have a look for Mrs. Poole? She had a wound at her temple you might also look at."

"Did she? I do wish I could have stopped her for you. Poor woman."

Bridey sought out Edith and promised her a packet she couldn't afford to go up and help watch over the nursery.

"Isn't Gigi there?" Edith said.

"Yes, I — When they wake, they'll be too much for one and" — she lowered her voice — "especially for Gigi."

Edith nodded knowingly, pleased.

On the road toward the village, Mrs. Arbuthnot sat in the front seat. "This is a lovely motorcar, Dr. Hart," she said. A Sunday drive. They drove slowly, watching for Mrs. Poole in the road, among the trees, in the fields.

"Necessary expense, getting out into the country all hours," he said. "And the weather. Your visitor. Was she all right? Aside from the wound, I mean. All right within herself?"

"She was confused," Bridey said before Mrs. Arbuthnot could speak of it. "And banged about. She spoke of falling through a floor, and I think she meant it literally."

"With her son," Mrs. Arbuthnot said. "A little lad she hadn't allowed us to bring along."

"Ah," Hart said. "Heartbreaking."

At the outskirts of Galmpton, the houses faced into the road, watchful. Somewhere nearby, children played. They drove a loop around the village before turning into a narrow lane, cottages bearing down, a chapel rising above. Hart stopped across the street from the church, where a small sunken shop clutched at the descent of the hill, its door propped open.

"There's a bit of commerce here, if you want to ask after your Mrs. Poole," the doctor said. "Should I come with you? The locals can be a bit . . . wary of strangers. I've had a hell of a time — pardon me — gaining their trust."

His expertise was dead men, Bridey suddenly recalled.

"That won't be necessary, Doctor," Mrs. Arbuthnot said. "We thank you for your assistance."

"If someone brings your Mrs. Poole to my surgery, I'll ring the house. Or if you locate her, I should gladly come 'round Greenway to see to that wound. Shall I wait to drive you back?"

Mrs. Arbuthnot demurred. "Nurse Kelly and I will have a pleasant walk."

As soon as Hart's motorcar drove away, Mrs. Arbuthnot turned brusque. "Let us find Mrs. Poole and be done with this. And then I'll have a word with you."

Helpless Bridget, cornered Bridget. "Yes, missus," she said, not at all certain which crime she should be scolded for now.

31
JOAN ARBUTHNOT

Galmpton

Standing in the lane with the doctor driving off, Joan thought of Mrs. Poole grasping her son's hand at Paddington Station and tearing him away from the safety she had offered. A boy of five? It can't be. It can't be true.

Several times in her life, Joan had found herself thinking the same thing. The death of her parents had opened inside her a great well that would never again fill. George, her first husband, taking up with her when he might have had anyone. It couldn't be true.

And then his death, the well deeper still. She had trouble believing it, even yet.

By the time Malcolm came around to her rescue, *she* might have had anyone, with George's fortune now hers. And if the so-called brotherhood of photographers George and Malcolm had come up with were still laughing, they stopped then, didn't they?

"Mrs. Arbuthnot?"

"Yes, let's go."

They walked toward the shop. In the window was more of the War Office propaganda that had got her into this mess. *Leave Hitler to me, Sonny,* a poster on the street in London had said, a soldier holding out his arm to shield a little boy. *Don't do it, Mother,* said the one about leaving evacuated children in safety. As though it were always the mother's fault, no matter which way the bombs fell. At the end of this, they would blame the war on Hitler's mother, for giving birth to him.

The shop was tight and dim. The man at the till said he hadn't seen anyone of Mrs. Poole's description. "We don't see strangers here. That is," he said meaningfully, "we didn't used to."

She had suffered the likes of him enough for the two lifetimes she'd lived. She was only the daughter of a Channel boatman, one of too many mouths to feed. She knew what it was to lie in bed hungry, the shame of it still in her bones, in her blood. A shopkeeper? In this backwater?

"That's a terrible shame," Joan said. "As strangers often have money to spend. When they feel welcome, that is."

Outside again, Bridey smiled from behind

her hand. *"Missus."*

"Well, he was a bore, wasn't he?" When Malcolm walked into a shop, keepers the world 'round tripped over themselves to serve and please him, to help him spend *her* money. George's money. She studied the skin of her hands. There was always something about her that gave it away, wasn't there? She had been George's housekeeper after he parted ways with his first wife. Some had thought it a euphemism, something he called her to excuse her presence in his home, but no. And now the war had made her a vagabond. If only she had ever been a *good* housekeeper, she would know how to run Greenway as she should. "As though he wouldn't accept my dirty London pounds, if he had anything I wanted."

"Did you want something?" Bridey asked.

For the moment she only wanted to find Mrs. Poole. A sort of despair threatened, a cloud. These children might have been her and her family — they *were,* they were all the same — and she hadn't kept one of them safe. She hadn't been allowed to.

"I wanted to save them all," she said. "Even one child lost —" She wouldn't speak of such things, even to a nurse. Not her own secret heartbreak, not to a girl who had so many siblings at home. She had heard the house gossip that Mrs. Christie had suffered a similar loss, and didn't want her name chewed over in their mouths, too. Anyway, she had her brood, one way or the other.

Bridey clasped her hands tightly to herself.

They checked at the churches and at the school but a woman in her garden was more helpful, pointing out the direction of the nearest train station. There was a hotel there, she said.

"Have you checked the Manor Inn? Up the hill as you were going, on the way to Churston Station."

"Isn't it Sunday?" Mrs. Arbuthnot said.

The woman shrugged and went back to hanging her linens.

The public house was cool and still. A single customer in farmer's clothes sat alone at a table. He was a large sort, unkempt, one of his hands in wraps. Bridey shrank beside her at the sight of him. Joan slid awkwardly onto a high chair at the bar, feet dangling. The barman glowered. "Help you with something?"

"On the Lord's day, sir," Mrs. Arbuthnot said. "I suppose the local wardens are aware you're serving on a Sunday?"

"One of those, are you? We're boosting morale, we are." His eyes shifted toward Bridey. "Half-pint, wasn't it, my lover?"

Bridey studied a sketch framed on the wall.

"We're not here for custom," Joan said, though as she recalled why they'd come, she thought she *could* have a whiskey. "We're looking for a woman who might be a danger to herself." She described Mrs. Poole as well as she could. Long hair, dark. She hadn't had a good enough look at her. Hadn't paid attention. "She was rather beleaguered, scraped up. She's searching for her little boy."

The barman's expression didn't soften. "One of them brats saved from London."

She wasn't sure of his tone. "This one might not be saved."

"Good riddance," the customer at the table piped up. The bandage on his hand showed through with blood. She felt sick to look at it. "One less piece of refugee trash come to scrape the village clean."

"I beg your pardon," Joan said.

"Eat up all the rations," he said, "so Dodge here can't put together a proper feed."

Dodge seemed surprised to hear it but said nothing.

"I think you'd rather blame the Ministry of Food for what rations you can and can't get," Joan said. Honestly, she was rather tired of helpless, complaining men while the women got on with it. "The children are due their rations as you are yours. And you might as well blame the King or the country itself —"

"Here now," Dodge said.

"— for not being large enough or temperate enough to grow all the food we need year-round for every English man, woman, and child."

The man shifted his weight and glanced in Bridey's direction, then looked again. "Are *you* the one —"

But Joan wasn't finished, not by a far sight. "It makes as much sense as blaming a four-year-old child for it," she said, "who's only been boarded here while his mum is working in a factory to make aeroplane parts and his daddy is fighting for all our bloody lives in France." She gulped, breathless. "Aside from that, *you* look well fed and all."

"*You'll* not to talk to me like that."

"And why not? You, who have taken liberties to decide who *I* am."

"My family's farmed this land since the Conquest and should have carried on a thousand more years."

The publican set down a glass of water for her, smeared with fingerprints. "Lydell

Michaelsmith," he said, low. "He's —"

"I don't want my name in her mouth," Michaelsmith crowed.

"Well, we agree there," Joan said. "Come, Bridey."

"Scramble away, that's right," Michaelsmith called after them. "As ever, evacuation for the cowards."

Joan turned on her heel. "What's this you're saying to me? Evacuation such as at Dunkirk, sir?"

"Now wait a minute," said the barman, sounding quite serious this time.

"How dare —" Michaelsmith started.

"I do dare, sir, to point out that you are calling mere children by filthy names," Joan said. "Is it cowardice to scramble for one's life, sir? Is it cowardice to point out the futility of war and the damage it does?"

"I wasn't calling the *children* names," he said.

"Ah, so your epithets are for me, are they? You also feel comfortable striking out at women as well as children. Brave man, yourself. Well, sir, *I* am in service to this nation just now —"

"Proper war work taking care of wet nappies —"

"And what sacrifices have you made, yes, I will ask —"

"Please, madam," Dodge said, coming around the bar, his hands out as though he approached a panicking animal. But the animal was behind him, frothing now and shouting things after them as Dodge escorted them to the door.

"Forgive him, madam, as he's only recently lost his son. At sea. And he's had a bit too much to drink."

"In the middle of the *day,* sir, a *Sunday,*" Joan said.

"We're only trying to keep a roof over our heads, same as anyone," Dodge said. "He's had his last, as he's out of money."

She looked over Dodge's shoulder at Michaelsmith. The man was a pathetic pile of flesh, but those were the very people emboldened to point fingers. "I forgive Mr. Michaelsmith for his grief, but not those making excuses for his attacks. You'd best call his minder, if he has one. He should be brought home."

"Yes, madam, you're right."

They checked in at the train station and the hotel at Churston, before turning back toward Greenway. Joan was hot and cross and tired of Bridey's sidelong looks.

"What is it, Bridget? Do speak up."

"Will you call the authorities on that innkeeper?"

"I don't know." Joan's heel had begun to rub in her shoe. Her own daddy had liked a pint on his only day off, Sunday. "Uncharitable attitudes — even more reason to find Mrs. Poole. Where *could* she have gone?"

They walked on, and then Bridey made a noise in her throat. "The ferry."

The sun bore down on them the rest of the way back toward Greenway and the ferry quay. Joan's blister had her limping down the hill, thinking of Mrs. Mallowan's bath.

"I wonder how London is treating Mrs. Christie," she said.

"I don't know, missus."

It was all the girl ever said.

At the gatehouse, they stayed true, continuing down the hill to the ferryman's cottage and the quay. A stinking air came off the river.

The ferry was moored, and the man said he couldn't say who he'd seen and not seen. "I seen all kinds, missus."

He wore a rounded cap that had not kept the sun from creasing his face.

"She would have been upset, sir," Bridey said. "She would have been rather undone. Crying, talking to herself a bit."

Joan followed his gaze down the river, where a bend kept Dartmouth tucked out of sight.

"Aye, maybe I did see someone like that," the man said finally. "This afternoon? She went over to Dits'm."

"Across the river?" Joan cried. "Why would you allow a disturbed woman near a river?"

"She was already near the water, m' lover," the man said, and Joan couldn't help but recoil. "She wanted to get away from here," he said. "And tha's where the ferry goes. Who'm I to say? There's naught to do in Dits'm, if'm honest, so she might've gone on."

Joan gazed across the river but there was little to see, even from so close a distance. An inn and a few buildings sat at the waterline. Houses clung to the side of the hill.

"I only know she had a little money and di'nt mind where she went. Tha's what she said. Di'nt mind this river. Funny thing, though."

Joan's blood went cold. "What?"

"Only she kept calling it the River Styx, and tha's a long way from here."

32
BRIDEY

Dittisham and back

On the passage to Dittisham, Bridey couldn't decide how to ask the ferryman about Thorne, not in front of Mrs. Arbuthnot, who she couldn't have thinking her a gossipmonger or a tell-tale. But then her employer said, "I suppose it's been rather a nuisance, all this business with the man they found."

" 'S good business for me, and that's a fact," the ferryman said.

"Do you mean people coming to have a look? How vile."

"We've had all sorts through the quay, but then it's been a season like that, months now. Bueys coming through to join up with the navvy in Dar'mouth, some, but others, too. Many strangers on these shores."

"What do you ascribe that to?"

"Eh?"

Mrs. Arbuthnot raised her voice, as though

the man might be hard of hearing. "Why do you think so many strangers are coming through this, uh, well, it's a small town, isn't it?"

"I wish I knew, missus, but I don't mind the coin."

Dittisham had a pier and beach, an inn, and not much else. They tried the inn and walked up Manor Street, but no one they encountered had seen Mrs. Poole. She had vanished.

They had to wait for the ferry to cross back to Greenway. Only a bit of its roof was visible from this viewpoint.

"Perhaps she went back to the house," Mrs. Arbuthnot said.

Bridey had no such hope. Hope was not what she felt for someone such as Mrs. Poole, or her son.

At Greenway again, they let themselves in the back door and Mrs. Arbuthnot hurried off to ask Mrs. Scaldwell if their visitor had returned.

This was optimism, she supposed.

Bridey took the stairs to the nursery slowly, methodically, bracing herself for something she couldn't name. Something had changed inside Greenway, some outside influence had been let in, some poison.

At the landing, she paused and listened at

the sounds coming from the nursery. The children had found diversions without her; she was glad. It was better they could do without her. They would need to.

But how soon?

She had the sudden urge to turn around, slip out the back door of the house, and make her way to the nearest train for London. She should never have come. Caring for children, reminded constantly of what she had lost, what she would never again have — and to lose one. Well, he hadn't been entrusted to them, but little Sam Poole was still a heavy burden.

Was it her? Was she the bad luck brought upon this house? Or —

Quietly she crept along the passage to their room and surveyed Gigi's side. In the chest of drawers they shared, Gigi's drawer was still almost empty, but she had at last put her things away. Bridey petted a jumper, admiring the feel of the soft fabric. This wasn't utility. Gigi hadn't used her ration book to buy this.

An ear cocked toward the corridor, Bridey sorted through it all, sampling fabrics between her fingertips. Silks instead of rayon, when most silk was gone to parachutes. Was that *lace*? Good wools, too — was this what cashmere was? Nothing remade or mended, nothing knitted at home. Everything perfectly tailored to Gigi's slim figure by a professional hand.

Now she went to the cupboard. Dresses and skirts in the new trim style that heralded the end of gatherings, of pleats, of ruching and trimmings. The end of embellishments. Bridey spotted Gigi's cape hanging at the back and brought it out to have a look. Why had she never noticed? Gigi's cloak was rather nicer than hers — nicer than any other she had seen. It was dark blue with cherry red lining, as it should be, with the same reversible double-breasted button tabs to close it at the front. But where Bridey's was stiff boiled wool and three-quarter length with the initials of St. Prisca's Hospital embroidered onto its stand-up collar, Gigi's was supple and flowing, longer than it should be. No hospital name marked it.

Was it even *blue*? Bridey pulled the edge of the cape out. The hem was stiff, weighted. Some of the girls at St. Prisca's sewed a few coins into the hems of their capes for emergencies, which had the additional benefit of keeping their hems from flipping up in the winter wind.

But it was not a few coins that lined this hem. Someone unskilled with a needle had done the deed, too. The seam that had been ripped was closed with a few amateur stitches, little Xs in a thread that didn't quite match. They had managed not to ruin the entire garment, though. Bridey rubbed the hem between her fingers. It was paper inside, wasn't it? Documents of stolen identities and maps to buried treasure, she supposed, more of Gigi's intrigues.

She could do a much finer job of it. If, say, a stitch popped.

The work of an instant. Bridey pulled the thread, two stitches, three, and worked a lump of the lining's contents to the opening.

They were ten-and twenty-pound notes, folded intricately to overlap and slide into the lining like a snake.

She felt along the hem. No good at figures, but could it be thousands of pounds? How would a nurse come by such a bounty? And hiding it. She supposed there were good reasons for hiding money. They were hearing things out of France now, people forced to take what they could and flee. But if one had to hide a boodle such as this, it's possible the money didn't belong to them.

Bridey fetched her needlework and found a near match for the thread color. But she couldn't fix it up well, could she? With precision and speed, and with shaking hands and her blood coursing through her veins, she reconstructed the clumsy stitches and returned the cloak to the cupboard.

In the playroom, Gigi sat on the floor among the children, her legs crossed prettily at the ankles.

But she was a prop on the stage. Around her, the children played jacks and tea party, raced tiny war machines across the floor. One of the babies was attempting a first crawl a few feet away. Gigi, posed, seemed to notice none of it. When the ball from the jacks set bounced against her, she said nothing. Maureen and Pamela darted to chase it.

"Nurse Bridey!" Maureen called out.

Gigi's eyes turned sharp and she scrambled to her feet. "Where have you been?"

The girls rabbled around to tell her about the midday meal she'd missed. Mrs. Scaldwell had come up with something from a ministry pamphlet where a small potato was turned into a piglet with radish ears, stuffed with something that should have been sausage but wasn't.

"Shall we put our things away and go for a walk?" Bridey said.

The children hurried for a place at the door.

"I don't think we should," Gigi said, pulling at her lip. "It will rain soon, I think." The windows showed the fine late afternoon.

"It's lovely. I know because I've already had a nice *bracing* walk back from town, looking for a surprise visitor."

"Was it . . . was it someone for Mrs. Arbuthnot? As you thought?"

"*You* suggested it might be," Bridey said. No one would come looking for *her*. Dull Bridget. "There was another caller. For *me,* actually." She thought it fair to characterize the doctor's visit in such a way but felt heat rise in her cheek to remember his gentle touch where Mrs. Poole had boxed her.

Bridey sorted the infants between them — why shouldn't they have a pram? — and led the group outside to begin the longest way around the estate she could think of, across on the top path to the far end with the view of Dartmouth, down the hill, and back past the boathouse and the battery. The children knew the way. The girls went in a crocodile, hand in hand, Doreen stopping to pick flowers as she found them. The boys, of course, turned their pleasant stroll into a military parade to present their arms, which were sticks, little Edward running to keep up and reminding her of Sam.

Gigi fidgeted until the children ran ahead. "Who was your visitor, then, if not the constables? Tom?"

"You might forget about Tom," Bridey said. "I know people beyond Tommy Kent."

"People beyond Tommy Kent who can be expected to show up at the end of the world for you?"

She was defensive, scared since the night in the sheep pasture. "Who are you expecting from London, Gigi?"

"I don't know what you mean."

"You're afraid of something," Bridey said. "You armed me to say you weren't here!"

"I never should have been," she said, then softened. "A suitor. A most ardent one."

"That's all? I never heard a girl say a bloke was too devoted," Bridey said.

"Haven't you?" Gigi said. "I believe I have. Tommy Kent, was it?"

"*He's* not in love."

"We've been at Greenway a month," Gigi said. "How many letters has he sent?"

The baby in Bridey's arms squirmed and fussed. Why had she called for a walk when her feet already hurt? "You said you once asked people to open up and tell you their thoughts and fears, but you never admit your own. You're the sphinx. This is not who you are, you said. Who are you, then?"

Gigi wouldn't look in her direction.

"Tell me one true thing about yourself," Bridey said.

Gigi took a deep breath and shifted the other baby against her neck. "His name is Nicholas. Nicholas Thorne."

"Who's — Gigi, no. Not the man in the river?" She didn't know what to say. "You knew it all along."

"Now you," Gigi commanded.

"One true thing about *yourself*," Bridey said.

"The fact that I know Thorne's name is a fact about myself," Gigi said. "If you think it through."

"Is he your lover?"

"No!"

"Your brother?"

"I used to have one of those, until I was disowned," Gigi said.

"What's that at home? Cut out of father's will?"

"Cut out of father's life. But I suppose the will as well."

"If Thorne's nothing to you, his name is not about you," Bridey said.

"He was . . . a colleague. Once."

"You *worked* together? The observing job?"

"Yes, as a matter of fact."

310

Bridey remembered the intruders draping themselves across the children on the train. Were they *all* observers? Willa, too, then? The sullen one who went to Dartmouth. Engaging the full carriage of travelers as they walked away, noting book titles and newspaper headlines. "You all pretended as though you'd only just met."

"It's rather the point to never speak of it."

"Is it?"

"Answers to questions change when people know you're writing them down, when they might be held accountable for what they say or think."

"An old colleague on the same train and you coming down with us," Bridey said. "Rather a coincidence."

Gigi said nothing.

"What's this job exactly?" Bridey said. "What do you do?"

"I chatted up people in the market, that's all," Gigi said. "The pub. What they're worried about, what they're complaining of, how their morale is holding up, that sort of thing. I listened. I could talk to anyone."

"My *mam* could talk to anyone," Bridey said, gritting her teeth through a sharp jab of grief. "How's that a job, though?"

"Well, I gave a report, you see, and the information was valuable to someone, and . . . that's the job. I was paid."

All the local talk of fifth columnists, of infiltration by Germans to the interior of the country, and she was paid to listen in at pubs. "Are you a *spy*?"

"No!" Gigi said. "It's anthropology, like I said. We're studying British people in their own natural environs. It's . . . catching history while it's happening, capturing the everyday so that history doesn't leave out small lives."

"*Small* lives." Like hers.

"You know what I mean, Bridey. Those who don't rise to the newspaper headlines."

"All to sell — what was it? Soap flakes?"

Gigi looked away. "Just an example, in peacetime."

"And in times of war?"

She took a breath and squared her shoulders. "Gauging moods. Listening for the common man's opinions."

"Which opinions? What they like for their supper?"

"Dissent, I suppose."

They had come to the boathouse, but the children had already turned toward the battery, through a steep grade in the path.

"Dissent," Bridey said, grasping at weeds to pull herself over.

"It means —"

"I know what it means." There must be something to her face that people did not like, something of the innocent to her.

"It's only listening to the stories they tell, Bridey," Gigi said. "It's not espionage, for either side. I *suppose* it might seem like spying, if one didn't understand. Or if one had something to hide. Having someone asking questions would feel like the walls coming down around you."

They stepped onto the platform of the battery. The children crawled onto the backs of the cannons, shouting and tussling and calling for the nurses to watch, to adjudge who could sit where and for how long, and whose turn it would be next.

"Asking *questions,*" Bridey said. "Mrs. Bastin said Thorne was asking all sorts. You think that's how he died. Doing what you're still doing? Gigi, why in God's name —"

"I don't *know* it's how he died. It's only making conversation, isn't it? Not an offense for the guillotine, is it?"

"Isn't it?" Bridey took a breath and plunged in. "Do you know who wants these reports? What makes you certain it's not Germans?"

"Are you daft?" Gigi said. She turned so she had her back to the children. "Mass-Ob is — it's crown, all right? I'm not supposed to say, but it's for the Office of Home Intelligence. For the King by way of Churchill."

"Churchill —" But she believed it, suddenly felt the pieces lining up to fit together. Spy or not, no matter what Gigi turned out to be, she could not be what she had said she was all along. "You're no nurse at all."

33
BRIDEY

"No, I never was," Gigi said. "There. That's one true thing about me."

Bridey, stunned, could only think the children were cared for by not one but two fraudulent nurses. They'd be sacked and rightly so.

"I tried to tell you," Gigi said.

Her shock boiled over into anger. "When? When you nearly fainted at the sight of blood? I should have known. Your finger-nails."

Gigi held out her hands. "What of them?"

"They're rather hard to maintain if you're working a busy ward in wartime," she said. "But you didn't know that."

"I would have trimmed them, at least."

Her disinterest in the children and their care. The money sewn into her cloak. Her cloak! It was not a nurse's cape at all but a fashionable version for ladies who might want to pretend.

"Why did you say you were the other nurse?"

"I needed to be on the train. It was a matter of — well, grave national importance." She sounded like someone still playacting. "And personal, as well. I had to get out of London — honestly, Bridey, I understand how Mrs. Mallowan must have felt, running off as she did."

"You? You think *you* know her desperation? Her pain?" Hadn't the woman lost her mother, her husband, and her security, all? If anyone should know Mrs. Mallowan's state of mind —

She braced herself for the wave of grief she knew would come, sucked herself in, deep within her own skin.

"Look at you. At least I'm capable of feeling someone's pain," Gigi hissed.

Bridey held her guts in, hand over her mouth.

"You pulled me up into the train, and rescued me," Gigi said. "You believed I was the other nurse and I went along with it. For one reason or another, I've kept going along, rather successfully —"

"You *haven't*. You're a *rubbish* nurse," Bridey said. "I only noticed you at all because I thought you were Mrs. Poole —"

"Who?"

It was her fault. Gigi would still be on the platform and maybe she should be.

"Mrs. Poole. The woman who took her son back and she's just been at the door — oh." She sank, shaking, on the low battery wall. Through the opening created by Gigi's deception and by the memory of Sam Poole, her little brother had climbed through, whole, her sisters, and her mam.

"What is it? Should you see the doctor?"

"Don't be ridiculous," she whispered. Her girls came around to see she was fine, hand her leaves and stones they had collected.

"Thank you," she said to the girls and held the gifts in the palm of her hand. "I'm fine — I keep forgetting what it means, truly. Her little boy. The same age as —" Her youngest sister. "As James," she said instead. But her sister was too much there, playing alongside them, and now Sam Poole, too.

There was no room for him here or within her, or for Gigi to ruin everything.

The girls set a table of pebbles at her feet, ladies at tea. "Why did you *stay*?" she said.

"It was safe," Gigi said. "From the man I mentioned. That's why I had to leave London immediately." She sighed. "And then it was confining, isolated from town and seeing to their schedules and needs. And then —"

"Then the man in the river was discovered," Bridey said.

"After Nicky was found, I stayed because I was scared to do my work. He'd asked too many questions or asked them of the wrong person — I didn't know if we *should* go on. We're not spies, Bridey. We're file clerks and census takers."

Nicky, was it? Now she knew who he'd been waiting for that morning the foxes screamed.

But then the boys were yelling and scuffling on the ground at the far cannon. James and John, fists landing, and Edward knocked aside and crying. Bridey hurried to intervene, infant still on her shoulder, while Gigi stood by, as always. *Are you? Are you capable of feeling someone's pain?* The boys wanted to be stopped and scolded. The girls wanted the fight to end. They all wanted sure ground and, if Gigi could feel their pain at all, she hadn't ever acted on it.

After peace was established, they trudged up the hill, everyone a bit bruised and sore in spirit.

"I'll pack my things," Gigi said when they reached the house.

"Let me *think* a moment," Bridey said.

If Gigi left, what would happen? Was she truly in danger from the man from London or was it the wish man all over again, stories and haunts? And if Gigi went, she'd have the children to care for, all. It was too much for one person. Her nerves were already coming apart like embroidery floss, fraying. Was she likely to impress Mrs. Arbuthnot if she was short tempered with the children and they came back from every outing as they did today, with sleeves torn and lips bloodied?

Couldn't she have one thing for herself? All she'd survived?

She couldn't think what to do. National importance? It seemed another kitchen story to her, the Devil after them.

"I want to meet the observers and hear the whole story."

"It doesn't make you —"

"Any safer, yes, I know. I have to know who I'm protecting, don't I? If I'm to do it."

"Why would you want to protect —" Gigi's look on her had a new quality. "All right. I'll find a way."

At the house, there were letters. Another from Tom and one for Gigi, notable only in how quickly she grabbed for it.

The children were tidied up and put down for a rest, the ripped clothing put in the darning basket. In their room, Bridey picked up Tommy's letter. She didn't mind not knowing where he was, in truth. There might be some thrill in filling in the unknown with daydreams — but he might say *something* to her, all these letters. These were dangerous times, a time when souls might be laid bare. He could surely find more to say than what he'd had to eat, how much rain they'd had.

Gigi had never come in.

She's not gone off? It was Bridey's decision whether she stayed or went. The cloak still hung from its peg.

She wasn't in the nursery rooms, or down in the kitchen. Bridey worked herself around the house, searching in places Gigi might be and in places she shouldn't. The morning room and the drawing room in one wing, the library in the other.

In the dining room, the shutters were drawn to spare the carpet. At the head of the grand table, Gigi's careless posture was somehow regal and slattern at the same time.

"You shouldn't be here," Bridey said.

"That's what I think as well."

Bridey edged in. She had never been to the dining room before, and wished she could see the details. The room had a curved wall and — was she seeing things?

— bowed wooden doors set into it. "Bad news?"

"You haven't heard the church bells ringing the Armistice, have you?"

"Well, there's news of the world and then there's news from home." She held onto a chairback, not daring to sit.

"The only news now is news of the world," Gigi said. "Haven't you noticed? We're making terrible efforts to save the children, the future, *saving England,* but the men we'll ship over by the cargo load. Saving England for what? For whom?"

"And the women —"

"England has no use for women. Well, only one use."

Bridey listened to the silent room around them. "*Have* you had bad news?"

"I'm nothing but bad news, Bridget," Gigi said. "I might have said back at Paddington and saved us both the trouble." Gigi pulled her knees to her chest in the chair, her face hidden in shadow. "Never mind. I'm talking nonsense because I'm imprisoned in this gorgeous house and of no use to anyone." Curled up in darkness as she was, Gigi was hunched and nearly monstrous. Bridey thought of Mrs. Scaldwell's story, of the gnarled wisht woods that hid devils.

"They want you to stay where you are."

"I've nothing to do but read murder stories."

"You could try being a nurse," Bridey said. "And being some use to me."

Gigi lifted her head. "Don't you want me to go?"

If she protected Gigi's lies, her own were safe. And the only worse thing she could imagine than having to care for children to earn back her life was to care for them without the promise of Gigi's friendship.

"I need your help with these small lives," she said.

34
BRIDEY

*9 May 1941 — almost six weeks at
Greenway*

Later in the week, Bridey woke to find
Gigi's bed empty.

Morning had become regimented: faces
and hands, fresh clothes, heads checked,
tongues stuck out for color, teeth brushed,
hair combed — even the boys. Breakfast in
tin plates and cups and then tidying up the
rooms and today, even without Bridey prod-
ding the boys, everyone was on best behav-
ior, to be allowed to go on the outing to the
beach.

Bridey sent the children sorting through
everyone's jumpers and jackets, and caps
and bonnets, too, for the weather was not
as fine as she would have liked. The wind
rattled the windows and the youngest child
clung to her, wet and teething and cross.
Mrs. Scaldwell had been appealed to for a
lunch hamper, and Hannaford for a ride in

the car. The Arbuthnots had just decided they would come along, after all, which put off the journey while they saw to their own kit, to his easel. It was all rather a great deal of work, and when Gigi finally appeared, she had the nerve to say so.

"A great deal of work but none of it yours," Bridey said. "I said I needed help, remember?"

"I was making a few arrangements for a visit to the boathouse," she said.

"Not your observer friends? Scaldwell will have their guts for garters if he catches them on the grounds."

"They're coming after Scaldwell's rounds, midnight," Gigi said. She glared at the infant in Bridey's arms. "How else will we meet? We can barely get a moment away, with that little monster's fangs coming in."

Bridey hushed her. "Can you watch the others while I speak to Mrs. Scaldwell about the hamper? It will need to be heavier with the Arbuthnots along."

In the kitchen, Mrs. Scaldwell welcomed her with a sigh at the infant grizzling in her arms. "I've already heard," she said. She had thick slices of coarse brown loaf open on the table, and a knife spreading something horrible and orange. Shredded carrots held together with pickle, something learned from the wireless. "Himself won't like what I've put in, but that's what's on offer. He'll soon have sand in it, this wind, and blame me for that, as well."

"Thank you, Mrs. Scaldwell." The woman could be lighting fire to Bridey's skirt, and she would have to thank her for it. Everyone, it seemed to her, required her to pet and fuss over them, not just the little ones.

She was almost to the stairs when Bridey heard the children laughing. She stepped back into the corridor. Were they on the hill? Gigi had taken them out? All? It was the first time Gigi had ever taken on the children of her own volition.

Bridey stood in the corridor and listened to their cheerful racket. She knew their parents must break their hearts over the silence. Any bit of joy now was victory.

Bridey dandled the child in her arms until he quieted. They were lucky, weren't they? Even with the raids they'd had, with the awful things happening, the body at the quay, the pantry theft, with Scaldwell breathing down their necks and the Arbuthnots strict and peculiar, they were alive, far from the center of things. A lovely home and healthy children. And when this was over, she could expect a place at St. Prisca's, the renewed respect of Matron Bailey, all she had ever wanted.

But she shouldn't be happy, shouldn't allow herself to plan a future when some hadn't made it through, still more wouldn't. Would they ever be allowed to be joyful again? To get back to the way things had been? She thought they might have to renegotiate public life, the dreams they'd put on hold. England couldn't be the same. How could it?

She didn't dare cut through the entrance hall to use the front door, not in daylight with the Scaldwells about and not crossways against her luck, anyway. She bounced the little one in her arms down the service corridor and out the back door and intercepted a young man skidding an old bicycle to a halt on the gravel.

"Telegram for Mrs. Joan Arbuthnot," he said.

"Oh, no." Bad news came by telegram. She'd brought it on, thinking of luck.

"Naw, not from the War Office. *This* time." The boy had front teeth too big for his mouth but he sounded as world weary as a pensioner. "Is that one of them? One of the 'vacs? He looks like any other kiddie."

"He *is* any other kiddie. She'll have to call in a reply later. I'll have it."

Until it was placed in her hand, Bridey had every intention of delivering the telegram directly to its recipient. Mrs. Arbuthnot had sons but she'd said they weren't at the front. They were the right age and even so . . .

Not from the War Office.

Couldn't it be about her? Matron Bailey's reach extended, finally, to grab her by the scruff of the neck? Or —

The telegram, slipped into her sleeve.

Upstairs in their bedroom, Bridey kicked the door closed, bounced the baby as he began to complain, and tore the message open clumsily with one hand, irrevocably.

Mishap train missed stop

Advise nurse still required stop

Matron Higgins, St. Saviour's Hospital for Children

Outside on the hill, the children raced and played, and Gigi held the other little baby boy up against the sky to kick and laugh.

Bridey read the telegram again. Were they getting more help? No —

Mishap train missed stop.

Like words thrown together in a hot soup pot, the meaning bubbling, then bursting.

They had been at Greenway six weeks, and here was the beginning of the end. How ardent a suitor was this Matron Higgins?

How soon before Gigi's lies caught up and all their secrets were spilled on Greenway Road?

35
VERA SCALDWELL

Greenway, at the back door

Vera thought they'd need one of those open-topped charabancs used with tourists at the seaside to take the children, nurses, Arbuthnots, all, to the beach. The mistress's car was hardly large enough, and Hannaford shouldn't offer it in any case. He had it out for a wash, Frank said. A wash, she said. Why not wait for a warmer day? You'll see, he said. The mistress's bath could do with a freshen, he said.

Could it now? Vera carried the bucket and mop upstairs, closed the door, and pressed her back to it. Sad state of affairs that to find a moment's peace, one had to find it in the bathroom with a bucket.

She could have Edith do the scrubbing, but she didn't mind the work and Mrs. M. was particular about her bath. *As she was allowed to be, heavens.* A woman was allowed to be particular. Vera put her back into it.

A woman who earned her right, that is.

Mrs. Arbuthnot, now that one played at houses, didn't she?

Playing the madam, but no management of those nurses, coming home all hours. A lot of high feelings, all in one place, and no one to call it off. It was all heading for a tumble, Vera was sure of it, but what shape would it take?

She sloshed the mop back into the bucket, then pulled it out and wrung it, gray water running over her hands. Later her hands would be red knuckled, the skin sore, cracked.

She caught sight of herself in the mirror over the sink. She wouldn't allow a woman looking such as herself in the door, for fear she'd nick the silver. Vera let the mop lean against the wall and centered herself at the mirror, turning her chin one way and the other.

Vera Scaldwell prided herself on being the woman no one had to wonder about. But did they not wonder about her, or did they not think of her at all?

Mrs. M. relied on her, though, and she was satisfied. Frank — well, Frank relied on her, too. It was enough, most days.

In the mirror, Vera saw the ledge over the bath that Mrs. M. had ordered Mr. Bell, the architect, to install.

"For apples, God love her."

She liked apples, too, and they weren't a luxury here, the way they were in other places, not yet. The trees in the gardens would turn out plenty soon enough. If she could keep the villain pinching their preserves from ripping the trees, roots and all, from the ground under their feet, the orchards would see them through. The orchard, the peach house. The kitchen garden like the one her mum once had.

Vera sat on the edge of the bath, and an old memory came to her. Her mum had put something from the garden into the water for their bath, Saturday nights. And then put a new kettle to warm the water for her own wash at the end, the air steaming and petal-soft as she poured. "Go on, Verie." Gentle nudge out of the room. As a little one, she had hated being left outside the door.

She should have more patience for those small ones upstairs. She knew she should. Children shouldn't be separated from their own, not in times like these. It showed the cracks of the world, letting it happen.

Frank's mum had died when he was a tot,

his da put in the workhouse and the children sent on, Frank and his older brother to a boys' home. On Sheepwash Road in Sussex, she couldn't forget that. He never spoke of it, but she was sure he looked on the children billeted here with more kindness because of it. Her own family had suffered a bout of the cholera and the workhouse as a result, and the shame of it lived in her bones.

When she had the chance to be gentle, it was that shame that rose up and wouldn't let her. She looked down at her dry hands, dirty nails. They had worked so hard here, and now —

Vera went to the door, meaning to open it and get back to the kitchen, or to go to their room and have another look at the mistress's last letter. It was impossible, what she'd written. She'd never do it.

Instead, Vera's hand reached out and turned the key.

Back at the bath, she opened the taps, running the water hot as the pipes would allow and letting her clothes fall to the floor. When she had the five inches per the Civil Defence, she stepped in and lowered herself.

Indulgent, was what it was.

Hairpins out, she lay back, sinking, sinking until her head was below the waterline.

The mistress had taken all her cream hair shampoo to London or she'd have some of that, too.

Vera sat up and found the right spot for resting her head and neck, closed her eyes. The mistress had taken a great deal with her when she left, and would have it all. There were those who could make any decision they wanted, and the rest — they had the rug pulled out.

There was a noise in the hall. Vera turned her head and caught a shadow under the door — two shadows, side-by-side, a pair of shoes. It would be Edith or Elsie, with a question. Not a moment's peace.

"Who's there?" she said. "I'm cleaning Herself's bath."

But the shoes at the door only moved on, floors creaking and shadows sliding, revealing a sense of height and weight that was not Edith or Elsie.

"Frank?"

That Arbuthnot chap, prowling. Of course. The wind must have sent them back. They'd be stomping up the stairs and sending down demands.

Briefly, though, she thought of the wisht man. She lay back again but the water was no match for the chill that had come over her.

36
BRIDEY

To Elberry Cove, Paignton
In the car, they were piled in layers, children across their laps and in between them on the long seat, girls stacked upon one another and boys crouched at the women's feet. Little Edward spent the trip waving wildly to other motorcars from the back window. Mr. Arbuthnot, moaning about his easel in the boot, sat up front with Hannaford.

The drive was noisy with giggles and complaints among the children, but the men sat silent until Mr. Hannaford cleared his throat. "Broadsands Beach, that's Mrs. M.'s favorite."

"Why aren't we going there, then?" Mr. Arbuthnot said. "If it's good enough for the *mistress.*"

"It's a longer journey," Bridey said. "Not all of us being quite as comfortable as others."

Gigi, next to her, snorted. Mrs. Arbuthnot

should have scolded them but was not listening. "Have you had any letters from Mrs. Christie?" she said.

"She's putting her poisons to good use at the infirmary. There's no poison left in the house now, is there?" Hannaford's eyes flashed with mirth in the rearview mirror. "The Mister Mallowan's off translating Arab, his *speciality.* That's what Alice has from Elsie."

"Was a secret of this war ever truly secret?" Mr. Arbuthnot huffed.

Hannaford had it from his wife, who got it from his sister Mrs. Bastin, who would have the news from Mrs. Scaldwell, who got it from *Mr.* Scaldwell, who received the letters. Estate business, he never let anyone else read them.

Mrs. Arbuthnot sat back in her seat. Gigi slumped in hers. She hadn't wanted to come. A sharp little elbow poked at Bridey's leg while Beryl wriggled in her lap. She wouldn't mind the chance to stalk the beach and clear her head.

Mr. Hannaford parked the car and toted the food and blankets down so that the nurses might carry the youngest to the cove. Once they were clear of the trees, a sharp gust stole their breath.

"Maybe only an hour," Mrs. Arbuthnot

said to the gardener, keeping hold of the sun bonnet she'd worn. "Perhaps just wait for us in the car park."

Hannaford couldn't do it, he said, but made a second trip for deckchairs and the infernal easel, and the Arbuthnots settled in, one of the infants asleep against Mrs. Arbuthnot's shoulder. Bridey sneaked a treat for Hannaford from the hamper in thanks — a slice of Woolton pie, topped thick with mashed parsnips, that must have been meant for Mr. Arbuthnot.

At the far end of the cove stood an old ruin and a wall. They set off into the wind across the shingle beach, stone and pebble, letting the children run. But someone got a speck in their eye, and soon Edward fell and scraped a knee. Gulls cried overhead.

"Shall we have a walking tour of *hell* next?" Gigi hissed to Bridey when the crying had stopped and the oldest children were far enough ahead. Bridey had an infant on her hip and held Edward's hand while Gigi folded her empty arms and kept pace, only to have someone to complain to.

"You didn't have to stay."

"I did. Company orders, or I might ruin —"

"And you always do what you're told." She hadn't all the pieces, not until she'd

336

heard the full story from the observers. Bridey looked down at Edward. He was the age to repeat every living word one said. "What plans would you ruin by abandoning your post? You here, Willa in Kingswear. Thorne stationed in Galmpton? Another at the Naval Academy, wasn't it?"

"I just collect opinions," Gigi said. "I don't have them."

"You did say what you collect is valuable to someone." In this lonely place, this small community of people, what could be so valuable about the stories they told? "Why would the opinions of *these* common men and women matter so much? Why here?"

"I can't tell you," Gigi said. "I mean that I don't know. I have a guess but that's all it would be."

"Let's have it, if it's a guess and not state secrets."

Gigi gazed along the shore and out to sea. "My prediction is that this little remote spot is about to have a big place on the world's stage," she said. "I think Greenway is going to help end the war."

"Sounds like an opinion, which you don't have," Bridey said.

"Even so."

Bridey hitched the baby up against her. Edward dragged at her other arm to pick up a shell or stone. "What sort of scrape was it? The man in London. I thought it was a love affair but . . ."

"Well, it was, but don't say that in front of Willa," Gigi said. "All right, do you remember when I said you could take in information you weren't looking for, doing what we do? In London I had a fling with the man who owned the pub we frequented after hours. The Friar's, hole in the wall. Without meaning to, I stumbled upon some of *his* after-hours dealings. He's a devil, Bridey, and a clever one."

"What sort of dealings?"

"The criminal sort," Gigi said. "It's better that you not know, but — a murderer in plain sight, using the damage of the war to his advantage."

"How's that? War profiteering, the real kind?"

"And exploiting those who had too little to begin with," Gigi said. "And should the need arise, burying the bodies in the rubble Hitler left behind."

"No."

"He somehow learned who we were because, even though we weren't collecting . . . well, we picked up a signal without meaning to, and it was about us."

"I don't understand. You heard things

about yourself?"

"Whispers that we were — well."

"Spies, fifth column," Bridey said.

"German sympathizers. Jews."

"Sexually deviant. Half caste," Bridey said into the wind.

Gigi's jaw was tight. "The sorts of things that other people tend to make their business. We were stonewalled from the places we'd been observing, chased off from the Friar's. Then our flats were broken into, our things smashed. Evicted, arrested. Some of them have families, you know. They couldn't take the chance. Me — well, I was clear of that at least. Mass-Ob assignments were shuffled and shuffled again, but it made no difference. In the end, those who had no other choice — the misfits we are — were sent here."

Bridey smelled the sheep pasture, felt the mud on her cheek as they hid from a car without its headlamps covered. It was someone from London she feared, all this time? I'm not here, she'd said. I'm sorry, she'd pleaded, whiskey breath. Sorry for —

"Can we climb, Nurse? Nurse? Can we?"

Bridey looked up. The tide was out a bit, the lower stones of the wall showing the water level they might expect if they dallied. James and John hadn't waited and were clinging to large boulders at the base of the ruin, slabs of rock showing their tilted layers, covered in slippery green moss.

"Come down from there," Bridey called. The girls were lined up along the wall out of the wind. James and John jumped from the rock, imaginary parachutes, and raced back and forth, daring the water to get their shoes wet. Bridey tried to get them back, but her voice was getting lost in the wind. Or they were ignoring her. The baby in her arms startled awake and started to wail.

Gigi stopped to pick up a pebble and studied it in her palm.

The wind whipped Bridey's hair out of its pins and lashed it across her eyes. It was every woman for herself, was it? Except someone must look after the children. Someone always had to mind the children, and that someone was always her.

She hated what she had become and withstood and allowed. Bridey turned her back on them all and ate her rage whole. Far along the coast, past the Arbuthnots and this cove, a curl of the land arched and trailed off into the sea. Bridey rocked the baby against her and set her sights on the quiet of another place. Someday, somewhere, there would be silence and she could have a good night's sleep and a thought in her head again. Gigi's secrets would sink her own plans but just now she was saving England. She was *saving* England. She was keeping these children safe and their parents contented and —

Behind her, the girls started up a row, and her patience snapped.

"Gigi, for the love of holy God, will you see to them?" She left off the pleases and I'm-sorries and the would-you-could-you. She sounded absolutely mad but no one had heard her, surely, because of the wind howling in their ears. Bridey reached out for Edward —

Edward was gone.

He was not at her feet, not along the wall with the girls, not climbing the ruin again with the older boys.

"Where is he?" Bridey walked to Gigi and put the baby into her arms.

"Who?"

"Edward."

"You just had him," Gigi said.

"But he's —" Not with the girls, not with the bigger boys. Not back with the Arbuthnots and the open hamper. No one else was on the beach. On a windy day like this, no one else was such a fool as to be near the shore —

Bridey turned to the sea and took a lurching step.

There was something in the water, something bobbing against the tilted stone.

She was running across the shingle, thinking of the drowned man who was not drowned, before the figure in the water resolved into a small boy, facedown, with arms flung out like an angel.

A terrible noise cut the rush of the wind in her ears, a cry of terror. Her own. She splashed through the shallows into the cold water, up to her waist, up to her shoulders to reach him, and her feet almost coming out from under her, too. She pulled him from the water and splashed to the beach as the baby screamed, the girls gathered around, crying and calling for her, all wanting comfort she couldn't give.

Bridey clutched the sopping boy to her, pounded his back. He was not breathing. He would not breathe, and his lips were gray. *His mum.* She pounded his back hard enough to feel it against her own breast. Her arm hurt with it. His mum, home in London, and they were to save him. They were *saving* them, and if they couldn't keep them safe, what was the point? If they couldn't save them — Maggie-Helen-Simone-Michael-little Evangeline —

But then Edward convulsed against her

342

and spewed water and bile down her dress.

Gigi collapsed on her knees in front of them, clutching the other screeching 'vac. "He's breathing," she gasped. Her eyes were wild as she sought Bridey's agreement. Her forgiveness. "He's alive."

The wind howled.

Sorry for —

Sorry for risking Bridey's life, too. For risking all their lives to save her own.

"You don't think Thorne asked too many questions," Bridey said through chattering teeth. "Or the wrong ones." Edward shrieked, the end of days, struggled and fought. She held him tight. Across the shale, the Arbuthnots hurried in their direction, holding their hats and the last infant. "You lured a murderer down from London. To Greenway. To these children."

Gigi couldn't look away from Edward. She sat back on her heels. "I'm sorry."

"You're the poison in this house." Bridey leaned into Gigi, Edward clamped to her and kicking. "You are not a nurse, and you're a danger to say you are."

The Arbuthnots ran up, gasping. "What happened?" Mr. Arbuthnot demanded. Mrs. Arbuthnot shuffled the infant in her arms to him and wrenched Edward from Bridey.

"What in heaven's name?" she cried.

"How could this have happened?"

"He was there and then he wasn't," Bridey said.

Gigi laid her hand on Bridey's arm.

"I lost him," Gigi said. "It's all my doing."

Bridey was not sure who she meant, little Edward or Thorne or someone else entirely. She sat back, slipping in the cobbles, and let the girls cling and cry. *All. All were lost.*

37
JOAN ARBUTHNOY

Home again

Everyone was fatigued, nerves frayed and pebbles in their shoes, the nurse and the child saved both soaked and shivering. Joan hadn't decided if anyone deserved praise for heroics or if everyone needed a good spanking, but she sent up silent thanks she didn't have to tell the parents one of the children had drowned.

At Greenway, they tumbled into the back corridor, a parade of noise and bother, dirty, cold, crying, the entire range of human misery and filth. Scaldwell, proper as you please, held the door as though they were the mistress's own treasured guests.

"When you have a moment, Mr. and Mrs. Arbuthnot," Scaldwell said.

A little white dog ran around them, barking uproariously, cheering some of the children into joyful hysterics and alarming the baby at Joan's shoulder. One of the older boys saw his chance and made for the dinner gong while Scaldwell, who was particular about the instrument, only watched as the boy raised the hammer and struck. Joan grabbed him before he tried a second time, and Malcolm — "Please don't worry about the hamper, darling. Mr. Scaldwell, whose dog —"

She had missed a turn, for it was Mrs. Christie's dog — Mrs. Christie who stood in the entrance hall, silver haired, tall and foreboding. Strangers stood alongside, tweeds for her and golfing plaids for him, that insufferable sort. Upon seeing Joan, Mrs. Christie turned away.

"What is it, Scarsdale? Let's have it," Malcolm said.

"Malcolm," Joan cautioned. The nurses and children watched from the stairs. They could not see Mrs. Christie, and her husband hadn't. "Gigi, please take the children up and see they get washed and down for a rest. Sort their clothes for a soaking — Bridey, no. You stay for a moment."

"This one needs his nap, too," Bridey said over the sleeping child in her arms. She hadn't let Edward go since she'd got him back, and had expertly got him to calm down. She was sodden, dripping.

"He'll get to his bed shortly. Mr.

Scaldwell, let us convene in the kitchen."

Mrs. Scaldwell stood at the stove. She looked up and stared a long while at Malcolm, heaven knew why. "Are you just back?" she said. Then she noticed Bridey and Edward, went to the scullery, and came back with a deep soup pot to put on the hob.

Mr. Scaldwell said, "What's happened?"

"One of the children," Joan started in a low voice. Her heart fluttered to say it. A child truly could have died. On *her* watch. "We've only just managed to avoid — a catastrophic outcome."

Scaldwell looked suitably serious. "Misadventure?"

Bridey wouldn't look up from the boy. "I let go of his hand for a moment," she said. "A moment. You know how fast they are and how many and Gigi —" Her face was red and bulbous with crying.

"I'll have to call the parents," Joan said. "I don't know what they'll do."

Or what should be done. Should something be done?

Joan wanted to punish someone, she realized. Was that the war sneaking in through a crack? Turning her from one kind of participant to another? Men made war and women and children suffered it. What if their suffering turned to cruelty to be served down the line until the smallest and most powerless took the brunt?

Behind her there was a noise. She turned her head to find Malcolm lighting up one of his stinking cigars.

"Barely a chance to sit down, let alone get a sketch," Malcolm said.

"All right," Joan said. "Bridey, take the child up and see to them all. I'll be up to help."

"I'll bring up something warm," Mrs. Scaldwell said.

Bridey quickly took her leave.

"What are we to think of all this?" Joan said. "Malcolm, put that out."

"Do you think the nurses are not up to the task?" Scaldwell said. "I would have thought *that* one could manage."

"That's the issue," Joan said. "I don't know. What should we do? But we can't mind ten children in this house without them both."

At the stove, Mrs. Scaldwell cleared her throat.

"Ah," her husband said.

"Yes, Mr. Scaldwell," Joan said. "You had something you wanted to say?" Announce, more like. He was the trumpeter making way for the queen.

"You might have noticed the mistress home," Scaldwell said. "As you came in."

Malcolm coughed into his hand. "Er, yes." He hadn't.

"Indeed," Joan said with effort. "It will be a pleasure to have her home."

"She's here to show the home to some potential buyers."

"Greenway? For sale?"

"It appears so."

"Well, why haven't we been offered the chance to buy it?" Malcolm said.

Mrs. Scaldwell laughed, once, like a dog's bark. Her husband's eyes shifted away, uncomfortable.

Joan would not have her husband a laughingstock in *their* company. "I'd rather think of days ahead when we return to our proper home, Malcolm," she said. "Wouldn't you? As *comfortable* as Mrs. Christie's home is, you understand."

Mrs. Scaldwell sucked her teeth.

"The acreage," Malcolm grumbled. "Could be a nice retreat for us when all this mess is over. We could come to terms, of course, Scarsdell. You staying on to wait at table and the like."

Now everyone in the room was angry and Joan knew Malcolm wasn't serious about buying the place. "The sale," Joan said, "is early days, I suppose? But if it *did* sell, what might that mean for us? For the children, I mean."

"Haven't the foggiest," Mr. Scaldwell said.

"But I mean — we rented for the year and it's only been six weeks. Where will we go?" Her dismay sounded like one of the gulls from the beach.

"You'll stay for now," Mrs. Scaldwell said, as though she herself granted the favor.

"Yes, of course you'll stay," Mr. Scaldwell said. "A sale will take some time. It might not happen at all, in fact, and you've rented the house in good faith."

Good faith sounded like words transferred directly from Mrs. Christie's mouth. Letters must have come and gone, buzzing with evidence against them. She had never been invited to take part, to have a say. Staying in this house, Joan felt that she, too, was one of the infants under care, always scuttled out of the room when the grown-ups needed to talk.

"Rented for a not-insubstantial amount of money, I might add," Malcolm said.

The Scaldwells stared at him, as though he'd spoken out of the mouth of a second head. As though they had ever had any *money.*

"This seems all rather sudden," Joan said.

"I should talk to Mrs. Christie myself."

"If Mrs. *Mallowan* wants to sell her house, I suppose she'll do it," Mr. Scaldwell said.

Was he enjoying himself?

"You'll be out of a home, too, I suspect," Malcolm said. "It's not so big a home to need a full-time staff. Not these days."

Mrs. Scaldwell's back was stiff at the hob, stirring broth.

"Malcolm," Joan said.

"It's a new world out there, my dove," he said. "And it's not you and I who need to learn it."

38
BRIDEY

In the nursery

Everyone had hot broth and a cool flannel, while Edward had a water bottle in his bed.

Bridget caught the fleeting scent of her brother in the boy's room and nearly gagged with grief. She set herself up at the boy's side and only knew the doctor had been called when he spoke from the door. "How's the patient, Sister?"

Bridey thought she might have cringed. Mrs. Arbuthnot had lost all confidence in them, then.

"Not as bad as all that," Dr. Hart said. "He looks a good color. Let me have a look?"

She should be grateful to turn the child over. Hart moved in, brought out his stethoscope, pressing it with gentleness to the boy's chest. He shone a small torch into Edward's eyes, left and right, but the boy only grimaced and slept on. "He seems to have weathered it. His lungs sound clear. You'll watch for signs of infection and notify me?"

"Of course."

Hart had turned to study her. She'd changed into dry clothes but her feet were bare and her skin windblown and tender.

Her hair wet against her neck.

"Has something else happened?" he said.

"Negligence," Bridey said. "Mine."

"I find that difficult to believe," he said. "You seem highly competent."

Any other time, such a compliment would have warmed her as well as sunlight, would have turned her toward him as though he were the sun itself, but he didn't know she spoke of mistakes that had happened long before their acquaintance.

"Have you ever had a reason . . ." she said. "I'm sorry. Impertinent."

"Have I ever had a reason to . . . ?"

"I don't think I've put a foot right since I arrived."

"A reason to doubt myself?" Hart said. He folded the stethoscope into his bag. "Quite often, and many times recently. Four good men who should have had years left have died in this county in the last six months. Disease of the heart, the liver, most likely — some ailments I couldn't name, even now. If I didn't know better —" He stopped and looked at her. "I know what they say about me."

Bridey lowered her eyes.

"Some of my patients have invisible wounds that will not heal. Like the farmer with the cut hand at the pub. Michaelsmith. I've been tending to him especially since — His son."

"I heard," she said. "The poor soul." But her words seemed hollow. *Were* hollow.

"Sleeping draughts and the like, though nothing seems to give him peace." Hart's attention drifted toward the sleeping child. "I can leave something for you, if you like."

She had not thought of the darkness of her room, how doubt would find her vulnerable there. "Thank you."

"Michaelsmith suffers as so many do," he said. "There is no cure for the anger and loneliness of loss. Many of the patients I see, the people I meet, suffer it, and it's all I can do to see it, acknowledge it."

She kept herself still. Had some word got back?

"All I can hope for," Hart said, "is that I can say I have done everything I could to ease suffering."

"I'm sure you have," she said.

"No, you don't understand," he said. "It's

internal work, and nothing you can say will save me. Do you see? As nothing I can say will save you."

She thought there were a few things he might say, anyway.

"This area is lovely but isolated, and they don't often get the best on offer. Of anything. They have no access to it. They can't afford it." He looked perturbed now. "But why shouldn't they have a good doctor?"

"They do," she said.

He blinked away. "Your confidence in me is . . . but do I doubt myself? Yes, and gladly. Someone who didn't doubt himself — would he try anything but the first remedy he thought of?"

"Are you saying your doubts make you . . . better? Sir?"

"Call me Oliver, if you like. Bridget, isn't it?"

"They call me Bridey here."

"Do you like being called Bridey?"

Not since it came from the mouth of her littlest sister.

"Not — no," she said.

"Then I'll call you Bridget, shall I?" Dr. Hart took a last look at Edward and packed in his case. "My doubts make me human. Would you want to be under the care of a physician with no doubt, no humility at all?

An automaton? A monster."

Bridey looked back at her feet.

"A person who doubts will pay the proper attention, will make the proper adjustments." He stood and set his bag on the chair to dig through it. Bridey remembered the thrill of assisting him, of dipping her hands into the store of implements and drawing out just what was needed. The delicate glass syringes, needles lined up in their leather pouch alongside the scissor-handled clips. Hadn't one of the clips been rather posh, with a spangle at the end? What would one use such an implement for?

But now he pulled out a stoppered vial and rattled the pills inside. He held it up, checked the bottom of the glass, and held it out to her. "One of these before bed tonight. Only one."

Bridey accepted the vial. They'd given these blue pills to soldiers with battle fatigue, and she didn't want them for herself. Suddenly she was thinking of Matron Bailey's warnings to her: her striving, her need for control and perfection. She had been warned, and still it had done her no good. Where had it got her? What had it almost cost them all? "How do you do it?"

"Hmm? Do what?"

"Learn to let doubt in."

"We question ourselves, understand what we do not know and learn from it," he said. "Operate, if you will, from the heart rather than the mind only. If we do all this, we may yet build a better version of ourselves. Worth a try, anyway."

"Worth a try," she agreed. But she was not a nurse, only someone with closed heart and fist, and she could not see that she deserved the chance.

Edward and Maureen's mum and granddad arrived late, rushing down from London in a borrowed motorcar and the old man cursing the Bronze Age roads. They would arrange a room at the inn at the Churston train station, wouldn't be talked into a night at Greenway. Apologies offered but not accepted. Mrs. Arbuthnot had her bring the sleeping children down one at a time then sent her to pack up their things. Bridey went quietly to avoid waking the rest, who had already required warmed milk and more comfort than usual. She had seen to the boys as well as the girls.

By midnight, the house was quiet. Diminished.

She should go to bed, put off taking the blue pill she shouldn't need. She should sleep in the girls' room and Gigi —

Gigi was not in their room. Bridey looked through the nursery rooms, then searched downstairs, listening to the stillness of the house, room after room of solitude and protection — just as she had the first night, before she had understood quite where they were and who kept them safe.

No one.

It was a thin thread that kept them tethered to the earth, a single strand of her embroidery floss, easily snapped. *No one keeps us.* They were all small lives, nowhere near the center. Tossed about by the gale of history and hardly noted for having endured.

The hall was dark, the kitchen. The house itself was in mourning for a child who had lived.

She searched the front of the house, the library, the dining room, all the places off limits to them. The kitchens, checked again. The larder, the pantry, even Mrs. Scaldwell's sitting room behind the scullery where they had never dared enter, through the old bakehouse with its dusty ovens. Bridey ripped open the back door. "Gi—"

Someone was smoking at the coal house walls, sitting on the crumbling last step that had once led to a terrace and the south walled garden. The same step on which

Nicky Thorne had waited one early morning.

"Who are you looking for?" It was a man's voice, and in a flash of understanding, she knew that he had come for them, whomever it was Gigi feared.

The wisht man was real.

"Bridey, who are you looking for?"

This time she recognized the voice. "Mr. Scaldwell, it's Gigi. Have you seen her?"

"She was having a walk."

"A walk?"

"She's off toward the road," he said.

"At this time of night?" Bridey stepped out to stare into the darkness toward the stables.

"It didn't seem to me a fine idea, but she's her own person."

"That she is." Gigi had brought the danger of her life into this house, when she might have walked away. They were supposed to *save* the children, not —

But hadn't she done the same?

No one else would save them. No one could.

"You shouldn't blame yourself," Scaldwell said.

"I don't." She pawed at her arms, rubbing them warm. The wind had been tamed.

"Ah." He looked toward the stables now,

too. Past the stables, the road to Galmpton. "That does make sense."

"What? What makes sense?"

"Midnight walk with nowhere to go. Makes sense, if your closest friend holds you responsible for such a thing."

"She's not my closest friend." She hadn't any friends, close or otherwise. Tommy Kent came to mind, unbidden.

"You might be hers," Scaldwell said.

"I am not." She would go to Willa, wouldn't she? That was it. Gigi would search out Willa in Kingswear.

"If I'm honest," Scaldwell said, "I've always considered the two of you one person."

She wasn't the only arrogant one, was she? "And the children all one baby with its mouth open and its fists pulling down the china?"

"That's Arbuthnot you're thinking of. I like children."

She couldn't even say the same.

"Vera had a stranger in the house while you lot were at the beach."

"Dear God," she said. The bootprint at the back door the morning the foxes screamed — someone really had been in snatching jams.

"She'd the door locked, thank Christ."

The man from London, unnamed, unseen? "What did he look like?" Bridey said.

"You know who it is? I'll wring his neck for scaring my wife."

"I don't know who it could be." She looked down the road. They should all be in bed, not stalking the moors.

Later, on the stairs, she realized — *wring his neck.*

She went to check the children again, and in the girls' room stood in the window next to Doreen's cot. It was just possible to see the opening in the wall where the butler took his cigarette.

Couldn't Scaldwell be the man Doreen had seen? He was rather the most likely to be skulking in the woods at odd hours. His patrols gave him the freedom to stalk the grounds for any reason, and no one to question him.

She had always thought Scaldwell a fussy man, someone speaking with standing he hadn't earned, but trustworthy at least — but who could know? Who could sort it out? She was exhausted.

In their room, Gigi's bed was empty, still unmade from the previous night. Bridey checked the chest of drawers for her clothes, the cupboard for her dressing case. Her cloak still hung on its peg, its hem still stuffed with money.

She would be back for it. She would be back, and they could come to some kind of understanding.

Bridey opened her own drawer, took out her kit, with bandages and the few tools she had managed to put together. She'd secreted the blue pills in their vial there and now took them out for a look. Hart had given her four, perhaps because that was how many the vial still held, perhaps four nights' rest was the prescription, or the upper limit. She didn't know — she hadn't learned enough.

She saw herself on Greenway Road, hands and knees, and put the pills away. She couldn't afford doubt just now, nor oblivion.

39
BRIDEY

Middle of the night, the boys' room

Bridey woke curled in Edward's cot to shouting in the corridor.

They had 'planes overhead, low, close. Bridey sat up, tore away her coverings, and hurried the boys out. Mrs. Arbuthnot had one of the infants, was trying to manage both. "Where were you?" she wailed.

Downstairs they put out blankets like a picnic but no one was fooled. An explosion went off so close the china rattled in the cabinets in the next room and pictures in the entrance hall popped off the wall. Behind the shutters, the windows shook in their frames.

"That's Dittisham, that is," Mr. Scaldwell said, looking out. *Dits'm.* The loops of his braces dangled from the trousers he'd pulled on over his nightclothes. "Why bother with Dittisham?"

Their ears rang with another explosion,

very near, and the children whimpered and clung. "Better than they bother with us," his wife said.

The Arbuthnots in their worn robes and drawn expressions seemed like ancients wrung empty of wise advice. Bridey was keenly aware of Maureen and Edward gone.

"Nurse Bridey," whispered Pamela. "Where's Nurse Gigi?"

"She'll be back," she said. But she wasn't sure.

"Is that —" Scaldwell at the window. "I think some blighter's out on the estate in this. Well, he's welcome to it, tonight."

After the skies quieted and they had the all-clear, Bridey and Mrs. Arbuthnot led the parade of sleepy-eyed under-fives dragging blankets and soft toys. Behind them, Mr. Scaldwell placed the portraits back on the wall, picked up a knocked-over walking stick.

Bridey fell into her bed in the early hours of dawn but dreamed the walls came in and smoke filled her lungs.

By morning, Bridey's confidence that Gigi would return had cracked.

"We had a dead man at the quay not so long ago," she appealed to Mrs. Arbuthnot as they saw the children through their morning rituals. "Mrs. Scaldwell says there was a stranger in the house —"

"These women and their folk stories, scaring themselves and each other." Mrs. Arbuthnot, in a borrowed pinafore, was soaked through.

"*I*'m worried."

"Give her until midday," Mrs. Arbuthnot said.

"And then what, missus?"

"We'll have to ring the police, I suppose." She smoothed her hair back, caught sight of Bridey in the mirror. "Bridey, good Lord. Are you well?"

She'd imagined throwing herself at the mercy of the local bobbies for the death of the soldier. "I'm sorry, missus —"

"I'll see to the children, if you would like to lie down," Mrs. Arbuthnot said. She looked around at the children eating their porridge at the plank table. "Only eight," she said. "Seems nearly manageable."

And this, also her fault. Bridey swept down the hall to be sick.

Willa. Willa was the most likely person to know where Gigi had gone, but then she didn't know Willa's last name or where she lodged in Kingswear.

She righted herself and went down to the kitchen. The Scaldwells had not seen Gigi.

The butler sipped his tea, looking at her over the rim in a way she didn't like.

Bridey went out to the drive and hurried around the corner of the stone wall toward the gardener's yard. The round-topped door in the wall stood open. She had never seen inside.

"Mr. Hannaford?"

He ducked out of the low-roofed bothy where his tools must be kept, wiping hands on a rag. They had no relationship to speak of, only he had been party to the catastrophe at the beach and the damp, sniffling ride home.

"You haven't seen Gigi, have you? The other nurse?"

"Can't say I have. Is there trouble?"

"I need a favor I have no right to ask," she said.

He was only happy to put off his work. Mr. Hannaford checked with Mrs. Scaldwell about other errands in the village, and at the gate, he touched the horn twice until his wife came out. Mrs. Hannaford looked past him to Bridey and shook her head.

On the road, they had time to chat, but didn't. Bridey cleared her throat a time or two before Hannaford asked her how she liked staying at Greenway.

366

"The grounds are especially lovely," she said.

"They're a bear to keep," he said, but pridefully. "Bit of an escape from city living for your lot."

If one wanted an escape. "And the house is quite beautiful."

"All right for some. Our cottage is as tidy as a pin and as small, but it's enough. How old are you?"

"Twenty," she said, from surprise more than anything else. "Sir."

"My son's a bit older," he said, gazing across the fields. "It's not a bit lucky to be his age now, or yours."

"But especially his."

"Aye," he said.

In the village, he set her down at the train station at Churston. "You don't need me to wait for you?"

"I can make my own way back." It was the Manor Inn she wanted but it was best to start from a spot that wouldn't start up rumors back on the estate.

The Churston stationmaster hadn't seen Gigi, he said. Or Willa, when Bridey described her, carefully.

She climbed the incline and walked the bridge over the tracks, pausing at the top to watch a train puff its way toward her.

There was a train to Kingswear, wasn't there? She walked toward Galmpton, calculating how it might be done.

At the Manor Inn, the front room was dull. The man with the stitched-up hand sat with his head down in the corner. His linen bandage was only a week old but filthy, dark with grime or blood. Others murmured quietly in their pairs or groups, even as they looked up to watch her pass. Sunday best, black hats and bands. But it was not Sunday.

"Is it church?" she said when the barman — Dodge, wasn't it? — didn't hurry to ask her business.

"Funeral for another man not yet fifty."

"Another one?" The poor doctor. "Who was he?"

"Albert Kendrick. I'd say you couldn't know him, but he was in here spending the money he earned taking a load of 'vacs to Greenway House, so there you are."

"The cart driver?"

"That weren't his job, miss. He was after doing you a favor." Dodge wiped a rag across the bar listlessly. "He was that sort."

"I'm sorry for you. He seemed in the spit of health to me."

"He was, miss —" He seemed to want to say more. "You're a nurse, they say."

Bridey fought back the matron's voice in

her head. "Yes."

"They say — they say the doctor doesn't know what he's about, miss. All these friends of ours, that's the result."

People who took no care of themselves always assumed that medicine will fix them up, that the human machine couldn't simply break down. "I rather think it was something within himself, sir. Disease can be swift, invisible."

"Aye, but," Dodge said, not comforted or convinced. "This weren't invisible, miss. He had bruising. Fell and hit a rock, they say, but his neck —"

"Bruises?"

The barman, misty-eyed, straightened up, cleared his throat. "What will you have, then? To the memory of Bertie Kendrick."

She hadn't meant to have a drink, but ordered a half-pint to raise. Then she asked after Gigi.

"Your woman from last time?" Dodge said, glancing over her shoulder at the sleeping man in the corner. "She's missing still? Or again?"

"Actually, no." The day they'd sought Mrs. Poole seemed distant rather than a matter of only days. "I mean another dark-haired woman. She's —" How to describe Gigi? "She's comely, striking. Difficult to miss." If he remembered *her,* he would certainly remember Gigi.

"They do a lot of running off from that house," he said. "Must have got the notion from the mistress of the manor. I don't think she's your one, but there's a pair at t' other side."

40
BRIDEY

They were tucked up against the inside wall in the next room, out of sight.

Willa stood at the sight of her. "Where is she?"

"I thought you would know," Bridey said, coming across the room until Willa's companion stood. "You," she said.

"Do we know each other?" he said. It was the other fellow from the train, the one with the sour expression who had stood by as she administered to Thorne's dead body on the quay.

"Bridget Kelly," she said.

He frowned at Willa. "Wasn't that the name that —"

"Yes."

"Is it not her name?" She'd had to be called a baby name that broke her heart while another woman claimed her true name and twisted it into something ridiculous? What else was there to learn? "She's pretending to be a nurse, pretending to be someone she isn't, listening in on —"

"Yes, all right." Willa grasped her arm and pulled her toward an empty seat at their table. A deck of playing cards was arrayed there, some kind of game. "You're smarter than the last time we met."

"Is she in danger?"

"We were pursued here," said the man, "so I would say so. Or did she not speak of the trouble we dragged down from London?"

"I thought *you* might be the trouble she dragged down from London," Bridey said. "If I'm honest."

"I know I look it," he said. "I can't help it. Henry Kenworthy-Jenkins."

She shook his offered hand. "Is that *your* real name?"

His expression reformed into something like mirth. "I wouldn't carry it otherwise. Far too heavy. This lot call me Jenks."

She set down her glass. "Where can she have gone?"

"She was supposed to meet us last night but she never showed," Willa said.

Midnight at the boathouse. Bridey was glad she hadn't tried to keep the meeting, with bombs falling in Dittisham and Scaldwell at the window.

"Our butler said he saw someone —"

"*Butler!*" Jenks said. "She got herself a soft place to land, then. You should see the squat I'm in."

"He also said," Bridey went on, "that Gigi walked away from the house on her own. But she never came back."

Willa swept up the cards and shuffled them. Jenks watched the cards with a sheen of sweat on his lip. "This is bad," he said.

"Gigi tried to tell me the story," Bridey said. "But she was trying to spare me details — or hide how dangerous she was to the rest of us."

"The story," Willa scoffed.

"You tell me," Bridey said to Jenks.

"You know about Mass-Ob? Yes? How Gigi picked out a pattern centering around this pub we used to meet in? Accident of the trade," he said. "She picked up the real business of the place."

"And the real business, exactly?"

Willa sighed and laid out the cards in a solitary game.

"Black market, to start," Jenks said. "Then, well, it picks up weight and momentum. The more deals you do, the more people know, the more word gets 'round. It's a tough business to stay in, crime, without seeing the chance for — how do you say it? In business, like?"

"Expansion?" Willa said.

"Exactly. No stagnation for this fellow." Jenks sat back with a cigarette. "He expands his services, puts some unseemly people on the payroll to build and protect his empire — but a booming business is difficult to keep quiet. The wrong sorts hanging on, getting greedy, and everyone liking their drink so much." He looked at her. "People died. Anyway, somehow we weren't discreet enough, or perhaps we met there too often. Then the tables turn, and the Friar —"

"The Friar?"

"The pub's the Friar's Poison —"

Bridey winced. If she hadn't called Gigi poison, none of this would have happened.

"After the bloke in *Romeo and Juliet,*" Jenks said.

"He's a meddler," Willa said. "If he'd only stayed out of it —"

Jenks said, "He was trying to stop a feud, wasn't he?"

"By killing off both Romeo *and* Juliet," Willa said.

"No. No. Juliet killed *herself,*" he said. "Anyway. Ah. So we've just been calling the owner the Friar. His name is Clement but he's nearly beside the point, see, because we don't see him, we don't hear from him.

Instead he used our tricks against us, had his people whispering in the pubs and streets that we were — that we were anything he could think of. And he had an eye for Gigi. You can imagine what kind I mean."

Bridey glanced at Willa, who kept herself busy slapping down cards.

"And they believed it all? The people who heard the rumors, I mean."

"Some of it was easy to believe," he said.

"Or absolutely true," Willa said.

"Well," Jenks said. "People don't mind a rumor either, not when it fits the shape of the anger they already have and can't find a place for. They're barely hanging on, and here's a group of degenerates — they used other words — doing just fine for themselves. The same all over." Jenks had forgotten the unlit cigarette in his hand.

"I had convinced myself that the man didn't exist," Bridey said. *Gigi's* wisht man. "That he was a story."

"He's real enough," Willa said.

"And I'll tell you now — there's not a thing to do about him," Jenks said. "Men like that one don't topple, and if they do, the next one's waiting to take his place. But he's set someone on us, hasn't he?"

"It'll be a lieutenant," said a man's voice.

Bridey turned, stared. "Not you, too." It was her hero from the train, the veteran home early with a hitch in his walk and his simple, homespun walking stick, like a limb only recently fallen from a tree.

He laughed. "Sorry for the misdirection, but we do try to keep things to ourselves, especially in transitional times. Llewelyn Nevins, Nurse Kelly. Call me Lew."

"We could have taken separate trains," Willa said.

"It didn't seem necessary," he said sadly. "I still wonder if we're shuffling two decks together." Willa looked up. "Thorne might have only got into a tussle with someone here that night, nothing to do with Mass-Ob at all."

"The local men are rather restless," Bridey said.

"Someone here?" Jenks remembered the cigarette and reached for a match. "He's the one we thought they'd like. Good-looking chap, amiable —"

"Wealthy, though," Bridey said, thinking of the reverence, sometimes bitter, sometimes protective, of the *mistress,* the manor house. Fine for some. "They have a complicated relationship to wealth."

"*He* wasn't rich," Jenks said.

"Where did you get the idea that he was?"

Lew said. "Was he waving cash around?"

"No," Bridey said. "I'm not sure why I thought Thorne was wealthy."

"Only —" Lew started.

"What?" Jenks said.

"I don't want to start a story," Lew said. "But some have it that the Friar lost a lot of money recently. I wonder if it could be why he's so set on vengeance."

"Gigi doesn't need money enough to steal it," Willa said.

"There's always greed," Lew said. "And a love of nice things, now she's cut off from Daddy and Mum."

Bridey looked away, thinking of the luxury among Gigi's things, the pound notes stitched into her cloak. But was it fair that Gigi could be picked apart, weighed and balanced from all angles, when she couldn't speak for herself?

She didn't mention that Gigi had left all those nice things behind. It was more evidence that she would come back, or it was more evidence against it — she couldn't decide.

"Well, Thorne had not two farthings to rub together," Jenks said, striking the match. "At least it seemed that way to me. Enough to stand a round of drinks, maybe. He wore cast-offs from my closet." He started to laugh but swallowed it, painfully. The match went out in his hand, and he put it and the cigarette into the ashtray. "I should have taken him 'round to my tailor."

Bridey glanced at Willa. "Jenks is the one to the manor born," Willa said.

"Lot of good it's done us," Jenks said. "If I had the inheritance now, we should all be hiding in the family hall instead of here."

"Hiding?" Bridey said. "That's the objective? I thought you were listening for —"

"Hush," Willa said. "Listening means you have to know when to stop talking."

Bridey stared at the cards in front of Willa, but there was no pattern to the game she could see. Was even the game of solitaire a deception? "But what is there to do?"

"Do?" Jenks said.

"You can't hide for the rest of your life," Bridey said. She looked from one to the other. "Can you? That can't be the goal. Gigi can't hide for the rest of her life."

"What if she has to?" Lew said. "Where might she go?"

"For one thing," Jenks said, "she's no good at it, is she? Hiding inside that pretty face."

"Well," Willa said, picking up Jenks's cigarette and a new match, lighting it in one go. "She's better at hiding than we thought. Where is she?"

41
BRIDEY

Manor Inn

Willa and Jenks said they would scour the
town. Lew had use of a car, he said, and
promised to make a few inquiries in Paignton. Bridey would go back to Greenway.
"Perhaps she's come back already," she
heard herself say, and recognized Mrs. Arbuthnot's hope from the day they'd
searched for Mrs. Poole.

Bridey sat at the table after the others had
gone, her half-pint still half full. She could
see out the window into the street, where
life went on.

They had *two* missing women. That was
something she hadn't considered until the
barman Dodge had pointed it out. Two
missing women, one dead man. A dark
syndicate — was that the right word? —
bearing down on the team of observers,
perhaps someone sent to report back on
them or the Friar himself here to do them

380

harm. All of it happening at ground level while the war raged on, barrage balloons flying overhead and, if she listened, enemy 'planes.

There was a shuffle of feet in the room behind her. The man with the cut hand stood in the door, loose in the knees. He hadn't dressed for mourning.

"You jabbed me with a ruddy needle," he said.

He took a chair against the stone wall of the hearth.

"You were more relaxed for it, sir," she said. He had set himself between her and the door. "How is your hand? You should have the stitches pulled out in a few days' time but the wrappings could do with a freshening."

"I'm not letting that sawbones anywhere near me. Highway robbery," he muttered at the floorboards. "He takes his fee one way or t' other, I'll tell you that. And still I've not a wink of sleep, for all his potions and poisons."

He'd only just been sleeping in the pub. "Insomnia," she said. "It's a natural side effect."

"What would you know about what ails me?"

Michaelsmith, that was his name.

"Grief, sir. Trauma. Exhaustion. Battle fatigue, even at the home front. Sleep is the first loss, then we're weary for it, less able to fight off other symptoms. Like despair."

He made a noise in his throat. "Stand a despairing man a drink, will you?"

"Lydell," came the voice of the barman. "Don't make us send you home."

"We're only about having a chat," Michaelsmith said. "Could you stand us a pint, Dodge? You know —"

"Not hardly," said the voice.

"The drink might be the problem, sir, if you'll forgive me," Bridey said. "It's known to unsettle a man's sleep."

Michaelsmith rubbed at his eye with the heel of his good hand. "Maybe I like my sleep unsettled."

"Does your boy come to you in dreams?"

He glared. "Dreams! Nothing so soft as that, my lover. He don't come for tea, does he? His ghost don't come 'round for a *pint,*" he spat. "No, he's garroted and stabbed, shot up, shot down, blown to bits. He dies a thousand deaths a night, and any one of them might be the right one. I'll never know. They've no body for me to bury."

Bridey felt the familiar pressure in her ribs, the hardness inside her pressing outward for escape. *Blown to bits.*

Michaelsmith said, "I heard a man tell how he dug up one of them garden shelters after a blast and found the family — man, woman, children, all — sitting pretty as you like under the rubble, not a mark." He wiped his mouth with the back of his hand and glanced longingly toward the bar. "What is that? What kind of death? I don't know which is worse. Knowing. Or imagining."

Until now she had always presumed to have lived the worst of it. Knowing what had happened to her mam, knowing too well what her siblings had been reduced to, had seemed the worst punishment the war might exact. "Knowing is terrible," she said. "Knowing means you have a picture in your head you wouldn't wish on an enemy. To keep it out, you have to play games with yourself —"

"Games," he scoffed.

"To keep yourself from thinking on it always. You harden yourself to keep it sneaking in when you least expect it. You swallow it whole before it consumes you. And then it lives inside, where no one else knows how it sickens you, how it grows roots in your stomach and branches like a tree up your throat until you're choked."

Michaelsmith wiped at his mouth again.

"Imagining might be worse but I wouldn't know," Bridey said. Her beer was warm. She pushed it away. "You can always imagine something worse than what might have happened. Have you tried imagining something better?"

"An easier death? Should I imagine him ninety-five, going at old age?"

"If you like. Were you at the funeral today?"

Michaelsmith blinked away from her. "I've had enough of mourning."

"I only mean that you might imagine the worst," she said, "or you might imagine that — say his fellows cared for him, talked to him gently and held his hand, said a few words of last rites. They say a man dies with his memories rushing through his mind, like a picture show." Something caught in her throat. None of her dead had ever been to a picture show or, in some cases, had many memories at all. "He might have thought of this place. He might have had a pint with you."

"He wouldn't have thought of this place." But Michaelsmith had grown contemplative. "He wouldn't think of me — only his mam. We lost her when he was a boy."

"My condolences."

His eyes were black and shining in his

face. "Are you sure you won't stand me a pint?"

She didn't think he meant it. It was only a thing to say. A safe thing. "I might have enough for a cup of tea."

"Bah," he said. "Never mind."

"Or I can stand you some new wrappings for your hand, if you show me to Dr. Hart's surgery. There's blood there," she said accusingly. "Your stitches haven't pulled, have they? What have you been doing —"

"Butchering," he growled. "A man has to feed himself."

But he stood when she came near, and they left together, Dodge watching with a squint.

42
BRIDEY

The high street
They made an unlikely pair, perhaps, for the children playing in the schoolyard stopped to stare and the woman pegging out her wash, who had seen them, surely, would not turn her head or say good morning.

"This is the way to Dr. Hart's surgery?" Bridey said loudly. Answering questions that hadn't been asked.

"I told you it was," Michaelsmith said.

Close up, the man had a rank, salty stench to him. Meaty. Bridey glanced at the man's wrappings as his arm swung. "What sort of livestock do you have?"

"Eh?"

"The butchering you were doing."

"No livestock to speak of. I have wheat and hay, and a patch just for my own table," he said. "This were fox."

She must have flinched.

"They're vermin, same as a rat," he said. "Doing Herself a favor, stalking her wood."

"Herself? Are you saying you hunt on the mistress's land?"

"The *mistress*. Oh, aye, writes lies and claims title," he said. "I'm not saying a thing — only they've thirty acres and don't bloody live there, do they? And would they make sport, even if they did live there year 'round?"

The image of Michaelsmith dragging the hides of foxes by their tails through the misty woods of a morning gave her a sour taste at the back of her throat. *Sport.* Bridey heard it in the creaking voice of Mrs. Scaldwell. And here, finally, was the wisht man from Doreen's window, flesh, bone, blood.

Michaelsmith turned off the high street up a narrow lane and gestured at the house that had emerged from behind tall hedges. A standard sort with timbers, old, or made to look it. In hard times, perhaps it was too bold, too well cared for when bombs were dropping, the paint fresh, everything trim and pretty. *Was* there a wife? A small sign near a side door announced where patients might enter.

Inside there was a small antechamber, close quarters. The door snapped behind

them and Michaelsmith's fetid scent filled
the room. Should she tell a grown man to
bathe? He'd have an infection in that hand.

"Hart," Michaelsmith barked toward the
open door. "I've come to see your summer
home paid for."

Hart soon appeared with a serviette
tucked into his neck to cover his tie. "Michaelsmith, I'm afraid — oh, hello, Bridget."
He pulled the serviette out. "You caught me
at table, but come in." He made a face.
"Lydell, we talked of hygiene. It's essential
if we're to have your wounds healed."

"I wondered if we might bother you for a
new dressing for his hand," Bridey said.

"Lydell, did you hire a personal nurse?"

Michaelsmith glanced toward the door
with regret.

"Come through," Hart said.

It was a simple room with a hard chair for
the patient and a screen blocking most of
the view of an observation bed at the back.

Michaelsmith sat in the chair. "I'll not
submit to this with a woman in the room."

"She's a nurse, Lydell, and presided over
the original surgery. You might not remember."

"He remembers," Bridey said. "Shall I
wait in the vestibule?"

"Lord, save us. Lydell, you wait here."

Dr. Hart showed Bridey through the next door to a rather cramped clinical space, a sink and a metal table but nowhere to rest. "It will be more comfortable for you to wait just through here," he said, leading her through to yet another door. "Help yourself to the teapot if you like."

She found herself ushered and abandoned inside the man's home, standing in a simple kitchen with a table and two chairs, and a tall cabinet crowding in. On the table sat the remnants of Hart's midday meal, a few bites of veg and a lamb shank picked clean.

Bridey sat down but the look of the gnawed bone unsettled her. The teapot was cold.

She stood and looked in on the scullery, the greasy pan still in the sink, then moved on to the next room, a dining room with a draped table and the doctor's bag as centerpiece. The next room was a sitting room focused around an elaborately designed fireplace. She sat in the second-best chair, at its edge, and imagined the room cozy with a fire in colder months. Oliver — she was supposed to be calling him Oliver, wasn't she? — reading a newspaper like the one resting on the other chair now. The wireless set would give the latest news or the gramophone would turn — opera or orchestra. Vera Lynn singing as Bridey dusted the bookshelves.

It was a pretty picture, her life folded so easily into his. His life, his work, his home.

She stood and went back to the dining room, took out the chair at the center, and resettled. Less comfortable, obviously, but proper.

Bridey waited, nothing to keep her attention but the décor, which here was sparse and suited a bachelor. The sideboard held a few pieces of good china and a dish in an iridescent blue that caught her eye. But she had chosen the room for its lack of personal effect and now suffered it.

At her shoulder sat the doctor's bag.

She would have liked to have another look at the contents, but that was rather sneaking — she might as well take herself up to the bedroom and riffle through cupboards. Tuck herself into his bed.

Bridey blinked away the image that came to her and went to the sideboard to admire the blue dish. It was an unusual piece given how staid the rest of the house was kept. An heirloom, perhaps, a family piece. She took it down, gently. It held bits and bobs, but these were the sorts of things that gave a glimpse in, didn't they? What someone gave pride of place to, or couldn't toss out? The dish held a pocket watch forgotten and unwound, a few penny nails and a pair of cuff links, a silver tie clip, an old key or two, a striking man's ring with a black square of stone, a pipe — surely he didn't take tobacco? Things better sorted into a valet in his bedroom.

She needed to stop thinking of his bedroom.

She withdrew from the kitchen just as a telephone began to ring somewhere along toward the surgery. She heard Hart's voice calling out, muffled, and went to open one of the doors between them. "Yes, Oliver?"

Blushing. That's what she deserved for letting a daydream squeak through.

"Could you get that? Just finishing up."

The phone jangled loudly from the corner of the clinical room. "Hello, Dr. Oliver Hart's office."

"Put the doctor on," said a man's voice.

"He's unavailable —"

"An emergency, this is, and police are already called." She knew the voice. "Is this Mr. Arbuthnot?" she said.

"Who is this?"

"It's Bridget, Mr. Arbuthnot. Bridey."

He said nothing.

"The nurse? Hired by your wife?"

"Where have you been, girl? Joan's worried herself distracted over you. She's just run across someone on the grounds and fell down the blasted hill — only broken her arm."

It would be Gigi that had her worried and he was mixing them up. She didn't have to ask. "I'll tell the doctor. We'll be on our way."

43
BRIDEY

In the observation room, Michaelsmith stood remade, clean hair and a new shirt, a bit too tight for him. A washed neck, too, and a better smell. In his fresh bandages, he walked to the door and helped himself to the outside.

"Lydell, go home and see to your fields," Hart called after him.

"Is he going back to the pub?"

"I imagine so. Alcoholism — well, I'm sure you've seen your share of it."

She'd seen it most closely in her own da.

"Enough to last a lifetime."

"Lydell said you offered to pay for his services?"

"Oh, I am sorry," Bridey said. "I'll see to it right away if you give me the cost."

"No, no. Let's share today's efforts as our alms work, shall we? Your guidance to get him in before gangrene set in, a bit of my time and an old shirt. I only wondered why you made the bargain." He glanced down at her hands. "My bag?"

"The telephone call was from Greenway," she said, handing it over. "Mrs. Arbuthnot might have a broken arm."

He moved quickly, gathering supplies, and led her down to the street and his motorcar, parked in the lane. He held the door for her. "What do you think of it?"

The car, he meant. "Sporting. Is it new?"

"As new as one can have just now," he said. "I'd have had an easier time getting my hands on a tank."

They drove the first mile in silence. Bridey kept an eye out for Gigi.

"It was the right thing to do," she said.

"Eh?"

"Bringing that wretched man to see you," she said. "It was the right thing. That's why I did it."

"I thought maybe you wanted to speak to me."

Bridey was grateful for the control she had cultivated, not to give herself away. "I do enjoy our conversations. To talk with I really only have Gigi." She turned to the window.

"Did I hear your friend has gone away?"

"How did you hear it, if you don't mind my asking?"

"Whispers at the funeral this morning,"

he said. "Some from the estate were there."

Many campaigns, it seemed to her, were convened in whispers. "Which from the estate?"

He glanced at her. "Farmhand from one of the estate tenancies and his wife. The . . . Bastins, I think?"

"Did they say she'd been at the ferry?" Again she'd gone to the village when she might have checked at the quayside first.

"I didn't hear details."

"I'm hoping she'll see sense," Bridey said. "Before it's too late for the Arbuthnots to forgive her. It's also rather a lot of work for one nurse. I *can* do it but . . ."

"I'm sure you can. Or someone with your skills could be useful to a hospital now," he said. "A Red Cross infirmary, a St. John's detachment."

"Or in private practice," she said.

"Difficult times to find the wage," he said. "At least down here. Many of my patients pay me in parcels of mutton. You saw my dinner plate? Delivered the man's child. I'll have lamb three meals a day until it spoils."

Bridey pictured the mean, buff-colored ration books that ruled every ounce they ate. "Things needn't be so . . . professional," Bridey said. "There are arrangements that might forgo a wage, if you had need of a nurse."

Hart was smiling out at the fields. "Bridget, are you proposing to me?"

"Well," she started, sure her face was in flames. But as soon as she allowed the shame in, she was sick, doubled over.

"Are you all right?" Hart glanced between her and the road. "Shall I stop?"

"No, hurry on. I'm all right. There's Mrs. Arbuthnot to see to."

"I should have a look at you, as well. Where's the pain?"

"I'm only nauseated a bit, nothing serious. See?" She sat up as well as she could. "I'm quite all right."

The gates to Greenway stood open.

"Acute pain shouldn't be ignored," he said as they drove the lane toward the house. "What if it's your appendix?"

"It's not my appendix."

"Have you eaten? Have you —"

"It's all in my head, Dr. Hart." One true thing that would ruin it all, but she could see now that no arrangement could be made. He was too handsome a man to settle for a nurse rather than adoration. She would have to get back to the original plan — if she was allowed to. "Nothing to trouble yourself about."

"Psychosomatic? What are the triggers?"

"Please, sir."

They rounded the curve to find a police motorcar parked ahead.

Hart braked hard, the wheels sliding in the gravel. The motor died. "Why are the police here?"

She'd forgotten the police had been summoned and was having her own reaction. "Someone on the grounds, he said," Bridey said. "Or because Gigi is missing. Or found."

He turned his head. "Found would be ideal — but you don't mean . . ."

"We had a murdered man on the quay," she said. "She could be dead."

Hart put in the brake. "Isn't she your friend? How can you utter the words as though it matters not a whit to you?"

"Because if I allow myself to have the slightest emotion, you will think my appendix is bursting." But in saying so, she had made the allowance and couldn't stop the knife in her stomach or her reaction. "I'm going to be sick."

He opened his door and came around to hers, released her. She turned in the seat and leaned out, choking and crying. Hart knelt and produced a handkerchief. She wouldn't take it, wiped at her nose with the cuff of her blouse.

"No emotion at all?" he said.

"I'm not a specimen for study."

"You're an interesting case, whether you like it or not," he said, glancing toward the police vehicle. "Are you not able to experience even happiness? Thrill? What are you left with?"

"I don't deserve happiness. Or thrill."

"Deserve?"

"I shouldn't be alive, so how much does it matter if I'm not, even still on my feet?"

"I think it matters a good deal," he said. "Making it through this madness should make survival sweeter, not its opposite. Life should be lived to its fullest. What would you have said to Michaelsmith if he'd said such a thing? That he shouldn't be alive?"

"I am not Michaelsmith."

Hart's look roved over her face. "Everyone deserves happiness, Bridget. And thrill." And then he leaned in and reached a hand toward her, held the back of her head, a finger grazing, soft, against her neck. She was too surprised to know what was happening and then his lips were pressed to hers. Her eyes were still open, and his, too. He pulled back, studied her. The finger against her neck distracted her greatly. He pulled her up out of the car to her feet and wrapped her in an embrace, startling and strong, the scratch of his chin against her cheek something she hadn't imagined. This kiss was less tender and could have been exciting —

He pulled back. "No thrill at all?"

— if it were not so diagnostic. "Not if you want me to keep my guts."

"You're a fascinating girl, Bridget."

"Girl!" she shrugged out of his arms.

"I believe you're half my age, and this afternoon makes me a cad I would only warn you about."

Bridey smoothed the front of her dress. If someone was watching from the house . . . "I don't need your warnings. I look out for myself."

"That, I do not doubt. I am not in the market for a surgery nurse or a young wife who couldn't love me. I'm sorry."

"It's not that I couldn't," she said. "Only that I don't want to try."

"And why is that?" he said. "I'm not what they say I am in the village."

"No, of course — it's only that loving someone opens one up to . . . risk. I don't think I can risk anything else. I won't survive it."

"All love opens us up to loss."

"I agree," she said. He had never been told

he wasn't worth the risk before. He would have traded love for its showy cousin, worship, she was sure. But she hadn't the spirit for that, either. "Let's go see to Mrs. Arbuthnot, poor woman."

The corridor was dim, the house quiet. "Hello?" Bridey called.

Mrs. Scaldwell came out of her sitting room. "At last. She's upstairs in their room, Doctor," she said, a queer expression to her. "Bridey, the police are up front. They'll want to talk to you."

Bridey stood absolutely still. "About —"

"Gigi," she said. "She's not back yet."

But this was good news in its way, not to be delivered another body.

"I'll assist the doctor first. Someone has the children?"

"Mrs. Bastin and one of the Jackson girls are with them."

Upstairs, Bridey knocked at the door to the Arbuthnots' apartment.

Mr. Arbuthnot opened. "Yes, yes, come in. She's waited long enough."

Mrs. Arbuthnot lay fully clothed, shoes dangling over the foot of the bed. In repose she was ten years older, awkwardly settled with her arm on a pillow.

"Isn't there something more comfortable for you to wear, Mrs. Arbuthnot?" Bridey

400

said. "A nightdress, perhaps? Is it here?" She reached for the cupboard nearest her.

"Not *there*," her husband exclaimed rather more harshly than warranted. "I'll see to it. Don't you have something for her pain?"

Hart nodded and Bridey reached for his bag. In the front pouch, the leather wallet wasn't in evidence, but a thick gold chain lay loose below the bandages he'd stuffed in. She opened the back pouch, found her quarry, and laid out the wallet of syringes, scissors, and clips, chose the slightest syringe, and went to have it rinsed in the kettle water. She used the family stairs, front of the house, and heard voices talking in the morning room. The police, she supposed, and was so exhausted by her deceptions and omissions, she thought of walking into the room and putting out her wrists for shackles. The dead soldier at St. Prisca's deserved as much. Was she not a murderer, in her own way? A poisoner, even if only in error?

She wouldn't, but the thought did occur.

When she arrived back to the room, a bit breathless from the stairs, Mrs. Arbuthnot was still in her dress and shoes, but sitting up. "My corset, Bridey," she whispered. "Could you . . ."

Mr. Arbuthnot cleared his throat, and

401

Hart stepped back from the bed.

As soon as the woman had the morphine — Bridey checked the vial three times — she would usher these helpless men out and get her employer settled softly. This was the thrill, not of being adored, of being loved, but of being needed.

44
SCALDWELL

Greenway grounds

Frank stalked the grounds: the walled gardens, the greenhouse, the top path along to the summerhouse. Across the property and through the stations of the cross, hail to his mistress, his feet carried him by rote. He wouldn't find the nurse, of course, but he could avoid the doctor, at least.

"They were," Vera had said as he went. "I tell you he was snogging her. The least passionate kiss I ever saw, but snogging indeed."

It was none of his business, though it made him think. Bridey was as young as his own daughter, and Hart old enough not to end up a medic in Belgium.

Frank had been thinking a great deal about which men had gone to war and which had not and what they were saying in town about God's own punishment for the ones left to face their neighbors, whose sons hadn't gone, who might have gone themselves if the conscription ages had been lowered even a few years. Heart trouble and the like for men who had been as fit as bulls, or had seemed it. Trouble inside, nothing you could see.

It gave a man pause. And now Kendrick dead as well.

Elsie Bastin had come back from the funeral that day full of talk from the village, and she had surely doled out whatever passed for news coming from Greenway. The nurse leaving in the night and all. The house for sale with no offers to buy. Probably his fault for thinking anything in the letters the mistress sent with her directives for the estate could be kept to the house. They had always felt left out down here, outpost at the end of the empire, hungry for what could be had from the outside.

And now they had its opposite. Strangers in the village, the townspeople getting their backs up.

"Hard to look for outsiders when we've so many," one of the old ones in the Home Guard had said, last muster. His hands gnarled so that he couldn't hold one of the rifles if it ever came his turn.

"You wait," said another ominously. "This is just the beginning."

But this was the one among them known for his bitter pronouncements and doom-saying. Frank didn't know what to think. They had enough to worry about, keeping everyone fed and dogfights roaring over the Channel. When he needed to know more, he hoped he'd be told — but that felt like a resignation.

At the apex of the top path, he checked the perimeter of the summerhouse, and turned to gaze down the hill and across the estuary toward the sea. If Greenway House was sold and they had to leave, this was what he would think of, standing here, gazing out over the best view the area had to offer. It didn't matter it was not his when naught of this world was theirs for long.

He strode down the far end path into the woods, keeping an eye out only to say he had. The dark-haired nurse was gone, and he knew it better than anyone.

What had Arbuthnot said about her? That she had the scent of danger about her, secrets and tempting looks.

Frank had thought the old man ridiculous then, afraid of little girls. Afraid of waif-thin women of twenty-odd who had to creep up and over every impediment men like Arbuthnot had put in their way. Men like himself.

There was something to it, though, he had to admit. Against all odds, Arbuthnot had the prescience of a sea captain sensing a storm brewing long before the first cloud.

But that assigned him too much courage and the women too little.

No, Arbuthnot was more a rabbit, tensed in the high weeds to danger in every sound. Trembling, nervy, eyes wide, and — once in a while, through pitiful, all-encompassing fear — justified.

He wished he had never come to Greenway. He wished never to leave it.

At the ferry quay, Elsie hailed him for a cup of tea.

"Ah, no. Won't bother you," Frank said, looking at the sky. It might rain, and he didn't want to be caught out. But he had a thought, and a plan sprung up before him. "Only stalking the grounds in case — you know. In case the young lady . . ."

Elsie brightened. "I'll bring it out, shall I?"

The Bastins had two chairs in the small garden behind the privet, and Frank waited there, watching the heavy traffic on the river through the hedge. Servicemen and surveyors and the like on the Dart, it was said. Just the beginning but of what?

"Father hasn't been taking his feed of

late," Elsie said, coming out with a tray. "So we have extra. I think it's no milk for you? Tell me if I'm wrong — there's a jug."

"That's right," he said, surprised. He had never given Elsie Bastin, Hannaford, as was, the slightest consideration but that might have been his mistake. "Thank you."

"Stalking the grounds, you were saying? In case?"

"Ah," Frank said. "In case there was an accident or . . . Mrs. Arbuthnot had a tumble, says she saw someone lurking about."

"*Goodness,*" Elsie said. "I'll come up and help out. Her down and the nurse . . ."

"Still missing, yes."

"And you think she could have . . ."

"You never know," he said, with just the right tone.

"I hadn't considered the possibility she might have done herself harm — but now you suggest it, with all the goings-on . . ."

Frank spotted the other nurse, the plain one left behind, coming along the hedge. Time to change tack. "And the funeral this morning, Mrs. Bastin," he said loudly. "Was it everything it should have been?"

Mrs. Bastin had her cup halfway to her mouth. "Ah, yes?"

"Oh, I'm sorry," the girl said at the gate,

and both Frank and Elsie stood to welcome and invite her in. "I didn't mean to disturb."

"You're most welcome," Elsie said, offering her chair.

"Is there news?" he said.

"Mrs. Arbuthnot is resting," Bridey said, and sank into the seat. Frank gestured Mrs. Bastin into his. "But — no. I was hoping Gigi had been through here."

"The police already had a nose around," Elsie said. She had a habit of looking toward the high window in the cottage where her father lived, as though including him in the conversation. "We've not seen her and no one rang the bell last night. She might have made her own arrangements, of course." Now she glanced knowingly in Frank's direction. "I'm sure she'll be embarrassed at the trouble when she comes back."

Bridey didn't seem so certain.

"Have that cup of tea, my dear," Elsie said.

"Mrs. Bastin," Frank said, "you were saying about the funeral this morning? A proper send-off for Kendrick?"

"Moving," she said. "And a nice table after, at home, if you could ignore the cousins fighting over the scraps."

"The food?"

"The valuables," she said. "One cousin claims the other's already nabbed the silver, and the first says only because the gold pocket watch and chain is gone. Bridey, take a bit of sugar, my dear, you look wretched." Elsie looked between them, satisfied. "Where was I? But yes, squabbling. We've seen a bit of it of late. The family shows up, the body's not even cold in its grave, and they're all keen for that thing no one thought to want until now. Granny's hatpin. Uncle's onyx ring. Now it's missing, it's an hair-loom."

"If these thieves come to the house for more than jam, I'll see to them myself," Frank said.

"I hadn't even thought of the jam," Elsie said. "Do you think it's the same ones?"

The first raindrop fell into his teacup. "Here comes the rain. We should be heading back up the hill, shouldn't we, Bridey?"

In the woods, they felt few drops, but heard the rain patter on the leaves above. Frank measured his steps to allow Bridey to keep pace, but still she fell behind, lost in thought. Had she heard him planting his gossip with Elsie, suggesting Gigi dead at her own hand?

"Was the police interview all right, then, Bridey? Not too difficult, I hope." He did feel bad about the police having to come, but it couldn't be helped.

"I'm sorry?"

He stopped to let her catch up. She had lovely eyes — he had never noticed. That was probably the other one's doing, the sun too bright to see the moon in daylight. Something the mistress had said once.

"What did Mrs. Bastin say . . . what about a hatpin?"

"Never mind Elsie," Frank said. "Let's go see if your friend is back."

"No, I don't think she will be."

Scaldwell turned his face up the hill. The white house was grayed with the curtain of rain. If he said nothing at all, he might not have to lie to her. "Why do you think so?"

"She was never meant to be here," Bridey said. "Now she's gone, she has no reason to come back."

45
DOREEN

December 1941, six months later
One day when it is cold outside, strangers
come and take Pamela away.

That's the day one of my mittens grows a
hole. The red string starts short but I can
see my fingers inside. Hello fingers!

We march the path to the boathouse to
look at the water and see if it's ice. The
string is longer, *whushing* in the wind like a
kite's tail. We visit the battery. The red string
is long now, and my fingers poke out. I show
Nurse Bridey and she says we must go back
to the house but the boys don't want to go
back to the house and there's a tussle.
That's how boys do. Since the thing that
happened in America, something with
aeroplanes, and a pearl, and a place that
grows a strange sort of apple from a pine
tree, says Beryl, the boys only want to play
war. They won't play jacks or Statues or
anything else. Inside the house, they only

have a few small metal soldiers and a tank and some lorries, and that's all they will play with. They frown over them and when they are asked to do a chore or to wash their hands or to come to the table, they have a strop or cry.

That day we arrive back at the house to find the strangers, a Mr. and Mrs., and they take Pamela. Nurse Bridey takes my mittens. "Maybe Saint Nick will bring you new ones," she says, but Beryl says Saint Nick won't know where to find us and it's a problem.

Pamela is back before bedtime, and I am happy. She has a new coat and new boots and new tall, warm socks and tights. The next day, Tina gets a visit.

For days, people come and select a child, and sometimes my friends come back the same day, their lips red with sweets and their pockets full, and sometimes they are gone for hours until I know they are not coming back. Then they do.

"It's our mums and daddies," Beryl says when it's her turn. Beryl is the oldest and the bossiest. But now she shares a bit of the sweeties she brought back.

"Your *real* mummy and daddy?"

"Of course!"

"Are you going home then?"

"Not until the war is over," she says.

The sweet she gives me is sharp in the side of my cheek. I do not think of Mummy and Daddy as much now, only when we take out our picture books on Sunday and I remember that I have not always lived at Greenway. Only when a letter comes and Nurse Bridey says, *It's for you, Doreen! Nanny and Grampy say hello!*

The candy is stuck to my teeth. "When will that be, the *end* of the war?"

"Don't know. Daddy said the Americans are in the muck now. That's what he said."

"What's muck?"

Beryl won't say so I think she doesn't know, either.

The next day or the next after that, some people come again and this time they are for me. They aren't strangers at all. It *is* Mummy and Daddy, they say, and let's get your coat. At the door, Nurse Bridey hands me a pair of gloves that are not mine. "Until we can darn yours," she says. The gloves are red but too big. But Nurse Bridey has been sad and cross since Nurse Gigi left, so I don't say they are too big.

But they are too big.

Mummy wears her best coat with a ring of fluffy fur like a fox around her neck and Daddy wears his Sunday suit, and we go in a motorcar to a town by the sea. There's a shop where Mummy chooses new shoes for me and socks. I have a new coat, too, with six buttons, two by two down the front. It's a lot of the tickets in Mummy's ration book, then Mummy brings out a brush and makes my hair shine and curl and puts in a hair clasp. Down the street, in another shop, the man says, "Shall we make a family picture, darling?" Daddy hands over more pounds. His mouth is closed straight. When he sees me looking, he smiles and picks me up so that my new shoes dance on the air.

"We've missed you, Sugar," he says like he always did, and I think yes, I miss them, too. And then I do miss them, and I do miss them terribly.

"Peter, what in the world did you say?" says Mummy because I am crying and I want to go home. "We can't go home just yet, darling," she says.

"To *Greenway*," I say. "To Nurse Bridey and Pamela and Tina and the monkey puzzle tree."

"Well, that's fine," Daddy says.

Mummy and Daddy take me to eat but there's nothing for pudding.

In the motorcar, Mummy is crying.

"Edie, she's safer here."

"Is she?" Mummy says. "They had bombs

up the road in May!"

"Once. Do you remember May in London, Edie? Would you have wanted her there? During the worst night we've seen yet?" He glances back, makes a face to make me laugh.

"It's only that she . . . she has a whole life here without us."

"I did notice," Daddy says. His mouth is straight again but he doesn't look back now. "Happy Christmas. Nobody gets what they want."

46
BRIDEY

Spring again, one year at Greenway
Bridey stood James up against the inside of
the cupboard door in her new room and
made a small tick, hardly noticeable. They'd
grown enough the siren suits had been
repurposed and some hems let out on
trousers and dresses.

"John, you next." He stood as tall as he
could, his expression concerned he wasn't
as big as James. Beryl next. They had eight
children, seven walking now, but finally a
pram.

They also had Mrs. Arbuthnot's daughters
in to help. Two young women in whose
company Mrs. Arbuthnot never tired. In the
face of so many eager hands, Bridey's duties were diminished. She had a shift each
day to see to their health, and spent more
time when there were fevers and bad tum-
mies. It was not enough to fill the days and
she had to wonder if she could collect the

glowing recommendation she needed to rejoin her stalled life — if that life was still her goal. She was waiting for something else to happen, she supposed.

The Arbuthnot girls — their name was Davison, their father's name, but this is how she thought of them — had taken over the old room she had shared with Gigi, and Bridey had moved down to a cramped single room between the elder Arbuthnots and the Scaldwells. She had never considered what close quarters the Arbuthnots shared with the Scaldwells and what it could mean. A message sent, one which she only now understood. The children were guests. The Arbuthnots were servants.

And now so was she. Her new room was a small T-shaped space with a single window overlooking a magnolia north of the house and the path from the quay. She didn't mind at all that her room might have been the smallest, that if she forgot to close the shutters, the morning sun baked her in her bed. At the least, with the extra help, she had more leisure time.

When each child had been measured, the Arbuthnot girls collected the group for a romp outside. In the silence their departure left behind, Bridey couldn't think what to do. She was grateful she didn't have to play and pretend, didn't need to keep her face right for questions she didn't want to answer, or remember who she said she was, who she said she would be. She could do whatever she wanted for an hour or two. She could walk down to the river on her own, at her own pace, speaking to no one, scolding no one, reminding no one to stay out of the puddles and nettles. She could sit on the boathouse terrace overhanging the Dart and watch the birds, have a moment of quiet.

The river, however, was teeming.

The attack on Pearl Harbor had changed things, brought to the area billeted American GIs, bright new uniforms and smiles brighter still. They took up a great deal of space wherever they went and passed through the quay at all hours. Elsie was beside herself, nervy since her father, Old Hannaford, had died in the autumn. But no wonder. She was alone in the house during the day now, listening to the near daily dogfights overhead and the ferry bell clang, a hollow song.

On the boathouse terrace, Bridey slipped off her shoes and extended her pale legs in the sun. She pulled her skirt up a bit. Nothing improper. When the local fishermen waved, she returned the greeting, knew a few of them by name. When some Americans heading down the estuary toward Dartmouth cat-called from their patrol boat, she ignored them and laid back her head.

The people of Galmpton hadn't known what Americans would be like, finding most of them rowdy and oversexed. They had pocket money, more rations than the Brits. The local children followed them for chewing gum and sweets, and the young women awaited the next dance, when they could hear the latest music brought over. Glen Miller, Duke Ellington. American presence in the war was a boon, but for some, especially their own men, Americans were too present indeed.

"Hey, there you are, little sister," an American accent called, his delight carrying across the water.

Bridey sat up. He was a black man, a foot up on the gun-wale of a boat taking a slow prowl downriver. His attention was focused on an incoming craft with a Wren in the bow.

"You must have taken me for someone else." The woman's back as straight as if she were the admiral of the fleet. "Private."

"My mistake, ma'am," the soldier said,

but still watching her as his vessel churned on.

Bridey stood and leaned on the handrail to make sure. It was Willa and another Wren at the helm. The boat sat low in the water, piled high with several large, stuffed sacks. Mail, perhaps.

Bridey lifted her hand, but she needn't. Willa had directed her conveyance brought in, the engine cut out so that she floated right up to the boathouse's waters.

"No news, then?" Willa said.

"I would have sent word," Bridey said. "If I'd had any."

"It's been months," Willa said.

"Just shy of a year," Bridey said.

"It's not like her."

How wretched were those whose hearts could be grasped and pulled from their chests. "I wouldn't know. I wonder if I ever met the real woman who called herself Gigi Kelly."

"You're a hard one," Willa said. "So you aren't bothered by two missing women and a dead man? I'm surprised you can sleep at night."

"Your lot was convinced the trouble had nothing to do with Greenway."

Willa glanced at the other Wren. "I was never convinced. Remember Thorne's assignment. What if he gathered information in the wrong room? As we did in London."

With Gigi out of the house, she hadn't had to worry about shadows, about wisht men prowling the woods. The intrigues had come to a halt. With the two new girls helping, she barely had to worry about anything. She found herself impatient at being drawn in again, to have Willa's worry handed to her to keep. "But even Gigi seemed to think it was — the Friar."

"Well, I guess that leaves you hoping she was right," Willa said. "She took herself off, then? With no word to me?" Willa gestured to the other Wren and turned her shoulder as their launch pulled away. "Personally, I have no hope left."

The wind had picked up and Bridey couldn't feel the sun on her skin anymore.

She took the middle path up the hill, wishing she had the answer. She couldn't let it in, could she? The cracked vessel she was could only take on so much. And Gigi had gone off without a word to her, as well. But she wanted to *know,* to have the mystery of it solved, neatly, like one of the mistress's books.

She'd finally got through some of those books over the winter, with Gigi gone, the group of charges down to eight, and everyone healthy and contained in the house. The books were full of ghastly stories, but she was strangely comforted by them. Murders on trains, in river boats, on a golf course, and in country house libraries and drawing rooms — all brought happily to justice. She could see now why Gigi had spent so much time inside the books while she waited to hear from London, why she thought questioning the inhabitants of Greenway could lead her to truth. In Mrs. M.'s books, solving murder was the work of an afternoon, and the satisfaction great in the knot unraveled and tied again into a pretty bow.

But Bridey had spent many afternoons, many late nights and early mornings awake, the curse of idle time. She couldn't make sense of what had happened to Gigi.

If Willa hadn't heard from Gigi, where had she gone? Had she taken herself off? If she'd been in trouble, was it already too late to help her? Had the man from the Friar's pub caught up to her? Or had she suffered something inside, as so many men in the Dart Valley had succumbed to?

Mystery and secrecy. It was well and good for the mistress to spin her yarns, for Hart to celebrate doubt. But it was a thin gruel on which to survive.

Or perhaps she was starving for something else.

Gigi gone, Mrs. Arbuthnot happily ensconced with her daughters, the children kept busy — she was reduced to shelling spring peas with Mrs. Bastin and Mrs. Scaldwell in the kitchen for entertainment. But she knew they waited until she left to speak freely. In the winter they'd only needed the doctor in once, for a cough John couldn't shake, and then he might have been any workman from the village plying a trade, certainly no special friend of hers. When she thought of him, of that kiss and his finger against her neck, she wondered if she hadn't made a mistake.

As she entered the house again, she thought she heard music, the wireless. But the music reached down the stairwell: piano music, gentle fingers on the keys like a fairie song, an enchantment. Was it coming from the children's quarters?

Piano music?

"What do you think you're *doing*?" She burst into the girls' room, expecting to flap the children away from the bench and return the instrument to hibernation.

At the bench sat a silver-haired woman, her posture good under a sagging gray jumper. The figure cut off playing and turned to look.

The mistress was home.

"I'm so —" Bridey didn't know what to do with her hands. "I'm sorry to interrupt, missus, er, Mistress Mallowan. I thought they were messing about. The children. They're very keen to have a chance at the piano."

Of course it wouldn't have been the children, playing so well. What Mrs. M. must think of her. "It was wonderfully done," she said.

"I don't play often," the mistress interrupted herself with a little cough, "anymore."

"You could play the Royal Albert."

"Oh, no," the mistress said.

She was shy, it was said. "I thought it sounded lovely. It's a shame the house isn't filled with music all the time. Ma'am."

The mistress pushed the bench back from the piano and gazed about the room. "It's a perfect house, isn't it?" she said without pride.

She couldn't want to sell it. If it was at the center of her life, a dream she had attained, why should she let it go? Perhaps it was sold already, and they would all have to leave. "Do you mind the children here, missus?"

"Not at all," she said, taking in the girls' cots, in a row, the cupboard with their names. "Perhaps I'll write a story about a war nursery someday."

"Oh no —" Bridey slapped her hand over her mouth.

The mistress smiled.

"I only meant that you've kept the children safe and to write them into a *story*," Bridey said, wishing she could shut her mouth or be consumed in flame and turned to ash on the spot.

"I do understand you."

"I wonder what they will remember," Bridey said, for something to say. "As young as they are."

"One never knows," the mistress said. "I've always thought children see the world quite differently." The dainty cough again. "Quite differently than we expect or remember."

"Perhaps we'll loom large in their memory," Bridey said, but she didn't think so. She hoped they didn't remember too well being away from their parents. She hoped they would remember only that they had playmates and fun, that they were cared for. That they were —

She couldn't love them. "Shall I put things right for you, missus? Before the children come in?"

Mrs. Mallowan stood up. She was a tall woman, but not a commanding presence, precisely. In fact, she seemed almost apologetic for taking up the space she did. The front of her gray jumper drooped under a heavy silver broach.

Bridey moved out of her path and turned back at the last minute, the mistress in the doorway, thinking of the silver broach, the accent of wealth worn for no other reason than the display of it. It reminded her of something. What was it? Not her own mam, of course, never had she owned anything so fine.

The piano draped and the bench replaced — only then did Bridey wonder if she had missed her opportunity to know what had happened to Gigi. Just once she might have had the courage to speak up, to ask the great lady how a mystery was solved.

47
BRIDEY

The Greenway kitchen
Mrs. Scaldwell was busy, three pots boiling on the stove, but alone.

"Can I help?"

"A year of eating and now you can cook?"

"I can be told what to do," Bridey said, suspecting that was Mrs. Scaldwell's favorite sort of help, anyway.

There were peas to shell, lettuces to wash. Bridey dug in but kept her silence to see what Mrs. Scaldwell would say.

"It's a different thing altogether," Mrs. Scaldwell muttered after a few minutes.

"When the mistress is home?"

"The standards I have to meet. She's never living by rations in London."

Bridey looked up. "Isn't she?"

"Rest'rants," the cook said. "In rest'rants you can get a meat meal and keep your ration ticket for home."

"What? For free?"

Mrs. Scaldwell gave her a scathing sort of look. "Paid for, in cash, if you have it. And some do."

"Oh." She had always assumed there was another life that could be purchased, but she couldn't be angry about it. She couldn't allow herself to be angry about anything, or where would she stop? What did it matter to her if the mistress adorned herself with a bauble in her own home? If someone like —

Thorne! Thorne had been wearing a silver tie pin on the train, a rather nice one. That's why she had thought him wealthy. But the connection in her mind, which should have been an itch scratched, was not satisfying. Some other idea that wished to be pulled to the center bothered at her. What was it?

"I've never been around anyone with money," she said.

"The Arbuthnots haven't told you how rich they are?"

"Are they? I never thought they would be. Not the way —" She shouldn't gossip.

"Right. The rich like they are, those are the ones scrabbling over a half crown. What about your friend?" Mrs. Scaldwell said. "The *doctor* always seems to have plenty. I know he's not paying the lady that does for him well enough, but he has that big house. That fine car."

"He's not *my* friend," Bridey said.

"Ah now. Why haven't we seen him about lately?"

"Mrs. Arbuthnot's arm is healed," she said, tearing the lettuces vigorously. "The children have been quite healthy."

Mrs. Scaldwell stirred at the hob, said nothing.

"The doctor says he is often paid in material goods," Bridey said, remembering the bone on his plate, the ornaments loose in the blue bowl. They might have been payments, too. "Perhaps that's why he has plenty."

The lettuces were washed, the peas hulled.

"I haven't seen Mrs. Arbuthnot this afternoon," Bridey said.

"I sent her to help Elsie in the garden," Mrs. Scaldwell said.

"You didn't!"

The cook smiled over her shoulder. "To plant potatoes. She's got two extra mouths in this house now. She'll need to pull a bit more weight."

Bridey looked around for something else to do.

"I didn't mean you," Mrs. Scaldwell said.

But this rather confirmed for Bridey that the chatter had begun. Why did they need a hospital nurse, then? Healthy children, *fewer* children, and two daughters to mind them?

"Let *them* tell you when it's time to go," Mrs. Scaldwell said. "Unless you have plans of your own?"

"I don't have any plans," Bridey said. "I had some, but . . . I feel as though I'm neither here nor there, do you know what I mean? In the middle — except I don't mean the *center* — I mean the opposite."

"Sure, you don't have the other one to have a laugh with."

The pain in her stomach was immediate.

Mrs. Scaldwell turned at the stove. "What in heavens — Are you all right?"

"A stitch from climbing the hill," Bridey said through clenched jaw.

"That's a stitch like I've never seen. Should I call the doctor?"

She was already pulling off her pinafore. "No, please,"

Bridey said. "I'm fine." But she didn't sound fine. "I'll go and lie down. Stretching out will help."

Bridey stood, her knees quaking and her back bent. Mrs. Scaldwell watched her go.

It answered one question, posed by Willa. She did care about the plight of one of the women gone missing. She cared too much.

In her room, she took out Gigi's cloak,

430

wrapped herself in it, and lay on the bed until the pain finally subsided and she could think of Gigi as a concept and not a friend and of the facts distantly. She put them to herself like Willa setting out her hand of solitaire.

It was Gigi's whereabouts she cared to know, but she couldn't help thinking it was Thorne's death in which the matter rested. He'd been observing in Galmpton, setting off the locals. He might have been listening within the wrong room. But which room would that be? The Manor Inn was a public place. There'd hardly be dark schemes laid out in the side room. Had he listened at the wrong table, overheard a plan, a confession? Perhaps he had asked too many questions altogether. Or perhaps he had chatted up the wrong person — a single question asked of someone with a secret might have been one question too many.

There was a rap at her door.

"Hello?"

"Mrs. Scaldwell, Bridey, with the doctor."

"I told you I was fine."

"But that was a lie." Mrs. Scaldwell opened the door. "I have pots boiling so I trust you'll not need a chaperone?" She ceded the doorway to Hart.

"Madam," Dr. Hart said, studying the floor.

"I told her I was fine," Bridey said. "And I am."

"May I come in?"

"You already know my malady," she said.

He took it as an invitation, leaving the door wide. He gestured to the cloak. "Are you chilled?"

"It was Gigi's."

But her body folded in half against her will, her knees suddenly at her chin. "Close the door," she panted, teeth grinding.

He closed the door and approached again. "*This* is psychosomatic? Let me listen to you, at least."

She unclenched herself and lay back to watch him sort a few instruments from his bag. She stared at the bag and an odd sense of memory distracted her from her pain. Something shimmered just out of reach, a moment she had already lived, and she was there as well as here.

"May I?" The stethoscope was cold through the fabric of her dress. Heart, lungs, stomach. "From, er, which location does the pain emanate? Precisely?"

"Not the appendix."

Kidneys, liver, bowels. The flat circle of the instrument traveled along her ribs, across her stomach, his fingers grazing over her.

"You'll find nothing except I haven't had my lunch yet," she said.

His attention sparked nothing inside her that resembled passion, but she felt better for receiving his assessment, his touch confirming the shape of her.

Heart lungs stomach kidneys liver bowels, the pieces of her, like a butcher's guide of a lamb for butchering. The roving instrument pressed to her skin had mapped her body, but she didn't know why it mattered to her to think of herself this way. When he put the stethoscope away in his bag, her attention hung there again.

He pulled up a chair. "I don't think I'm the doctor you need."

The words hung between them, bunting on a string. Another woman might have needed him to be clear whether he spoke of marriage, but they understood one another. That he was not the *man* for her either was not the open question before them.

"You could do with a rest," he said.

"I have enough rest." She thought rather that her idleness might be driving her mad. But he meant —

She sat up. The leather wallet of syringes and clips, the vials of morphine.

"I don't want a sedative." She'd be out of her own control on morphine. She hadn't been a person out of her own control in a long time — what would that look like? She hadn't even had the pills from the night Edward had almost drowned. Now they offered compromise. "I could take one of the barbiturates later, the blue pills you left. I still have them. I could take one tonight."

Tonight, for sleep. But not now, because she had caught the strange feeling again, that she was in one place and another at the same time. She was both here and at the quay, and all the people Thorne had questioned had gathered to see his body.

Hart agreed reluctantly, and stood to pack his bag.

All the people Thorne had questioned.

He hadn't asked questions in one room, or listened at a single table. He had roved the village like the doctor with his bag. Doling out questions and picking up bits and pieces, collecting stories and laments from all over the parish and ward until a body of knowledge had formed. But what had the constellation of what he'd learned looked like? What had he alone understood?

"When you tended to Nicky's body —"

"Who?"

"Ah." She'd forgotten she shouldn't know

his name. "The man on the quay. Someone said his name was Nicholas Thorne. Did he have anything on his person, in his pockets?"

"Why should you worry yourself about the contents of the man's pockets?" Hart said. He wouldn't look at her.

The tie pin.

She was suddenly very worried about it. Surely — not Hart. Not a man of *medicine,* not a man whose patients trusted him. A pocket watch and chain as payment? Something for the blue bowl?

She had seen it. She'd seen it all: pocket watch among the penny nails, chain forgotten at the bottom of his black bag. Uncle's ring, missing, in the blue dish. The tie pin among the medical clamps in the implement wallet in his bag. A different sort of collecting, a magpie taking what was shiny.

"Are you all right?" he said. "You do need a rest, Bridget."

Heart lungs stomach kidneys liver bowels. All the internal problems of those who should live many more years. Except Thorne. Except Bertie Kendrick, who might have hit his head on a stone in his garden, but had marks on his neck. How far would one go, to claim payment? How far would one go to keep silent the incomer whose

435

questions laid bare the presence of a murderer?

The doctor's area of expertise. It was dead men.

"That's it. Your breathing is *labored*, Bridget." Hart reached into his bag again and pulled out the leather wallet, a vial. "I'm afraid I do have to insist, or I won't have done my job."

"I'll scream," she said.

"What? God sakes, what's come over you? Is this about — I'm sorry for the kiss. It was rash. But I do recommend something to help you —"

"Just go." It couldn't be. No doctor would commit such crimes, not a doctor who cared so much —

The doctor takes his fee, one way or the other.

"Go," she said.

Some of Hart's precious doubt passed over his face but he said nothing. She watched the sleek leather of the bag leave the room, knowing more than she had, or wondering if, like so much of what bothered her, it was all in her mind.

48
JOAN

The kitchen garden that afternoon

In the kitchen garden, Joan scratched at the hard soil with the little hand tool Mrs. Bastin had given her. A pail of potatoes sat on the path.

"I'd always thought that was the end product. Not the seed."

Mrs. Bastin ignored her. She was on hands and knees, up to her chubby elbows in soil.

"What are those flat shrubs against the wall there?" Joan said.

The other woman swiped at a strand of hair as she looked up, leaving a smudge at her temple. "Peaches, trained up the stone."

A peach couldn't be had for love nor money. Joan's mouth watered. Even onions, now that they were cut off from the islands and Spain, would be dear, and apples, but they would have them at Greenway. "When are the peaches ready to eat?"

Mrs. Bastin sighed, sat back on her heels.

"July? As late as August."

Looking into the trees, Joan caught the tail of a fleeting thought and let it drag her down. *There is no guarantee of August.*

Her nan would have said someone walked over her grave, a shiver up her spine like that. That's all they were doing, wasn't it? Walking over the graves of each other's kin.

She dusted her gloves. "It'll be here before we know it." Maybe they would all be home by August. These peaches could rot in place and spoil the ground for all she cared.

Mrs. Bastin grunted, back to digging.

Joan had only wanted the work to be made more pleasant. "How long have you lived at Greenway?"

"Forever. Born across the way in Dits'm."

"I hadn't realized. You've been here far longer than your mistress."

"Father was here the longest. Before he went."

She'd rather lost track of the woman's loss. All this desire to care and comfort in the nursery but she hadn't spared any for the people who lived on the estate or at the farms. These were the ancestors in whose dust she dug.

She had at one time supposed Elsie Bastin the pantry thief, a little too pleased with herself. But why shouldn't she be? She had a home, a real home with roots that dug all the way to the heart of the place, and that was no small thing.

Joan went back to her patch, her hands cold and her attitude turned inward and sharp.

All day long, Joan thought of Mrs. Bastin, her ancestral grounds and family all around her, and swallowed her envy until she thought she might choke. Joan had her two youngest foster daughters with her now, but her natural daughter, her foster sons — it was all she wished for, to have them all together again.

And then to find the mistress had arrived, unannounced.

Unannounced to *her*. Scaldwell always seemed to know when she might arrive.

That night Mrs. Christie had her meal in the dining room, alone, not to be disturbed. They had theirs in the kitchen as usual after the children were in bed, her family and the Scaldwells. Bridey had taken to solitude and it was just as well.

"Is there any more of that rhubarb?" Malcolm asked pleasantly. They'd had a supper of something Mrs. Scaldwell had made from a recipe on the wireless, all the ingredients standing in for something they weren't. Nothing one should want more of, and she'd already given him her portion.

"No," Mrs. Scaldwell said.

There was more, as a matter of fact. "It was a lovely meal, Mrs. Scaldwell," Joan said. "The rhubarb was tart." Did it ring of criticism? "Refreshing."

Her ill humor sizzled under her skin. Greenway was a lovely home but not large enough, and it was her doing, bringing the children here and tying all their fates together with one string, too tight and the knots fraying. But what right did she have to regret or worry?

Joan didn't have to wonder the Scaldwells felt the same way about them.

Malcolm pulled out a cigar and the girls went up for bed. Joan had stood to help clear when Mrs. Scaldwell approached the table from the scullery and bumped her husband's shoulder with her hip.

Mr. Scaldwell cleared his throat. "I've had a talk with the mistress this afternoon."

Malcolm stiffened next to her.

"Yes?" Joan said.

"The Admiralty," Scaldwell said, "is requisitioning Greenway and all its buildings and lands."

Joan sat shakily. "When?"

"Soon, if they have their way. The Mallowans are taking this up the chain of command," Scaldwell said. "For themselves, they prefer the damage small children might cause next to that done by sailors."

Joan allowed her chin to dip to her chest. How much of her life had she promised to this arrangement? She only meant to do some little good. Maybe the requisition would force the children back to their parents' care, freeing her and Malcolm to find their own foxhole for the duration.

But she couldn't abandon them. Their mothers had held her hand and thanked her, and given her their trust. She couldn't help but think of little Sam Poole.

"We appreciate Mrs. Mallowan's efforts to fight the order." The stench of Malcolm's cigar made Joan sick at her stomach. "I've had few responses to my inquiries last year, when we thought the house might be sold. I suppose I should — I should follow them up? How long do you think we have?"

"I wouldn't wager on any time at all. I'm sorry." Scaldwell did seem regretful.

"You're out, too, aren't you?" Malcolm said.

"Likely," Scaldwell said. "And one wonders if the house itself will survive."

"I'm sure the house will somehow keep standing without you opening and closing the shutters."

"I don't mean without me," Scaldwell said. "Only, it seems to me many of the houses in the area are filling up with soldiers and sailors, aren't they?" His thoughts seemed to take him far away. "Something's happening. We can only hope it's the end that's coming."

"A victorious end," Joan amended.

"Yes."

But she would take any kind, and perhaps Mr. Scaldwell would as well.

"There is a bit of the rhubarb, if you'd like it," Mrs. Scaldwell said. Smoothing things over.

"I've lost my appetite." Malcolm stood and pushed in his chair.

In their room, he stormed back and forth. "The cheek of that man. Who will you bother?"

"It's out of his control. It's always been out of *his* control," Joan said. Tired. "I'll write to everyone, I suppose. All the big houses will be filled."

"What good does money do, I ask you," he muttered. "We might have stayed at home —"

"And be trapped there? Have you heard from anyone on Jersey? Have you heard from anyone since it fell?"

Malcolm was as surprised as a kitten at

her tone. "They're in the wind, like us."

"They might be, darling." But she wondered.

Malcolm slipped out of bed in the dark hours. Joan reached for him and when she woke, it was a minute later or hours and he was still gone. She turned onto her back and studied the empty ceiling rose above. That was the way the lady of the house liked it, Mrs. Scaldwell had said once. All the central lights had been taken out when the house was redone, the ceiling roses left decorative and purposeless. "She likes lamps and candles," Mrs. Scaldwell said. "Flattering light. It's no use against the dark, though, is it?"

Joan agreed with her. For someone who liked to read as much as Mrs. Christie, for someone who wrote stories and might reckon with what one might call metaphor, the empty, ornamental detail was an odd choice.

She got up to look for her dressing gown. Perhaps Malcolm was ill and needed her. All that rhubarb, one didn't have to wonder. She couldn't find the dressing gown in her own cupboard, hadn't seen it in a while.

She went to the cupboard Malcolm used and opened it. A sheet had been rolled up and stuffed into the shelf. Had he torn up more household linens for paint rags? Scaldwell would have him for it. She pulled out the wad and stared, understanding only after a moment what it was she saw.

A few hours later, Joan sat fidgeting at the little table in their room with a stack of Greenway stationery she'd pinched from the library. The first letter was to the Ministry of Health, alerting them to the situation and asking for guidance. Then the Women's Voluntary Service. Perhaps the children could be absorbed into another nursery.

The third?

Who will you bother? Joan took a breath. She needed a different tone for this letter. Who was to say Mrs. Christie was the only skilled writer in residence at Greenway House?

Dearest friend.

She started with the nearest circle, those most likely to feel obligation. Close friends, old friends. She had never been a woman of society, had not been invited or allowed. No tea-rooms or parlors, no season in London, no societies. Not when it might have mattered and set her on a different path.

She sat back in Mrs. Agatha Christie's own chair and wondered which path she might have preferred.

But she knew people, and some of them might be called upon for a name or suggestion, a whisper in the right ear.

When she ran out of chummy friends, she turned to distant ones. Acquaintances, friends in common. Dear sir, dear madam. If you might do me this kindness. Her hand began to cramp.

Joan put down her pen and kneaded at the pain. The lady who lived here directed servants through the many houses and apartments she owned, let, rented, refurbished, and kept her own correspondence with agents, publishers, foreign and domestic. She picked up the pen again.

To whom it may concern. If you might be able to assist.

The words began to grate at her, the wheedling tone. Her neck felt tight.

She was going begging, that's what it was. She did not feel the power of using the great woman's paper and pen, only the scrape against her dignity, again. Always. She should have been expected to be sorted by now. Instead, she was forced to reach out in every direction, toward any meager connection like a Jane Austen heroine left a pittance in her father's will.

Joan's hand stilled over the page. Ink gathered in a pool on her last word. She crumpled the note and dropped it into the bin.

It was easy to forget, huddling from the bombs in someone else's home, that she had some funds at her command.

Not enough funds to keep Malcolm from hoarding jars of preserves in the cupboard of their room like a little match girl, apparently. If the Scaldwells found out . . .

A not-insubstantial amount of money was exactly what she had. Enough money to fight over, to cause rift.

Some still thought she shouldn't have had her share of George's estate, that she and their children had somehow not deserved to have security. She hadn't spent it down. She'd nested on it, a golden egg. Making their lives pleasant now and then —

The jars of preserves in Malcolm's cupboard rankled. Stealing from their generous host and hoarding them against — what? Was anything ever enough?

Joan took up a new sheet of the letterhead and smoothed it with her hand. *Greenway House, Churston Ferrers, South Devon. Churston connection, 81243.*

How to state it? To whom.

This is the last will, testament of one Florence Annie Arbuthnot, she wrote, and just

446

this once, she did not think of Malcolm at all.

49
VERA SCALDWELL

Greenway, 14 May 1942

By mid-morning, it was up and down the lane from the farms to the quay that the King and Queen were visiting Kingswear.

The ferry had gone out and not come back, Elsie Bastin reported when she arrived to help with the midday meal. A crowd at the quay waited in the hopes of catching a glimpse.

"Are they wearing their finest?" Vera said. "In case the King starts knighting folks?"

They both had a laugh and then Vera sent Elsie to the kitchen garden to see what was harvest ready. She came back with an armful of bushy green leaves.

Spinach? The children would wail and gnash their teeth. One of them had refused her barley soup and gone to bed without her tea the week before. In the Scaldwell house, that might've been a spanking, but it was not her house or her child. These children grew bold in the house, as though they meant to outlast the Admiralty.

Were the children any different since they came, though, or was it perhaps the rest of them wearing down? Even the nurse left behind had a new guarded look to her.

"Who thought they might go to have a look at the Queen, then?" Vera said.

Elsie washed the spinach dreamily. She wouldn't get it clean, with that attention for it. "They was wearing their hats, going out, like. Like it was Sunday." She straightened, looked stricken. "It's not Sunday?"

"Thursday, my lover." Vera took over at the sink.

Elsie wiped her hands and went to the window.

"You'll never be able to see down to the quay," Vera said.

"I know! Was only thinking . . ."

"Thinking what?"

"It might be nice to see the King and Queen, mightn't it?" Elsie Bastin looked young to Vera just now. "What do you suppose she's wearing? A crown?"

"She'll have a smart hat," Vera said. "Maybe a veil, short and smart, like a posh lady visiting. You know."

But she wouldn't know. The only posh lady they knew was the mistress and she didn't go in for nonsense and fuss. She had a mink coat she kept near her in case of an air-raid siren, and a string of pearls for special occasions, but otherwise she dressed in old jumpers and flannel skirts. When she came to Greenway, the mistress was usually on holiday, celebrating her birthday and a book draft finished. Another Christie for Christmas ready for its wrappings and bows. She might read a bit from the latest to the family after dinner, and the master always guessed at the endings until all was revealed. *And if he got it right, wasn't she mad?* She wasn't one for extravagance, not in clothes, and certainly not while at Greenway. It was her escape from all that, the place where — she'd said many times — she was most herself.

Vera was always most herself, and hadn't realized she might have another Vera Scaldwell for a suit to put on when needed.

"They came to Dartmouth in '39," Elsie said.

"Pardon?"

"The King and Queen. They came to Dartmouth before the war."

"Did you see them?"

"No, but Mrs. Dodge at the Manor Inn says she did. They brought the princesses, too, she said. The Queen wore a hat. No veil, but a —" Elsie's hands swirled around her head to show a swooping cap, high in the front. "Pinned back at the top with a shiny bob. Probably *real,* I never thought of that. And the princesses wore little matching coats and bar-rays —"

"Hmm?"

"Hats like Mr. Arbuthnot wears, but to match their coats. That must have been darling."

Vera had come to stand near her, the meal forgotten for a moment. She shouldn't care about such things. Who should care about such things? She was fifty years old and there was a war on. "They are rather pretty girls." Vera couldn't start wishing for grandchildren too soon but she'd not mind another little girl to buy buckle shoes and ribbons for. Wouldn't mind a baby name for the child to call her. All the women she knew looking forward to grandchildren made a study of it — what special name would they have, just between them, granny and child?

"What do they do when they visit, did Mrs. Dodge say?" She doubted the keeper of the dirty sink water at the Manor Inn had got anywhere near the royal family. She'd seen a newsreel or a photopage in a magazine.

"They saw the naval academy and the boys there were shown off, like sheep at the fair," Elsie said. "And they planted trees."

Vera thought she had misheard. "They planted —"

"Trees. The land man there will have done the planting, but they throw in a few inches of dirt to make it a ceremony. The King planted a purple beech, the Queen a golden beech. Princess Elizabeth's was a whitebeam, and Margaret's was a scarlet chestnut."

Vera felt herself start to laugh and choked it back. Tried. "Why in the world do you remember all that?"

Elsie's face had been wide open and reverent but now it closed as firmly as a door slammed. "The gardener's daughter, amn't I? I know trees."

"Oh, of course. Of course. I didn't mean to offend, only —" She tried to think of what to say.

She should not require friends. She was a married woman with work to do. She had no time for lingering confidences over tea, for gossip. Didn't want them.

And yet.

Vera ran more water over the spinach in the colander.

They weren't at Greenway in '39, and now

they may not last the year. Or the mistress would get her way against the Admiralty. Or a bomb would fall tonight and the people at Greenway would be the people she died with. In these times, what truly mattered? Getting the floors to their greatest and fullest shine? Keeping another woman's house clean couldn't be the only accomplishment of her lifetime.

Diana was her accomplishment. Diana was everything: crown and scepter, the rule of the land. Her daughter, in whose memory she would reside someday. Her child, the tree she had planted.

Vera turned off the tap and let the spinach rest in the sink.

She had not given the same consideration for the children of other women.

She had a terrible feeling in her stomach, as she often did since Douglas's death, that she had not paid the right attention, had not instructed well or showed her love precisely enough. That everything she had done would still turn to dust in her hands, sand in her mouth. Vera glanced down at the spinach leaves. It would still grit in their teeth. They wouldn't have it, not after the barley incident.

She didn't like barley, either.

"We should make a treat for the children,"

she heard herself say.

Elsie looked up, showed a hesitant smile, then the empty socket of a missing tooth. A favorite smile, the smile of a friend. "Should we?"

What had she set aside? They'd had some bramble jam in the pantry from last summer when the sugar rations had been raised for harvest time, but the last jar had been snatched as so many things had. They'd moved as much as they could from the larder to the pantry to keep better watch.

But when she reached the pantry, the door stood open. Not again. It boggled the mind, the selfishness —

She tugged the string for the light and stared. "Elsie," she called.

The missing jars, all of them, were lined up in front of the locked cupboard. Preserves and peas and apples and pickles, all in a row.

She thought of a kind of biscuit her mum used to make, rolled dough, a sandwich with jam showing through a cut-out, bright as a church window.

Elsie came to stand next to her. "Is it real?"

"It is, and it makes a special occasion. We'll have to put on our finery, shall we?"

Elsie laughed and said she would. She

would put on her jewels and celebrate as though the royal family had come to the very front door.

50
BRIDEY

That night

The children were sticky from the treat Mrs. Scaldwell had made and wouldn't go to sleep. Only a few hours later, they had 'planes overhead, as low as they might be flying past their ears.

The sirens in Dittisham had begun to wail, the rising and falling of warning. Mrs. Arbuthnot appeared in the corridor. "I suppose we should bring them down?" They had become accustomed, exhausted, but Bridey insisted. Yes, they should bring them down.

Beryl, Tina, Pamela, Doreen, and the boys carried pillows under their arms, and some trailed the blankets from their cots. Mrs. Arbuthnot grabbed the baby a little too harshly and woke the poor thing. The child howled as they marched down the family stairs to the entry, past the portrait of the mistress, age four, past the portrait of the stern nanny of Mrs. M.'s own childhood, into the morning room and through.

Bridey settled the children in piles of bedding in front of the fireplace and, after taking each to the toilet, dropped into the couch behind them. Mrs. Arbuthnot eagerly handed over the crying infant. Bridey jostled him back to sleep while Mr. Scaldwell checked at the shutters.

"Brixham, I think," he said. "Again."

Mr. Arbuthnot had a cigar out, Sunday picnic for him. "Brixham's hardly up the road."

Scaldwell looked over. "If you light that cigar, so help me . . ."

"Ah, you think you have authority, do you?"

"I like my chances, *sir,* if you would like to test it."

"Dear me, I wouldn't want to tangle with a member of the Brixham Home *Guard* —"

"Malcolm, put the cigar away," Mrs. Arbuthnot snapped. In the light of the candle Mrs. Scaldwell had lit, her face was pinched. "Think of . . . the children's developing lungs. Bridey?"

"Yes, missus," Bridey said. "The smoke's not good for them."

"*Bombs* aren't good for them," Mr. Arbuthnot groused. "Or for any of us, but

Churchill has his cigar."

"When you lift a finger to save humanity, you can have yours, too," Scaldwell said.

Arbuthnot dug himself out of the chair, bluster and indignation.

"Malcolm, please," his wife said, without conviction. Her daughters exchanged glances.

Mrs. Mallowan hadn't even come down. She preferred, Scaldwell said, to be up in the high stories of the house if it were to collapse.

After the all-clear, after putting the children back to bed, Bridey went to her room and pulled out her kit, her bandages and packets of aspirin, and drew out the bottle of blue pills. She had not slept much since her visit from Dr. Hart, had spent all her time within Greenway House, studying the mistress's books for ideas. How was a villain revealed?

She opened the bottle and shook one of the pills into the palm of her hand. She couldn't take one. What if the sirens started up again, or if one of the children became ill? What if the pill worked too well and she couldn't rise in the morning?

What if it stunned her into thinking she should take more than one?

What if she took more than one?

Bridey put the pill back in the bottle, the bottle back into the kit, and herself to bed. What she wanted was a clear head, though she felt she may never have one again.

Bridey woke to shouting. She sat up but all was silent.

She had dreamed of the old family flat on fire, charred remains of all she loved, and the smoke in her nose and throat. Was it *her* thrashing and shouting in her sleep?

But she did smell smoke. She kicked back the covers and went to the door. Bare feet in the corridor, then the stairs, yes it was smoke, the stairwell filled with haze.

She tucked her face into the crook of her elbow and trailed the smoke down to the ground floor, past the kitchen and pantry, past the gong, and into the front hall. It came from the left, from the library — no, from the inner hall, a sort of sitting room reserved for the family. In that room, a comfortable-looking chair smoldered.

Bridey ran to the kitchen, flung open the door to the scullery, and finally found a stew pot to fill with water and carry back. Mr. Scaldwell stood at the bottom of the family stairs, slippered and groggy, his demeanor all but poised to demand of her what the blast she was doing when he caught the scent.

"Did we have a strike?"

He followed her to the chair and watched as she poured the whole of the pot into it.

"An enemy within." He reached into the seat of the chair and pulled out the short end of a soggy cigar. "I would like to be enraged but I'm not nearly surprised enough. I don't have the blood for it."

"He nearly set the house on fire."

"I dare say it is not the first fire this house has seen," Scaldwell said. "But he might have killed us all."

She'd not had enough time to consider it, to follow the smoke to its ultimate conclusion. Her teeth chattered.

Scaldwell reached for the pot. "I can take over if you would like to return to bed."

"I'm quite awake now."

"Perhaps some tea, then."

In the kitchen, he made the tea and set two cups on the table. "An old man falling asleep and dropping his lit cigar like a baby dropping its dummy. If that doesn't say something about the state of this country, old codgers in nappies at the gears . . ."

She concentrated on keeping her hands steady to pour milk into her cup.

"Ah," he said, "you think *I'm* an old man,

is that it? I'm not so old as that." He stirred his tea. "Aye, maybe I am. Old enough to have been in the tangle last time."

"Oh?"

"But still hearty," he said. "Rhymes with foolhardy, though, doesn't it? Best not call my own bluff, as many funerals as we've had, these parts."

Bridey worked at keeping her face blank.

"Something inside them gave out," he said. "That's what they've been saying."

Heart lungs stomach kidneys liver bowels.

"If you're worried after your friend," he said, "you can rest easy that whatever took these men didn't take her."

He couldn't know that.

Gigi had been gone a year with no word, and she thought of her less each day. Now, she was thinking of the doctor's bag, filled with tools to save and used to carry home treasures. And in between —

"Why does a person kill another?" She remembered the soldier at St. Prisca's. "Other than an accident, say?"

"Other than war?" Scaldwell could be thinking of deaths he had meted out, too. Some, encouraged to kill. "Greed. Lust. Wrath. There are more but I can't — pride. Envy?"

She didn't know what to do about the

461

doctor, if anyone would believe her. If, in taking her account, certain questions might be asked in London. She was not a trustworthy person. She had to stop it, though, didn't she? If she could stop suffering —

A stab in her gut, thinking of Gigi. But Gigi would have put herself first, too. Every woman for herself.

"I think I will try to lie down a while," she whispered. She left her cup for someone else to tidy. It wasn't like her. It wasn't at all who she was.

51
BRIDEY

On the grounds

That day looked to be fine, and Mrs. Arbuthnot's daughters wanted the afternoon. Bridey was only too happy to be pressed into service again. She left the smallest boy in the nursery napping with Edith nearby and took the older children for a walk.

They marched along the top path, good little soldiers, along the crumbling loggia below the summerhouse to the view to Dartmouth.

"Why did Nurse Gigi go away?" Pamela wanted to know.

The Arbuthnot daughters had been gossiping near the children again, repeating the story that Mrs. Bastin had brought from town, that Gigi had been seen in Cornwall a few weeks back. It had stirred her hopes that Gigi had come back — for her money if nothing else. But she hadn't arrived. "She had something she needed to do."

"Did she go back to London?"

"No, not there." London was a place they couldn't go.

They walked down the hill to the river and back toward the house, past the old ruins where the girls sat crowded into the niche of the wall and the boys used the old open-roofed shelter in their ongoing game of war.

She should be happy they were so well adjusted here and not mind what games they played. It seemed to her, though, the boys acted out what they couldn't understand. What none of them could understand. Who got saved? Who was left to fend for themselves?

When one decided that certain lives were more important than others, what followed, inevitably it seemed to her, was murder.

She found it difficult to imagine Dr. Hart making those judgments, playing God. He had wanted the people here to have a good doctor. It didn't make any sense to her that he would play with their lives or his own reputation.

She kept the blue pills safe in her aid kit, however. Not as medicine any longer, but as evidence, if she got the courage to accuse.

She did not think she would, and thought of doing as Gigi had. Leaving it all behind for someone else to solve.

On the hill again, the children raced ahead.

"Nurse Bridey," Tina said as the house came into view. "There's a visitor."

A motorcar sat on the curved drive at the top of the hill. "So there is." She started to lead them around the house, but Mrs. Arbuthnot came out and beckoned.

"Bridey, a moment." She seemed nervous. "Mrs. Scaldwell will see to the children."

Mrs. Scaldwell never saw to the children and Bridey had never entered the front door, like a guest. Entered by the front door when she had left by the back —

The two policemen stood in the entry, their caps under their arms.

Her luck, run out.

"What's happened?" she said.

"They might have found Gigi, my dearest."

Mrs. Arbuthnot used sweet words on the children, not on her. But it was her other words that caught her out. "They *found* her?"

"A young lady of her description," Mrs. Arbuthnot said with meaning.

"Dead." Bridey lurched, legs folding up, but one of the constables was ready and grabbed her. She was planted in the morning room and a cup of sugary tea put in her hand before she felt required to speak again. "How was it done?"

The policemen didn't know what to think of this. One of them blinked at her but finally answered. "Drowned, most likely."

"Drowned?" The surprise of it made the cramp in her side disappear. But she was still dead. Bridey held herself still to keep the teacup steady and her guts in place. Hadn't she said she would never let another person burrow into her heart? She imagined Gigi showing her the plan for Hitler: mustache, knee, gun. She had wanted to end suffering but was only causing it.

"The body was found in the sea, Bridey," Mrs. Arbuthnot said. "They think she may have . . . she might have done herself harm."

"Was your friend . . ." The constable couldn't find the right words. "Would she . . ."

She hoped for a better question, concentrated hard on his mouth for a better question to come from it.

He started again: "Did she leave everything behind when she went?"

It couldn't be Gigi. Could it?

"Everything," Mrs. Arbuthnot said, then lowered her voice. "Not right in herself."

Mr. Arbuthnot lurked in the hall.

"We'll speak to you, too, sir," the other policeman said. "Does anyone have a photograph of her?"

"Is the body fresh?" Bridey said.

The policemen stared. "A recent death," one said. "She was seen passing near the village there, Salcombe it's called, not more than a week ago."

"No, we have no likeness of her," Mrs. Arbuthnot said. "Isn't that odd?"

As though Gigi had never existed. None of them had. When they were turned out and scattered, who would remember that they had once all converged here? But maybe that was true of every life not fit for the history books. The *small* lives. The children would grow up, bless them, given the chance, and forget they'd ever stayed at Greenway, and maybe the house itself would fall to ruin, forgotten. Maybe the *village.* Or the very country. It was not so unlikely, now, to think they lived in the last days.

The men asked for Gigi's address back in London, but she came up empty-handed there, too.

"I could ring the hospital," Mrs. Arbuthnot said.

Bridey hiccoughed with a half-sob of

467

laughter. They all looked around at her.

"Which hospital then?" one policeman said.

"The hospital she — oh, I'll have to see if I have the name," Mrs. Arbuthnot said. "She came recommended."

Bridey rushed in. "Is it possible she was murdered?"

"What's this?" They looked keen now.

Mrs. Arbuthnot sank into the nearest seat and Mr. Arbuthnot rushed to her.

"We had a murder at the quay last year," Bridey said.

"You think the same bloke might have killed your woman?"

"You said she drowned," Mr. Arbuthnot said, fanning his wife with a newspaper.

"She might have been pushed," one of the men said. "Or —"

"Or she might have been dead before she entered the water," Bridey said. As it had been with Mr. Thorne.

"The doctor will have to say." They'd come for easy confirmation and hadn't collected it. Bridey hoped it would be a different doctor. They might get to the bottom of this, if only they didn't ask the killer himself how the victims had died.

The men sized up Mr. Arbuthnot and asked if he'd come to identify the body.

"Me?" he said.

"It should be me," Bridey said.

The policemen didn't like it. Mrs. Arbuthnot watched them argue about the right and the wrong of it, then stood up. "We'll both go. Malcolm, you stay here and protect the household. Remember Mrs. Scaldwell's intruder."

"I *could* come, I suppose," he said.

"No, too right. You're better suited here. Mr. Scaldwell?"

He'd been just outside the door and didn't seem bothered they would notice. "Yes?"

"Would you get the gentlemen more tea while Bridey and I gather a few things, just in case? If you would be so kind?"

Mrs. Arbuthnot led Bridey down the service corridor and up the stairs to the landing to their rooms. "Do you think she drowned?"

Bridey held herself tight, all her muscles, *Gray's Anatomy* pages of muscles tightened to keep herself in one piece. She would come apart. She would blow to bits.

"It's not just that you don't want to think she took her own life?" Mrs. Arbuthnot said. "It might seem the coward's way out, but certainly Gigi might have been —"

"She's no coward."

"Someone killed her, then."

"Someone," Bridey said. There was the matter of who, but did it matter? Was it Hart? Was it the Friar from London, come for his money and revenge? Here was an end, no matter its name.

52
BRIDEY

On the road to Salcombe-by-the-Sea
The body that might be Gigi had washed
up on the shore below a treacherous cliff
further south along the coast, a woman's
body battered against the rocks, and so
that's where they had to go.

In the back of the police motorcar, Bridey
fidgeted with the handkerchief she'd
brought from the house, only realizing now
that it was the doctor's. She stroked the fine
stitching of the monogram and then balled
it up in her fist. She didn't cry. She turned
her head and tried not to be sick as the car
barreled through curves in the tight lanes
and through rushing hedges. As each small
village slid into view and the car might slow,
she had a moment of relief to imagine what
the women in their gardens thought as they
looked up from laundry baskets. She could
be anything. She might have done anything.

"Might we stop at the next town for a

stretch?" Mrs. Arbuthnot said when they'd been on the road forty minutes.

The policeman in the passenger seat looked back. A bead of sweat rolled down the fat of his cheek. "We need to get on, ma'am."

"Surely we could spare even ten minutes?" Bridey knew she was nodding in her direction.

No one would mind the break. The police had driven hard to fetch them, and Mrs. Arbuthnot had hurried to make arrangements, sending for the oldest Jackson girl at the lower farm to help her daughters with the children. The others, from the cottages, from town, would soon hear. Some would come to the house to lend a hand and to have the news from Greenway lips.

At the next village, they drew in front of a public house and stopped. One of the men hurried inside but the other stayed back and leaned on the bonnet, watching as Bridey and Mrs. Arbuthnot took a slow turn along the road and back.

"It can't be her." Mrs. Arbuthnot's eyes were red rimmed.

"It can't be," Bridey agreed. She had kept herself still and controlled so far. Perhaps she didn't appear worried enough.

"Just because we haven't heard word

from her . . ."

The unspoken thing was that it very well could be her. A year at Greenway and another body to see.

A sharp pain poked at her. Bridey put her hands to her knees and looked at her shoes, dusty from the road.

"Still ailing?" Mrs. Arbuthnot said. "Let's get you a cup of cool water."

Inside the pub, men watched from the bar as the women sat on either side of a small table. Bridey was reminded of the day they had gone to the Manor Inn seeking Mrs. Poole.

She sipped from the cup placed in front of her, eyes roving. No one paid her any attention. Next to Gigi, she'd known exactly who she was and how little she mattered, and here it was the same. Invisible Bridget. How had Gigi gone unnoticed, Gigi who attracted stares wherever she went? Covetous, curious, looks of knowing judgment?

Mrs. Arbuthnot said, "Whom do you suspect of murdering Gigi?"

Bridey's breath caught. She had said too much, back at the house. "I don't know, missus." Thinking of the doctor, Hart, and his ill-gotten baubles, and then of the bootprint at the back door. The man the others called the Friar. A devil in real life or in a story, what did it matter? The devils went on, didn't they, and the rest of them were crushed under hooves.

Back in the car they had another hour of hurtling down narrow lanes and rushing through hedgerows until they reached the sea and the body that could not be Gigi. Bridey sat back and closed her eyes, squeezing the handkerchief in her fist.

An inn sat on the high overlook of the crashing waves, twenty minutes on the other side of Salcombe in a spot the police, local men, had referred to as Soar. The place was a location out of one of the mistress's novels, beautiful and perilous. Bridey remembered a book open across Gigi's lap, and the wind stole her breath.

At least the air carried a bit of mist from the waves smacking against the rocks. Bridey stood at the top of the rise over the water, bracing herself, cool droplets on her cheek.

Mrs. Arbuthnot took her by the arm and led her to the inn and inside. The lobby was long and narrow, with a dining room on the left set for breakfast for twenty or more, and a closed door on the other side. As they approached, the door opened and more policemen, more men with caps under their elbows, emerged. Eyes cut toward them and away.

"The lot from Churston," one said to the other, but where it might have been a question, the words lay flat. Or Bridey only heard them this way, listening as she was around the sound of her own blood pounding in her ears. She concentrated on the open door, willing the body beyond to be someone else, the same way she kept the aeroplanes in the air during raids. Remembered Gigi pumping air into a baby bag and wondering if there wasn't someone better suited —

"Miss?"

The sea of men, dark sleeves, parted so they could pass. It was a parlor of sorts, a large room meant for holidaymakers and cream teas. The hearth stood dark and cold, a small stone figure of a black dog nearby. A piano had been pushed toward the window that faced the water, and before that, a platform built, a plank resting on two chairs, and a sheet draped over an uneven form.

Mrs. Arbuthnot's grip tightened on her arm. She did not know Mrs. Arbuthnot well, and now probably never would, but she seemed like a woman with more below the surface than could be guessed. An iceberg of a woman that she and Gigi had only drifted into.

One of the policemen stepped forward to assist with the sheet, which made a reverent whisper as it fell away. Mrs. Arbuthnot's arm jerked in Bridey's, and she slumped to the floor. The crowd of men hurried to help Mrs. Arbuthnot to the nearest couch, someone calling for a jug of water.

"I'm so sorry," Mrs. Arbuthnot said. "I didn't think — I wouldn't have thought —"

The body lay unattended. Bridey felt her resolve crack and moan against the pressure of everything she felt.

She stepped forward and gazed down at the form on the plank, taking in first the blanket, wound around the body like a nest and shroud, darkened by damp at the edges. Covered, demure. A tendril of her long dark hair had fallen out and dripped into the rug.

After a moment, the face.

The face, whose edges had barely begun to turn soft.

Bridey's breath caught in recognition. Even in death, so lovely. She had not been in the water long. Where had she been all this time?

"Are you all right, miss?"

"Yes — no." Her legs went weak. But this was only a slab of flesh, emptied of spirit, which had been released. When the soul had no home to return to, was that freedom at last?

Could it be?

If I had the chance to end suffering, I would have to try.

She was not here. She was gone, beyond suffering. This spirit was already mist in the air.

"I'm sorry," Mrs. Arbuthnot was saying across the room. "I don't think I can . . ."

"Mrs. Arbuthnot." Bridey felt the room shift toward her. "Stay there. One of us should be spared."

"Oh, Bridey. Is it her?"

"Miss?" one of the men said. "Can you help us?"

"Yes," Bridey said, taking the handkerchief out of her sleeve. Like a conjurer, making it all go away. "Yes, it's her. I'm sure of it."

She had feared coming apart and now allowed the breach, the snap of all her reserves. All her own edges went soft and the men came running. Bridey poured herself across the body and let loose the torrent of her grief.

53
BRIDEY

On the road from Soar

"Is this the way?" Mrs. Arbuthnot said.

"Yes, ma'am," the man behind the wheel said.

"If you're sure." She didn't sound sure herself.

Bridey opened her eyes to a desolate vista.

"It's a different way than we came," the policeman said.

That was bad luck, if she'd ever heard it.

"This road avoids some of the twists and turns," he said. "For the young lady."

"That's kind of you," Mrs. Arbuthnot murmured. She sounded as though she would have liked to have been consulted.

"Thank you," Bridey said, sitting up. She unpinned her hat and used it to fan herself. "I'm feeling much better."

Mrs. Arbuthnot's head turned in her direction. Perhaps she should have grieved or slept all the way back to the house. She might have been allowed to accept a cup of tea and an early bedtime. She lowered her eyes. "My stomach is feeling better, anyway."

"It was a difficult task," Mrs. Arbuthnot said. "I'm sorry you had to do it."

The man in the passenger seat had turned to see her. "What will happen now?" Bridey asked him.

"Well," he said. "We'll talk to any witnesses, last to see her, that sort of thing. Perhaps someone saw her before she, er, went in."

"I meant what happens to her body?"

The driver raised his chin to see her in the mirror.

"They'll get her back to her people in London," the other one said.

"I don't think she had any people," Bridey said. "No one to go home to, that's what she said."

"That's a little more difficult then. Someone will make decisions for her, in that case."

"A pauper's grave?" Bridey said.

No one said anything.

"In Salcombe?"

"What does it matter, Bridey, if Gigi had no people to visit a grave in London?" Mrs. Arbuthnot said.

"She has me."

"These things can be quite dear."

Mrs. Scaldwell had spotted the Arbuthnots for the kind of wealth who couldn't spare a farthing. "Well," Bridey said. "There's the payment coming to her. For minding the nursery."

Mrs. Arbuthnot pursed her lips. "Yes, I suppose you're *right,* but of course we'll have to replace her, won't we? I can't spare her full payment when she only worked a —"

"She can have my portion," Bridey said. "I mean — both our portions can go toward a proper burial." She would open the hem of Gigi's cloak, as well. A ransom she was sure Gigi would have been willing to pay.

Mrs. Arbuthnot blinked at her. "I can make inquiries for you, if you like."

"I'd like to see to the final details myself." She would make sure it would be just and right.

But in the instant she allowed pride to sneak through her defenses, all the seams were split. She clutched at herself and knew she would be sick this time. "Please," she hissed.

"Pull over," Mrs. Arbuthnot commanded.

"Eh?" One policeman turned to look, but the driver did not ask questions.

At the side of the road, Bridey threw open the door and dove for the verge. She heaved until all she could produce was bile, until she was empty and shaking, making her think of the soldier back at St. Prisca's who had shuddered under care.

She hadn't the courage for what she must do.

Mrs. Arbuthnot came to stroke her back. "Where is your handkerchief?"

"I've misplaced it."

"Never mind. Sir?"

Another was produced between the policemen, plain, white, serviceable. When she thought she could manage the last miles of the journey, Bridey held the cloth to her mouth and accepted help back into the car.

They were quiet the rest of the way. Bridey leaned her head against the window and pretended to drowse. She did doze off, because when the car stopped, she woke from dreams, where she had chased Gigi through the woods, over the stile and across the fields, field after field and no village appearing. She had to catch herself, quickly, as she woke, to keep herself contained. Had she spoken in her sleep? Her head ached, and her mouth and stomach were sour.

As the police motorcar pulled away from the back door, Mrs. Arbuthnot held Bridey's elbow. "One moment."

Bridey could barely stand. "The children . . ." But she had no duties there now. She had only stayed to see Gigi home and now —

"Why would Gigi go to that place? Did she know someone there?"

"No one she spoke of. I didn't know her that well."

"You were thick as thieves," Mrs. Arbuthnot said. An accusation. "Whispers in the gardens, laughter along the paths."

"We passed the time."

"Passed the time well enough for the display at the sight of her body? On the road today? Well enough you'd pay for her burial and see to the final details yourself? What happened to her? You clearly don't believe she walked into the sea, Bridget."

Bridey heard the shift. One Bridget, only Bridget.

"I thought she'd gone back to London. To be more useful to the war effort."

Mrs. Arbuthnot studied her. "I wish she had. You may go to your room. My girls will see to the evening rituals." They started toward the door. "But the children's *health* . . . I suppose I should ask after another nurse —"

"Send for two."

Mrs. Arbuthnot pulled up short. "You don't mean to leave? The children need consistency in this time of upheaval, and they'll look to you."

"You're their constant, missus," Bridey said. "I admire what you're doing here, and the children will —" She could barely say the words. "They'll be fine without me."

"But why?"

"Begging your pardon, the assignment isn't to my liking. It's too isolated, I suppose."

"Isolated and safe —"

"Having identified a body today, missus," Bridey said, "I'll have to disagree."

"Compared with London, we've been spared. Bridey, they need you. I suppose, well, *I* need you."

"I'll stay on until you're settled at the next location."

"We're still fighting the requisition."

"But we'll lose," Bridey said.

"We can't be defeatist."

"I only mean with the Admiralty, missus," she said. Gigi had been right when she'd said the house on the river was better suited for sailors or soldiers than the likes of them. Gigi had been right about a lot of things. "They'll have the house if they want it. We're in the way of the plans they have, and they won't upend the scheme even for a lady like Mrs. Mallowan. Send for two girls. I'll stay on until they arrive, or you're settled in the next place." Bridey braced herself to say what needed to be said. "I won't leave you in the lurch."

Mrs. Arbuthnot looked at her strangely, then turned and led them to the door. "She must have been disturbed in her mind."

"She must have been. If I'm honest, missus —"

"Yes?"

"I've been thinking and I hate to say it —"

"Do just say it, Bridget."

"If she had stayed," Bridey said, "might she have been dangerous to the children?"

"Oh." Mrs. Arbuthnot's hand faltered reaching for the door. "Well. I would never — Let's keep that between ourselves."

"Of course, missus."

"You're sure you won't stay on? The war can't last the winter, they're saying."

They had been saying it for three years now. "No, missus."

Mrs. Arbuthnot despaired of her, she could tell. "Right, then. Go and lie down."

Bridey went through the door, the corridor, weightless. On the stairs, she realized she had not come in by the same door she'd left again. More bad luck, and it was all she deserved.

54
BRIDEY

Edith caught Bridey at the landing. "You've a gentleman caller, miss."

Why did she think of Tommy Kent?

"Who?" It wouldn't be Hart. Would it? She turned back.

In the front entry, Mrs. Arbuthnot stood sentry outside the morning room, still in her traveling coat and hat. "You have a visitor, or do you wish me to send him away?"

Bridey looked in. "Jenks."

He turned and stood, reached for her hand properly. "Miss Kelly."

"I —" She couldn't remember his full name. Mrs. Arbuthnot watched with keen interest from the doorway. "Could I introduce you to my employer, Mrs. Arbuthnot?"

"Arbuthnot," Jenks said appraisingly. "Pleasure. Henry Kenworthy-Jenkins, madam."

"From —"

"Indeed."

The mental image of some large house had passed between them.

"Would you like some tea, Mr. Kenworthy, uh, Jenkins?" Mrs. Arbuthnot said, removing her coat and taking Jenks's hat. "We've only just — Mrs. Scaldwell? One moment."

Mrs. Scaldwell peered into the room, accepted the things thrust at her.

"Could you work up tea for Bridget, please?" Mrs. Arbuthnot said.

"For Bridget?" The cook looked in again.

"And her *guest.* A trying time just now, could you, please?"

"Yes, of course." Mrs. Scaldwell scraped the room for details as she went.

"Now," Mrs. Arbuthnot said, taking a prim seat at the edge of the settee next to Bridey. As careful as she was, the cushion underneath Bridey shifted unpleasantly and her insides leapt. "Now, to what do we owe the pleasure of your visit, Mister — uh . . ."

"Call me Jenks, ma'am. Much easier to get to the end of."

She wouldn't be able to do it. "And were you and Bridget friends in London?"

Jenks looked at Bridey uncertainly.

"She means me," Bridey said. "We've only met recently, missus. In the village."

"Ah yes." Mrs. Arbuthnot had scolded her

for traipsing off but now seemed mollified that such fine company might be had in Galmpton.

Bridey felt the expected thing coming at her like a train. "Gigi introduced us," she said.

Mrs. Arbuthnot lowered her head. "Perhaps you would like a few moments."

"Thank you," Bridey said.

"I'll see where the tea is."

Jenks waited until Mrs. Arbuthnot had left the room. "Is there something happening?"

"I'm sorry," Bridey said. "I've only just arrived from identifying a body of a woman found off the coast near Salcombe —"

"You won't say it's . . ."

"I won't say it if you prefer I wouldn't. They believe she took her own life —"

"That's impossible."

"Of course it's impossible. She would never —"

"I mean that it's impossible that she's dead."

Bridey looked toward the doorway. Empty. "What do you mean?"

"I've been to London since we last met," Jenks said. "The home office, some old friends . . . ?"

The observers. "Yes."

"They contend the Friar's never left

London, and there's not a whisper of anyone coming this way. Other than the five of us."

"No one from London was ever sent after you?" Perhaps Thorne had picked a fight at the pub after all? And Gigi had jumped at mere shadows?

"They did seem to know where we were, mind." Jenks rubbed at his furrowed brow. "*Someone's* here, reporting back. Odd to be the one *observed*. But I know when the front mat's being pulled out. It's time to shove off, me. They're sending me over. Bad time to have a little boarding school French." He leaned forward on his knees. "I came to tell Gigi. I supposed I thought . . . I thought she might be back."

It had to be done. "I'm sorry, Jenks."

"She's not really dead?"

"I don't know what to tell you."

"You're a nurse so I suppose you know what you're about but is there any way —"

"I'm not a nurse," Bridey said.

It was out of her mouth before she knew she would say it, but she didn't scramble to swallow the words back. The welcome had worn out, as Jenks had said.

"I thought they said . . ."

"They did say. But I lied," Bridey said. "I was training, you see, but things got mixed up at the hospital and — I killed a man."

She had not said it quite so boldly before.

"Is this a confession?"

"It was an accident. Vials mixed up, or I gave too much. I don't know. I was never sure what I'd done to make him shudder and kick as he did."

Jenks's foul look eased. He leaned forward. "Shudder and kick, you say?"

"It was awful," she said.

"What did he do? Did he cry out?"

"Yes, and then —" Too weary to remember another death scene.

"And then every muscle in his body seized at the same time?"

Bridey looked up. "How could you know that?"

"Was he foaming at the mouth?" Jenks said. "When the fit passed, had he, uh — excuse me — er, relieved himself? Down his trouser leg?"

"I didn't — I was dismissed in a hurry and never — You said 'fit.' "

"Have you never seen someone in the throes of a seizure?" he said. "Epilepsy, I mean. My brother had spells, awful to witness."

"Epilepsy." She'd heard of it but hadn't seen it. She hadn't finished her training — she'd barely begun. There were countless conditions she hadn't encountered in the time she'd lasted, or perhaps she hadn't always spent her attention where it should have been. Always looking ahead, always striving. "Is it deadly?"

"It can be. There are powders for it, now."

Hadn't the matron said the soldier had died? Or had that been her own interpretation? But if he hadn't, if the man only suffered an episode of a survivable illness, then why had she been made an example? Why had she been sent away?

Bridey remembered feeling small, accepting the matron's complaints. That she was haughty — arrogant, that was the word. That she played God. That she was trying to patch up patients without care, with a clenched fist and a heart that was closed off behind a locked door. Well, it was true enough, but there were no remedies for her disease. The best medicine — for grief, for battle fatigue, come to that — was time.

A rest cure. But she never would have agreed to it.

She hadn't agreed to it.

She went along on the evacuation for the sake of her return. She never would have put herself among small children, who only reminded her of everything she had lost. She never would have turned her attention outward the way it had been, not she, who had been curled around to protect her own soft flesh. As lonely as her life had been in London, she never would have given it up.

"What are you thinking?" Jenks said.

Unless she'd been forced to give it up. Unless Matron Bailey had seen the opportunity and taken it.

The matron couldn't have lied and said the man was dead? It was too cruel.

But how many lives had the matron saved by making her believe she had taken just one? By shunting her off for garden play and cleaning behind ears?

She should have been angry.

But he lived. She was not a killer. He lived and so would those he went on to help, the thin thread that pulled through all their lives not snapped at all, but secure. Her confession had absolved her of all her sins. Most of them. "I was just thinking about dear, dear Gigi," she said, and it was one true thing.

55
SCALDWELL

Greenway House, 18 September 1942

Frank Scaldwell let himself out into the courtyard. Above, leaves rustled in the trees. A storm would come in the night, perhaps. Best get his turn through the grounds over with.

A little rain wouldn't deter a fifth-column man, would it? A German invader?

He'd heard some little gal had been handing out white feathers in Plymouth. As though it was her call who could go and fight and who was a coward. He'd heard she'd handed a feather to a veteran of the Great War and he'd had his fun with her, asking next time for the whole goose.

Frank started on the path to the top garden, small steps, his left knee a little stiff. Slowly. One unseen root might send him sprawling. What good to anyone to have him laid up, or worse? Imagine dying in the war by falling down a hill in the night and breaking one's neck.

Home Guard or no, there'd be no parades for a man like that. No honors at his burial.

These days, one had to think about the end. One's own but also the deaths that caught one by surprise, wedged under one's skin. Certainly he'd been gutted by the loss of Vera's nephew but for him it was the nurse's death, Gigi. Young woman, bright. How had it happened? Four months since they'd heard of her death and he still didn't understand. He'd put her out of the mistress's car at the station for the north train as she'd asked, safe and sound. Then she was found dead and further south. They spoke of suicide but he hadn't found her melancholy at all. They'd had a good talk about the estate and his duties, the Home Guard, the trespassers on the grounds. She'd thought he meant the fellow who'd been killed, but he set her straight. It had only been some blighter with a twisted ankle, using a fallen branch for a walking stick and hoping for a shortcut to the quay.

Perhaps she had been a bit melancholy, as she'd grown quiet then, and rode the rest of the way to the station in silence. He thought Greenway was a place people didn't want to leave, even when they thought they must.

Now the night was coming quickly and he

wished he had a walking stick himself. Why hadn't he brought a torch? He went slowly in the dark, feeling his way through the turns of the path as though he'd been born to Greenway land.

And now he would have to leave it. The Admiralty would take the house. The requisition moved forward and soon a crew of sailors would turn his mistress's fine home into a barracks.

He'd sensed it all along, that the mistress, working every connection, making every argument, would lose the battle. Soon, the children and their keepers would be cast off to another spot, and their shores would become a barricade. Greenway, a last defense.

Frank didn't know yet where he and Vera would be sent, or if anyone would think of them at all.

He followed the zigs and zags of the far end path down the uneven grade back into the woods, puffing breath. He'd *like* to see a German attempt these grounds.

At the boathouse, he checked the saloon, had a lookout from the terrace. For some reason he got the feeling someone had been there, a chair moved, a magazine turned over. He couldn't pinpoint it but went below to check the old plunge pool more carefully than he would have. All clear.

Of course all clear. What did he expect? To find a Nazi hidden in the bath, flicking through one of Mrs. M.'s books?

But he might, mightn't he? That was at issue, whether or not the Jerries might stop bombing them from above and come in for a dance. He never thought they would, but then he never thought he'd hear of their churches bombed, their towns gutted. For a moment, he put himself in the place of a younger man, a man who waited for his true life to begin, but had the time ahead for riches, for a piece of land to call his own, for all his potential to be realized.

He might have told the Register count taker he was three years *younger* and still been safe. But he hadn't. He had stretched his age in the other direction, lied. Was there a white feather for him and all? Who kept score?

If he had trouble living with himself, he only had to think of Hart. They'd traced a handkerchief of his from the nurse's body to his surgery, and found a set of trinkets from the houses of dead men. Bodies would be exhumed. The village wagged their tongues, trying to suck all the poison from the story. He'd never liked the man but — a murderer?

The noise began as a gnat at his ear. A mosquito. He swatted it away but the sound grew until he understood.

The air-raid sirens at Dittisham began to scream.

Frank raced back up to the terrace and looked out along the river. The 'planes came roaring overhead, chewing the air toward Dartmouth. He hurried back out into the trees, breath quickened. The droning grew small and was gone. The trees quieted around him until the night creatures began to make their noises, cautious.

The girl he tried to help was dead. The coward's white feather was as much as he had coming.

When he recovered himself, the night had closed in. How long had he stood there?

He hurried up the footpath and when he reached the battery, he crouched at the wall, one hand on a cannon. Cannons left over from the wars of long-dead men. It made no sense to him, that another generation would choose slaughter. They were not meant to fight their lives away. They couldn't be. He looked out over the water, gathering his wits in the blessed silence.

Across the river, a small light glowed.

His righteousness rose up and swallowed the last of his fear. What fool in Dittisham broke the blackout orders? Why not light a beacon for Nazi 'planes to attack by?

Was it Dittisham? Frank marked the far shore. The light seemed to be coming from the middle of the river. Something caught on the anchor stone? As he watched, the glow moved, danced. Almost as if —

Fire.

Frank stepped back from the battery's edge and watched the floating candle of the boat drift down the river. He closed his eyes and waited out the thrumming of his blood in his ears.

He'd make the full rounds, down to the quay, up to the road to Maypool, the next estate. They had 'vacs there, too. He wouldn't be able to sleep tonight anyway, not with boats blazing down the bloody river.

He would need a torch. The switchbacks to the quay were tricky in the dark, with a steep grade besides.

Frank was still on the middle path when he heard the gnat start up at his ear again. No mere pest. He fought the hill and the pain in his creaking knee and ran.

56
BRIDEY

In the house

Mr. Scaldwell's shouts rang up the stairs but Bridey couldn't hear what he said. Then the sirens in Dittisham began to wail, the rising and falling of warning. The bell at the quay joined in. An aeroplane groaned overhead, flying low enough to rattle the windows.

Mrs. Arbuthnot swung open the door. "Bring them down," she said, breathless. "Quickly."

Another 'plane approached. Something in the angle, the approach, was different than they'd had in a while. The noise of the 'planes still hummed in her teeth and bones.

She helped Mrs. Arbuthnot's daughters hurry the children down the family stairs and into the drawing room. They made a nest of the blankets and cushions and huddled all together, the youngest in Bridey's lap, a tot just starting to pull up on furniture to walk. Even Scaldwell came down among them, and his haunted look gave Bridey a fright.

They were forced compatriots who might live and now die together, as much a family as any she could claim now, as much a home as she had to go to. She clutched the baby to her.

Even if they got through the night, where would they all go? It boggled the mind to imagine Greenway a military headquarters. She'd once proclaimed that the children couldn't get too accustomed to living at Greenway House — but she had. She cared for it as though it were her own. It belonged to her — and Gigi. But she knew that wasn't quite right. The place didn't belong to them and never would, but somehow — in some small way — they belonged to it. They belonged to Greenway, and though she had planned to leave, wanted to leave, she wondered if she ever truly would.

"Nurse Bridey," whispered Pamela. "Are we off to another house?"

"Yes, soon," she said. "Be still."

"How will Nurse Gigi find us when she comes back?" Tina said.

"She's not coming back," Bridey said. Mrs. Arbuthnot glowered from the settee. She hadn't wanted to tell the children.

Hadn't wanted to tell the parents, more like.

"She's never going to mind us anymore," Doreen said.

"No."

"She didn't want to?"

"She would have stayed if she could."

Tina took a heaving sigh. The others plucked at the blankets, sniffled. James and John started to tussle and when she scolded them to stop, John hid his face to cry. Bridey remembered Mrs. Arbuthnot warning her: *Don't love them.* But the problem wasn't that she had loved them, was it? It was that they loved her.

She should never have been allowed near them. But because she had, they loved her, and she —

She loved them in return. She did. How had it happened?

Gigi. Gigi, alive, had changed her, and Gigi, dead, had changed her further still. She thought of her sisters and brother, her mam. *Could* she think of them? She took a breath and let is out, emptied herself, and was fine.

In a flood of feeling, she loved the Arbuthnots for bringing her here and the Scaldwells for keeping this home and the Mallowans for making a place such as this hers, if only for a moment. And now she was free, for the soldier had lived, and the village was safe from Oliver Hart, and Gigi —

The German aeroplanes came 'round again, screaming as they dove low over the house. Beryl slapped her hands over her ears. Bridey held her breath and looked down into the baby's sweet face, filled his vision with her loving gaze. It wasn't fair. He had lived his whole life here, his parents strangers. He deserved a chance to live. They all did.

An explosion went off all around them. Had it lifted the house into the air?

A crash — china in the next room. Shattering glass fell, all directions.

"Pull the blankets over them," she yelled. Mrs. Arbuthnot and her daughters stretched coverings over as many as they could. Bridey felt debris flying at her back and curled herself around the baby.

The house shook with another round, Mrs. M.'s collections falling from the walls all around. Another explosion sounded downriver, followed by the scream of enemy 'planes rising out of range. The telephone began to ring and the children wailed, all of the women taking as many into their arms as they could. They stayed in place until all was silent and the children started to fall asleep. They stayed a long time, listening to their own breath in the dark.

The children in bed at last, Bridey went down to the kitchen.

Mr. Scaldwell sat at the table, a glass of something dark near his hand and a bottle at the ready.

The edges of the blackout shades showed nearly dawn. "Get them to bed," Bridey said, "only to have them up in an hour."

"Maybe they'll sleep longer," he said. "The night they've had. Poor mites."

Bridey sat heavily at the table. She'd never before heard him use gentle words for the 'vacs, for anyone. "We've had the same night."

"Drink?" he said. "Might help you sleep."

"I might never sleep again," she said, thinking wistfully of the blue pills she would never take. She should toss them out, poison in the house with children.

He stood and got her a glass, filled it an inch from the bottle. "I saw what you did tonight."

The sip she took ripped down her throat like a knife, and she came out coughing.

"Second drink tastes better," he said.

"It would have to," she said. "What did I do tonight?"

"Protected that little one with your own skin."

Had she? It had all been rather chaotic. "Have you heard anything?" she said.

"They're saying at the quay that the shipyard in Kingswear was hit," he said. "Noss and Sons. It will take years to get it up and running again."

"Was anyone killed?"

"Twenty or more." He took a drink. "In a few hours we'll start to find out they're people we know, their brothers and sons."

"Or their sisters and daughters."

He poured her another inch of fire, with a nod. "Cheers, sisters and daughters and mums and — good friends."

"Yes."

"I never said. I'm sorry about Gigi."

She closed her eyes, letting the alcohol roam her veins. When she opened her eyes, he canted in her direction, waiting. "We hadn't been friends for long, but — thank you."

"You identified her body for the constables."

"Yes."

"And paid for her burial."

"I'd rather not speak of it."

"Of course, of course. Well," he said. "May she live on."

She looked at him.

"In our memories." He raised his glass. She tipped hers, drank deeply. "I hear you're leaving us."

"Everyone is leaving you," she said. "Or . . . where will you go when the house is taken over?"

"Wherever they tell us."

"Good soldiers, we are," she said.

He watched her take a drink, almost hungrily. She couldn't help wondering about Mr. Scaldwell, though she had until the night Gigi disappeared considered him as much a part of the house as the rug in the morning room, an egg timer in the kitchen. That night, he'd given her reason to wonder. *Was* he a good soldier?

"You know who I've been thinking of?" he said. "Whatever do you think happened to that poor mother who came to the house?"

Bridey brought the glass to her lips, found only a drop. She set down the glass and he reached to pour her more. "No," she said. "Thank you."

"What was her name?" he said.

"You mean Mrs. Poole."

"That was it. Where do you think she went?"

"The trains run both ways," she said.

"Her little boy —"

"He died," Bridey said.

Scaldwell poured another inch for himself. "She didn't have anyone else?"

For a moment, Bridey was confused which woman they spoke of. She shook her head to clear it. "She said she didn't. Mrs. Poole."

"What about Gigi?"

"She said something similar. No home to return to, a family that set her out. That's what she said."

"She said so many things," Mr. Scaldwell said. "How can we tell the truth from a lie?"

"What does it matter?" she snapped. Her eyes felt hot, the skin of her face tight. Anger was one of the emotions she hadn't been allowed in a long time. "What's the truth for, now? What should we use it for, a flag to fly in a parade? A bludgeon to beat her to death? It's too late."

They stared at each other. She had a strange feeling that they were not talking about what they had meant to, but her head was muddled with drink. Maybe he had meant it to be that way, to catch her out. She didn't understand his game.

"I heard in the village today that Dr. Hart was led away in irons," Scaldwell said. "Something about an onyx ring being returned to its owner's family."

"What's onyx?"

"A black stone."

"Is it valuable?"

"The gold setting would be a fine payment for the doctor's services, though the family doesn't believe it would have been offered as such. An heirloom, passed down generations, worn every day. Until the day he died."

"Of old age, I hope?"

"They never would have suspected the doctor, only —"

"I should go to bed."

"Only something of his turned up, alongside a body," Scaldwell said. "In Soar."

"Something of his, you say."

"His handkerchief," he said. "Tucked into her sleeve. Monogrammed."

"How elegant. She did carry things in her sleeve. Once —"

"How curious, though, that the doctor says he never met Gigi."

Hadn't he? Perhaps she hadn't learned soon enough not to play God. "Did they find heirlooms belonging to other families?"

"You can't believe for a minute he did the things he's accused of," Scaldwell said, his face red. "Is this some sort of spurned lover's revenge?"

"I don't know what to believe," Bridey said. "I suppose if the doctor is an innocent man, he'll soon find himself back in his surgery."

Scaldwell said, "*If* he is. This place deserves a good doctor."

"You deserve an *honest* doctor."

"What are you playing at?" he said.

"I should go to bed."

"Probably for the best." He took the bottle, stood, felt in his waistcoat pocket for the set of keys to the office, where the bottles were kept.

"Thank you for the drink."

"And the enlightening conversation," he said. "Take your time on the stairs going up. There's no doctor at all just now."

"We're down a nurse as well," Bridey said.

On the stairs, she took each step with concentration, with care. One of them had to get out alive, and if it wouldn't be Gigi, then it would bloody well be her.

57
BRIDEY

The next day

Bridey was in the kitchen garden with Mrs. Bastin when the post arrived and Scaldwell brought the postcard with the King's profile on the stamp out to her, special delivery.

He had read it of course, and stood waiting to see what she would say.

"Thank you, Mr. Scaldwell. I could have fetched it later."

"But what does it mean?"

"What does what mean? You've never been reading other people's post."

Mrs. Bastin had a laugh at that, because of course all the post that came to Greenway was considered his own until proven otherwise. Guardian, caretaker, monarch of this tiny realm — the manservant with no one to serve had made a squire of himself.

"It's only a postcard," he said.

"With *my* name on it." She turned it over.

He sniffed, glanced at Mrs. Bastin. "I

thought it might be for the other one. Is she not also Bridget Kelly?"

"You'd read a dead girl's post an' all," Mrs. Bastin chided.

But now Bridey had read the card. " 'When a lady loses everything,' " she read aloud, " 'where does she go?' "

"Oh," Mrs. Bastin cried. "What kind of letter is that? Is that some sort of hex?"

"It's from Gigi," she said. It had to be.

Mrs. Bastin let out a strangled noise. "All these weeks later? Was it lost in the post this whole time?"

Scaldwell glowered at Mrs. Bastin. "She sent it herself."

"What do you mean?" Bridey said.

"Frank Scaldwell," Mrs. Bastin scolded. "What are you on about?"

"Well, it's no greeting from the seaside," he said. "What's it mean?"

"I suppose," Bridey said, reading it again, trying not to let it break her heart. She barricaded herself against the message for now, only took in the words. It would do. "I suppose it's proof enough she jumped."

"Oh, bless her," Mrs. Bastin said.

"There's no mark," Scaldwell said, reaching for it. "That's her handwriting?"

She held it back. "I don't know her hand well, but I don't know who else would have sent me something so lonely. I can barely write my letters, myself."

"I'm the same," Mrs. Bastin said, kindly.

"Do you think the police will need this?" Bridey said. "Or can I keep it?"

Scaldwell turned and walked across the lawn toward the house. Bridey sat, her legs splayed, and read the card again.

"A lady what's lost everything would go to the workhouse, my day," Mrs. Bastin said.

"Lost all her money," Bridey said. "But what if she had no family, too? No husband. No protection at all?"

Mrs. Bastin's face was red. "Let's not speak of it, dear."

And so they didn't. But Bridey was certain Mrs. Bastin would speak of it again. It was just the sort of story she liked.

In the early evening, Bridey sat with the Scaldwells and the Arbuthnots in the kitchen, waiting them out so they couldn't talk about her. The telephone began to ring.

"That beastly thing," Mrs. Scaldwell said while her husband went to answer. "I wouldn't have a 'phone in my house."

They didn't have a house, though, and for once Mr. Arbuthnot didn't point it out.

Scaldwell's voice could be heard in the entry hall promising someone right away.

"What's this?" his wife said when he came back in.

"They need the nurse in the village," he said, eyes sliding to Bridey.

"What?" she said. "Who does?"

"You're needed at the surgery," he said. "The doctor being in the *prison.*"

"He deserves to be, if he did what they say he did," Mrs. Scaldwell said.

"*If* he did," Mr. Scaldwell said.

"Do go, Bridey," Mrs. Arbuthnot said. "If you can be any help . . . I don't suppose Mr. Hannaford could be so kind?"

"I'll drive you," Scaldwell said.

"Let me get my kit." She assumed Hart's surgery would have everything necessary, but it was better to be prepared in case they couldn't get inside. She had taken to wearing Gigi's cloak since the weather turned. It was made of finer stuff than hers and was warmer.

In the car, Scaldwell seemed to be gaining a head of steam to say something.

"Yes?" she said. "Was there something . . . ?"

"I'm sorry," he said. "About your friend."

"You said it already. But thank you."

"I said it before but — I mean it. I'm sincere. I thought — well, I don't know what I thought if I'm honest, but it seemed to me there was some shady dealings going on, and in the mistress's house."

"I would never play mischief with Greenway," she said. "I love Greenway."

He glanced over. "I believe you."

"Where will you go? If they make you leave, I mean?"

"We're talking of Australia."

"What?"

"It might not work out," he said. "But if the war has shown us anything — the war and all the other ways — it's best to take our chances when they come 'round."

As they pulled up to the doctor's house, the windows were incandescent, all the lights blazing into the lane. Scaldwell whistled and said, "Will you look at this? Where's the warden?"

A beaten-up farmer's lorry had been run into the verge, its door hanging open.

"They've no caps on their headlamps, either," Scaldwell said. "That's a citation."

The doors of the house were left open, front and side, the surgery door forced.

No caps on the headlamps. Bridey remembered the smell of the sheep pasture, Gigi begging forgiveness for bringing the Friar down on them all. She fought a chill. "Who called the house?"

"One of the villagers," Scaldwell said.

"They said a chap was looking for the doctor. I didn't think —"

"Whose lorry is it?"

There was a noise inside, a clatter, and a man's voice.

"Hello?" Bridey called. "Sir, are you hurt?"

"Is that the nurse?" The voice was deep, a growl.

"Mr. Michaelsmith?" Bridey walked inside the vestibule. The door to the surgery had been left open and, on its glass handle, a smear of blood. "Did you hurt yourself again, sir?"

"Should we go for the constable?" Scaldwell said.

"If you like," Bridey said.

Scaldwell hesitated but followed her through. The examination room with the bed was empty as well. Another open door, another slash of red.

"Where's the bloody doctor?" Michaelsmith shouted from deeper in the house. "I've need of him."

"I can help you, sir."

"I don't like this," Scaldwell said.

"It will take an age for the police," Bridey said.

"Who's with you?" A shadow moved in the next room, and then Michaelsmith's heavy tread announced the opening door. "Scaldwell."

"Michaelsmith," Scaldwell answered evenly. "Have you hurt yourself poaching on Greenway land again?"

"I've been hunting those woods long before you were leashed in its garden, and I'll be hunting those woods long after she cuts you free."

Michaelsmith's sleeve was dark with blood. "Let me see your wound, sir," she said.

"No man can see my wound."

"It's a good thing I'm not a man, then. Is it the same hand?"

"I mean it's invisible. I'm cracked through, and what tonic do you have for that?"

Was he drunk?

"Have a seat," she commanded, and was amazed when he did as told. When she pulled back his sleeve, his hand was wrapped in cotton from an old shirt, foul, frayed, and soaked through with blood. She reached for her kit.

"Here now." He yanked his hand back, stirring Scaldwell. "No jabs."

"It's only scissors, sir." She showed him, and drew his hand back under her control to cut away the bindings. The cut in his hand was infected still or again when it should have been healed over. "What acrobatics do you do, sir, that this wound is open? It's been months since you met that pint glass. You should take more care."

"It hardly matters."

She studied him. This wound hadn't festered for a year. It was fresh, renewed by the man's own blade. They'd had soldiers at St. Prisca's harming themselves to be removed from service and she'd heard of some bent on destruction of themselves this way, those who existed somewhere between living and dying.

"It matters if you want to run your farm, sir," she said. "Will you not submit to the syringe? Fine. Mr. Scaldwell, will you please go find a more suitable pain relief for Mr. Michaelsmith? Something in a glass, perhaps?"

Scaldwell's eyes flashed. "I'd rather stay and make sure he keeps sweet."

"Mr. Michaelsmith and I are old friends," she said. "Bring the bottle. Please." With the patient's attention turned to Scaldwell, Bridey made the shape of a telephone with her hand to her ear and nodded into the next room.

"If that's the case," Scaldwell said. He still hesitated but finally went, his footsteps quick across the floor toward Hart's telephone. She only hoped he might find it quickly, in case she was wrong about Michaelsmith, and they were not friends at all.

58
BRIDEY

At the receding of Scaldwell's foosteps, Michaelsmith scoffed. "What's he good for?" he said. "A butler. An organ grinder's monkey."

"He's more than that," she said, trying to remember what she knew of Mr. Scaldwell. She took off her cloak and lay it aside, then went to the nearby cupboard, found surgical spirits, fresh linen, a sealed bottle of boiled thread. If Hart had left behind his bag, she might have had all she needed easily. But she supposed it had been taken for evidence of his crimes. Everything in her sight nauseated her. "A husband. A father."

"Those are temporary occupations." Ah. His son.

"They are, quite often," she said. "I believe Scaldwell was in service in the last war. A rifleman."

Now Michaelsmith had interest. "Was he? What about this one? Why does he not serve his country now?"

"He's fifty if he's a day, sir. And he's Home Guard, anyway, on the prowl of the estate every night."

"Aye," he said. "I've seen him —"

He'd stopped himself saying more.

Doreen's wish man in the woods, and a mystery solved.

She cleaned the hand. "You've seen him while hunting in the Greenway woods?" Poaching, Scaldwell had said. Trapping foxes from the mistress's land as they screamed, and helping himself to the riches of the Greenway pantry, too?

"So what if I have?"

"Do you envy the land, sir, or the house?"

"Neither. If I can be accused of envy, it's a different sort of man than Mallowan I would envy. He lets his wife pay his way through life."

"No, he doesn't," she said. "He digs lost treasures out of the sand." She had the hand prepared for stitching but awaited the drink. Nothing would keep him sweeter than whiskey. "Lost worlds for us to remember and admire."

"Graverobbing."

Envy, plain and simple. Hadn't she spoken to someone about envy only recently? "Whom do you envy, then? The doctor?"

"Not him. I would never envy rubbish like him."

"Did he take something from you? You've broken into his home —"

"You wouldn't understand," he shouted.

Bridey glanced toward the open cupboard and the syringes there. She didn't know where Hart kept his morphine, even if Michaelsmith would submit to it.

Did time loop around on itself? That's what she felt — as if she had been here before, this moment. The morphine? She looked back at the cupboard, chasing the tail of whatever it was that hoped to speak with her.

The doctor. Morphine. Syringes?

"I would *like* to understand," she said.

The doctor, syringes.

Morphine.

Hart had confessed to the thefts from his patients, men who couldn't pay for his services — the owner of the onyx ring, the gold watch. Thorne. The cart driver. But he would not admit to killing these men or hurrying their illnesses. Now there was talk of bodies being brought up from their graves, of looking for signs of violence Hart would have had to explain away, like the finger marks on Thorne's neck.

But why would Hart not use the tools of

his trade if he had the desire to kill a man? Why should he resort to using his bare hands if he had access to sleeping draughts, morphine?

She took up the needle for Michaelsmith's injury and tried to thread it, but her hands shook.

Hart had taken Thorne's tie pin, no mistake. But Thorne's corpse, on the quay, still wore it. He would have taken it afterward. If he'd killed Thorne for the wealth in that diamond pin, wouldn't he have nicked it at the site of Thorne's death, before anyone could find the body and note it?

Hart had taken the other things, too. He admitted it, they said. But to kill a man for greed, wouldn't one take more? Not just a token from each, what one might deserve in payment for a patient who could not pay, but as much as one could slip away? All?

"You wouldn't," Michaelsmith said. "You wouldn't understand." His countenance cracked, folded in half. He held up his hands to weep into them, but she grabbed the wrist of the damaged one to keep it clean for the needle. In a single swift move, Michaelsmith turned his hand and gripped her wrist, and then reached up and had her by the neck with his uninjured hand, too. Her kit crashed to the floor.

"You *couldn't* understand," he said.

She did, though. The doctor had no need to use his strength on Thorne's neck. He had no need to use violence at all.

"Do you envy men," she choked out, barely able to form the sounds, "whose sons still live?"

He stood and lifted her so that her toes scratched for the floor.

"They live because they don't *fight,*" he growled. "And their fathers have a lot to say about how a war should be waged, while the rest of us shoulder the risk." His anger seemed to wane. He regretted having to snap her neck. "You wouldn't know a thing of what a man is expected to suffer if he lives during one of their wars."

"Women, too," she choked. Her head was swimming. "And children. My mam, my sisters."

Michaelsmith lowered her to her feet, hesitated. She thought she would die in his hand, his uncertain black eyes the last thing she knew.

He released her and she fell away, coughing, scurrying out of his reach until her back hit the bed. It was all so quickly over, she couldn't believe it had happened.

"Lost?" Michaelsmith said.

"My little brother, too." Her neck was

tender; her throat burned. Where was Scaldwell? "All gone."

"You spoke of them in the pub," he said. "How do you . . . ? I hurt — so profoundly, so that I don't know what to do with myself."

"How can it hurt you any less to inflict loss on someone else?"

"I'm a weak man," he said. His eyes caverns, cheeks hollow. "If I had any real resolve, I would join him." He held up the sliced hand. He had tried. Tried to bleed himself, tried to leave the wound open to decay.

"Would your son want you dead?"

"There's nothing left of him on this earth. Why should I suffer here without him?"

"I have asked myself the same thing. Many times."

They stared at one another. "What conclusion have you come to?" he said.

"I haven't. I'm still . . . gathering evidence," she said. "And if in the meantime I can do anything worth having been done —" *If I had the chance to end suffering . . .* "I have to try."

Michaelsmith sagged and grasped the chairback near him. "I've tried nothing but suffering — causing it."

He made for the door, crushing some of

her supplies under his boot as he went.

"Your hand!" The first thing she thought to say.

"Why should I care of gangrene when I go to put my old pistol between my teeth?" He blinked down at the mess on the floor, shattered glass and mercury. A glass bottle, unbroken, had come to rest near his foot. "I should have done it the moment I buried him. Bought the plots and put myself into the second."

"Wait." But he had not gone. He stood at the door, a man who could not hurry himself toward his weapon, had not been able to take the knife from his hand and gut himself. Bridey had seen the answer to his dilemma, but was it only more playing God? "You're determined to do it?"

"I don't know if I can." He hung his head. "I'm the coward, it turns out."

She thought of the matron's words, warning her that she would send more to harm with her arrogance. But if she sent only one? If she sacrificed one, as the matron had done? Whose suffering should end? Who decided mercy?

"That bottle at your boot," she said.

He looked down, reached for it. The blue pills rattled inside. She had never had a single one.

"What is it?"

"You should put those down, sir."

"What?"

"Please don't —" Bridey found that she was crying. "They're dangerous, sir, and must be handled carefully."

Michaelsmith held the bottle to the light. "Dangerous?"

"You should never take more than one at a time, sir, and certainly not all four at once." The crying hurt her aching throat and the pain only reminded her of Thorne, his collar too big for his neck. Did it have to be done? Did it have to be her? She would never again want the decision of life or death. Matron Bailey's tricks hadn't cured her of playing God. Michaelsmith had.

"All?" Michaelsmith's brow smoothed with relief, and his shoulders sagged. "Thank you," he said.

Scaldwell came in then from the street, starting to announce something. When he saw the destruction of the room, he went for Michaelsmith. "What — you blighter!" The larger man had the upper hand, landing a blow and sending Scaldwell tumbling into the cupboard. All of Hart's equipment and supplies came down with the shelves in a tremendous crash. Scaldwell came up, bloody-lipped and ready to fight, but Michaelsmith had gone. The butler stumbled after him, shouting out for others to stop him.

Bridey sniffled into her sleeve. After a few minutes, Scaldwell rushed back in.

"They'll have him, don't worry," he said, helping her up. "Did he hurt you?"

"He tried," she said.

"Is he the one, then? Not Hart."

"I think so. Yes." Her voice was hoarse, speaking painful.

"My God — but what stopped him?"

"I don't know," she said. One last lie. "I suppose he only wanted to stop."

59
BRIDEY

A few days later, at the boathouse
Bridey recuperated on the terrace of the boathouse, blanket tucked around her legs as the sun fell behind the hill. She had the mistress's library to select from, the latest across her lap and a lavender ribbon to mark her progress.

Lavender, the color of Doreen's siren suit stitch. The most natural thing in the world to remember.

Bridey suffered nostalgia for things still right before her in the in-between place she inhabited now — not a nurse to the children anymore, not a servant, not a guest. Not yet returned to London and somehow not quite at Greenway anymore, either. Treated with kid gloves by Scaldwell, like a sack of meat the wisht man had brought back from the hunt by his wife and Elsie. Like a waste of the rations by the Arbuthnots. She'd been offered a letter, heroics detailed and praise effusive, to take wherever she went. *When* she went, which would be soon. The children didn't understand, but the time had come to leave. The front mat pulled in, as Jenks had said.

Where does a lady go? She was no lady; she had no idea.

A floorboard creaked behind her in the saloon.

"Hello?"

A footfall, then a click. It was Lew, her hero from the train, come a long walk on his bad knee and cane. "Is the lady of the manor accepting visitors?" he said, standing in the doorway, blinking into the sunset. "Magnificent view."

"I'm going to miss it terribly," she said.

"Going somewhere?"

"Home. Or —" She waited for the rush of guilt and grief whenever she thought of the old home place, her family, but it didn't arrive. Not as it once had. Her grief would never be entirely spent, but spending some of it instead of bottling it up had cured some part of her circumstances. "Or what's left of it, I should say."

"Won't they miss you here?"

"Some will," she said. "But they're moving on, too. We're not supposed to know, but it's American officers of some sort taking the house."

"We know so many things we shouldn't know," he said.

She didn't point out that he knew things because he eavesdropped for them.

"Gigi said it would be like this," she said. "She said it should be sailors instead of us and now it will be." Military vessels prowled up the river as she spoke. Were they not supposed to notice? Charlie and Artie, the young men from the Manor Inn so long ago, must have known something of the plans. Had they ever *said* they were sailors? Or were they surveyors or sounders readying for this onslaught and whatever came of it? "She said Greenway would have a place in the victory."

"Did she?" he said. "Did she use the *word* victory?"

She didn't want to be jollied.

"It's a shame about the requisition," she said. "I'm sure the house has been through worse, when you consider the cannon set into the hill. But it's a lovely place, not a barracks. The mistress had it set up just so, just as she liked it. Curved doors in the dining room, the library full of books —"

"The bath with the ledge upstairs — what's the ledge for?" he said, laughing. "To keep her books dry?"

"Apples. That's what they say, that she likes to eat apples —"

The smile had fallen from his face.

When had he been upstairs at Greenway House?

She couldn't think of a thing to say about apples now. Was it Michaelsmith creeping along the corridors of Greenway, or had this man taken a turn? *Had* Gigi drawn the devil down from London to Greenway — not following behind as she thought, but on the same carriage? The Friar's lieutenant among them the entire time?

She thought of the money lining Gigi's cape.

Or perhaps he was acting on no one's orders, only taking the opportunity of an easy pay packet.

"I always thought apples in the bath sounded rather decadent," she said easily. "Luxury doesn't suit me, I suppose."

"No?"

"I sent Gigi's things to a foundlings hospital. Do you think she would have approved?"

Lew gave her a shrewd look. "Those nice jumpers of hers?"

"To make baby blankets."

"The only way she might be a comfort to orphans," he said. "You sent all her things?"

"All." The cloak's hem, emptied, and a bit of the money spent to bury a suicide in consecrated ground in London. The rest to charity. It was bad luck to keep ill-got money. It should be. "To charity. Nothing to her family, nothing to Willa or Jenks. To nameless orphans needing a second chance."

Bridey kept the cloak itself, the crooked stitches replaced just as they had been.

He tapped the tip of his cane against the terrace floor. "You know Bridget Kelly wasn't her name?"

"It doesn't matter what her name was."

"You're not the least curious? I thought you were friends."

Over on the quay, someone rang the bell for the ferryman. "We were friends," Bridey said. The truest thing. "I loved her."

"Well, that was a mistake," he said to the river.

"It always is."

60
BRIDGET KELLY

St. Saviour's Hospital, London, May 1944
Three ambulances arrived nearly on top of
one another, the men quickly arranged but
everything a muddle. Bridget made rounds
ahead of the doctor, sorting names and as-
sessing conditions, but at the last bed of the
ward, she reared back.

"What is it?" The young doctor approached. After hours, the other trainees
discussed this physician at length, trading
the same few known facts until they were
shiny with wear. He wasn't terribly handsome, but he was nearly their age, and when
he rolled up his sleeves, he had good strong
arms. Like a farmhand, one of the girls
would squeal.

Sometimes when others picked the doctors to pieces, she wondered what they
would make of Oliver Hart. Wasn't there a
moment, before discovering him a thief —
not a murderer, but an accomplice of sorts,

distracted enough by his greed to miss the signs of murder a moment when — he might have been hers? In disgrace, he'd given up his practice. Given up practice in South Hams, that is. A new name, a new place — Bridey had considered it for herself before coming back to London, Mrs. Arbuthnot's letter in her sleeve.

The patient before her now lay with his eyes closed and linen showing blood wrapped around his head. "I don't want to bother him."

"I'm awake," the man said. "I just have a terrible headache. One of his majesty's bloody jalopies ran me down." One of his eyes was swollen shut, but the other landed upon her. "Bridey."

"Tommy."

The doctor raised an eyebrow. "A reunion? What happened to you, soldier? Look into the light." The doctor waved his hand over Tommy's face.

"Two days' leave to see my mother, and I stepped into the street and took a truck to the side of my face."

He'd had a boyish look the last time she'd seen him, but now his rounded cheeks were gaunt, his eyes dull. They all of them had that look these days, the war dragging on.

"Where are you posted, soldier?" the doctor said.

"If I'm not ready for the streets of London, I'm hardly right for defense of the nation, am I? I'm a clerk down the street."

The doctor murmured something as he unwrapped Tommy's bandage to reveal a shallow gash and bruising. The bleeding wouldn't stop without stitches. Tommy looked at Bridey over the doctor's shoulder. "How have you been?"

She shook her head. "How is your mother?"

"She doesn't like you."

"I wouldn't like me, either."

"I did, though," Tommy said. He turned his attention to the doctor. "I liked her a great deal."

"Is that so?"

"She wouldn't marry me," Tommy said.

"Perhaps something for his delirium, Doctor," Bridey said.

"He sounds sensible to me," the doctor said, looking Bridey over as though he saw her for the first time.

Tommy watched Bridey the entire time the doctor's hands were on him. "Am I going to live, Doc?"

"Yes, and I'm afraid I can only eke out three stitches here. That's not enough to earn leave."

Tommy tried to laugh. "I'm not a dodger. Just an idgit who didn't mind where he was crossing."

"Right then. Since we're rather busy, I'll have Nurse Kelly here tidy you up. Three stitches —" He was away before he'd finished the sentence.

She brought the surgical spirit and a section of gauze to his side. "This will sting a bit."

"Is that what you tell all the blokes, Nurse Kelly?" He sucked his teeth as she blotted his wound. "It might have been Nurse Kent."

"I'm still a trainee, not a nurse." She'd started anew, ground level, ready to learn. What else was there to do?

"I go by your old house."

"Hold still now. It's not a house if there's no house."

"Is it because you think we'll live too near there? With my mother?"

"Hush."

Four stitches. She might have done it in three, except she wanted the scar to be minimal, a thing he forgot. Ten, twenty years from now, he would have to search for it in his hairline.

He watched her face as she attended to him. They had never been so near, not for longer than it took him to kiss her cheek.

"It's only because you didn't love me, isn't it?"

"It's not that I didn't love you, particularly." She administered fresh bandages and a length of linen to cover it all. His curly dark hair was soft against her fingers. "I always wished I did."

"Is it someone else?"

"There's no one else."

He laid his head back. "Am I that awful?"

"Of course not."

"Is it the shame of me in this uniform hit by a bloody bus?"

"Tommy —"

"You'd respect me more if I was shot, or torn up by a shell. Even a friendly."

"Tommy."

"That's what I do, you know, investigate the times we kill or maim our own. It's the most senseless thing I can think of — except being the bloke stuck at the desk, up to his ears in it. *Counting* friendlies, making excuses for the damage we do each other."

She should get back to work. She could hear footsteps hurrying, the ward sister calling for assistance. "It happens that much? I didn't realize . . ."

"When you hand guns to men who've barely started to shave."

"Accidents, then."

"Not all," he said. "Accidental, misguided, purposeful."

"That's awful."

"I would try very hard to make you happy," he said.

He would. "It doesn't seem fair," she said. "What if it wasn't enough to make me happy? What if you couldn't make yourself happy?"

"*You* make me happy," he said. "You always have. I know it's hard for you since . . . since. Why wouldn't you close yourself off after something like that? But I remember you from *before.* I remember you a laughing child in the lanes, Bridey, do you remember?"

"Yes." Her head hurt. She would get them both something for their headaches.

"Remembering you before, it helps me remember the me before, too, do you know what I mean? And it's like a — like a compass. Inside, like. If I can get back to that, or anywhere near it, maybe it's not all lost. Even if an awful lot is."

Across the room, the ward sister called for her.

"I need to go," Bridey said.

"I don't know." He closed his eyes. "Maybe I've put too much on that picture

537

in my head. Maybe it's too far gone. Or we'll have to build it ourselves."

"Build . . . what?"

"Everything back," he said. "As we should like it to be."

She thought of touching his hair again but didn't, leaving him to rest. For the remainder of the morning she was run off her feet, but now and then thought of herself as a young girl. So much lost. But not all. Up and down the ward all morning, she took every chance to walk by the bed in which he lay, the new center of the room.

61
WILLA CROSSLAND, WRN

HMS Cicala, Kingswear, 3 June 1944
Around midday, something in the River
Dart caught Willa's attention. A grinding
sound, metal.

She paused in the street below the hotel
that served as their headquarters and looked
down the slipway toward Dartmouth. She
was supposed to be inside, a direct order,
but what was that one little rule broken
among so many?

The river was crowded with wide landing
craft, three or four deep on each shore and
their decks crowded with vehicles. The Dart
was so thick with vessels that she might
jump from deck to deck across the water to
Dartmouth and not get her stockings wet.
The ships had packed in and then the
stream of men had poured down from the
hills behind the village, from their temporary
camps, from the train station, through the
streets in a steady and rowdy parade to the

shore and out into the ships and carriers. The Wrens had watched from the windows of HMS *Cicala,* as the hotel had been named in its service to the fleet, until the streets were once again clear.

When they'd first packed onto the ships, the men spent as much time above decks as possible, stripped to their waists and sunning themselves, tossing sweets to the children and letters home for the Wrens to post. Some had blown air into their issued prophylactics, tied them like balloons, and batted them around, having a fine time. They had brought jazz tunes to the river, clarinet and saxophone. The music so cheerful, you couldn't help but listen, to make light work. Willa knew every song by heart without trying, and sometimes realized she was tapping her foot. She would suddenly remember where she was, what was at stake, and think of Gigi, something she tried not to do.

Jenks had come to see her not long after Gigi had been found and had a lot to say, a lot of questions. Had she been in contact with someone back in London? Had she drawn attention down on them? She could have put the blame on him — he had family there, too, a woman and a nipper his father wouldn't want to claim, some said.

Well, when you had something like that against you, they could always twist you to get what they wanted, couldn't they? She'd had her mother, still living in the old neighborhood, where there was no such thing as a secret. Love had been her mother's weakness or Willa wouldn't exist; it was everyone's.

Well, her mother was gone now. She was free to name names, point fingers. She had no one left to lose, and no one left who could lose her. She had alerted Home Intelligence, made a full report of what she knew — but she didn't know everything. Had she somehow brought it all down on them? That's what Jenks had been suggesting, wasn't it? That one of *them* had caused all the trouble?

She'd been waiting to be summoned when all leave was canceled, all exercises cleared, and then thousands of men flooded into the valley. Time passed, the order of lockdown came, all the rowdy men stowed inside their ships, and the river went silent.

For days now the Wrens had been whispering in the corridors, looking fretfully toward the river. The air was charged, as though the string of a bow had been drawn back and held.

Held, except — there it was again, the

grinding sound, a low creak. Willa turned to the water, watching the gentle rocking of the nearest vessel, a large LST anchored to the old rusty iron buoy outside their office window. Inside, tanks, vehicles, men strapped in place.

All the Wrens in Confidential Books had known the details, had devised and couriered the codes and navigational chartlets the crews required to synchronize, launch, land. The date got around, as rumors did —

A low metal-on-metal sound. As though . . .

Willa shielded her eyes. The nearest landing ship, the LST that had been their vista, their neighbor and mainstay, had weighed anchor.

They were moving out.

All Willa's feelings caught in her throat and a sob escaped.

It was *happening.* The ship inched forward, and the few men on the deck waved to her wildly. Waving not with letters, not in greeting but . . . good-bye.

Good-bye. She nearly stumbled with the weight of it. She turned and raced inside, up the stairs and through the corridor, shouting.

"Willa!" A friend tried to catch her sleeve, but she slipped past.

"It's happening!"

She hurried into the station's communications center, footsteps collecting behind her. "Ladies," started a superior voice, but Willa passed quickly through. When she caught sight of a set of their flags, she grabbed them and burst onto the terrace. Below, the mouth of the river was still choked with ships, but the first of them were beyond the castles at each side of the river's mouth. They were in the Channel and sailing on.

It was not someday any longer. It was now.

Could it all be saved? They would find out

She gripped the flags, one in each hand, index finger just so. She heard others filling the doorway behind her, cheering, crying.

She raised the flags, *Attention,* pulled into a beginning stance, then lifted the flags into position. *George. Oboe,* beat, *Oboe. Dog.* Flags down, crossed in front of her to signal a new word. *Love. Uncle. Charlie. King.* G-O-O-D. L-U-C-K. Flags down, crossed. She positioned the flags low: *George.* Her right arm swung to nine o'clock. *Baker.* Flags crossed, end of word. *George. Baker.* Which meant Good-Bye.

It wasn't much, was it, for the last hope of England and the free world, these troops slipping out of the River Dart and into the battle for all their lives?

They would have been offered communion below decks, all the preparatory rites in case they did not return. Many of them would not. Tears ran down Willa's face and into the collar of her blouse, but she didn't stop to wipe at them. It would take all day for the ships to clear Dartmouth. There were hundreds of vessels to see off. Thousands of men.

Thousands of men and she was a traitor, thinking of one woman. But no, they all thought of someone else, the one left behind, the one they might not return to.

George Baker, she signaled again and again until the flags blurred and her arms grew tired. She did not stop. She wouldn't, not until she had used every bit of her strength. Behind her, the other Wrens had grabbed more sets of flags or waited a turn.

G-O-O-D. The flags wheeled and tore through the air. L-U-C-K.

62

SCALDWELL

On the Greenway Estate, 4 June 1944

Frank woke while it was still dark and couldn't coax himself back to sleep. A wind whipped up the hill and over the roof of the summerhouse, roaring like an engine. He could not grow accustomed to living here, not after the solid walls of the big house, the insulation of so many rooms. Vera murmured and turned over as he gathered his clothes and pulled the door behind him. He washed his face in the basin and looked at his dripping face in the mirror. The wind, insistent, but he had nothing to hurry him.

Most of the American officers staying in the house, Coast Guard, had packed up and disappeared days before. All along the river, the requisitioned homes and the sausages, the temporary camps, had emptied, and lorries roared through Galmpton, down to the quay. Platoons of sailors, phalanxes of soldiers, all flowed downhill from all directions, endless numbers of men, all streaming toward the river. Their little patch at the far end of the country had become the center of something great — the center of a storm, the center of the world, it had seemed.

When he'd last had a chance to gaze down the pasture from the summerhouse to the estuary, it had still been clogged with battle destroyers and the like, squat, hulking landing crafts. All of them pointing out to sea.

Now he walked to the front window and stared down the slope. He went out, leaving the door hanging wide.

The river was empty.

Ships had gone out before, of course. Maneuvers, practice runs. Frank had heard from Albert Dodge, the innkeeper, that some of the exercises down Slapton Sands way, where they had emptied full towns, had gone wrong. "Attacked by Germans right there on the beach where the mams take the tots for swimming," Dodge said into a glass he was cleaning. Frank could hardly watch him do it, it was done so badly. "Bodies on the bloody beach," Dodge said.

"It can't be," he'd answered. Slapton wasn't ten miles down the coast. The evacuation of all who lived along that stretch had been months ago. Who was left to tell tales?

One paid keen attention these days, after Lydell Michaelsmith had made them all fools. Bereft father, harmless enough. Hadn't they looked the other way as he prowled the county? A butcher of men, while Scaldwell worried over the estate foxes, good Lord.

Michaelsmith had scrawled the names of the men he'd killed, a confession, and escaped the noose by being found cold on his son's grave. Not a mark on him. Their neighbor a murderer, their doctor a thief. What had come of the notion they were all in it together? Had they become so worn down they couldn't take care of one another?

"Hundreds dead at Slapton, Scaldwell," Dodge had said. "Hundreds. I wonder if the government will ever come clean of it. Hurts the morale, you see, the truth does. What would we do without the sodding morale?"

Morale was low, indeed. His.

But now Frank sensed progress. Hundreds of ships, all of them gone at once? It was a sign that some great mechanism had been set in motion, and he was consoled to imagine it.

Consoled and shamed. Allowing young nurses to face off against killers and boys half his age to fight on his behalf. Here he stood on safe ground.

He was so tired and so fearful, but wouldn't they be, as well, those young men in the ships? Weren't their mums and dads holding their breaths back home?

Frank didn't realize he was crying until Vera put her arm around him.

"Are they off to save us all, then?" she said. "Good lads."

They put their heads together for a moment then went back to the summerhouse where they toasted the brave recent inhabitants of the estate and the Dart their good health and victory.

Afterward Frank took the top path over to see the damage done.

Greenway House stood high above the magnolias, as beautiful as it had ever been, as lonely. Its mistress in London, the master in Cairo or some such, the war nursery moved on, and the troublesome nurses —

But one of them hadn't moved on from here, had she?

At the house, Frank circled around back to see if Hannaford was at work yet, had heard the river was bare. He would check in with the Command staff who remained in the house later, and someday soon he would go through the rooms as he had not been able to do with the fifty American officers bunked there. Take note of nicks in the wall panels, damage to the paint. Some of that he could attribute to Arbuthnot, right enough, banging around with his easel and his leisure.

They'd have to remove the extra latrines, the smoky stoves in the kitchen, paint the library. One of the billeted sailors had painted a frieze of his flotilla's activities, including a bare-breasted slattern, using military-grade paint — grays and blues, as though he were decorating the belly of a destroyer.

When the damage was all tidied up, they could have the curved doors of the dining room brought out of storage and hung again. But it was too soon for a list. They must wait to see that the ships in the estuary turned the tide. If they did not —

It wasn't worth thinking about.

They would need to clean the house, top to bottom. To prepare for the mistress to return, to welcome back the victors? To close the shutters and drape the furniture for a new owner or until a brighter day? To see it yet bombed to ashes?

He couldn't predict, but it was his duty to always be ready and bloody ready he would be.

63
Bridey

Trafalgar Square, London, 7 May 1945
It was a Monday when surrender came.

Bridey rushed into the street and allowed herself to be dragged along in the crush of people toward the Column. Just an hour before, one might have thought the day was any other, but now the streets were wild and churning. Young people climbed the bronze lions, careless and carefree. Soldiers had their trouser legs rolled up to dance and splash in the fountains. Their girls, too, pegs as pale as the Portland stone of the Cenotaph.

Tomorrow Churchill would be speaking down at Whitehall. Tonight, the celebrations were their own making. The crowds would be at Buckingham's gates calling for the King and Queen. Every corner of the country would find its own way to demand ceremony and revelry. It had been a long time for solemnity and sacrifice. The bells of the churches all around rang and rang.

Bridey waded through the merrymakers. Perhaps an official parade had been ordered but tonight there were many parades, all directions, people hip to hip and glassy eyed. Tomorrow the ticker tape, the speeches. Tonight —

She caught sight of a woman weeping. Carousing as though she hadn't a care in the world but sobbing.

A man grabbed Bridey by the waist and pivoted around her. She made a clumsy dance partner until she shook herself free.

"And best of all, Hitler rots in hell!" another man nearby whooped, and many joined in to *huzzah* and cheer.

"I like his funny little mustache, don't you?"

Bridey stopped in the street, her feet almost out from under her. The crowd rushed around her on both sides, as though she were a stone in the current. The anchor stone from the center of the River Dart, a remnant of another time, another place.

Someone knocked into her shoulder, reminding Bridey where and when she was. She moved through the crowd to a side street.

A fête in the streets — what good was it? What good was waving a flag and pointing fingers into the air, when they'd lost so much? Too much. They would erect stone plinths to lay wreaths on for the men, and surely more bronze forms to the commanders. Where would they build the remembrances to the valor of the women who had died, who had protected, who had sacrificed? It was not just a generation of men who was lost or changed. It was all.

Nothing could get Tommy sputtering more quickly when she talked of it, but she wouldn't stop. He'd spoken of his compass for what was right but what she had was a thread that pulled, gently, in the direction she was meant to go.

Now she was tugged away from the gaiety, down the street, past the old places she had known, into the old neighborhood and to the churchyard. At her back, revelers filled the streets, whooping and singing and making a nuisance. She could not join in, though she stood before the results of a victory of her own.

On Samuel Poole's headstone, the dates for birth and death were far too close together.

Next to Sam's grave was the headstone that bore her own name.

She'd had to wrangle a bit, first to find the graveyard where Sam had been buried by kind neighbors, and then to negotiate this plot out of all others. Some of Gigi's hidden money had warmed the palms of leering men, sexton to gravedigger. But it had to be done, and the more notes she offered, the fewer questions anyone had.

She had not brought anything to decorate the graves, had no task to distract her from her thoughts. It was the woman sobbing in the street who came back to her. Amidst the flag waving and parades and dancing, she could not feel victory or even relief, not with so many sacrificed.

And then she was thinking of the long, wet tendril of dark hair dragging the floor of the inn at the end of the world. The wet fabric of the shroud framing the face whose features had only just begun to turn soft in the water, so that the drowned woman might be anyone. Anyone.

This Bridget Kelly, she thought, yet another. This Bridget Kelly would not mind what she was called. She had only wanted reunion with her son, and now she had it.

Bridey wished she had the words to say something. But she had lost the feel for her mam's God and knew she spoke to stone and soil.

In the end she said nothing, for the words would only be tossed into the roar of the world around her and swallowed. Who would she wish peace to? The victorious dead, the survivors, the innocent, and the damned? All of them. She closed her eyes. Man, woman, child. All.

64
DOREEN

Holmes Road, London, July 1945

The woman says we're home. The man calls her Edie, and when I do, too, to ask where home was, she says, "Why don't you call me Mummy? Or Mother, if you're so big now."

"Now, Edith," the man says.

"Peter, I can't bear it."

"Give her time, Edie, darling."

I'm six and a half. I wonder if I have been adopted and they don't want to tell me.

The mystery now is where have the others got to? Beryl, Tina, Pamela, and the others. They would be having afternoon quiet time now. I don't need a nap any longer but I've just woken in the borrowed motorcar, hot seat against my cheek and needing the toilet.

We're driving through a neighborhood but the houses are odd shapes and blacked at the edges. Or flattened. I ask politely, with all the pleases I'm supposed to, but the woman seems upset with me.

"She went away a baby," she says, her voice high and strange. "We're almost home, love," she says to me. "If you can wait just a moment."

Inside the front door, my case is placed down. The woman takes my coat and opens a door. The cupboard is small and the corridor crowded. The stairs are cramped and the sitting room so tight it could be a doll's house. Except it's not a doll's house.

"You're home now," Edie says. She seems to think I'll guess where the toilet is. She shows me.

Down the corridor, there's a room with one bed in it. It has a window, but outside there are no woods at all, no hill or trees, no river.

"Your very own room," Peter says.

They take me around the house and show me the things that are mine: clothes, all new. Some toys. There's a soft bear with black bead eyes. "You won't have to share with anyone," the woman says.

I gather the bear into my arms. It's the right thing to do, I can tell. The man Peter and the woman Edie leave. The room, so small, is suddenly too big and too quiet and everything in it is strange. Not mine. None of it is mine.

I wish for Beryl and Tina and Pamela, Mrs. Arbuthnot and the boys, and then I'm thinking of the big white house and the nurses and Mr. Scaldwell and the china cup of water on the stairs, and all the people who are mine instead of these ones. The Mother and The Father — like out of storybooks. In a story, sometimes the child is fattened up for eating in a cage, but I'm not sure which story this is. Is it the one with the wolf?

The Mother and The Father, like cut-out paper dolls ready to get dressed. I must be The Girl. The Daughter. And the clothes in the cupboard fit to me, flat.

Around me, the room is white and yellow and it has only one bed and for now I will play pretend. I will pretend it is mine and that I am me.

65

BRIDGET KENT

The Kent Home, Islington, 1 September 1945
In Margaret Kent's den, Bridget stood in front of a bookcase, sipping punch out of a proper china cup. After each sip, a wince. A bit heavy on the brandy. She ran a finger along a long row of book spines. *Aha.* Out in the front parlor, the formal room with the new settee no one would dare sit in, Tommy's mum stored only the smart sorts — the Lawrences, Huxleys, Garnetts, the Springs. But here among the second-best furniture was treasure: well-thumbed pages, spines cracked, familiar names. Sayers. Wentworth. Meade. Christie.

So the woman did like *something.* Stories and not just gossip.

"All right, Bridget?" her new mother-in-law called from the kitchen. "Did you get lost from the powder room?"

Bridget felt heat rise, neck and cheeks. One would think Mags, as her friends called

her, had never once used the toilet herself.
"Admiring your library. I didn't know you were a fanatic."

"Of *reading,* dearest?" Bridget could hear pursed lips, or imagined she could. "Can I freshen your cup?"

Bridget's head buzzed already. The wedding had been a Register Office affair, bride's insistence. But now she faced the reception, all Kent relatives and friends, no one from her side.

She had no side. Her prospects were a cup of punch, a slice of cake, a cup of tea, making small talk for an hour or two, and then — wedded bliss. With Tommy. Her husband.

What had she done?

She'd surrendered, that's what. Against the onslaught of charming promises and a clear horizon now that the war was over, Bridey had agreed to be a wife.

She abandoned the books and went to the kitchen. At the sink, Mrs. Kent handwashed delicate crystal cups from the punch set. In the next room, voices rose and fell.

"I don't need more punch, Mrs. Kent, thank you."

"Now, Bridget, we've talked of this. You may call me Mother or Mum, but Mrs. Kent won't do."

She never put a foot right in this house.

Since the engagement, spending time with Tommy's parents made her feel she was walking out into water, and just starting to lose touch with the sand below, just struggling to keep her breath.

She wouldn't call anyone else Mum.

"Now, darling, were you snooping?"

"No," Bridget said. "Only I noticed the bookshelves from the door." She *had* been snooping — observing. It was the only way to see people as they truly were. "Impressive collection of Christies."

"Those dusty things. Simon's mum leaves them when she visits."

"Oh." She couldn't hide her disappointment.

"I didn't know you were a *reader,* darling."

Bridget threw back the last of her punch. She had taken to reading, over time, seeking out secondhand shops, swapping with the girls at the hospital. She supposed that was over now. She hadn't had a chance yet to know which parts of herself she might be allowed to keep. "Did I ever tell you," she said, "that I stayed at the great lady's house during the war?"

"I *think* you may have mentioned it," Mrs. Kent said. "Now, will you take these cups out to the punch bowl for me? I hate to ask the bride but —"

"Of course. The bowl is empty, I think."

"There's always more. A hostess is prepared. Take note," she said. "Afterward, why don't you toddle out and see the guests? They're here to celebrate *you*."

The cups dispatched in the dining room, Bridey waded through conversation and deep-pile carpets the length of the house. In the parlor, the dining table chairs had been brought in and arranged. They were nearly full, and no one seemed to want to celebrate her, not one bit. The new settee sat empty, slipcovered and pristine.

She'd lost track of Tommy. Perhaps he'd gone with the men to the garden to smoke. Bridey sat on the edge of an available chair by the door.

"How are your strapping young men?" one of the women asked another.

"They're lovely, Kate, thank you, and how is your Geoffrey?" Kate's ugly goon of a son was somewhere outside, an old school chum of Tom's. When she thought of men like Geoffrey Hughes, Bridget hoped she never had daughters.

"Won-der-ful," Kate Hughes said. "As he got that promotion and pay-rise we were anxious over. What were we nervous about? They value him so highly."

Bridey had a headache and a nervous stomach at the thought of the party ending. She'd been to Tommy's mews court flat, of course, but not wearing a white suit and a gold ring. Not with the expectations that came with them.

"Good news, ducks," Mrs. Kent said, entering the room. "There's more punch, and my hand slipped just a *bit* with the brandy bottle." The crowd of them moaned and laughed. "Now have you all met our lovely bride? Bridget Kent, oh, I'm so blissfully happy, my dears, to have my son happily sorted to such a lovely young woman."

Mrs. Hughes's smile, manufactured.

"Tell us about yourself, Bridget," said one of the other women.

"Oh, there's not much to tell," Bridey said. "I — uh . . ."

"Why don't you tell them all about where you were in the early days of the war, Bridget?" Mrs. Kent said. "Special assignment at Agatha Christie's house, can you imagine?"

"I don't think —"

"I thought you were a nurse, dearheart," Kate Hughes said. "What great battles were fought at a storybook author's house?"

"Minding children, wasn't it?" Mrs. Kent said. Smiling at her friends, already plumping for grandchildren.

"So you *weren't* a nurse?" Mrs. Hughes asked.

"I was a trainee," Bridget managed.

There was conversation in the dining room. "Everyone?" Mrs. Kent called in. "Come and hear what my new daughter-in-law did during the war. You'll never guess." Groans were politely held in. Everyone had a war story. Everyone in the Blitzed cities had a bomb story, and everyone in the reception areas had an evacuee story. The room filled in, the last few seats claimed, faces turned in her direction. Even Mrs. Kent came and paid the ultimate compliment of her attention, coming to rest in her slipcovered throne. Bridget, eyes hot, at the center.

"Well, then?" Mrs. Hughes said. "Was there a *murder* to solve at Mrs. Christie's house?"

No one in the room laughed aloud, but Bridget could feel their mirth in the air. She caught a wry twist of a mouth here and there among them. She knew hardly a one, but she would. She had innumerable Sunday roast dinners ahead of her, Women's Institute talks.

"No, ma'am," Bridget said. The women felt free to titter now, but she knew they would stop. She took a breath and said, "There were two."

Bridey had another cup of punch, after all, and then she located her handbag and slipped out the door. She had managed to reach the corner in her court shoes before Tommy caught up. "Bridey, love, where are you off to?"

She didn't know. She'd been walking in the direction of her old shared flat, but her room would be taken now.

"Are you drunk?" He laughed and pulled her into his arms, but she fought back out. "What's wrong?"

"Is this how it's going to be? The men out in the street boasting and I'm inside with the ladies from the bridge club and the flower club?"

"You'll get your own friends," he said. "At whatever club you want to join."

She didn't think she'd made her point well. "I don't want to eat every Sunday dinner with your parents."

"All right," he said. But he was wounded.

"Tommy, I'm sorry. I wonder if this was a good idea."

"Bridey," he said, leaning in. "We haven't even made it *home*. You don't have to join a club or go wherever ladies go, all right?"

Where does a lady go?

She had never learned. There were so many things she hadn't done, and now she would have to negotiate every decision she would ever make factoring in Mags Kent of all people —

But suddenly she knew. She knew where a lady went, when she lost everything.

"I have to go," she said.

"What? What do you mean? Should we go, you know? Together?" He looked hopeful, sweet-faced, handsome in his dress uniform. He was a little drunk, too.

She went to him and pulled his tie, pressed her lips against his. She felt everything she should, and safe, too. Sometimes she felt too much and worried that she had done it again, risked loving someone *again.* Risked everything.

He groaned against her. "Let's go home. I've made it up for you." His mother would have cleaned it.

"You said you wanted to make me happy," she said.

"I do."

"Then can you give me this?"

"What, a chance to scarper?" He stood straight again, his voice higher than normal.

"Consider it my hen night, a little late. It wouldn't need more than a day. Or two."

"But that's —" He wanted to say it was insanity, or their honeymoon, or an embarrassment, or a scandal, all of these things. He didn't. He brought his parents' car around, her dressing case in the boot already, and, though he tried to talk her out of it, dropped her at the station.

66
BRIDGET KENT

The train north

On the train, Bridget caught the gaiety of the travelers, holidaymakers and weekenders and students, all jolly for adventure. She pulled out the copy of one of Mrs. M.'s books she'd brought in her case and tried to make herself concentrate. *Five Little Pigs,* though she supposed there would be no pigs or it would end badly for them. She soon read a passage that struck her soundly between the eyes. Mrs. M. was writing about Greenway, for here was the battery, the scene for a murder.

They hadn't reached Sheffield yet when the train suddenly went into a tunnel and she remembered waking to the dark of the train on the way to Greenway. A thousand lifetimes ago. In this tunnel, she kept her eyes open and hoped to catch a glimpse of her compatriots as the train shot out on the other side, a moment of unguarded emotion or slack, unfixed face.

At Leeds there was a delay. Bridey stood on the platform, gathering her bearings. A nice chap with an official sort of waistcoat directed her and she was soon in the telegraph office. A few words, spared. She could manage that, at least. *Train trouble Leeds. Stop. All well. Stop. Love &tc.*

Did it help Tom to let him know she'd be delayed, or was she somehow waving her defection in his face?

Another train, another station.

When she descended the carriage at last, she was stiff in her back. She might have had a taxi but by now felt like a walk. With a few fingers pointing her, she set off. It had rained recently, so the sandstone buildings were patchy, the pavement a bit slick on the hill down into town and then up again. On the way, she passed a teahouse and nearly diverted toward its door. But the voice in her head murmured, *where does she go, where does she go,* a hum almost constant.

Bridget passed Turkish bathhouses and lovely homes, dragged her dressing case across wide streets and up a long hill. She didn't know what to hope for. Perhaps she had gone to all this trouble for no reason, no intelligence to be had, nothing gained.

She regretted not taking the taxi by the time she arrived at the dark brick edifice at the top of its lane. Over the Victorian chimneys, low gray clouds scraped the sky. The Hydropathic, at last.

When a lady loses everything. But it was not any lady, but *the* lady. The only lady she and Gigi had known, when she lost everything, had gone to the Hydropathic Spa Hotel to reclaim herself.

Mrs. Mallowan, still Mrs. Christie then, had found peace here or anonymity or — *something.* She'd been able to get on with things, salvage all that was hers, find happiness. She had also suffered other tragic losses, Bridey knew. From this she might take that the trajectory of life was not always one direction. But it was also not only the highest and lowest moments, not only life that made headlines.

The man at the front desk turned her way, hesitated. She was unkempt, hair wisping and her stockings in ladders.

"Gracious, would you look at the state of me," she said. "I should have saved the walk for tomorrow."

The man's shoulders relaxed as he caught proper accents and embarrassments. A quick glance to find the gold ring on her finger. "How may I help you, madam?"

"I don't suppose you have a room for the night?" She had other questions, but it was better to start here, from expected questions, rather than those which would be unexpected. "For one, please. I'm caught out, an unfortunate train travel delay."

"My *dear,*" he said, casting his hand over an open book on the counter between them. "We do indeed have a luxurious room available for you, madam."

"Luxurious?"

"And reasonable, of course." He turned the book around for her signature. She wrote slowly, reading up the column until the clerk coughed with feeling.

"I had a friend who stayed here . . ."

"Madam?"

"A Mrs. Neale?" She hadn't known she remembered the name. She hadn't known she would ask after it.

"No, I don't think —"

"Teresa. Teresa Neale?"

The clerk took an almost imperceptible step back from the counter, as wary as he'd been when she first arrived. "No. None by that name."

"What about a Bridget Kelly?"

The man's eyes flicked to her signature in the book. She had signed her name as Kelly, forgetting. She was still wearing her wedding clothes.

Bridget had enough money for the room, just, but had to dig in her coin purse for a tip to the boy who escorted her up the steep, white marble stairs to her room. They'd given her a tidy little room for one, the single bed shoved into a corner. The *luxurious* rooms must have been full, after all. She sat heavily on the chair by the window and pulled the curtain aside to see the tops of trees, the roofs of houses, more chimneys.

She should have been on her honeymoon. *Tasting pleasures.*

Bridey bathed and changed and took herself back downstairs, some emergency funds from the secret slot in her dressing case now in her pocketbook. In the dining room past the front desk, it was late for tea and too early for dinner, but the kitchens came up with a warm plate of this and that, and she tucked in, the lone diner.

Her waitress took a long time breaking away from her conversation in the back before seeing if she needed anything more.

"Yes," Bridey said, "do you know if a Mrs. Mallowan ever stayed here?"

"I wouldn't know," the waitress said. "The front desk —"

"A Mrs. Christie?"

The woman's eyes flashed at this. "Not since *I* was here, madam. I think you might find a few around town to tell you a few stories."

"Right. Thank you. If I could have more hot water for the teapot, please?"

The hot water never came, but neither did the bill.

She wandered away from the dining room, looking out windows, trying doors. Behind one, she heard someone speaking curtly and was thrilled by the sense of listening in on a private life. Is this what it was like to observe, as Gigi and her group had? Did you learn how to live, listening at doors?

When the corridor ended abruptly in a salon, she turned back toward the lobby, where the desk was unmanned. Across, a wide doorway led to a lounge with high-backed chairs faced together, as though the Women's Institute meeting had just adjourned.

Outside, the gray skies opened up and pelted the cobblestone.

Bridget chose a chair facing away from the bar. Where would a lady go?

Had she come all this way to mourn, again? She had no other plan, had banked it all on coming here and seeing this place.

Pulled by an invisible thread through the whole of the country, and now undone.

67
Bridget Kent

The Hydropathic Hotel, morning
Bridget slept badly and arrived in the lobby the next morning tired and out of sorts, her neck cricked from the unfamiliar pillow. She went to the desk to order a telegram sent and struggled over the words. What was she doing here?

In the dining room, the hostess walked her to a large, fresh table past other diners enjoying their breakfasts communally. Bridget averted her gaze and when seated, asked immediately for tea.

She was still scowling into her empty cup several minutes later when the hostess seated a man across from her.

"Good morning," he said, too cheerful by half. He had a newspaper rolled up, Bridget was glad to see. She nodded.

"Did you sleep well?"

The hot water came, tea already steeping, gracious good Lord. "I did not, but it's no concern of yours." Could a woman not simply enjoy her solitude?

"It is, indeed, as I'm the manager of this establishment."

Bridget poured, wishing she hadn't said a word. "It's fine, really."

"Is there nothing I can do to make your stay with us better?"

She felt too grim, too spiteful, and then too desperate, quite like her old self, the girl afraid to speak for fear she might gut herself onto the linens. She was as alone as she'd ever been, and that was saying something.

At least she might creep home. Poor Mrs. M., to have struggled for her mind and dignity as publicly as she had. All the women and girls she had known, who had to spend so much time and effort being who everyone thought they should be, first, before being who they might. Desperate girls at the infirmary trying to avoid motherhood at all costs. Desperate mothers during the war, stripped of their children. Bridget thought of poor Mrs. Poole, whose floor had gone out beneath her. That lady, when she had lost everything, had gone to Greenway, reaching for Greenway like a drowning person grasping for a life raft —

The invisible thread tugged. "Do you know if a woman named Cecilia Poole ever stayed here?"

The man's concern cracked into a smile. "And how do you know our Mrs. Poole?" he said.

Bridget waited in the lounge where the hotel manager had placed her, all the compliments of the house. She didn't want any more tea — she was shaking with it — but she hadn't wanted to order anything from the bar. The teapot steamed and grew cold and the light in the lounge shifted as she watched the doorway, empty. Until —

A woman stood there, looking in.

She wore a swaying coat in champagne colors, light as bubbles, with a silk flower pinned to the front, as large as a clamped fist in the same pale shade. Her hair sleek and modern.

Bridget stood up.

Gigi, risen from the dead.

She hadn't been entirely sure she hadn't got it all wrong. But here she was.

She hadn't changed but for the hair, still fine-boned and small, with the walk of a much larger person as she crossed the room. The moment for embrace came and went.

"I could ask for more hot water," Bridget said, gesturing toward the table and empty cups.

"We can do better than that, surely."

Bridget shuddered at the sound of Gigi's voice, as though not a minute had passed, as though nothing had gone wrong. As though she had never waved Dr. Hart's handkerchief over a dead woman's body and proclaimed it someone she was not.

Gigi gestured over Bridget's shoulder, and they sorted themselves into two of the high-backed chairs, turned inward, knees almost touching, like girls.

"Why is it such a shock?" Bridget said into the void.

"You're real," Gigi said. She sounded relieved to have passed through the first words. A hurdle cleared.

"*You're* real," Bridget said. "I knew you were alive, of course. Well, I hoped you were."

"It's been long enough, I was beginning to think I'd dreamed it all."

"Rather a nightmare at times." She sounded, to herself, like someone else. Someone insulted.

"You're not here to be upset with me?"

She didn't want to be upset or angry or anything other than grateful that it had worked. Here was Gigi, alive, escaped with her life and free. But she didn't feel grateful. What she felt was cheated, and underneath, she could feel the sensation of a ticking clock. She was stealing time from her life to be here, to have it resolved.

"I wish —" She didn't know what she wished, and she didn't want to spend their short time hashing over the near misses and lost opportunities. "Tell me. Tell me what the last few years have been."

"Difficult," Gigi said. "Finding work, getting through the war. I wish I'd been a nurse."

"Me, too," Bridget said.

"You weren't?" Gigi threw back her head and laughed. "My God, we were both fakes? But you were quite good. Seemed to know what you were doing."

"Long story," Bridget said. "Eventually I became a nurse. An actual one. But —" She would have to give it up now. "Have you married? Had children?"

"No, none of that," Gigi said with a dismissive wave.

"Ah, so you must have . . . taken, er, lovers?"

"A great deal too many," Gigi said, looking away.

"I wish you'd written," Bridget said.

"I did!"

The barman cut in. Gigi had ordered them glasses of some dark, thick beer.

Bridget held her glass in front of her, no intention of drinking it, but then Gigi raised hers. "What shall we toast to?" Gigi said.

"The one card you posted? That's the letter you mean? 'Where does a lady go?' "

"You never responded," Gigi said. "I wasn't certain you ever got it." They had not toasted to anything.

"How should I have answered it?" Bridget said. "It had no return address, no mark! Granted, that helped when I used the card as your suicide note."

"Fantastic stroke of luck, that."

Bridget set her glass down. "It was nothing but a fantastic tragedy."

"Of course," Gigi said. "Poor woman."

A hard slant of light from the window cut across Gigi's face like a knife's gash. Bridget had no idea who this woman was. She never had. "Was I supposed to puzzle out where Mrs. Christie went all those years ago and — what did you imagine? That I would follow you? I had plans of my own."

Gigi glanced at Bridget's hand. "I hope it's not that doctor. Or did you find some feeling for Tommy finally?"

She'd wasted her time by coming here, wasted her time doing a kindness, making arrangements, making things right. "*You* might find some feeling, if you tried, Gigi."

The other woman glanced around. "No one's called me that in years. What a silly name."

"I always thought so." Bridget retrieved her glass and took a deep drink. "We all did."

Gigi looked down at her hands in her lap. Then she was smiling, and the dimple was just the same as it had always been. "Mrs. Arbuthnot thought it was ridiculous. On the train, do you remember? Mrs. Arbuthnot!"

Bridget felt the thaw begin. "*Mr.* Arbuthnot. And his awful cigar."

They compared a few names as they occurred to them.

"Mr. Scaldwell," Gigi said. "Did you know — I don't know if he would have said —"

"He helped you away, didn't he? He never said precisely." Bridget thought of the evening at the kitchen table at Greenway, Mr. Scaldwell asking after poor Mrs. Poole. He'd been so sure Gigi couldn't be dead, because if she were, he couldn't think himself the hero. They had each of them needed to think some good would come out.

"He took me to Paignton and put me on the train," Gigi said. "I don't think his wife would have made much of that, if she'd known."

"He was only saving your life," Bridget said.

Gigi sat back in her seat. "*You* saved my life. You murdered me as well as Mrs. Mallowan would have."

They were friends again. A quiet hum of satisfaction came over Bridget, drowsy in the high-backed chair from the sleepless night, the stout.

She wanted to ask more about the last few years, what they had given and taken, what total freedom to choose one's life felt like. Or she could beg her for the story, beginning to end, to find where they might have changed even one small move. They might have arranged it better, been reunited sooner. But their friendship wasn't for every day, was it? It was a war relic, kept under glass.

Best not to bother with what-ifs. *Heretofore* was the word Matron Bailey would have used. What could they be to one another now? If they had one day to spend, she'd rather hear Gigi laugh again. Remind each other of the march around the grounds, of the boys roughhousing on the battery cannon like soldiers in training, of the gap in the smile of Elsie Bastin, of the pantry thief, a mystery left unsolved.

It would be the easiest thing in the world to keep a light grip. The better to let go.

68
BRIDGET

Bettys Tea Rooms, Harrogate, that afternoon
The last pastries in the three-level tray called Bridget's name, but she didn't reach for another. Gigi sipped tea and looked out at the rooms over the rim of her cup. Was Gigi looking out for someone to avoid, in case she had to explain who Bridget was, or for someone to invite over, now that their conversation had dried up? The walls of the tearoom were golden and warm but Bridget could not be comfortable. She put her cup in its saucer and glanced at the scones.

"Do have another, Bridget."

She was reaching but halted. Greedy Bridget. "You should call me Bridey," she said. "I feel as though I'm being scolded when you call me Bridget."

Gigi selected a scone, slathered jam, took a dainty bite. "Didn't your mam call you Bridey? She used Bridget for howling at you?"

Bridget took the last scone. "You always called me Bridey and I like it the old ways." Clotted cream, then jam. "And I don't want to talk about my mam."

"All right, my lover," Gigi said it in the purring accents of Devon. "Bridey it is. What does Tommy call you?"

"*Tom* calls me —" The knife in her hand paused. "I'd rather not talk about Tom, either."

"What *would* you like to talk about?"

"I'd like to talk about why you're still here," Bridget said around a mouthful. "In this town. Who are you hiding from at this point?"

A woman at the next table turned her head, eavesdropping.

Gigi set down the pastry and put her serviette to the corners of her mouth. "No one." Careful tones, low so that Bridget had to lean forward. "I suppose."

"Why did you not return to Willa? I might not have worried if you'd only gone to her."

"Willa," Gigi said. "Willa was vulnerable to the influence of the people I was trying to avoid, and to the harm they might have caused her. We have to make our own way."

With sudden clarity, Bridey realized that Gigi had never meant to meet her again, either. The postcard had never been an invitation.

"Why did you never write again?"

"Why, why, why, so full of questions." Gigi stared at her plate. "You really should have worked with Mass-Ob. I thought you might be better off without me."

"I thought you were dead until I saw the body."

The tables all around them stared openly. Gigi reached for her handbag, threw a five-pound note on the table, and stalked out of the room. Bridget hurried to follow, apologies and prim smiles for the waiter, the hostess.

Out on the street, a queue of people waited for a table. Gigi moved quickly past them. Slow Bridget, breathless Bridget.

"Wait, Gigi, please! I never meant —"

Gigi turned, red faced with trails of black running down her face. "Never meant to what? Embarrass me in front of the day trippers? Oh, I'll never be able to show my face in Bettys."

Bridget reached into her clutch and pulled out a handkerchief. It was one of Tom's, plain, white. She held it toward Gigi.

"What's that for?"

Bridget stepped up and raised the handkerchief. Gigi flinched, then yielded, letting

Bridget mop at her cheeks, one side gently, then the other. Bridget thought of the sweet children back at Greenway, allowing her to comfort them, turning their faces toward her with such trust. Wasn't it strange they were out there somewhere?

The afternoon was coming to a close. The end was a feeling in her stomach. "Now I'm starting up," she said.

"Soggy messes, both of us," Gigi said.

"It could be a while again." Or forever, this time.

"I'm sorry you worried," Gigi said.

"I'm sorry I killed you."

Gigi held the back of her wrist to her mouth for a moment, but not from laughter. Bridget recognized it as the gesture of someone holding themselves together. "I never wrote again," Gigi said, "because I wasn't sure I deserved to have what I wanted. Everything I touched, Bridey, it broke apart in my hands. And then I had this new life, no ties, a sort of freedom I knew I could only ruin."

"You deserved what you wanted — but you had to stay safe, or it was all for nothing. Why didn't you take the money?"

"The money? I did," Gigi said. "I left you half in the cloak."

"Half! How did you ever know I would

find it?"

"Bridey," Gigi said. "Your attempt at bad stitching was far and away better than my efforts."

She didn't want to go. They hadn't spoken of the Friar, of Lew, of Michaelsmith and Hart — did Gigi even know all that she had escaped? "I'm sorry you had to give up everything."

Gigi pulled a face. "There was nothing much to give up, don't you see? If I ever went back to my old life, I'd have to reckon with that." She turned her back to the street to block her words and ruddy cheeks from a couple passing by. They knew her, by the curious looks, but didn't stop. "My death meant so little to anyone, and if someone *had* cared, my resurrection would only hurt them more. Do you see? The longer I waited, the more painful it would be. I got myself stuck in a sort of limbo here, in another woman's skin. That's why I stayed."

Bridget used the handkerchief for herself.

"There was only ever one person I thought might be able to take it in. Who wanted me alive again enough to accept that I was. To be happy I was."

"I was. I am."

Gigi looked away. "I'm sorry."

"For what?"

"For . . . everything. I think that covers it. But most of all for dropping away like I did. It was an awful thing to do. I never meant to disappear."

Disappear.

Bridget found herself doubled over, the old pain.

"Bridey, what is it?"

"Oh, Gigi."

"Shall I call a doctor?"

"Gigi, I think I've thrown Tommy over."

"What?"

"Left him nearly at the altar. I didn't mean to," she said to the hem of Gigi's coat.

"Darling, *what*?" Gigi was laughing, bent, too, now and gasping.

"It's not funny," Bridget wailed.

Gigi pulled her up. "What the devil are you talking about?"

"We're barely married and I dragged my trousseau across the country without him. It will be three days if I don't get back tonight."

"You should get back tonight, then." Gigi reached for Bridey's shoulders, sober and certain. "If you want to."

"I do. Oh, no, I do." Gigi's life of intrigue and secrets held no interest for her. *None of that,* she'd said. None of the things that had mattered to Bridey. They weren't the same person, never had been. "I never meant to . . . what have I done?"

"Let's undo it." Gigi walked to the street and raised her hand for a taxi. "Something of this must be salvageable. Leave your things and I'll have the hotel send it. Or I'll visit, shall I?"

"Gigi, would you?" Bridey imagined Gigi in their flat, dinner and a glass of something, Gigi advising Tom to grow a mustache. "Write to me. Write me more coded messages I'm too daft to sort out, and do send me dates you can come, and oh, I can't wait to introduce you to Tommy. And to his parents, my goodness you'll despise the bones of them."

"They sound delightful. Here we are, my lover," Gigi said in a Devonshire purr as the taxi stopped. She opened the door. "Away with you."

Then the door was closed and the window wouldn't open.

"Where to, pet?" said the driver.

"Wait a moment, please." Bridey opened the door and leapt out. "Gigi!"

The other Bridget turned back. "I'm Cecilia here, you cow," she said. "You'll have me investigated."

"It's just a nickname."

"It was never just a nickname. You should

589

be on your way —"

Bridey reached for her and crushed the big flower on Gigi's coat flat against herself, squeezed and held on until Gigi put her arms around her, too. They stood for a minute, the meter on the taxi turning over, money she didn't have and time she shouldn't spare. A lady went to her friends.

She held on until Gigi said, more gently, "Away with you. Get home and let me know you're safe."

69
BRIDGET

Toward London

The fastest train toward London went through York and then Grantham, other towns Bridget had never been to and now didn't want to see. She didn't watch the landscape as she might have, but instead kept vigil with the time, keeping her watch wound as tight as it went, and bothering the inspector with the transfer at King's Cross — a taxi, he finally suggested. Perhaps a taxi would be easiest and with baggage —

"I haven't any bags."

It was freeing. She didn't mind if she never saw the case again, and only feared that Gigi would go through her things and see how shoddy they were. Cecilia. She would write to *Cecilia* that she had arrived and have her throw out the lot.

She could start new. In so many ways, start new. She began to think of Tom. She'd sent another telegram, promising her arrival, but now she turned inward, fretting. She had done this damage herself, thoughtlessly.

No. She couldn't let herself off. Her acts against her one-day marriage couldn't have been more deadly, a strike to the core of their friendship, designed to destroy beauty and the firmaments of her life. Accidental, misguided, purposeful, she had ruined everything. She had ruined all.

Bridget dozed and then woke to find her seatmate gathering her things together. "Where are we, please?"

"Coming into King's Cross. You haven't missed it."

She waited for the train to arrive, realizing after a few minutes that she could hear a bitter whispered argument somewhere behind her, a husband and wife. She had never meant to become an observer, not in the way Gigi had been. What would it do to you to take in all the poison spewed when people thought they couldn't be heard? If you stood aside listening in, and never made much of your own story?

"Do you need help with your bags?" the woman across said.

Bridget had a moment of panic, then remembered. "No, thank you. Traveling light." She was disoriented from her nap, unexpected and deep. She felt as though she was still swimming up from the depths, still reaching for the surface to take a breath.

"I envy you." The woman had straps on both shoulders, and a case at her feet. Bridget looked her over. No wedding band. She didn't want to travel as lightly as that. Her stomach hurt. *A taxi would be the easiest thing.* The words filled her head, as though they conveyed some grand wisdom.

In the station, she stood and caught a breath. Her guts had been good and shaken by the swaying of the train and twisted by her anxiety. She could barely carry herself down the platform. A taxi.

"Bridey love!"

Tom stood on the platform with a fist of limp flowers.

"Tom? Tommy, what on earth?" She went to him, letting people flow around both of them. "What are you doing here?"

"I missed you."

"I missed you, too," she said, almost in tears with relief.

"No, I meant I missed you in Leeds, and then again at Harrogate, and —"

"Have you been following me around the country, Tom?" She tried to make the joke light and buoyant, but she was startled and unsure where they stood. "I was coming back to you."

"Well, I wasn't sure, was I?"

She looked at the drooping flowers. How long had he carried them? "It's not your fault that you weren't sure. I should have made you sure. Tom, I never meant to worry you. It was all a — a lark, I suppose, hard to explain without dragging you through the whole thing."

"You didn't meet another bloke?" He waited for her to smile, so she did.

"I never went looking to meet another bloke and that's a fact, Thomas Kent."

He watched someone pass close by and lowered his voice. "You hurt me, Bridey. I'm barely man enough to admit it."

"I know." She reached up and pressed a hand to his cheek. He relaxed into her palm like a cat accepting a stroke. "It was never like that. Please don't tell me I've ruined everything."

He took her hand from his face and held it. "It doesn't have to be ruined."

She nodded toward the flowers. "Did you bring those for me?"

"Depends," he said, looking deep into the flowers instead of at her. "I brought them for my wife, and hoped I'd have one."

"You do. You will. What your mother must think of me."

"This seemed like something that was you and me. I'm not saying it right. Do you know what I mean?"

"I do." She said it like a bride, and he handed her the handful of stems. "We should get these into some water. Twenty-four hours ago, perhaps."

"I'll get you fresh ones for home. I thought you might like to make a night of it."

Bridget gazed about the station, busy with people rushing to and fro, the air thick. When she turned back to Tom, his face was hopeful. He so wished to give her what she wanted, or what he thought she wanted.

"What I would like best is to go home, with you," she said. "Nothing would make me happier."

"That's easy," he said, and offered his arm. "Where's your case?"

"It's a long story."

"Only you, Bridey," he said, laughing. "I want to hear it, if you'll tell me. I always want to hear your stories."

"You don't need me telling you, most of them," Bridey said. "Because you were there."

"I like to hear you anyway," Tom said. "You always tell it better than it ever was." They walked along the platform together, no hurry.

"Well, I'll tell you. It has some lies in it." About a woman who lived two lives, and another who discovered a locked door in her heart and wrenched it open. She said, "About a woman named Bridget Kelly."

His genuine delight was dazzling to her. "The one and only."

"You would think that," she said, leaning into him and tugging him toward the exit and a taxi. The easiest thing. "But that's not half the story."

70

BRIDGET KENT

London, 13 January 1976

The first news of Agatha Christie's death reached Bridget the next day on the Tube, from the *Daily Mirror* held by a young lady with dark, flaking nail polish and messy hair. The announcement was in a small section at the bottom of the front page, sneaked into a late edition, but bold and blunt: AGATHA CHRISTIE IS DEAD.

Bridget realized the other passenger was looking at her over the paper. "All right?"

"Agatha Christie is dead," Bridget said.

"Who is she?"

"You don't know? How can you not know?"

"I'm only after the job adverts," the young lady said.

"I meant . . ." But it was too late to patch it up from a bad start. "Don't you know the stories? Hercule Poirot and Miss Marple. Here." Bridget dug into her carry-all and brought out the book she'd brought along. *Dead Man's Folly,* her favorite. Mrs. M. had written Greenway into the story, setting the murder at her own boathouse. How could she not use the boathouse? It did have a certain darkness, or perhaps that was only Bridget's experience.

"Never heard of them," the young woman said, chewing her gum with her mouth open. "You can have the paper when I'm done."

Bridget reached her stop too soon, though, and climbed the steps to the street in a daze. At the newsagent's, she purchased her own copy and carried it loose in her hands to the apartment. She rang the bell twice — these were the customs they had come to — and let herself in.

"That you, Bridey?" Her daughter-in-law had struggled to find the right thing to call her, trying out Mother Kent, as she had been forced to call *her* mother-in-law, but they'd struck gold at last. She'd also thought a good deal before the baby's birth about what to have the child call her. No *Granny* or *Nana* for her. She wanted something all her own. A silly name. A name to make them special friends.

Nicola entered the room, tall and striking as ever, long brown limbs on display in a short and sparkling frock. She stopped abruptly. "You're not ill, are you?"

"No, no of course not," Bridget said. "I would have let you know. You look gorgeous, darling."

"Are you sure — look, I'll make David stay home and we can just have a quiet evening —"

"No," Bridget said. Her boys needed so little from her these days. Grown men with hair longer than she liked and lives she couldn't be part of. David, her younger son, with a statuesque American wife met on a gap year, a *divorceé* they hadn't had the chance to size up before the wedding. An *elopement*. But now David was a father, fancy that. "I *insist*. I've been looking forward to it all week. It's — it's what I want."

The baby's cry rose up in the next room. "There's the little madam now," Nicola said. She had chewed the lipstick off her bottom lip. "If you're sure . . ."

"I've never been more certain. The headlines got to me, that's all." She put the paper and her bag down.

"You read the *Mirror*? Those headlines will get to anyone. Well, if you're sure . . . Now, she's had her nappy changed only ten minutes ago but that crying makes me wonder if there's not another surprise in store."

They went down the hall together.

Later, in the dark of her granddaughter's nursery, Bridey cooed the baby to sleep in the rocking chair. She kept rocking long after the little one was down, though Nicola didn't want the child to grow too accustomed to sleeping in someone's arms.

Not *her* arms, anyway. Nicola had a busy life backstage in the West End and all sorts of ideas of how an independent child ought to be raised, including an active role for David. Nicola was a gift to their family but Bridget didn't want the baby too independent. Not too soon. It was good for her to be held and loved. It had to be.

For a moment, Bridget was back in the darkened room of their old flat, one of her boys warm against her, feverish. Then she could have been at Greenway, rocking one of the infants to sleep to the sounds of the others sucking their fingers. Then she was thinking of Gigi, and what she would have made of the news. The news about Mrs. M., and the news of Bridget's life, too.

Bridget rose and walked the room, shushing the baby though she hadn't woken or made a sound. At the window, she looked down at the silent streets.

Dearest Gigi, buried now for the second time. A silent killer of some sort, which she had kept to herself. Just like Gigi, to keep a secret.

When she thought of their friendship, she wondered if most people weren't mysteries to one another. They'd had good years and bad, cards at Christmas, birthdays, photos sent of the boys as they grew, a photo of Gigi sitting in sunshine with a beautiful bronze-skinned woman, the name *Anika* written on the back. *None of that* she'd said, but one could be wrong. The odd letter passed between them, but time got away. It was never the same, nor could it be. And then —

She'd found out too late to suggest the gravestone be affixed with the correct name — the *other* incorrect name, actually, so what did it matter? Any name other than what she'd been called in Harrogate would have stirred too many questions. In London, Bridget might have arranged it, but in the end this Cecilia Poole had been laid to rest far from the bones of her son.

What was the lad's name?

Bridget gazed down at the rosebud mouth of her granddaughter. Sara. A stout, no-nonsense sort of name. At one point, Nicola had been keen on calling her Evangeline, and Bridget wondered if she could bear it. *Sara* was modern, unencumbered. All her own.

Samuel. His name was Samuel.

Samuel Poole had his mother next to him all these years, Bridget had made sure of it. She thought it an elegant solution, right if not just. The crossed names bothered her sense of tidiness, but she'd much rather have the names crossways and the bones right, mother and son together. She'd managed it.

An accomplishment she told absolutely no one. Except Tom.

"Bridey, no." He'd been scandalized, the war offices clerk of old who abhorred an error in the files. "Think of their families."

"*I* am their family," she'd said.

Now Bridget put the baby into her cot. Nicola and David would be home from the theater soon, a little drunk, in love. She'd make a dash for the door, in case they were in the mood to make her another grandchild. They would ask her to stay in the guest room, and though she'd love to wake up to more time in the rocking chair, she wouldn't stay. She had her home and Tom to get home to.

The front room had grown dark in her absence, her newspaper fallen to the floor.

She reached for it. *Agatha Christie is dead.* Public mourning for a woman who had thrilled so many. A big life.

It was too dark to read. Instead of turning on the lights, she folded the paper and sat in the dark.

Who of their party was left to mourn her? She'd lost touch with even Edith, from whom she had learned the fates of so many. Edith's last letter, in 1946, had contained the happy news that the Scaldwell daughter had married the Hannaford son. Such a tender thing to imagine. All must have seemed right at Greenway that day.

The Arbuthnots, the Scaldwells, the Hannafords they had known — all of them would have died without benefit of headlines. But wasn't that the truth for most, and all of the people who had mattered to her?

Remarkable that Mrs. M. herself was among the last of them living.

The 'vacs. They were the only ones left who might remember the sweet, brief season of their time at Greenway — to remember not the newsreels or headlines but the feeling of safety, walking in the woods, picking violets.

It was only right, as the children had brought them all there in the first place.

The children had knotted them all together, to one another, to Greenway and the long history of the place, to the others who might someday live there or visit. The mistress's daughter and her family would surely take on the house, if they hadn't already. They would have their own memories and secret pleasures, the things that made a house a home.

She drowsed, blackout curtains making the room dark until one of the 'vacs cried for her. She jerked awake, time-traveling as her son's apartment filled in around her.

"Coming, my darling," she called, rising on creaking knees. Getting her bearings, hurrying down the dark corridor with her hands trailing the walls. "Coming, my dearest, my lover," she crooned as she went. "Your Gigi is coming. I'm here."

It was a silly name, but then it had never been just a name, standing in as it did for chances grasped and stories rewritten.

She couldn't wait to hear Sara call for her, and to play the games of childhood one last time. They were going to be such good friends.

AUTHOR'S NOTE

During World War II, more than three million people, most of them children, were evacuated out of London and other major English cities to avoid German aerial bombings. Ten children were evacuated to Greenway House, the South Devon holiday home of Agatha Christie.

My goal for this story was to include as much fact as could be found about this moment in history, and where fact ran out, turn to fiction. Where the truth could be found, I have stayed as close to it as possible, but the rest is my imagination.

Very little has ever been written about the children evacuated to Greenway, but I am in particular debt to Doreen Vautour, the only one of Greenway's 'vacs to have stepped forward and shared what she remembered with the National Trust and the BBC.

The rest we know as fact, though minimal,

comes from Agatha Christie's autobiography. The children, all under the age of five, came from the St. Pancras area in London and were brought to Greenway by "a Mrs. Arbuthnot." Also in the party were Mr. Arbuthnot and "two hospital nurses." The Arbuthnots rented the house. Mrs. M — as Agatha Christie Mallowan was known locally — would have received them on their arrival but soon left for London to be with her husband, Max, and to offer her services as an apothecary (skills learned during World War I) at the pharmacy in the University College Hospital in London. A few members of the household staff stayed on at Greenway, including the butler and a cook/housekeeper, and the head gardener, Mr. Hannaford.

Some of the children's names were Doreen, Maureen, Tina, Pamela, and Beryl; we know this because of a cabinet still on hand at Greenway, the children's names still affixed to the cubbies where they kept their clothes. (It is not on display, but the National Trust's Jane Curtis kindly unlocked a door to show me on my first visit to Greenway.) The other children's names are lost to history, though Doreen, who became a valued resource for this book (and friend), says one boy was named Edward and was the little brother of Maureen. Doreen also thinks the nurses might have been two of Mrs. Arbuthnot's foster daughters from her first marriage, so I have used both of those scenarios.

The timing of the children's stay at Greenway cannot be entirely confirmed. They arrived as early as spring of 1941, based on what I learned about Christie's movements during this time. They were gone by October 1, 1942. When the house was requisitioned for its access to the River Dart for use in Operation Overlord — resulting in D-Day and the eventual Allied victory — the children were moved to Winchcombe in Gloucestershire, and then to Reading in Berkshire, and then, after the war ended in 1945, home to their parents.

I used public records, including the 1939 Register and a deep dive into Ancestry.com, to include the actual inhabitants of the estate and the community, though almost everything but their names is fiction by necessity. By triangulating archived information, my research confirmed the identity of "a Mrs. Arbuthnot" as Florence Annie "Joan" (neé Austin-Jones) Davison Arbuthnot; she traveled with her second husband, artist Malcolm Arbuthnot (formerly known as Malcolm Lewin Stockdale Parson; no record of an official name change could be found). They may indeed have had two of Joan's daughters from her first marriage with them, but I have given them somewhere else to be for simplicity's sake. Though not named in Agatha Christie's autobiography, original research for this book also confirmed the couple working at Greenway for the Mallowans at this time to be Frank William Scaldwell, a butler, and Vera Phyllis (Weaving) Scaldwell, a cook/ housekeeper. Their daughter, Diana Frances Scaldwell, may have also been on the grounds; again, for simplicity's sake, I have given her other wartime activities. The Scaldwells remained at Greenway at least until 1946, when the Scaldwell daughter married the Hannaford son, Horace Arthur Henry Hannaford, who had become the Greenway chauffeur. On the marriage certificate, the Hannafords still have possession of the Greenway Lodge; the Scaldwells name the house as their home. The Hannafords and Bastins are based as much as possible on fact, but the nurses are entirely fiction, other than they existed, according to Agatha Christie. Edith is a composite of the staff listed at Greenway when the Register was taken in 1939. The Register gave names to all the other families along Greenway Road, and revealed a few errors in transcription — or lies. Scaldwell's age was nudged up; Agatha's down.

Thoughts attributed to Agatha Christie are primarily sentiments taken from her autobiography. Other factual information about the house, the community, the war, nursing, etc., came from a number of research books. The most useful were authored by Mike Brown and Carol Harris, Ray Freeman, Judith Hurdle, Hilary Macaskill, Janet Morgan, Barbara Mortimer, Laura Thompson, David Williams, Max Mallowan, and, of course, Agatha Christie. Christie fictionalized herself and Greenway in *Dead Man's Folly* (1956); she wrote a war nursery into *Ordeal of Innocence,* first published in 1958.

I have tried to keep details about the house true to the time period — after the Mallowans' renovations, but before the US Coast Guard moved in — with help from the National Trust.

Mass-Observation was (and is again) a real social science research project in the UK. I have taken many liberties with how their field investigators might have been put to use during the war.

ACKNOWLEDGMENTS

Thank you to every person who, upon hearing about this book, lit up and said, "I can't wait to read it." Your enthusiasm was a beacon.

Thank you to Emily Krump at HarperCollins William Morrow for giving me the chance to turn a long-standing dream project into my next book, and thank you to the entire team at William Morrow, especially Liate Stehlik, Julia Elliott, Jennifer Hart, Brittani Hilles, Amelia Wood, Virginia Stanley, and Owen Corrigan.

Thank you also to my agent, Sharon Bowers (who thinks I can write anything even though "no one does it like this, Lori"), and everyone at Folio Literary Management.

A special heartfelt thank you to Doreen Valsaycer Vautour and her son, Peter Vautour, who trusted me enough to share information and stories about her time at Greenway. One of the greatest joys of writing this book has been to get to know Doreen in real life.

Thank you to Ann Cleeves for words of wisdom about terms of endearment in Devon, for reading a messy early draft for Britishness, and also for putting me in touch with Adrian Pitches, who tracked down the video of Doreen Vautour and her husband, Norman, touring Greenway under construction by the National Trust in 2008. Doreen had never been able to see the video, and now her family has it. With thanks to John Scott Paterson at the BBC, who sent the files.

Thanks also to Sophie Hannah who introduced me to (and gave me, perhaps, some standing with) the National Trust, who allowed my husband and me to stay in the small "bedsit" at Greenway House on a research trip. I can't thank enough the staff and volunteers of the National Trust and Greenway House, especially Elaine Ward, Sandy Howard, Belinda Smith, Lauren Hutchinson, Laura Cooper, and Jane Curtis. Our stay was so helpful in writing this book, getting details right and finding opportunities for fiction. Sandy gave me my first glimpse of the actual Greenway evacuees, a photo whose original is perhaps lost to history. Thank you also to the librarians and staff at the Churston Library and the Paignton Library and Information Centre both in Paignton, Devon, England, for helping me dig through the local history.

Deep gratitude to Ancestry.com for the rabbit hole where I found a lot of generative information about a historical time period on which I am not an expert. Thank you to Connie Sanders for her help when her family tree intersected, briefly, with this story. Her family connection was ruined by FACT but Connie generously helped me research the correct pair of Arbuthnots and ended up leading me through the twists and turns of what could be known about many of the characters in this novel who are based on real people. I cannot thank her enough. Thank you also to Sir William Arbuthnot, Baronet, and those who keep the Arbuthnot wiki updated. Malcolm is of absolutely no relation to anyone born an Arbuthnot, but the Arbuthnot family's inclusion of this "branch" of the family tree in their research was helpful.

Also thanks to David Kenyon from Bletchley Park for answering questions whose answers didn't make the final cut of the book.

Thanks to Lesley Marsh for her bad news about World War II uniforms that I had to write around, and to Tracy Day for the connection.

During the writing (and rewriting) of this book, I had the pleasure of discussing a shared love of Agatha Christie with Julie Hennrikus. I thank Julie as well as Sandra Wong, Sherry Harris, Faye Snowden, Jacki York, Tracee de Hahn, Kellye Garrett, Stephanie Gayle, Debra Goldstein, Edwin Hill, Vanessa Lillie, Alec Peche, Shari Randall, Barbara Ross, and all the volunteers who made my year as Sisters in Crime president a rewarding experience.

Many thanks and all blessings to beta readers. In addition to Ann Cleeves, Catriona McPherson, Susanna Calkins, Yvonne Strumecki, and Laura Jensen Walker, who each made the book better and closer to what I wanted it to be. And to Kirsten McCarthy, my little English friend, who invited me into her family and took me to Greenway to get this book started, all the love and gratitude. (She also gave it a keen British read.) Thank you to Duncan, James, and Josh McCarthy for welcoming us into their lives.

A special thank-you to all the librarians, booksellers, and reviewers who have put my books into the hands of readers, and to the readers themselves.

I am lucky to have so many friends and family in my life who got me through the many stages of this book and the many ups and downs of the last few years, but it's Greg Day who made this book at all possible. He's also an exceedingly nice bloke and the only person with whom I would have shared the Greenway bedsit.

P.S.
INSIGHTS,
INTERVIEWS & MORE . . .

■ ■ ■ ■

ABOUT THE BOOK

■ ■ ■ ■

A Q&A WITH
DOREEN VALSAYCER VAUTOUR

Doreen Valsaycer Vautour was very young when she was evacuated to Greenway. In 2008, she sent a letter to the National Trust with her remembrances and visited Greenway with her husband. The conversation below has been edited together from Doreen's letter and her emails with the author.

Lori Rader-Day: How did you come to be evacuated to Greenway?

Doreen Vautour: I can only tell you what I was told of this period. My parents were working full time — Dad with the London Fire Brigade. At eighteen months I was taken to a nursery (day care) in St. Pancras near King's Cross Station. The lady who ran this nursery decided, with permission all around, to take her charges out of London and look after them for the duration of the war. Permission granted and destination chosen, fourteen of us (four adults and ten children) set off for Devon in the West of England.

LRD: What do you remember most about staying at Greenway?

DV: My own personal recollections are very limited, being too young at the time. I remember the large house, the gardens . . . one tree we particularly loved was a huge "monkey tree" near the house. "My" bedroom was on the second floor [third floor, to Americans] overlooking the front driveway and lawn of the house. I recall being so happy to have my own window. Even today windows are important to me. On facing the house, "my" bedroom was at the far end of the building. By the way, this room (quite large) slept five girls in all and perhaps one of the nurses and even accommodated a piano with a bench. I remember the piano because we were not allowed to touch it, but of course we did when we could get away with it! We each had small cot beds, mine was in a corner close to the window. At times I would wake up in the middle of the night and, for whatever reason, would walk up and down my bed until I felt cold. I loved getting under the covers to warm up.

We ate and drank out of tin bowls, plates, and cups. We were served our food and we always had to wear a bib. Anything sweet was rare. We did eat apples.

We were very regimented, disciplined and orderly for meals, bedtime, health checks (lice, etc.), washing teeth, ears, and necks. One of the nurses had lovely long nails, and I was fascinated by the way the water would drip off them.

I remember the butler — he seemed nice — and one day I had to ask him to bring me a glass of water! We were not allowed in certain parts of the house. I recall talking to him and he was standing maybe three or four steps down looking up at me.

We all had to wear an outfit called a "siren suit." It was a one-piece jumpsuit type of thing and we each had our own. A color thread had been sewn around the peak of the hood for identification — mine was lavender. We wore these suits whenever we went out to play or for a walk. One day stands out in my mind so vividly. We went for a walk in the woods and were allowed to look for and pick purple violets. I was so thrilled. I remember walking through an archway into the wooded area. . . . Another outing was being taken to a beach by a river. It was a blustery day and we had to stay close to a wall for shelter. The beach was stony, and we were not allowed to go close to the water.

LRD: What was the experience of war like for you?

DV: I remember my Mickey Mouse gas mask and hated it! I have wonderful memories of my childhood during World War II and especially my stay in Devon. . . . Looking back after all these years, I realize I was extremely lucky. Honestly, I was totally unaware of the "war," just that it meant I could not live with my parents.

I have no other memories of the war and can't recall it ever being mentioned. But how lucky I was in that both my parents survived the war in London; and I have at times wondered what happened to evacuated children whose parents were killed. I did learn a lot later that my mother's family was very opposed to the idea of my "going away."

We did not stay at Greenway for the whole war. Because of planes being sent over the Channel it was decided to move us. . . . This brings to mind the night we children were woken up and brought into "the lounge" and made to sit in front of a lovely roaring fireplace. Planes were thundering over the house. We thought it was very exciting, but we moved very soon after this adventure.

LRD: What do you remember about going home afterward?

DV: I have fuzzy memories of going home, and I do know that it took me a while to get used to the idea. I had many troubled nights sleeping. . . .

My parents came to pick me up in the summer of 1945, and the only memory I have of that day was arriving home in London to this tiny little house and thinking how small it was. We were surrounded by bombed-out houses that had been hit by German raids on the Eveready Battery factory not too far away. For a long time afterward I really believed that I had been adopted by my parents and that they were too scared to tell me. I was six and a half when my war experiences ended. I consider, looking back, how fortunate I was. There are no scarring memories, and we were treated with such kindness. I recall missing my little playmates very much even though I was assured I was lucky to have my own bedroom. This period was not an easy time for me. I did not want to sleep in a bedroom by myself.

It is hard to tell my story because of the lack of continuity. It seems one could compare it to a patchwork quilt. Little memories being sewn together with love and fondness for lovely surroundings. This is how I remember my brief stay at Greenway.

■ ■ ■ ■

ABOUT THE AUTHOR

■ ■ ■ ■

ABOUT THE AUTHOR

Lori Rader-Day is the Edgar Award–nominated and Anthony Award–and Mary Higgins Clark Award–winning author of *The Lucky One, Under a Dark Sky, The Day I Died, Little Pretty Things,* and *The Black Hour.* She lives in Chicago, where she is cochair of the mystery readers' conference Murder and Mayhem. She is a former national president of Sisters in Crime. Visit her at:

LoriRaderDay.com
Twitter: @LoriRaderDay
Facebook: loriraderdaybooks
Instagram: loriraderday

The employees of Thorndike Press hope you have enjoyed this Large Print book. All our Thorndike, Wheeler, and Kennebec Large Print titles are designed for easy reading, and all our books are made to last. Other Thorndike Press Large Print books are available at your library, through selected bookstores, or directly from us.

For information about titles, please call:
(800) 223-1244

or visit our website at:
gale.com/thorndike

To share your comments, please write:
Publisher
Thorndike Press
10 Water St., Suite 310
Waterville, ME 04901